MURDER IN WIZARD'S WOOD

Michael J. Allen

Delirious
Scribbles Ink

Delirious Scribbles Ink

Delirious Scribbles Ink
P. O. Box 161
Fortson, Georgia 31808-0161
www.deliriousscribbles.com

Interior Layout ©2016 Delirious Scribbles Ink
Author Photo by Jim Cawthorne, Camera 1
Cover Design ©2016 Delirious Scribbles Ink

ISBN 978-1-944357-06-1 (hc)
ISBN 978-1-944357-05-4 (intl. tr. pbk.)
ISBN 978-1-944357-07-8 (epub)
ISBN 978-1-944357-08-5 (kindle)

Printed in the United States of America
10 9 8 7 6 5 4 3 2 1
Murder in Wizard's Wood / Michael J. Allen. — 1st ed.

MURDER IN WIZARD'S
WOOD

Books by Michael J. Allen

Scion Novels:

SCION OF CONQUERED EARTH
STOLEN LIVES

Bittergate:

MURDER IN WIZARD'S WOOD

For Mom and Errol who introduced me to books and dreaming...
For Ann and Aaron who taught me how to share those dreams...
and always for B, B & J.

CHAPTER ONE

Murder in the Woods

The body hung suspended, spread eagle between two birch trees. Wide, thin wounds stained its blue flannel shirt, orange vest and further soiled its mud-caked jeans. A susurrus hum surrounded it, flies feeding off the now drying blood. Their spawn hadn't hatched yet, but maggots weren't long off in the muggy morning humidity.

Jedediah Shine bent over, picking up the fallen NASCAR number three baseball cap. He swept his own wide-brimmed hat from his shaking head and swished it in a complicated gesture. His crinkled blue eyes glowed a moment over a pronounced frown.

No token.

He spat at the dead man's feet. "Dumb as you're dead, Ronnie Gerald."

"No reason to insult the dead, Da." A silky feminine voice replied.

He turned darkened eyes upon her. Her wild, crimson-silver locks nearly hid the slight point to her ears. The graceful features of her face did as much to reveal her elven blood as her hair did to hide it.

"Ronnie swore he wouldn't hunt my land without my token. How the hell am I going to explain this to Joe Franklin? It isn't even hunting season."

She frowned at Ronnie's corpse. "If he didn't keep his oath then he's trespassing."

Jedediah sighed. "Just so, but I hate saying it. Hate adding shame to his missus's tragedy."

"You'd rather lie?"

He scowled. Clouds shadowed the woods around them. "You know I don't abide lying."

A smirk played across her lips. "I seem to recall something about Santa Claus and a claim that kissing boys might cause my skin to turn plaid."

He stroked trimmed salt and paprika whiskers "A jolly bearded man did bring you presents."

She poked his stomach. "Fat and jolly."

"I ain't fat."

"And kissing boys?"

"It *might* happen, in the right circumstances."

1

She folded her arms across her chest and raised an eyebrow.

He laughed, a full boisterous thing.

"What're you going to do about Ronnie?"

"Someone played 'to the pain' with him a long time." He met the girl's gaze, tone sober. "I'm going to have a chat with them."

She tightened her arms around herself.

"Any idea who did this, Lanea?"

"They leave any arrows?" Lanea asked.

"Not so much as a feather."

"I don't know, Da. If they didn't want you figuring out their identity, why coerce the wood into holding him up like that?"

Jedediah put his hat back on, pausing to adjust it while he scrutinized her. *Easy to forget how young she is when she isn't acting her five decades. She's still just an adolescent, dressing up like a grown woman. Guess half-bloods aren't much different from normals in that.*

"If the woods share any whispers, I'm going to need to know." He scanned the nearby woods. "Drake!"

A reddish-brown dragon a bit smaller than a Great Dane bounded out of the trees. He paused at Lanea's side to curl a long, forked tongue around her wrist affectionately. She scratched his leathery head and shooed him toward Jedediah. Drake met Jedediah's eyes, tongue still hanging out of his mouth.

"Need you to maul that." Jedediah pointed at the body. "Don't be eating any, make you sick."

"No, Da. Desecrating a body's wrong."

Drake's head bobbed back and forth between them.

"I can't explain those broadleaf wounds to Joe Franklin without lying to him. If Drake tears Ronnie up a little, I can tell him truthfully that some creature had at him."

"But that's not what killed him," Lanea said.

"Never said it was."

Drake examined the corpse, cocking his head.

"Well, get to it, you lazy lizard," Jedediah said.

Drake's wings—wrapped so tightly as to seem part of his sides—unfolded from his body. A feeling of static electricity raised the hair on their skin. Kudzu and tree limbs suspending the body untied themselves.

Drake shot one last glance at Jedediah then Lanea.

Jedediah narrowed his eyes.

Drake pounced on the corpse. His wings mantled the body as his claws ripped into it.

"That's enough, Drake." Jedediah pulled a worn handkerchief from his denim overalls and cleaned the blood from Drake's maw. With a satisfied nod, he shoved it back into the pocket. "Go find somewhere to dig."

Drake cocked his head.

"Sheriff's boys won't question a hound nuzzling a dead body, but we can't have blood on your talons when they go looking for what killed him." Jedediah turned to Lanea. "I love you, girl, but why is it you bring problems with you when you visit?"

A mischief lit her silver eyes. "Are you suggesting that I'm trouble, Da?"

Moving faster than normal for a man in his forties, he snatched Lanea into his arms with a massive hug. "Hell yes, you're trouble, girl. You just ain't the cause of it—this time."

Her head shot up, cocked slightly to one side. Her smile faded. "They're here."

Jedediah nodded. "Yup. Told them to park over yonder at marker twelve. Go on now, don't want you involved in this."

"But I found him, shouldn't I be here?"

"Ain't no record you exist and no sense changing that now," he said. "Drake?"

The dragon bounded up and fell into step with Jedediah. Mud caked its skin, obscuring blood and reeking of stagnant water.

"Don't forget your glamour," Jedediah said. "And try acting more like a *normal* dog this time."

A sound which might have been described by the nearly deaf as a bark came from Drake's throat.

"If that's the best you can manage, I'm boarding you a week in a kennel to practice."

Blue lights flashed through the trees. Between the patrol cars and Jedediah, two brown-uniformed sheriff deputies peered around the forest like Japanese tourists.

Jedediah waved. "Over here, boys."

Both heads turned his direction. The older led the way through, stepping around lingering mud.

"Mr. Shine, that hound gets bigger every time I see him," the older said. "You sure you won't stud him out?"

Drake's tail wagged back and forth.

Jedediah laughed. "Ain't no bitch that'd want this old hound giving her pups."

Drake whined.

"So how're you doing, John? How'd a senior deputy and his little brother get sent out into this heat?" Jedediah asked. "Rile the sheriff again?"

The younger chuckled. "John ticketed the sheriff's new girlfriend."

"How was I supposed to know they bumped uglies? Hell, Eddie, she doesn't look a day over nineteen," John said. "You got something to show us, Mr. Shine?"

"Now, John, isn't it about time you started calling me Jedediah. It's not like you're still a kid sneaking onto my property to impress your first girl."

John watched his feet.

Eddie laughed. "Give it up, Mr. Shine. He probably still has nightmares about that hiding you gave him."

"He took it like a man, impressed the socks—and I dare say a few other things—off that girl of his."

John cleared his throat. "So, a body?"

"Yup, this way."

Jedediah led them through the woods as if on a Sunday stroll. He shared a new joke they'd already heard, then asked after their parents, wives and children. He hadn't gotten to new gossip before they reached the body.

"Ah, hell," Eddie said.

John let out a low whistle. "Any idea who it is, sir?"

"I ain't the type to be going through a dead man's pockets. Found this though." Jedediah handed over a ball cap.

"What was he doing out here?" Eddie asked.

Jedediah darkened. "Trespassing."

"What's he doing hunting your woods out of season?" John scanned the ground around them. "And where's his rifle?"

Jedediah shrugged. "No idea. Might've dropped it while running from whatever he riled. You're welcome to look around for it."

"Appreciate that, sir," Eddie said. "You found him like this?"

Jedediah pointed at Drake.

The disguised dragon lay in the mud, gnawing a fallen branch.

Eddie examined him. "Did he do anything to the body?"

Drake's tail thudded the mud.

"Probably would've gotten himself a stomach full if I hadn't been nearby," Jedediah said.

"What were you doing out here?" John asked.

"I like walking my woods. A morning jaunt keeps a man spry."

Eddie bent down and searched the body. He scowled. "Better than jogging."

John pointed a thumb at his brother. "His wife demands he run on a treadmill four days a week."

"She just wants me in good shape," Eddie said.

John shook his head. "High maintenance."

"And worth every mile." Eddie offered John a lecherous grin. "Beg your pardon, Mr. Shine."

"I remember being young once," Jedediah said.

All three shared a nervous laugh.

"Ronnie Gerald." Eddie held up an open wallet.

Jedediah shook his head. "Doggone shame. Guess that's why he was out here."

"What do you mean?" John asked.

"He's got a missus and three little ones."

"How's that explain anything?" John asked.

"Revenuer beating down the door? Man's got to provide for his family."

"I thought he had two kids," Eddie said.

"Wife gave birth to a little girl last month," John said. "You sure keep up with people."

Jedediah shrugged. "What's a farmer got to do once the crops are in the ground but mind other folk's business? My grandpappy used to say, 'keep your fingers in the dirt, your ear to the ground, and your eyes wide. Trouble might still call, but it ain't sneaking up easy.'"

"Good advice all around," John said. "Look, we're going to be at it for a while. You don't have to stay."

"All right," Jedediah fished two bronze whistles from his overall pockets. His handkerchief tumbled to the ground. "Take these, one each in case you got to split up. Blow on it and it'll bring Drake running and me with him."

"I'm sure we'll be okay, Mr. Shine," John said.

"Just the same, make an old man happy," Jedediah said. "Drop them in my mailbox when you're done."

Jedediah strolled away, Drake at his heels.

"Mr. Shine?" John said.

Jedediah faced back around. "Yup?"

John turned Jedediah's bloody handkerchief over in his hands. Eddie's eyes shot between Jedediah and the object, face drawn and stance tense.

Caution undercut John's tone. "You dropped this."

Jedediah smiled and extended a hand. "Sure enough did. Thank you."

John didn't offer it. "Is this Ronnie's blood?"

"I'm sure it is, and afore you go asking, I did tell thee that Drake found him."

A puzzled expression crossed Eddie's face, and he furrowed his brows.

Jedediah swore inwardly, hoping the deputy missed his second mistake. "I mentioned being near enough to prevent Drake taking a bite out of poor Ronnie, but can't blame the hound for snuffling a corpse. Not a bloodhound anywhere in these mountains that'd pass something like that up."

"Why didn't you mention it when I checked Drake for blood?" Eddie asked.

"Is that what you were doing?" Jedediah asked.

"I suppose you're right," John hesitated, then extended the handkerchief. "Still would've preferred you mentioned it."

"You sure you don't want that as evidence? Maybe come full moon, I grow claws and hunt my property."

John chuckled nervously. "It's more than a week until the full moon."

"You want to look me over for blood?" Jedediah let the offer hang a minute. He took back the handkerchief and shrugged. "Guess not then."

"Knew you were old, Mr. Shine," Eddie said, "but I took you for a farmer, not King Arthur's personal confidant."

"What're you talking about?" John asked.

"He said thee—like some play or something."

"He did, didn't he?" John laughed. "Too much time selling fake dragon hide junk at renaissance festivals?"

I'm a damned fool. Just because these boys are easy going is no cause to get lazy and give away secrets. Jedediah smiled to cover his inward cursing. He bent at the waist into a formal bow. "I suppose it befits me not to speak thus to officers of the crown. Pity, I pray thee milords, for thy humble servant. If thou wilt forgive me, I must away."

Both deputies burst into laughter.

Jedediah straightened up and stuffed his hands in his pockets. "For the record, boys, I only sell genuine dragon hide."

He left them laughing.

Empty shadows parted beyond deputy sight lines. Lanea slipped into view.

"Used to be your full-blooded kin laughed when you tried that," Jedediah said.

Her jaw tightened.

"Told you all that practice would pay off."

"Often," she forced a grin, "barely without taking a breath."

"Something you wanted?"

"Whistles?" She asked. "I figured you'd watch them through a mist mirror."

Jedediah smiled. "Ward tokens to protect them while in the woods."

"Like the packets you give hunters you let in during hunting season?"

"Yup." He inclined his head. "But these carry a proactive bite against Fey indulging their prejudices."

She raised both brows.

"These hold the spell better than paper and are a lot easier to hand over than rune stones to ward off bad spirits. A couple of our newer Fey immigrants are a mite aggressive when it comes to normals. "

"As opposed to the local centaur?"

A scowl conquered his face. "We can't go jumping to conclusions, girl. Get me some evidence or give me time to talk to the tribes."

"Deputies almost caught you out."

"They're good boys, both, but they can't catch me for doing something I ain't had nothing to do with."

She didn't reply.

"You waiting for something else?"

She fidgeted with her fingers. "I wanted to talk to you."

"Uh huh?"

"It's," she hesitated, "about Trevor."

"Stay clear of that boy."

Color flashed in her eyes. "You don't even know him, how can—"

"I'm a wizard, girl. I don't like him."

"But, Da!"

Jedediah held up three fingers. "You're not my first daughter this century and I ain't called it wrong on a boy yet."

Drake's hackles rose. He darted away from the brewing argument.

"Jewel and Esme never got as old—"

Jedediah bristled. His soured expression stopped her cold. He radiated enough power a giftless normal could've felt it. "Jewel reached her twenty-first and you got two score more to be so mature. She thought me wrong, married that boy no matter what I said.

"You're good, daughter, and no mistake, but Jewel was a power even without a drop of Fey blood."

His jaw tightened. Sparks leapt from him

Lanea stepped back.

"She could've burnt him to ash, could have set him in stone or just held him in a mirror mist so slick and easy it'd have made you look like a dress-up fairy."

Lanea scowled.

"Jewel loved that no-good layabout way more than he deserved and he beat her to death for it." Jedediah took a deep breath. "If I tell you I don't like the boy then I've got good reason. Is that clear, girl?"

Lanea folded her arms. "All right, let's have it then. What's the reason?"

"If you ain't got sense or spell enough to see, then I guess you're going to make the kind of mistake that leaves a mark."

Her mouth fell open. "You won't tell me?"

"I shouldn't have to."

"You're going to make me figure it out? Make this into some kind of lesson?"

"Nope. I'm telling you your old Da don't like him. That should suffice."

She snorted. "Right, because you always listened to your elders."

Jedediah's smile faltered. He recovered it and shrugged. "I've got to be getting to the house."

Lanea smiled. "Time for *Gunsmoke?*"

"*Maverick.*"

"You know most people just watch reruns or buy those old shows on DVD."

"Television these days puts in all those blasted commercials for stuff like," he grimaced, "feminine products. Some things a man doesn't need to be knowing about."

"Right, you're what, four centuries old? What don't you know about?" When he didn't answer she finally said, "Of course. You don't ever change."

"Coming from a Fey-blooded, that's a serious accusation," Jedediah said.

"You don't deny it."

Jedediah chuckled. "I change every morning, right after my shower."

Lanea threw up her hands after the fashion of adolescents down the ages and disappeared into the trees.

She'll linger, hope I mumble something thinking her out of earshot. He shook his head and chuckled. *Kids never learn. They never stop trying to best their parents. Well, I ain't some lazy papa giving away false wins to soothe her ego. She wants to prove herself? She'll earn it—eventually.*

CHAPTER TWO

Dragon's Eye View

Drake exited the woods to the farm's cultivated edge. Local laws allowed year-round hunting on private wild lands if a farmer owned enough cultivated land. It allowed protecting crops or livestock from wild animals. Of course, most hunting on Jedediah's property protected the wild from civilization.

The dragon loped along, no longer bothering with the glamour that made him look like a bloodhound. Jedediah strolled some ways ahead, meandering the paths around the planted fields separating woods and farmhouse. Drake bound across the fields, leaping high in an attempt to glide.

Jedediah turned, glowering. "Too good to maintain a glamour with normals about?"

Drake shrank back.

"And trying to draw more attention with your dismal flight attempts." Jedediah pointed. "You turn right around and get rid of those talon prints."

Drake lowered his head and turned back.

"And you best not have damaged any of my crops, you great gormless lizard."

Drake darted back through the rows—peanuts, sugar cane, corn, and cotton—like an enormous rock lizard. He swept his tail over shallower gouges, cautious not to make other marks with the growing cluster of spikes on its end. Where his landing or launching had left deeper impressions, he unfurled his wings and invoked terramancy to fix the area. Neither method proved sufficient to repair the plants he'd crushed.

Drake stared at the bent and broken peanut limbs. He snorted. Tiny smoke wisps curled from his nostrils, withering the plant further. Drake glanced from the plants to the retreating wizard.

If I don't fix the plants, Jedediah will stop letting me eat human food. There'll be no more Cherry Coke. Drake shuddered. *I dread even imagining how merciless he'll be in lessons unless I fix these.*

He loosened his wings, reaching into his gut for his internal echo of the Dragon Springs. He sunk his talons into the power and narrowed eyes at the damaged plants.

Heal...

Prickles shot across the fine hairs on his leathery scales. They stood as energy leaked from his grip in tiny countless static discharges.

Grow...

Tiny motes of power dusted the plants like pollen, slowly forming a glowing aura. The broken plants shuddered, their leaves brightened, but the breaks didn't mend.

Heal! Grow damn it!

The gleaming plants exploded upward, growing years' worth in moments. Stalks surged upward, fattened and turned brittle. Leaves sprouted, spread and withered.

Drake stared at a swath of dead, overgrown foliage and cursed. *Ancestors, he'll never let me have Cherry Coke again!*

A scent—sweet and spicy like cinnamon from yesterday's baking—caressed his beak. He raised his head and inhaled deeply. *Lanea. She's not close, but close enough. She'll help me.*

Drake darted out of the rows onto the path around the field. Once free to move without threatening more crops, he unfurled his wings slightly. Power tingled its way down his limbs until even their tips felt electrified. His talons melted away, shifted into pads, feeling as if he'd stuffed his feet into shoes too small.

He sprinted after Lanea. Flute music reached his ears, quickening his heartbeat. It died abruptly and her scent soured.

Drake slowed his approach, voices reaching his ears long before he tiptoed to the clearing's edge. Two beautiful elves flanked Lanea. Long, flaxen hair shamed their silver-green silken garb.

"If it isn't the farmer's whelp."

"What're you doing here, Chalet?" Lanea asked.

"Trying not to die of embarrassment after that little bit of shadow stepping you bungled earlier," Chalet said. "I've seen one-legged toddlers with more grace, haven't you, Thestle?"

"It wasn't as bad as her music," Thestle said. "The farmer have any fresh cotton to stop the bleeding by chance?"

Heat blossomed in Drake's chest.

Lanea's scent grew spicier. She leapt to her feet. "Have you got a message, Chalet? You know, Da, forbad—"

"We're not centaur," Thestle said. "We go where we will."

"And unlike you, he'll *never* see or hear us," Chalet added.

A growl rumbled from Drake's gut out of his mouth.

All three gazes jerked his direction.

Lanea blushed.

Chalet and Thestle bowed to one knee.

"Greetings, Elder," Chalet said.

"Honor to thee," Thestle added.

Drake stalked forward and jabbed his beak against Chalet, threatening to topple even the graceful elf with his aggression. *What is your business on Master's lands?*

"Are you not master, Elder Lord?" Chalet asked.

"A wise student honors his teacher," Lanea said.

"Silence, half-breed," Thestle said. "We're not aroused by forbidden fruit like Treevoran."

She reddened further, fists tightening. A scent of impending rain filled Drake's nostrils.

Drake snapped his tail forward, sweeping Thestle's feet from him. The emerging spikes lay on Thestle's chest. He pressed his beak against Chalet. *I asked a question.*

"Forgive us, Lord," Thestle said. "The half—"

Drake bared a mouthful of long, serrated teeth.

"Wanderlust called our feet, Elder Lord," Chalet said. "We're journeying south to the ocean."

Without Master Jedediah's leave to travel his domain or even glamour to keep hidden while normals are about?

"No normal would've spotted us," Chalet said.

Thestle snorted. "Even this one wouldn't have if we hadn't wanted her—"

Drake's eyes narrowed. *You'll apologize to Lanea and then—*

"Apologize?!" Thestle said.

Lanea touched Drake's wingtip, giving him a significant look.

Drake withdrew his touch from the two elves. *Yes?*

<Leave it, Drake.>

They owe you an apology.

Her scent soured. *<It doesn't matter. If you learned speech you wouldn't have to touch them you know.>*

He smirked. *I'm trying, but flesh shaping is hard.*

<Tried augmenting with magic?>

I'm not allowed. An image of Jedediah appeared in their minds.

She sighed. *<Typical, Da.>*

He touched both elves without removing his wing from Lanea's reach. *You will apologize to Lanea. Then you will seek Master Jedediah, apologize for trespass and secure his permission to travel his lands in your journey.*

Thestle bristled.

Chalet lowered his head to Lanea. "Forgive us, Mistress Shine, if words from our lips brought you discomfort."

"Forgive us, Mistress Shine," Thestle said, "for trespass on lands your father claims as his."

Drake tail snapped across Thestle's head, leaving a gash across his perfect brow.

Thestle spoke through a taut jaw. "And forgive us for expressing opinions you took as insult. Your skills have grown since last we met."

Drake curled his lip, showing more teeth.

Lanea curtseyed. "Thank you, cousins, for your diplomatic words."

Leave on your task. Drake thought at them. *While I show you forbearance in deference to Lanea's presence.*

Chalet bowed. "We obey, Elder Lord."

Thestle bowed and they slipped into the nearest shadows as a parting insult.

Drake growled.

Lanea ran a hand through the frills behind Drake's head. "It's okay. They're not all like that. You looking for me?"

Drake showed her images of the broken crops.

Her fine eyebrows rose. "You know Da nearly hided me for helping you last time."

Drake whimpered.

"I can't help, not with him still riled over Trevor."

Master's right about Trevor. I don't like his scent.

"Not you too." She planted both hands on her hips. "Trevor loves me."

Drake wrapped his tongue around her wrist, careful with the barbs. *I tried healing the plants.*

"Try pyromancy? Warm and encourage growth?"

Drake projected incinerated plant images.

"Made any progress with aquamancy or terramancy?" she asked.

Drake lowered his head.

"Ianyss?"

She'll make me fertilize half the wood.

The accompanying images made Lanea laugh. "Face Da or help fertilize her flock."

Drake sighed. *It's beneath me. I'm Elder Fey.*

"Ianyss won't make you suffer as long."

Drake wrapped a wing around her. *Come with me?*

Lanea fidgeted.

Please?

She sighed. "It's like having a fire-breathing little brother."

Drake's eyes hardened. He unwrapped his tongue and looked away.

She laughed. "Fine."

His tail tip swung back and forth, leading her off at a jog.

Behind him, she slipped from shadow to shadow, shifting with the rhythms offered by breeze and branches at the fast pace. *She's getting very proficient despite Thestle's and Chalet's claims.*

He chuckled, a gravelly noise akin to a growl.

Jedediah wouldn't raise an eyebrow at a true master practicing.

"Never stop practicing, Drake," Jedediah said. "Stop whetting the blade and its edge will fade."

He proves it in actions too. Drake sighed. *Not that an occasional day off wouldn't be nice.*

They arrived at Ianyss's glade in no time. The dryad was nowhere to be seen. He sniffed the air, her scent lingered everywhere, the warm, clean scent of wood and home. He glanced at Lanea.

"Not here?" she asked.

Drake shrugged.

Lanea laughed, a musical thing that brightened the glade.

Shrugging wasn't a natural movement for a dragon on four limbs, but one he'd picked up from Jedediah and his daughter. The first time he'd done it she'd laughed too, so he kept doing it.

"So," Lanea said, "shall we knock?"

Drake sighed and walked around behind the dryad's oak, trying to obscure Lanea's view even if she knew what he did.

Old man's modesty is rubbing off on me.

Ianyss stepped from the oak's trunk opposite Drake and his offering. Smooth grey bark formed sultry curves, alluringly kept modest by strategic growths of moss. Spanish moss hung loose around her shoulders, framing a face most wood carvers would kill to manage with chisel and file.

She smiled at Lanea. "Day's blessings, forest child."

Lanea glanced away from the lovely dryad. "Hello, Ianyss."

Drake sidled around the tree.

Ianyss met his gaze. "Should I assume by this offering that our little dragonling has need of my services?"

Good thing cold-bloodedness keeps me from blushing. He frowned at Lanea. *Why does Ianyss's presence always make her blush?*

He laid his beak against the dryad's leg.

I do.

"You know what I'll ask in return."

How many trees?

Ianyss scrutinized him, maintaining her gaze for several minutes. "Ten score."

Drake felt faint. *Two hundred trees? But, I'm Elder Fey, lesser Fey are our servants.*

Ianyss frowned. "Would an Elder Fey make such a mistake? Again? If you're so great, my little Lordling, why do you care?"

Drake's head drooped. *Jedediah.*

"A mere mortal, or talented kine in your mother's words," Ianyss said.

The ridges along Drake's spine rose. *Don't call him that. Master's not some herd beast meant only for slaughter.*

Ianyss's fine brow rose. "It seems, Lordling, if you honor your teacher you need my *lesser* services."

Drake sighed.

Ianyss smiled. "This once, Lordling, I'll settle for five, to honor what your teacher does for we Fey."

"That's still an awful lot of trees for just a simple healing," Lanea said.

"One you could perform," Ianyss said. "If you'll not help Drake openly, you could share in his bargain in other ways."

Drake looked at Lanea pleadingly.

Lanea smiled her father's grin. "I think I'll stay clear of this."

Ianyss turned to the dragon. "Have we a pact?"

We are agreed, one hundred trees to mend the damaged crops.

"Always be mindful, Lordling. The greater you are, the more hurt you can cause Mother," Ianyss said. "If I must help you again, each injury shall cost greater penance to Her children."

The sun lay low on the horizon when Drake approached the farmhouse. Cars on the nearby highway reached his ears, but the wood separating farmhouse and road kept them from view.

He owed Ianyss more, but only so much could be done in a day. He approached the farmhouse's rear earthbound. He passed a combine and other farm machinery lined up for appearance sake, rounding the u-shaped greenhouse and entered Jedediah's boneyard. Refrigerators and toilets, water heaters and old junkers, the seeming junk concealed many of Jedediah's secrets.

From the outside, it appeared a two-story antebellum farmhouse typical of old southern farms. Whitewashed slats clothed its walls. A wide covered porch wrapped around all four sides on first and second floors. A few angled walls had been thrown in to round out its otherwise square shape. A railed platform topped its peaked roofs alongside a bronze owl weather vane perching atop the metal pyramid capping the chimney.

Drake climbed up the back porch and nosed at the door.

He locked it. Drake growled in irritation.

Jedediah never locked the doors. Reasons to lock them seldom arose out there in the country. His irascible personality combined with an exaggerated reputation for brutality against trespassers discouraged all but the most desperate thieves.

Lesson or punishment. Drake bristled. *Or both. I hate feromancy.*

He unfurled his wings, shook them out once and concentrated on the door. He reached into his core. Static electricity gathered around him. Magical fingers felt the door, the knob, the lock. They wrapped around the slippery mechanism. Drake tilted his head, rotating it in the same direction he wanted to rotate the door's bolt handle.

Jedediah's warning reached through the door. "Damn it, Drake, less power, more control!"

Drake's grip slipped. He panicked and threw more power into his spell. Magic clamped down not on the small locking mechanism but the larger door. He demanded the spell tighten. It did. Power crushed the wood like an empty Cherry Coke can, forcibly imploding the door.

CHAPTER THREE

Trouble Comes Knocking

Jedediah glowered at the remains of his back door.

Drake cowered like a beaten dog on the door frame's other side. The old wizard shook his head and walked the other way.

Drake whimpered, but he ignored it.

Disappointed silence sometimes affected a pupil better than anger or lectures. He'd lost doors to pupils before. Dragons made difficult students, more so from certain parents.

More arrogant than teens at their worst. More powerful than human or Fey-blooded. Petulant children indoctrinated to lazy mindedness and brute force. He stopped midstep and looked over his shoulder at Drake. *He's better than most, especially considering his mother, but he's still got no control. He'll end up halfway decent if I can teach him to think instead of balking when faced with problems meant for those with two legs and arms.*

Foolish of me to accept another student, especially from that power hungry bitch Stormfall—life debt or no.

Drake caught up and pressed a beak against Jedediah's thigh. *<I'm sorry, Master.>*

Jedediah turned to him, brows high. He stepped away to ease shielding his thoughts from Drake.

Well, I'll be a one-winged pixie in a dust devil. His dame bred him for power and status—though I've no idea how another dragon stood her long enough to do the deed. He maintained his disapproving expression. "You'll fix this yourself. You, not another Fey."

Drake's eyes widened.

"You really think I wouldn't catch wind of a dryad in my fields?"

He strode away, putting the door from his thoughts. *Drake will fix it. Maybe it's better she forced him on me too young—give or take the extra grey he's caused these last several years.*

He sighed, considering other problems.

Three solid knocks struck his front door. He squared his shoulders, conjured a smile and opened the door. "Everything all right, John?"

John cradled the pieces of Ronnie Gerald's rifle. Hoof marks marred the wooden finish.

16

"You wouldn't happen to own any horses, would you, Mr. Shine?" John said. "Maybe exercise them with a ride through the wood?"

"No, why do you ask?" Jedediah said.

"It's just," Eddie said. "No horse could've ripped him up like that."

"Not one horse on this property in decades, and I'm a little short on claws at the moment." He inclined his head at John. "It being a week to the full moon."

"This is serious, Mr. Shine," John said.

"I should say it is, poor Ronnie Gerald—good reasons or not—got himself killed trespassing on my land by Maker only knows what." Jedediah glowered at the rifle. "I can only guess what broke that rifle, but now I've got to get mine and make sure there's nothing dangerous stalking my woods."

"We're just trying to do our jobs," Eddie said.

"By pestering me instead of notifying his widow?" Jedediah yanked off a work boot and sock. "You see hooves?"

John's jaw tightened. "We're going to have to check the property for horses, wild or otherwise."

"I gave you leave to do so, boy, so be about it." Jedediah pointed at Eddie. "You, get Joe Franklin on the phone and tell him I want a word once Ronnie's Missus has been properly consoled."

He slammed the door shut and indulged in silent curses developed over several centuries.

Shouldn't have aimed my temper at those boys. I'll make it up to them later.

Hoof marks implicated the centaur tribes, not that other Fey on his lands didn't enjoy subterfuge for mischief or malice. His land hid and protected the combined communities of magical creatures from the same cruelty he and his people had suffered centuries before at the hands of European conquerors. It usually protected humanity from what would happen if they poked that particular badger's warren.

Some Guardian I am, letting a normal die on my lands.

Jedediah pushed away the selfish indulgence. Many normals and Fey died on the huge expanse of lands bought and maintained as a reservation—far fewer than if either group competed with the other for the territory.

The charm he'd given Ronnie, John and Eddie prevented them from falling prey to one Fey or another.

As long as the damned fools don't leave it at home.

Lanea'd discovered Ronnie's body early enough to prepare it and return it to the family. He'd buried other remains that would've fit in a coffee cup.

Need to reward that girl. I'd hate for Ronnie's Missus to pine for years thinking her man up and left.

The old wizard strolled into his study and took down a long faded white box. The top, while faded, had started out with more color than the sides. Both "Risk" and "Parker Brothers" remained faintly visible. He opened the box and unfolded the game board onto a table.

He shuffled through the cards. He held Eastern United States up. "*Artog il America ren southeast.*"

Jedediah laid it upon the board. Its map swirled. Colors shifted, bled then reformed into a map of southeastern America. Brightly colored sections interspaced large dull ones, highlighting his properties.

Jedediah picked out several green triangular prisms from the box and tossed them onto the map. "Show me the tribes."

The small wooden game pieces melted, changing shape into centaurs and Indian braves. The centaurs galloped over the map, their human counterparts jogging behind with mile-devouring strides they could manage for days. As they spread out, the areas they traveled stretched and expanded—a satellite image zooming in for a closer view. When the pieces finally came to rest, a pair of tents grew up around each of the figures accompanied by the subtle sound of beating drums.

Jedediah scanned the map, picking figurines of centaur, human or combined camps from its farther edges. The map magnified the remaining area, and Jedediah eliminated more one by one. Two camps remained close enough to have had a hand in Ronnie Gerald's fate—one human and one centaur.

Jedediah scratched his beard. *Is it fair to exclude the Ossahatchee? They've got horses, and they've sure never got over that forced resettlement. Guardian lands saved some of them from relocation, but many still resent their hidden boundaries as much as they might public reservations.*

Shelves housing a vast assortment of books covered one study wall. Cookbooks stood alongside old TV Guides, history books, refrigerator user manuals, a tome on animal psychology and several Mad Libs. An eclectic collection of models separated the books enclosed in plastic cases. A buggy, rickshaw and stagecoach rested alongside cars from every era. An old red biplane rested near their center.

The Fleet Hoof tribe lived closer. He'd see the Ossahatchee elders at their festival soon enough. He shook his head. *I'm making excuses. I've lived away from the centaur tribes too long. If they're hunting human blood once more, it's my duty to stop them.*

Jedediah cursed and strode upstairs. The smooth wood floor creaked as he topped the stair. Jedediah touched a small portrait hung in the hall and then an old tinned photograph hung next to it on his way past. His bedroom appeared as expected in an old farm house. A four-post bed dominated the room. A real goose-down comforter and several feather pillows lay in disarray on top. A bureau with a pitcher and basin rested under a large double window. A pair of open closet doors dominated the opposite wall.

Jedediah strolled to the doors, shut them, and knocked. "*Ostinari.*"

The doors opened, revealing another room countless times the size of the actual closet. Circular department store-style clothes racks dotted the room. Clothing hung upon them organized by era. At the far end, crudely sewn animal skins gave way to leather and broadcloth. Victorian waistcoats and trousers led to denim overalls. Nearest to the door, a dozen pairs of neatly creased slacks shared space with freshly cleaned sport coats. Accessories of every description hung from the walls. Hats, bags, and belts shared space with ornate weapons— few ceremonial.

He stepped in front of a taller clothing rack designed for full-length gowns and flipped through several ornate robes. He paused at one, scratched his beard and snorted. After a few more he turned away. He pulled a buckskin outfit from another rack.

With a one-handed flip of a strap clip, Jedediah sent his overalls to the floor. He pulled the vest on first, leaving it open and sat on a nearby bench. The vest mismatched his own Maykujay roots, but fit the more conservative style among Fleet Hoof.

He pulled the trousers on, stood and pulled them the rest of the way up. He tugged them together and tried to close the leather laces. Another tug attempted to bring them higher up and then together. Jedediah grunted, exhaled and held his breath. He tugged again.

Cursing the air blue, he considered altering his age to one with a thinner waistline before deciding it didn't matter. Fleet Hoof would be under scrutiny, not him. He stripped off the buckskin and pulled the overalls back on.

He paused at the front door, a prickle spider-walked up his spine. A sudden urge to lock it struck him.

What's the point? I've got no back door.

"Drake!" Movement caught his eye. The dragon lurked just out of sight behind the living room recliner. "Stay here and guard the house."

Drake whined.

"It's your fault I can't lock up. You'd better fix that door if you know what's good for thee. And stay out of the ice box."

Jedediah stopped in the yard and leaned to his right, stretching out one leg. He felt a twinge in his calf and continued stretching until both legs warmed and loosened. He extended his arms down, palms flat as if trying to quiet a crowd, and chanted softly until his eyes glowed. Mist curled around his work boots.

Jedediah stepped forward. A fluid stride traversed a dozen paces instead of one. The second crossed another dozen. Jedediah picked up the pace, gliding down paths between fields in a fraction of the normal time. Mist lingered behind, marking each footstep until it faded into night. He eased the pace at wood's edge, picking each cross-country step.

He wove his way to mile marker twelve. Jedediah paused at the highway's edge. A watchful deputy's silhouette hid in a dark car just up the road. A finger flick, a burst of light and several strides helped him cross unseen into the opposite woods.

The night air cooled, though humid enough to encourage perspiration. Woodland sounds scurried from or toward his path without noticing his passage. Dark shapes watched him from darker shadows, seeing in the blackness even better than he did.

They didn't frighten him. At worst, most represented pranks or mischief to a wizard. Even predators like shadowcats knew better than to rile someone of Jedediah's abilities. His lands protected truly dangerous Fey too, the true horrors from darkest folklore. Those he hid in his deepest wilds, as far as possible from normals that might make a tempting distraction.

He stepped from his properties through those of a neighbor before coming back to his own on the opposite side. The silence—magical and otherwise—caused a shiver.

Foreshadow and omen.

CHAPTER FOUR:

Centaur Tribal Council

Distant drumbeats caressed his ears. His steps fell unconsciously into sync. They rose with each stride. Flickers of orange danced in the distance.

Jedediah released the mist, approaching at normal speed. Two centaur shadows watched but didn't intercept him. He paused just outside the fire lit borders of their camp.

"I seek Fleet Hoof's council."

A palomino centaur emerged from a forest of hide tents. Overlapping layers of hardened leather protected his chest and muscular arms. He held an arrow on the string of a massive longbow, but appeared otherwise at ease. "What want you here, wizard?"

Jedediah raised an eyebrow. "I believe I just told you."

"You've no business here, *human*."

Jedediah pulled his hat from his head and raised his voice to other ears, unseen but focused upon him, "I, *Lyanthen Ah Lah'Phriel, Feihtor Ah Mythela'Raemyn,* Guardian of the borders succoring the Fleet Hoof, seek regress for injuries done unto me. Step from my path, brother, that I may approach the tribal council. Now."

Uproar met his demands. Young warriors rushed out crying objections and insults, some bare-chested while others dressed in buckskin vests. They cursed Jedediah in the centaur tongue.

Jedediah reached out. A black walnut staff leapt to his hand, riding a blinding arc of lightning up from the ground. He presented it defensively, ready to fend off any attack.

No one loosed on the old wizard.

A white bodied mare parted the angry warriors. Soft white leather covered her age-bent torso. Feathers and polished stones decorated three braids of her silver-white hair.

"Step forward and be recognized, *Lyanthen Ah Lah'Phriel,*" she said.

Jedediah bowed, not taking his eyes from the centaurs and addressed her by her formal name rather than the familiar. "I seek the council's face, Waphri Ah'Raemyn."

She nodded. "You will be heard."

"Thank you, WaphRae," Jedediah said.

WaphRae led him into the camp through tribeswomen garbed in doeskin or woven tunics. Several concealed their human-like torsos with form-fitted, hardened leather. A few, mostly young mares, went bare-chested without any sign of embarrassment.

Jedediah's cheeks colored. *Transfers from other tribes.*

Outrage and insult, curiosity and respect met him. Centaurs inclined their heads with greeting, deference or friendly smiles. One older centaur struck fist to chest. Murmurs coursed the trailing warriors.

Tent arrangement remained as it had during his years among the tribes. Familiarly marked tents remained—some advanced inward by their owner's achievements. New tents replaced those burned with their fallen warrior. All circled the massive council pavilion in concentric rings.

WaphRae held up a pavilion flap for Jedediah, setting off more murmurs. He ducked inside and she followed. Furs and skins carpeted the inside. Woven tapestries and painted skins hung from the walls. Four centaur rested around a central fire, having just finished their evening meal if the wooden bowls and cups close at hand were any indication.

Jedediah searched their faces. "I had hoped to speak with friend and Elder Tharus A'Lyathin?"

"TharLya hunts the spirit lands," WaphRae said.

Jedediah bowed his head. "May he best the great stag and outrace the mustang."

A chestnut roan spat venomously at Jedediah. "Why have you invaded our hunting lands, *human?*"

"*Lyanthen Ah Lah'Phriel* claims injury, VelSera," WaphRae said.

I remember this one, Velith'Seravin, troublesome colt—Ronnie's kind of trouble. Well, shit. Jedediah bowed to him. "I walk Mother's land. I wouldn't have come seeking redress if her people's sins hadn't demanded it."

VelSera snorted and stamped, but did not respond.

"Claim your injury," said a greying sorrel stallion.

"Grant me permission, Bauth Illos'Elirymn, to show you."

The stallion inclined his head.

Jedediah swung his hat through several gestures. Mist rose from the central fire, first mimicking smoke before revealing its true nature. It swirled, curling in on itself and reflecting the dancing flames beneath it. Colors solidified. Mist twisted and hardened. In moments Ronnie Gerald's corpse hung before them, tied spread eagle between two phantasmal trees.

"Someone slaughtered this man within my borders. A hoof broke his weapon," Jedediah said. "I seek truth and his killer's face."

"Any human trespassing within our hunting territory deserves death," VelSera said. "Whomever's arrows cleansed him from the wood enacted Mother's will."

Jedediah's brow rose. "Then let us address the tribe. Any warrior doing Mother's will would be coward not to proclaim it publically."

Velith'Seravin met Jedediah's unwavering gaze.

VelSera turned back to the others. "This two-legger has no right to demand answers of the tribe."

"Wrong." Jedediah calmed himself as the power-enhanced echo of his voice died. "I am of the tribes, raised among Mother's colts and fillies. When I first hunted with them, Strength held hunting territories."

"As it should be," VelSera said.

"The sun has set on those days." Jedediah matched each elder's gaze. "We who serve as Guardians protect your borders, walking in courts you may not go and wrestling laws you don't bother learn. Though it wound your warrior heart to recognize these lands under my protection, nevertheless it is *my* strength and not yours that keeps these borders. It is my blood and sweat that buys them away from normals that would cut it all down and slaughter the tribes."

"They can try," VelSera said.

"Can you fly, VelSera?" Jedediah asked.

"Do *not* speak the familiar, I am no friend to *humans*."

Jedediah addressed the others. "The normals have great flying steeds, metal spearheads to rain fire upon the lands if war came to them. They have eagles that watch from above the clouds and," Jedediah fixed Velith'Seravin with his glare, "pig-headed ideas about who is beneath them or their equal. They would cut up the tribes on metal beds to learn what made them and steal their magic if they learned of it.

"I am the Guardian of these lands. I hide you from their eagles. I keep them from your secrets, and I shoulder scrutiny and punishment when there is bloodshed within my borders."

VelSera waved dismissively. "You are the yearling crying ogre."

Jedediah bristled. Electricity sparked around his frame. "Head-butting granite is easier than granting you wisdom. Over three centuries I've protected this tribe and those like it. I do not speak false, and I'll not be treated like a colt not yet grown into his hooves. Nor will I tolerate warriors killing on *my* lands."

"You threaten us?" Bauth Illos'Elirymn asked.

Jedediah took a deep breath, suppressing the sparks through force of will. "BauthEli, I came seeking truth delivered from this council's hand. I'm a guardian of many Fey, protecting them to practice the old ways. In careful balance, I protect the Fey from humanity and the normals from those within my borders."

"No creature's rights supersede the tribe's," VelSera said.

Icy wind swirled through the pavilion, dousing the fire. Only the softly glowing mist displaying Ronnie Gerald lit the tableau.

Jedediah glowered. "Mark me. I am centaur—*Feihtor Ah Mythela'Raemyn*. Many times I've judged, sentenced and punished among the tribes. None—centaur, elf, nor human—shall endanger those I protect."

VelSera whipped an arrow from his quiver and loosed it with the speed of a lethal wind. A flash of sound and light exploded within the pavilion. In its aftermath, a chipped stone arrowhead dropped to the ground, followed by the ashen remains of VelSera's arrow shaft.

Jedediah held out his staff, a corona of electricity outlining him. While still garbed in his simple overalls, a ghost image of silver robes wrapped him.

WaphRae beseeched him. "Peace, *Feihtor Ah Mythela'Raemyn*, please. We've heard you. Give us time to seek your answer."

The fire flickered back to life.

Jedediah set his hat upon his head, adjusted it and inclined his head to the elders. "I will await your decision. As is custom among the tribes, I reluctantly grant two moons."

"You grant?" VelSera asked.

"I beseech you, employ wisdom and even greater haste. These cowards must be brought to justice lest they undermine the safety of all the assembled Fey. " Jedediah scowled at VelSera. "Don't force me to return unbidden."

CHAPTER FIVE

Mischief & Mavericks

Jedediah trudged home not bothering with magic for the return trip. *Hells and damnation, what's wrong with me? It's not the first time one of the Fey declared war on the normals. But, that, that, centaur. He's lucky I didn't fry him down to his hooves.*

Jedediah sucked in night air. He patted his pockets, extracting a pouch of shredded mint. The scent wafted under his nose as he tucked a wad in one cheek, softening his anger's edge. *I shouldn't have threatened a tribe. I'm supposed to protect them, not make things worse being pig-headed and short-tempered. Worse like the years ahead with that normal-murdering, mule fart on the council.*

With Velith'Seravin replacing Tharus A'Lyathin's conservative voice, he might be forced to entreat the High Tribe.

The last thing I want to do.

The mint continued its calming effect, far more desirable than slipping into Elizabethan English when nervous, angry or frustrated.

As vices go, it could be worse. He chuckled.

He'd known many wizards who hid their anxiety behind Tolkienesque pipe smoking—long before the actual writer. Old Justin had loved the noxious thing, and he'd grown accustom to it.

Chewing's private, doesn't invade peoples' space or glue stink to everything like an angry badger.

Mint and Velith'Seravin's arrogant tones warred all the way back to the farmhouse. Anger clung to him, though no longer sufficient for electrical sparks to escape his control.

Drake snored at the back door's still ruined foot.

Jedediah stepped over him. He ascended the stair, lingering long enough to touch the hall paintings before heading to bed.

He awoke to an all too warm late September morning. Humidity stalked the day from around corners, not quite out in the open but ready to pounce. Jedediah checked the Grainger's calendar on his refrigerator door. Circles surrounded today's date and the coming weekend. Tiny notes filled their squares.

Drake peeked around the door frame.

"Yes, I see you. No, I'm not angry, and yes breakfast will be ready in a minute," Jedediah said. "You still have to fix my door."

The only magic welcome in Jedediah's kitchen involved a good skillet and fresh spices. A half-dozen fresh eggs went into the skillet. Fajita chicken and black beans lingering in the refrigerator joined them. He chopped an early tomato, tossed it in with some sharp cheddar and added a dollop of sour cream. He flipped half of the concoction over his shoulder directly from the pan.

Drake snatched it from the air.

Jedediah slid the rest onto a plate, warmed some leftover fried potatoes and sat at a small kitchen table. He unfolded a newspaper with practiced, one-handed ease, ate and read. He turned the page, muttered and read until he'd cleared his plate.

Jedediah glanced at Drake, laying on fading, yellow linoleum, eyes half-lidded. "Fix the door or you're staying here this weekend."

One eye opened. Drake huffed smoke from his nostrils and gave the wizard a single nod. Issue settled, Drake closed his eyes the rest of the way.

Jedediah took a moment to clean up both kitchen and himself, traded out his flannel robe for a fresh shirt and jeans and headed into his den. Opposite a massive stone fireplace, an eighties projection television carcass rested in one corner. Its missing screen displayed its innards.

Jedediah dropped into a plaid Barcalounger and propped up his feet. An ancient TV Guide lay open on a cheap serving tray converted into a side table. Jedediah checked the decades-old schedule and grabbed a boxy, two-button remote control. It clacked loudly when he pressed a button.

Mist swirled into the television's cavity. Lightning flickered behind it like a tiny thunderstorm as it settled into a uniform grey. The opening scenes of the original Maverick television show flickered to life on its surface.

Jedediah smiled wistfully, folded his hands behind his head, and stared transfixed at the old western summoned across time. A doctor interrupted the program, expounding the virtues of his beloved Camel cigarettes.

"They'd lynch you for saying that these days, doc."

The commercial ended. Bret and Bart Maverick concluded their frenzied race to cash a check. Jedediah clicked the remote again. Gunsmoke's episode wasn't as good, but Jedediah clicked the TV off with a smile.

Drake waited in the bed of his old red Ford pickup. They drove through the thick trees flanking Jedediah's gravel drive. Jedediah waved at a deputy parked just off the road near the drive's exit, unable to remember his name.

The deputy waved back.

Drake hung his head over the truck bed's side, overlong tongue lolling out.

Jedediah picked up a few groceries at Piggly Wiggly—packing the cold items in a Styrofoam cooler—and headed to the Britt David Park sports complex. He backed into a spare parking place and the two strolled through parents and teenagers. The former bickered in the open like adolescents over umpires' calls. The latter hid in the brush, pretending at being adults.

Jedediah shook his head.

"Hey, Jedediah!"

Jedediah turned.

A thick-bodied man with thinning hair huffed toward them, baseball cap waving.

Jedediah met him part way, hand extended. "Afternoon, Russell."

"I'm so glad you remembered this time," Russell said. "We've got two umpires out. I can't believe they'd miss the Labor Day bi-city tournament."

"Probably had enough *fun* this summer." Jedediah chuckled. "Anyway, I'm sorry about last weekend. Where would you like me?"

Russell pointed. "Open up field three. Maybe it'll shut the parents up."

"Three it is. Little league, softball or high school teams?"

Russell checked a schedule. "Softball. Watch your temper tonight."

"What do you mean by that?"

"I know you're not normally hot-headed, but these parents are already angrier than an incontinent bear in a briar," Russell said. "Don't let their stupid rile you. Oh, can you umpire a special game this weekend?"

"No. Got a fair. What's happening this weekend?"

Russell pointed. "Special game for the Auburn talent scout."

Jedediah followed his gesture.

A tall man—slightly shorter than Jedediah—strolled into their midst. His clothing fit well, accentuating the fluid motions of his excellent physique.

"Marc O'Steele meet Jedediah Shine."

Marc pushed a lock of blonde hair out of his face and extended a hand. "Nice to meet you, Mr. Shine."

"Jedediah will do. You got your eye on some of these boys?" Jedediah asked.

"Girls, too." Marc smiled. "Got a kid out here?"

"Nope, just helping Russell out."

"Brave man," Marc said.

Jedediah shrugged.

Russell followed the conversation, his head swinging back and forth. He cleared his throat. "Sorry to cut this short. They're ready for me at one and Jedediah's needed at three."

"I'll walk you over, got a question about the shortstop on field two." Marc inclined his head. "Some other time, Mr. Shine."

Baseball games stretched into the evening, softball and hardball finals played under field lights. Jedediah watched part of the last game before strolling off in search of Drake.

Where's that fool dragon got himself?

Night's fall emboldened the teenagers, one or both sexes brazenly pushing things in the shadows.

What happened to decency? Getting a hand under a squaw's shirt at my age meant one less hand or a sealed marriage pact. Weren't no premarital sex back then, having sex married you.

Jedediah turned off the path, shortcutting through the brush toward the parking lot. Several trees in, he parted a brush line to find a tiny clearing. A girl reclined against a tree, seated atop a wide rock at its roots. A boy knelt in front her with his jeans around his ankles, struggling to tug down her tight jeans.

Jedediah cleared his throat and fixed the boy with a stare.

The boy flashed him an insolent sneer. His date blushed, grabbing for her pants. He resisted her, stalemating their tug-of-war.

Doesn't care that she's embarrassed—as they both should be—just waiting for me to go on my way.

In the old days, Jedediah could've seized that boy and dragged him before her father and a shotgun future. Evidence suggested modern girls equal instigators of sexual Russian roulette. He didn't want to believe it. True some Maykujay women younger than the girl in front of him had hunted mates as craftily as any young warrior, but by innuendo, flirtation and shows of skill.

They didn't toss their ankles wide and ring the dinner bell.

No young woman deserved to be preyed upon by the likes of the half-naked boy glaring his direction. His kind didn't care what they put a girl through as long as they got what he wanted.

Like Trevor. Why can't Lanea see why he's after her?

Heat plumed through his torso.

"Don't think the girl's interested," Jedediah said.

"Not with some old perv watching. This ain't your business. Now screw off."

"Pardon me for strolling in a public park," Jedediah walked out of the clearing. He smirked, muttering a spell. "I'd wish you a good night, courteous as I am, but you won't have one with that little problem plaguing you..."

...for the next several months.

Memories met him beyond the brush. Little Jewel playing as a girl. Jewel wearing her first dance dress. A shadow fell over his face. Jewel lying battered, bruised and bloodied by her husband's drunken temper.

He gritted his teeth. *Sometimes all this forensic science gets in the way of good old fashioned justice.*

He rejoined the path. Something flickered out of the corner of his eye. Drake hunched down behind a Coke machine, tail tip wagging.

"Blast it, Drake!"

Drake slunk down. A pile of Cherry Coke cans lay discarded around his claws.

"You magicked those from the machine, didn't you?"

Drake pressed himself closer to the ground.

"You know the money from those machines pays to keep these parks open," Jedediah said. "Stealing from kids, that's what you're doing, and you know better. That stuff is terrible for you."

Drake bit off the end of the can between his claws. He chewed it, swallowed and looked up at Jedediah hopefully.

"Bull, you're just a sugar addict." Jedediah shoved a pinch of shredded mint leaves into his cheek. "There ain't enough metal in those cans to do a cursed thing for your scales. I swear you're half goat. How are you planning to explain this if someone sees you?"

Jedediah yanked a wad of money from one pocket. He unfolded several ones and pressed them against the Coke machine's face. They dissolved into the machine. "Come on, then."

Drake followed for a few paces, then darted back and snapped up the cans in a few swallows. He chanced a look at Jedediah.

"Don't do it."

His shoulders hunched, but he extended his wings. A can of Cherry Coke dropped into the dispenser. He curled his long tongue around it, hooking its barbs over the lip and darted to catch up. Mid lope, he pushed a fang into the can's side and sucked at the contents. The can disappeared before they reached the truck.

Drake leapt into the bed, slamming his beak into an invisible wall. Drake yelped.

"Serves you right."

"Jedediah." An aged, dark-skinned Pillsbury Doughboy in a brown sheriff's uniform strode his way.

I'd never do it, but I swear he'd giggle if you poked his stomach.

Joe Franklin Tomlinson smiled easily, never hurried and could out polite an old lady in church. He'd been Jedediah's friend—knowingly and not—for almost all Joe Franklin's life.

Jedediah smiled. "Evening, Joe Franklin. Shouldn't you be retired by now?"

"You willing to sell that old fishing cabin?" Joe Franklin asked.

Jedediah shook his head.

"Got a minute, Jedediah?"

"This about Ronnie Gerald?"

"Could be. My boys have been gnawing that bone all week. They're stumped. Hoped you might remember something."

"We've been friends a long time."

Joe Franklin nodded. "Since before your pappy...before the war did him in."

"Yup."

"Still don't understand why he went at his age."

"Thought he could make a difference."

"I looked after you best I could when he passed," Joe Franklin said. "I'd really appreciate some help here."

"If I had something you could use, I'd let you know. You know that."

Joe Franklin stared into Jedediah's eyes. "Even so, you need to be nicer to my boys. They're doing a hard job."

"Seems reasonable."

"Right, well, fishing some time? Been a while."

"Sure. It's my busy season, but we can find a weekend I imagine."

"Good. You'll let me know if you find anything about Ronnie?"

"Yup."

Jedediah climbed into the truck. He nodded to Joe Franklin and drove home.

How come it feels like Ronnie Gerald's going to haunt me, one way or another, for a long time to come?

CHAPTER SIX:

Namhaid's Number One

One—the man's Namhaid codename—tapped his fingers and watched a blank screen. He checked the chat room's lower right corner a third time. Security level remained Priority Four.

Priority Three allowed the Namhaid American cell leader communications with his fellow leaders. Two provided communications between leaders and operatives and level one let operatives of a given cell cooperate—though never operatives of other cells.

It struck him as inefficient at times, but it protected the Namhaid's anonymity top to bottom.

Only Zero called a Priority Four meeting.

Either a good omen or a very bad one.

Zero represented the Namhaid's Board of Directors. No one but Zero met the board and few met Zero and lived to tell about it. An order from the unseen Zero demanded obedience, period. Something One's predecessor had forgotten.

The computer beeped:

```
Zero has signed on
Zero: Good evening, One.
One: Hello, sir.
Zero: Have you scouted the target?
One: Yes, but I don't understand how one person could be so
important?
Zero: You know of our feud? The betrayal which gave birth to
the Namhaid?
One: Yes, sir. My father and grandfather ranted about it
often. Sir, forgive my caution, but my cell at least is breaking
profit records. Is revenge against a single clan good business
at this point?
Zero: Your profits cannot compare to this theft.
One: The gold on that land is probably long gone.
Zero: Gold isn't always yellow metal.
One: Sir, may I ask what we're after then?
```

31

Zero: Imagine an underground railroad allowing free travel to a dozen global destinations. No borders, no customs, no one to stop men or shipments.

One: Not possible.

Zero: I've seen it personally.

One stared at the screen. *He's a fanatic, a zealot. What can I even say to him?* He leaned forward and typed.

One: If you say it exists, sir, then it exists. How has such a thing remained hidden?

Zero: It does. That is sufficient.

One: Meaning no disrespect to the Board, but why this plan? It's too complicated. Why not just kill him?

Zero: You've read the file?

One: I have, but really, so men have died, plans failed. That hardly supports the superstitious warnings in the file. Their restrictions don't hamper us. We've the finest weapons of modern military science and expert mercenaries the globe over.

Zero: So believed those now dead. Think what you want, One. Direct action is not the answer. The Board invested considerable resources into buying the right people. This plan leaves Shine impotent, no one to retaliate against, no room to sidestep fate. We're sending Two and a pair of my personal enforcers. Follow the plan. Leave the rest to us.

One: Another cell leader, sir?

Zero: Consider her a temporary partner. She'll play a part you cannot, all explained in the briefing she's been asked to deliver.

One: Yes, sir. We're watching the property now. We're only waiting for someone to take the bait.

Zero: Excellent. The Board has considerable faith in you, One. Please, don't make us regret it.

Zero has signed off.

One rubbed his eyes and exhaled. *Ugh, it's like working for Vader.*

CHAPTER SEVEN

Trouble Comes in Threes

Drake's doleful eyes pled up at him like an oversized puppy.

"My back door's still broke."

Drake whined.

"You stole from that Coke machine.

Drake whimpered.

Jedediah cursed his own good nature and the good mood renaissance fairs always put him in. "Fine, you can come."

Drake brightened.

"But the moment we get back from the Alabama Renaissance Fair you're fixing it, you understand?"

Drake nodded.

Renaissance fairs offered Jedediah periodic opportunities to be himself. He could dazzle children with magic, speak old English and share his joy with fair guests and regulars he'd known for years. Most of the circuit regulars stayed at the same hotel each year. He'd be welcome friend and story teller in their midst—family.

So why magic my way home when I can join them?

He wore his seventies again as he had during the eighteenth century. Long silvered beard draped down atop his dress robes, the slight red left in his whiskers counterpoint to the dark wood of his wizard staff.

He walked the fair as a wizard, spectacle for delight of many a child's eyes. Drake loped after him, cloaked in glamour and focused on his role as bloodhound.

He's putting in extra effort, of course who knows if it's honest effort or just contrition to get more Cherry Coke.

A young man in his early twenties stopped feet from him. "Jedediah Two-Hawks?"

Jedediah turned.

The same metallic-looking burgundy vestment and pants offset a silvery undershirt. New ranks of black symbols descended the sleeves to no longer scrawny biceps. He spread his arms, golden glove covering one hand opposite a hand bare save a gold ring. "By the Quasar, Two-Hawks, it is you."

"I see you've discovered the gym these last two centuries," Jedediah smiled. "It's Jedediah Shine now. Good to see you, Alden."

"Two centuries? But you're younger," Alden said.

"And you've aged what, three years? I like the goatee, by the by."

Drake's beak followed the conversation back and forth.

Alden ran a hand through close-cut auburn hair. "It looked good on you...that first time."

Jedediah beamed. "Imitation is the sincerest flattery."

Alden knelt and cupped Drake's head. "Aurei'Phriel?"

"Firewind sleeps beneath the Hawaiian Islands. This is Rydari Phriel, his grandchild."

Alden stepped close and lowered his voice. "What century is it?"

"Twenty-first."

Alden frowned. "Really? I'd have expected more advancement."

Jedediah laughed out loud. "This is a Renaissance Fair—a re-enactment of the medieval age."

"They find your medieval age desirable?"

"It's more a fantasy of a misremembered past."

Alden smiled. "Ah, I thought the smell tamer. Good as this meeting is, you know Shanriel."

"She still riding you hard?"

"A mentor's duty."

"Yup. If the old battle-axe turns up, she'll know from me you're hard on the job."

Alden chuckled. "Thanks, don't forget I still owe you."

Jedediah's brow rose, "Discourteous to die while you're indebted to me?""

Alden grinned. "Old man taught me an honorable man repaid his debts."

"So he does."

They shook and headed into different crowds.

Jedediah paused near a familiar troupe of troubadours and dancers. The gypsy-spirited youths made their living traveling from fair to festival. Their leader, Theophanie, spun into view, catching sight of him. Her smile ignited a Fourth of July pyrotechnic bonanza. She added a curtsied flourish to her dance just for him.

Tall and graceful, her mischievous brown eyes pierced the soul. He'd never seen her without long tumbling curls and ankle-length dresses, but he knew her every curve.

If I'd only met you younger, little gypsy.

Jedediah flourished a hand, fingertips drawing a silvered rose from nowhere. He tossed it at her feet.

"Amazing!" A ten-year-old boy beamed at him.

"I thank thee, young master. Have thee a gladdened heart for the arts of a poor prestidigitator?"

He nodded, an echo of the mid-thirties man holding his shoulder. "Come on, Mason. The man's not performing."

Jedediah held up a forestalling finger. He searched his robes, sparkling dust trailed each motion. A rolled parchment appeared, unraveling to display a scribed invitation. "Not now, I fear. This shall grant thee witness to many magical feats this night."

"Thank you," Mason turned to his father. "Can we, Dad? Please?"

"We'll see. You know how your mother bitches when we're late."

Mason froze mid-turn back to Jedediah. Wide eyes locked on Drake. "Dr-Dra—"

"Come on, Mason, leave the hound alone." Mason's father pulled him away.

"But, Dad, it's a..."

Mason's words dispersed in the crowd.

Jedediah frowned after the pair. "Come on, Drake."

They returned to Jedediah's stall. Jennifer perched on a stool inside it, a pose practiced over several summers. Bright, pretty and with a natural comfort among strangers, she drew people into his stall with ease.

Lucky to have her.

"Howdy, Jenn, anything new?"

"Sold some amulets and a wand. Almost sold that dragon scale armor, but his wife insisted they still had a mortgage to pay instead."

"Easy come, easy go." Jedediah shrugged. "Why don't you take a break?"

Jenn stood, adjusted her bustle and grinned her way out the booth. "Back in a bit."

Jedediah's evening performance went well. He didn't spot Mason despite a conscious effort. He whistled while he strolled. Double checked his stall locked tight and headed to his hotel.

Fair folk filled the hotel foyer, some still in costume. Many waved him over.

"Be back down in a moment," Jedediah said.

Drake whimpered. His eyes nearly crossed with the effort of glamouring himself both invisible and disguised in case he accidentally appeared.

Jenn leapt from a couch back over Theophanie, bouncing over to Jedediah.

"Mr. Shine, Theophanie's got a spot for me next summer."

"Aren't you finishing your degree?" Jedediah glanced down, shifting his leg to touch Drake's wing. *Concentrate, Drake, keep it up.*

<Trying, Master.>

"Yeah, end of this semester," Jenn said. "I want to do the circuit before job hunting, a celebration break, you know?"

"Yup."

She leveled innocent hazel eyes at him. "So, with all the events you do, maybe you need some more help? I'll need money to take off the season."

"I've got the Cotton Picking Fair first of October and Ossahatchee Fest later that month, but I've got help booked for both."

Her face fell.

"Think you could get over to Atlanta in December?"

"I guess, but Theophanie said December's a dead month."

"Usually, but they got some new medieval dinner show thing."

Drake whined softly.

"Heard they opened that up. The Florida one had a village set up, with an armorer and all this cool stuff," Jenn said.

"They asked me to perform for some Winter Solstice Festival on account of their druid going out on maternity leave."

"Thought that was a guy," Jenn said.

Jedediah grinned. "You'd be surprised what robes can hide."

"Something you want to tell me?" she asked.

"Nope."

"If you're doing a performance, why would you need me?"

"They're setting up a full, week-long fair to drum up attention."

Jennifer beamed. "That would be so great. I really need the money."

Jedediah glanced at Theophanie.

She raised her brows.

He winked then turned back to Jennifer. "You go tell that troublemaker I guarantee you'll earn enough to take a gypsy year off."

"Really?"

"Yup."

Her arms leapt around him. "Oh, thank you, thank you."

Jedediah chuckled. "Go on, girl."

She bounced off toward the others.

Jedediah glanced down. Drake's eyes squeezed shut.

"Stop pretending it's a strain."

Drake pressed against him. <*I can't hold this much longer.*>

"Need more practice then. Shall we join Theophanie?"

Drake growled. He bolted into an open stairwell door.

Jedediah chuckled all the way to his room.

A sheriff's deputy yawned, squinting at the rising sun. His hand hit the squad car ceiling. The car rocked side to side as two pick-ups roared past overflowing with dogs.

His radar gun blinked eighty-eight.

He reached for the ignition, but stopped.

Joe Franklin ordered me to sit and watch. He'll have my butt if I go chasing speeders, budget cuts or no.

He glanced down at a disposable phone in one cup holder.

Besides, I'm getting paid a year's salary to call in anyone stopping in the area.
He peered through the thick wood. Red seemed visible and he couldn't hear their engine anymore.

Should I call? Maybe I should drive up there and check. He shook his head. *That'd piss off Joe Franklin and might scare these guys off.*

"You should've seen the thing," Billy said.

Billy's cousin, also in his early twenties, glanced around at the roadside in the early morning light. "Don't see no tracks."

"Maybe it's a bit farther up, but I swear, Matt, the pig's huge."

"You sure we're allowed to hunt pig without a permit?" Matt asked.

"Heck, yeah. Pigs breed so fast, they don't even need a season," Billy said.

"Maybe, but this is Shine's land. You remember what happened to Paul."

Billy snorted and pointed at the dogs. "That's why we brought them. You and I set them loose over here, they'll smell the pig and Derrick will nail it when they chase it out the other side."

"If you say so," Matt said.

"Come on, you know we need the food," Billy said. "It's pure luck I spotted it before anyone else."

"There," Derrick pointed.

The other two looked. Large, fresh pig tracks trailed into the wood. Billy pulled a rifle from the gun rack and checked that it was loaded.

"Go on. I'll blow the whistle when we let them go," Billy said then guffawed. "Eating high on the hog tonight."

"You're not funny, you know that right?" Derrick climbed into his pickup.

"Shove it," Billy said.

The red truck's blue and white partner sped past the torn deputy fifteen minutes later. He picked up the disposable cell phone and pressed the speed dial.

It rang once.

"Hello?" someone said.

"Looks like someone's here," the deputy replied.

"Understood. We're already set up."

"Want me to—"

"Go get some breakfast."

The deputy's stomach knotted. "This candid video thing is legal right?"

Silence.

"Are you going to want me—"

"Thank you for your assistance."

"This TV stunt of yours is safe, right? Nothing bad is going to happen?"

The line went dead.

CHAPTER EIGHT

Magical Romance

Treevoran's lips touched hers, intensifying the tingle playing whack-a-goosebump all over Lanea's body. His mouth caressed hers. A tongue tip flicked her lips, almost demanding access past them. His hands burned against her cool skin.

This is so...no, I have to...oh but it feels so...no, breathe, push him away.

Her lips parted to stop him. Treevoran deepened the kiss.

His heat melted her closer into his arms, making it easier for him to explore wantonly.

I have to stop.

Her lips didn't stop, they begged for more and took it when it didn't come fast enough.

A gunshot exploded in the distance.

She jerked backward.

Oh so handsome Treevoran blurred. His true features, silver-haired elven perfection lurked under an afterimage of a more masculine, auburn-haired man with proper facial hair.

The glamour shifted, occasionally becoming something very much like Treevoran's true likeness. It altered again as conflicting thoughts on what truly attracted her altered the image.

More gunshots.

Treevoran pressed his lips to hers.

She shoved halfheartedly. "Trevor, stop. That's gunfire."

"Who cares?" He kissed her.

"I do. I'm supposed to be watching Da's lands, protecting the normals."

Treevoran's shoulder rose in the sexiest shrug she'd ever seen. "Let the normals work out their own problems."

He caressed her cheek, burning fingertips tracing their way across her mouth until her lips felt aflame. His mouth quenched it.

Another couple gunshots coughed irregular patterns.

A splash of cool water hit her face.

Treevoran spluttered, water running down his cheek to coalesce into a tiny pixie. The image of the pixie shaking a finger at him blurred as another watery, transparent girl formed on her nose.

"Mistress. Trouble in the wood." The pixie's piccolo voice said.

"Ugh, get off me." Trevor swept the pixie from his face. "I hate dewdrops."

The water Fey caught itself midair and started cursing at him in earsplitting squeaks. More dewdrops flittered between them, facing off against Treevoran while Lanea's flitted down to tug her toward the noise by a pinky.

"Mistress, you have to come, hurry."

Lanea's lips ached, cool, alone and reluctant to speak words she knew they must. "I have to see what's going on."

"Don't you love me?" he asked.

Her skin tingled.

The dewdrops fell silent.

I promised, Da...another kiss would be nice. It's cold without his hands...no, someone might be in trouble.

"Love is so much more important than babysitting *normals.*"

Dewdrops flittered down onto his shoulders and gazed adoringly.

"Just one more kiss from my beautiful princess?"

The dewdrops sighed, each presenting their lips.

"I guess, one more kiss, but then I have to see what that's about."

Treevoran smiled and pressed his lips to hers. Her skin tingled. His hot touch melted her deeper into his embrace. Lips and fingertips consumed her world.

Normals bled from her thoughts until a deputy charged into the clearing, wild-eyed and out of breath. "You have to run. It's insanity. There's—"

His expression worsened to crazed on sight of them and the dewdrops. Lanea opened her mouth to find out what happened, but Treevoran covered it with his own.

I need to...oh, his kisses are so...wait.

Treevoran's movement opened one of her eyes. He waved a hand at the stunned deputy. A blast of rainbow light knocked him from his feet.

"What did you—"

"I've protected you, love, he won't remember a thing." Treevoran's kiss muddled her thoughts. Magic swelled around them, hazing the area and surrounding the clearing in a thicket. "And now no one will interrupt."

Da's wrong about him.... Kisses ran her neck. *He's wonderful....* Fingertips caressed away her cares. *So good to me....*

Everything but Treevoran faded from importance.

CHAPTER NINE

Suspicions

Jedediah ambled out of his boneyard toward the farmhouse, setting sun streaking the sky at his back. The sound of wheels on gravel swept by him on the wind. He changed directions, heading around the greenhouse toward the front door. A tiny pink sprite rocketed up to him and almost up his nose, glowing bright even in the daylight.

"Jedediah, Jedediah," she squeaked.

He raised his brow and offered an open palm. "Are we acquainted, little one?"

She landed on the offered hand, light fading to expose a little-winged fairy the size of his fingernail. She traded pink light for red cheeks. "No! Th-that is to say, no, sir, but the dewdrops helped watch your place and I thought I should help, Great Wizard."

Jedediah frowned. "Why're the dewdrops watching my land?"

She clasped both hands together, wings fluttering enough to lift her just off of his hands and moaned one word. "Candy."

Jedediah chuckled.

"I have news, there are cars coming—"

"Up my drive. I know."

Her smile flickered but reignited. "They're—"

"Sheriff's boys, I wager."

Her face fell. "How did you know?"

"Only folks that visit these days."

She sniffled. "Does that mean no candy?"

"Don't usually pay for information I already have." Jedediah patted his pockets, coming up with a battered box of cinnamon imperials. "But, I like your gumption, so just this once."

He offered a tiny red candy half her size. She seized it, hugging it to her chest like a long lost baby. In an instant, she blazed pink and rocketed off, thank you's repeating over and over along a trail of sparkles.

Jedediah laughed and rounded the greenhouse.

Joe Franklin leaned against a police cruiser parked in the circular drive beneath his front porch. Two more settled to a stop on either side of the ring.

Jedediah put a hand on Drake's head. *Something's up. Go take a sniff, see if you can track down Lanea. Stay nearby but out of sight unless I call.*

Drake nodded and loped off toward the back door.

Joe Franklin tipped his hat. "Evening, Jedediah."

"Something up, Sheriff? News about Ronnie Gerald?"

Eddie and John stepped out of their cars upwind of him, but kept behind the open doors. Tension wafted off of them—sour and spicy aromas whispering through the breeze.

Jedediah frowned.

"Looking a bit grey there, Jedediah." Joe Franklin said.

"Just a bit of costuming. Your boys planning on drawing on me?"

"Why would you think that?" Joe Franklin asked. "I just thought we'd have us a little chat."

Jedediah waited. *Hell, he's working the dumb country boy act. What happened and where is that blasted girl?*

"Where were you this morning?" Joe Franklin asked.

"Why?"

Joe Franklin strolled over to him and presented his cell phone. Several pallid faces stared up at him. "You know any of these boys?"

Jedediah furrowed his brows. *First one might be familiar, but not the other two.*

"Jedediah?"

"I don't know two of them. That one there though, I don't know him personal, but I might've seen him around."

John's tone bit steel. "You don't know them?"

"Now, John," Joe Franklin said.

"I just answered that question."

John marched over to Jedediah. "Have you spoken to any of them? Recently?"

"No," Jedediah said.

"John, we talked about this."

John shoved a hand under Jedediah's nose. "Then how'd they have this?"

A small, dirty bronze whistle identical to the ones he'd given John and Eddie rested in a small bag on his palm.

Jedediah inhaled. Faint scents lingered around the plastic. *Dog, wild hog, gunpowder, horse, no centaur...shit, Ronnie Gerald and not a whiff of magic.*

"Well?" John asked.

Jedediah met Joe Franklin's gaze. "Your deputy's a mite upset, so I'm guessing by those pictures and his temper that something bad happened to those boys, but if he doesn't pull his hand out of my face I'm going to be forced to repeat a whooping I gave him as a kid."

"Assault my boys and I'll arrest you," Joe Franklin said. "John, take one step back please."

John did so.

"I recognize the whistle, but I never gave one to any of those three in the pictures," Jedediah said. "You find them on my land?"

"You haven't answered my question, Jedediah."

"Don't bother, Sheriff," John said. "He'll just lie. It's not like he makes a secret of how he regards trespassers."

Jedediah bristled. "I'll do no such thing. Need I remind you, *deputy*, trespassing is against the law?"

"So is murder," John said.

Joe Franklin stepped between them, hands up. "That's enough out of both of you. Your whereabouts this morning?"

"Alabama Renaissance Fair."

"Sheriff's been right here all afternoon while we looked things over," John said. "We've got deputies up and down the highway. You didn't come up the drive. You walk here from Alabama?"

"Slow up there, John," Joe Franklin said. "You got any witnesses?"

"Jenn Remer worked the booth with me all weekend. There're some roving performers, too. I've also got credit card receipts from this afternoon's sales."

Joe Franklin frowned. "That's one of them portable machines, right? Could have been used anywhere?"

"Well, it plugs into a phone line," Jedediah said. "You want to tell me who's been hurt?"

"You know cell phones can do that," Joe Franklin said.

"So I've heard."

"Eddie?" Joe Franklin said.

Eddie ducked into his cruiser and presented a long plastic bag containing a double hexagon-barreled shotgun. "This your gun, Mr. Shine?"

Few hexagon-barreled shotguns existed anymore, which pretty much made it his, but he checked it over through the plastic anyway. He pointed to the weapon. "That's my mark there on the stalk."

"Got radioed about a shooting. We found that there gun on your property," Joe Franklin said.

"Not much of a surprise," Jedediah shifted his weight. *Guessing they didn't pull that from my gun cabinet.*

"You admit it?" Eddie asked.

"Admit what?" Jedediah asked.

Lanea rushed around the edge of his porch only to backpedal out of sight.

"We found your shotgun laying in the woods, shell casings, three men and seven hounds dead around it," Joe Franklin said.

Jedediah braced himself against the swooping sensation in his stomach. *More men are dead, maybe with my gun.* Lightning careened around his rib cage, images of

Velith'Seravin's gloating sneer flashed across his eyes. *Looks like I've got a centaur's ears to peel back—or off his head.*

Joe Franklin watched him.

"What'd you give Simons? LSD?" John demanded.

Jedediah frowned at Joe Franklin.

"Deputy who called in the shooting," Joe Franklin said. "He's...a little confused at the moment. Found him unconscious not far from the scene."

Glamour? Why not kill him? Jedediah loosened his jaw. "So, what happens next, Joe Franklin?"

"Be nice if we could have a chat, Jedediah. I'd like my boys to get a good look in and around your place too—nice and friendly like."

"In other words without a warrant. You arresting me?" Jedediah asked.

"We should bring him in, Sheriff," John said.

Joe Franklin held up a forestalling hand. "Let's not get ahead of ourselves."

Can't have him taking too good a look at me like this—his memory's too good. If I can get that girl to help, I can slip this age, but only one reason he'll let me change before our chat.

"I've got nothing to hide. Let me change and I'll ride up with you to your office."

"Right here's just fine, or inside once you've invited us in," Joe Franklin said.

Jedediah glanced toward Lanea. He didn't know where she'd been when whatever happened. Her magic fooled the deputies, but Joe Franklin had developed keen eyes over three decades of police work.

Joe Franklin doesn't know her as anything but a migrant farmhand and I don't want him looking any deeper.

"If you and your boys are going to start accusing me of things, maybe we should do this all by the book," Jedediah glared at John. "Wouldn't want no pups yipping about unfair treatment."

"You leave my boys to me."

"I'll need to fill out a police report for the break-in and someone stealing my shotgun—keep things all nice and legal." Jedediah shrugged. "Need to pick up some groceries anyway. You don't mind if I change first?"

Joe Franklin sized him up. He took a deep breath and smacked his lips. "People died out here today. Might be killers are hanging around somewhere with more mischief in mind. Set my mind at ease if one of my boys escorted you, for your own safety."

Jedediah scrutinized the sheriff. *So you think you've got yourself a scent after all. I'll play your game, but only so you don't get in between me and the culprits responsible.*

"Thirty-seven please," Jedediah said.

The other three men looked between each other.

"What about thirty-seven?" Joe Franklin asked.

"Must have been about thirty-seven people saw me up in Florence today. Come if you're coming, Eddie," Jedediah glared at John. "Don't want to risk any guns going off by accident while I'm washing my face."

Jedediah led Eddie into the master bathroom. He ran the water until it warmed, waiting for his limbs to tingle. He pushed his face into the water, gritted his teeth and tried not to cry out. Hidden in his hands and then a towel, Jedediah's body reversed its aged appearance, growing younger to his late thirties. His hair and beard colored and shortened. Jedediah hoped either Eddie inattentive or Lanea glamoured him to prevent Eddie's noticing.

Jedediah straightened up and checked his appearance in the mirror. With a grunt of satisfaction he turned. "I'm ready to go."

Jedediah's eyes touched portraits on his way back outside. "Gun cabinet's in the den, as you well know Joe Franklin. Maybe your boys can find the thief's fingerprints. Shells are its bottom drawer."

"No locks?" Eddie asked.

"Locked tight and normally the doors would stop most people too," Jedediah said.

"Why wouldn't they now?" Joe Franklin said.

"Back door's missing. Might've had wood rot I guess, damn near disintegrated on the hinges."

CHAPTER TEN

In the State of Denmark...

Lanea watched the sheriff's cruiser pull out behind Jedediah in his old burnt-orange Dodge Charger.

John and Eddie strolled around to the back porch talking.

"I don't get it," Eddie said. "If the back door's off its hinges why come around front?"

John scratched his jaw. "Could be he heard us coming up the drive."

"Good ears for an old guy."

"Look at the door. Hinges are bent. Could wood rot have caused this like he said?"

Wood rot? Really, Da? Would a little lie really be worse than such ridiculous suggestions?

"No idea," Eddie said. "It's wide open, that's for sure."

"Something squirrelly is going on, Ed."

"Sure this isn't just an old grudge? You talk nice about Mr. Shine these day—well mostly, but I remember how you went on after he whooped you."

"He's a nice enough old fellow when the mood strikes him, but—"

"But you don't put it past him to shoot a bunch of trespassers in a fury," Eddie finished.

"Look, I know how I went on back in the day, but I wasn't just angry. I was terrified."

"Come on, you were always a daredevil. Sure you were younger, but it couldn't have been that bad."

John shook his head. "I heard him coming and ducked into that old boneyard. Opened one of those old refrigerators to hide. He grabbed me so mad, truth on the Bible, sparks came off of him."

Eddie chuckled.

"I'm serious. People talk about the fear of God, but in that moment I'd have taken an angry God over Mr. Shine."

Not mad, John, scared. A rueful chuckle almost escaped Lanea's lips. *That upset, you're lucky sparks ended it.*

Eddie shook his head. "That's what this is about? Him scaring you a decade ago?"

"No," John frowned. "Mostly no. Something's going on out here and Shine's not telling us everything. Hell, I'm halfway tempted to search the boneyard while we're here."

Eddie chuckled. "What do you expect to find? Bodies hidden in the refrigerators?"

Worse, Lanea thought.

"We've got *carte blanche* to look around," John said. "Never going to get a better invitation than that."

"Let's get on with it then."

They turned toward the door.

Drake crouched before it, teeth bared, muscles tensed and wings raised. A deep resonating snarl rumbled in his throat.

Color leached from their faces. Long unused instincts kept them still, telling each that the slightest move meant a horrible end beneath Death's wings.

Lanea cursed. She closed her eyes, frantically searched for her focusing image and projected glamour with all her strength. She pushed it at them, wrapping it like cellophane between them and Drake.

Both deputies' postures relaxed ever so slightly.

She charged out, gliding across the porch in a whisper. She glared over their shoulders at Drake and placed a hand on each head.

Thank Mother normals are so willing to ignore horrible truths—even ones about to eat them.

She imagined rain, falling softly over them and eased glamour into their minds in its drizzle. Fear's inferno evaporated her little thoughtdrops.

"Damn it, Drake, calm down." Her voice came out as a harsh whisper. "Da gave them permission, and for Mother's sake restore your glamour. I can't do this with you radiating dragon fear."

Drake growled something she didn't understand.

She glanced at her hands, the contact holding the deputies still. She searched around her, finding an old bucket under a gutter spout. She reached out to the water, teeth clamping down on her lip.

The water had been in the bucket a while, going lazy and sluggish. She prodded it, eyes narrowed with focus. It inched out of the bucket like a garden snake.

Come here. Go there. Flow between.

The water split into a two-headed serpent, each slithering across the porch's boards. Small amounts dripped from it between slats, but she held it together without releasing the deputies' minds.

It clamped onto her bare foot, but hesitated when faced with Drake. She pushed it harder and it formed the touch connection. Drake's thoughts erupted into her head.

<Stupid mortals. I should rend the flesh from them. How dare they question Master? How dare they threaten his flesh? I should rip their walls to the ground, feast on their marrow and leave their children shivering in caves for fear of my wrath.>

Drake!

His eyes flickered to her, softening a moment.

Stop. Please.

<They took Master.>

Da seldom does things for reasons other than his own. Give him time before you start disemboweling deputies and make the whole thing worse.

Drake snarled and both men stiffened again. Even Lanea could feel the edge of fear pushing against her mind.

Drake!

The dragon folded his wings into his sides, replacing the radiated fear with his glamour disguise.

She exhaled, letting the water collapse to the ground. She eased her magic back into the deputies, quenching their fear to only fright.

Lanea removed her touch. She darted around the corner before she slipped up and they caught sight of her.

John, paler than moments before, cursed. "Damn dog startled me. He's not happy with us going inside."

Eddie pressed a hand to his chest. "Wow, nearly jumped out of my skin. If he'd been here earlier, no one would've snuck inside."

Drake whined.

"I think I'd rather use the front door," John said.

"What about the boneyard?" Eddie asked.

Drake's lip curled.

"Maybe next time."

"Right."

Lanea waited.

The deputies drove down the gravel road.

"Come on," Lanea said. "Let's see what they found."

Drake sulked behind her, body language still projecting menace.

Jedediah's gun cabinet remained closed. The shotgun's cradle gaped empty. Lanea twirled her fingers, unlocking and opening the cabinet without leaving fingerprints.

Drake snuffled the floor around the cabinet, his nostrils flaring.

Another twist of her fingers pulled the cabinet's drawer open. An open box of shells rested inside.

No way to tell if any are missing without Da. She checked Drake. "Find anything?"

He pressed his beak closer to the floor and took in a deep breath. His head shot back and then forward in a forceful sneeze. Flame shot from his nostrils.

Lanea bolted forward, but he licked the flames from the singed rug like a child scoops whipped cream off a sundae.

"Together?" she said.

Drake unfurled his wings and extended one to touch Lanea.

Drake's magic flooded into her, nearly forcing her cross-eyed. She tamed the raging current, guiding and sliding it around her like river banks until his strength lessened to a gentle stream. She reached out to the rug's threads. Old and set in their patterns, Drake's strength came as an advantage. She prodded and cajoled the threads into remembering their former life. She forced their growth, burning those she replaced as they wove their way forward. She expanded her focus, shocked at the intricacy she could manage with Drake behind her.

Come on, little ones, share your pigments.

Moments later, the rug lay as it had before Drake burnt a hole in it.

Lanea waited for the second sneeze, deflecting it enough to dissipate without singeing anything. She touched him. *Drake?*

<Something, but I can't make it out.>

What's with the sneezing?

Drake made his awkward shrug. *<Something awful has been left behind to disguise the scent.>*

His scent memory rushed into her thoughts. She sneezed, rubbing her nose. *Ugh, there's no way Da left something like that around with his sense of smell.*

Drake nodded.

Do you recognize the scent beneath it?

<I do, but I can't place it.>

She frowned. Aquamancy didn't automatically augment sense of smell. Between Drake's aeromancy and natural senses, it'd be best to leave it for him to figure out. *All right, keep watch and see if you can remember what it is. I'll go see Da.*

CHAPTER ELEVEN

Mist & Misdirection

Jedediah sat across the table from Joe Franklin. Two cups of coffee and several pecan rolls lay untouched between them.

"I've known you a long time, Jedediah. Maybe too long," Joe Franklin said.

"Have you known me to murder?"

"No, but that don't change the way things sit now."

Jedediah nodded.

"First there's the business with Ronnie Gerald. Sad, but maybe it happened the way you said. Maybe," Joe Franklin scrutinized Jedediah. "Now there's these boys and their dogs."

"You ever seen me hurt a dog?"

"Not once, but the shell casings have your fingerprints on them."

Jedediah didn't bother to keep the sarcasm from his voice. "The shell casings from my shotgun have my fingerprints? The shotgun from my gun cabinet? Well, that's certainly suspicious. Come on, Joe Franklin, you've seen me case my own shells. All those spent shells have a thumbprint on the butt?"

"You keep that gun loaded?"

"You keep yours loaded?" Jedediah asked.

"That cabinet of yours locked up? Where's the key?"

Jedediah folded his arms. "You know I keep that cabinet locked."

"In case some kid sneaks in?"

Jedediah inclined his head. "But killing isn't some boyhood prank."

"Where's the key?"

"Behind the crown on top of the cabinet."

"Where anyone could get at it," Joe Franklin said.

"I'm a hand better than six feet. I built that cabinet to suit me. That key's out of sight and reach of just about everyone in the county."

"You own a bow, Jedediah?"

Jedediah leaned forward, placing his hands on the table. "You saw it hung on my mantle four Christmas ago when you and your missus joined me for dinner—afore she passed."

Joe Franklin's eyes slipped out of focus. He nodded more to himself than Jedediah. "Arrows?"

Jedediah leaned back in his chair and cursed his own good habits. *If I ignored weapon upkeep, I could take down that old centaur bow and show him a string that'd snap on the first pull. Like as not, that bow will fire a hundred times without a problem.*

"No."

"A bow but no arrows," Joe Franklin said. "That's a might peculiar."

"Only if I bow hunted. A local chief gifted it to us decades ago."

"And if I told you that we found some arrows in your home?" Joe Franklin asked.

"You'd be a damned liar."

The sheriff's eyes narrowed. He chewed on his response, but swallowed his temper and continued in a calm tone. "The coroner thinks arrows killed Ronnie Gerald, not an animal."

"Something ripped him up."

"Drake could've done it. My boys said you admitted to wiping blood off him with your handkerchief."

Jedediah shook his head. "Drake didn't escape my sight long enough. Fool beast snuffled it, but paws don't shred like that and I doubt he got a single bite. How many of those shells had thumb prints on them?"

"Two."

"The ones I loaded before putting it away last."

"Maybe."

Jedediah and Joe Franklin matched stares, each trying to glean the other's thoughts. *I'm to blame for those men's deaths. I failed them, but I didn't kill them. Joe Franklin's doing his job, but I've had just about enough of this bullshit. I've got a centaur to break.*

Jedediah's temper bubbled to the surface "What kind of fool do you think I am, Joe Franklin? I threw a fit, slaughtered trespassers? In control enough to wear gloves but out of control enough to leave shotgun and shells beside the bodies?"

"I know you're no fool," Joe Franklin said. "That's the problem. Four murdered men, four, on your land. Ain't enough to say you did it, but too much to discount you. Maybe you lost your fool temper then covered it up. Maybe you arranged it all to look confusing, to play the fool."

"Right, a psychic episode woke me early with news of trespassing morons, so I raced back from Florence, shot them, staged the scene and raced back. Did you even call Jennifer Remer?"

"Yup. She said you got to the booth around ten."

"Fair opens at ten."

"No need to setup?"

Jedediah folded his arms across his chest again. "On the second day of a show?"

"Seem to recall you're an early riser."

"Most farmers are."

"Could be you hankered for your bed, came back, caught them on your way back north and killed them."

"Waste money on a hotel? Easier to call me killer than admit I might've enjoyed sleeping in on a Sunday morning?" Jedediah stood up.

"I don't like any of this any more than you do, Jedediah, but I need you to sit down and answer my questions."

"I came here peaceable. I answered your questions. If you ain't arresting me, then I'm going home to feed my dog."

"I'm not arresting you," Joe Franklin said. "Today."

"Escorting me home? Just in case I go into another fugue induced killing spree?" Jedediah asked.

"That reminds me, Jedediah. Why didn't we see you drive up when you got home?" Joe Franklin asked.

Jedediah hesitated. *Because we teleported, but telling you that opens several cans of worms, some the juicy incriminating kind.*

"The truck broke down. I had to hoof it the last bit."

Joe Franklin heaved himself out of the chair. "An escort might be a good idea—for your own safety. Why don't we swing by Al's towing and we'll get your truck on the way?"

"I drove, remember? Groceries?"

"We've got to corroborate your statement. How about instead you file those burglary reports while my boys meet Al at your truck."

Jedediah glared. He could feel the power building within him, but still managed to prevent any outward show. "Fine. I'm going to the little boys' room. You want to follow?"

"Nah, got a call to make."

Jedediah hurried to the bathroom. Two others populated the facility. He cursed.

He's gone to radio his deputies to check a truck that isn't there. Guilty or not, I need it to be.

He relieved himself for appearances and cranked open the sink's hot water. Steam rose slowly, fogging his mirror. The last occupant finished and left.

Jedediah invoked a mirror mist.

"Lanea," he said.

"Behind you, Da," she answered.

Jedediah whipped around. The faintest distortion righted his facing. "What're you doing in a men's room, girl? You ain't got no call watching men doing their business."

"I didn't *look*, but I needed to talk to you."

"We need to talk all right, but I needed you at home."

"To move the truck?" she asked.

Jedediah nodded.

"What about Drake?"

"Fool dragon can't even open a door, you think he can manage a spell like this?" Jedediah asked.

"He's got the power."

Jedediah frowned.

"Got any choice, Da?"

Jedediah turned back to the mirror. "Drake."

Three attempts later, Jedediah stared at Drake through the swirling reflective mist projected over the mirror. Lanea stood beside him, fingers dangling in running water and concentration on glamouring the men's room door from sight.

"You sure you know what I need you to do?" Jedediah asked.

Drake nodded.

"Then get to it, and make sure you concentrate. This is important."

Joe Franklin met him outside "Al's on his way."

And so is Drake, God help him.

Drake darted through the farmhouse.

Master's counting on me. Got to get it right this time.

He sped into the study, skidding on the waxed wood, leaving claw marks he'd have to fix later. He leapt onto a chair, front talons on its back, and reached out with his mouth to pull down the case-protected model of an old red pickup truck.

He darted out the back door and through the boneyard. Using his wings seemed tempting, but he couldn't risk dropping the model already slippery in his beak.

Got to hurry.

His wings unfurled slightly. Change magic coursed through him. He pushed it into his talons, altering them for running. His pace increased.

A deputy cruiser slipped in and out of sight through the woods offering Jedediah's farm privacy. It rolled up the old state highway without hurry.

He bolted away from them cross country.

They're too close to put it where Master said, but it'll be close enough for puny human brains.

He glanced at the deputies. Heat and moon-reflecting metal slipped between the trees. He lowered his head and put on more speed.

Drake ran full out, struggling to keep hold on the model when he remembered the gully. *I'll reach it before I can slow, got to jump it.*

He glanced toward the cruiser.

Too close to use wings. I'll be lucky to get the release spell off in time. He focused on his glamour, altering it on the fly from hound to buck. Drake jumped the gully with all his might—a perfect jump. He sailed high over the gully. His front feet hit the road.

The case slipped from his mouth and smashed into the pavement.

Drake wanted to howl. *No time.*

He knocked the lid from the case, scooped up the model and bolted to the far side of the road. He set the truck down faced toward the farm.

The cruiser came around the curve, headlights shining toward him from far up the road.

Drake bolted beyond the tree line. With a frustrated growl, he extended his wings and glared at the model. Magic swelled, but refused to reach out a connection to the truck.

The cruiser rolled closer.

Breathe, Master's counting on me. He breathed—in through his nostrils, out through his mouth. His heartbeat pounded in his ears. He held his breath and tried to shut it out. He tried again, focusing on the truck to the exclusion of all else. He still couldn't feel the germ of power within the model.

What if dropping it dispelled the magic? What if I've ruined everything? What if they take Master away for good? He shook his head, trying to clear his thoughts. *Focus, I can do this. I have to do this.*

The cruiser drove by, its wheel crunching the model case.

"What'd we hit?" Eddie asked.

"I didn't see anything." John asked.

"Should we go back?" Eddie said.

"Let's find this truck."

Drake *really* wanted to howl.

He pushed at his magic with everything he had. A sense of suffocation gripped him as if he pushed air from his body instead of the magic. Tiny sparks flickered from him, singeing the tiny hairs along his leathery scales. He put it from his mind.

Flight hairs aren't important, can't fly yet anyway. Hope the deputies think the flashes are fireflies.

The cruiser rolled to a stop.

Out of time. Drake narrowed his eyes at the truck, growled and shoved all the power he could muster at the model. Time held its breath.

Drake felt the kernel of power within the old truck model. His power flashed across the space, lightning igniting a fuse. The truck exploded to full size with a flash of light and a sound like a gunshot.

"What the hell?" Eddie asked.

"Passing car?" John said. "Blown tire? Hey, there's the truck."

"How did we miss it?" Eddie asked.

"No idea," John said. "Do you smell smoke?"

Idiot, idiot, idiot. Drake slowed his breath and extinguished his sparks.

"Probably whatever burned out on the truck," Eddie said. "Should we check if someone lost a tire up the road?"

"No, we wait for the tow truck. Let's check it out."

They approached the truck. It sat at an odd angle, partially in the gully. John bent over and whistled.

"What's up?"

"Axle's broken," John said. "Must've ground to a stop. Good bet the engine's burned up."

Eddie reached for his radio. "Okay, I'll let the sheriff know where it is."

"Don't bother. It's close enough. They'll find us."

CHAPTER TWELVE

Good Counsel

Jedediah saw Al's oldest Brent off with the truck for repairs and stormed back into the farmhouse.

Drake made himself smaller on the porch nearby.

Jedediah stopped just short of the doorstep. "Excellent work, Drake. You've proved what we've believed of you for some time. From now on, I'll expect nothing less."

Jedediah stepped inside, pausing long enough to hear Drake groan. A smirk played at the edges of his lips. He marched upstairs.

Great lizard got lucky, but that broken axle left Joe Franklin once more without answers. I don't intend to go without mine any longer.

He'd warned Jedediah not to leave town, probably heard it on television. Normals who couldn't travel the world to return a moment later stayed put. It didn't matter anyway. Guilty feelings or not, they had nothing on him.

His temper built while he rummaged through his closet. Items disappeared into a duffel, regardless of size: several outfits, a spare set of boots, a feather decorated spear, his ill-fitting buckskins and a quiver of arrows. He threw the duffel out of the closet onto the bed, almost hitting Drake.

"Sorry," Jedediah mumbled.

Drake eased forward until he could touch the old mage.

<Are we traveling, Master?>

"Yes. Haven't you worked out that mouth shift yet?"

Drake jerked back.

"Da," Lanea scolded. "Drake's done you a service, you could show more gratitude."

"I thanked him proper," Jedediah said.

She stepped into the doorway, folded her arms and glared up at him. "Where're you going?"

"To tear VelSera's fool head off and shove it up his horse's ass, him and anyone else responsible for this."

She blocked the doorway.

"Custom requires you to give them two moons. You taught me that. Besides you gave your word," Lanea said. "It's only been a few days."

55

"Look what they've done with them. I warned that fool VelSera not to force me to return early." Jedediah fixed her with his gaze. "I also recall asking you to stay nearby and protect the normals. What happened with that?"

She reddened. "I got...distracted."

His scowl deepened. "That boy's not welcome on my land."

"I didn't say anything about Trevor."

"Uh huh." Sparks flickered from his shoulders. "And you've got the nerve to ask why I don't approve. Move. I'm getting to the bottom of this now."

Lanea placed both hands on his chest and smiled up at him. "Do you remember when I wanted to slip ten-penny nails into the beds of those elves who teased me?"

"Handling that iron nearly sent you into a coma. No good would've come of it. Probably would've ended up branded a kin-killer."

"You tried explaining that, but I refused to listen, remember?"

"Too wrapped up in your fool temper."

"Yup," she mimicked.

"Girl, get out of my way," Jedediah said.

"We shelter the tribes. You can't just go declare war on them while in a temper," Lanea said.

"Then I'll kick them right off the property," Jedediah said.

Her eyebrows arched, emphasizing her elven features. "Guilty and innocent alike?"

"They killed three more men."

"And all those dogs."

He froze. *Why kill the dogs? Easy enough for a centaur to calm them.* He shook the thought away. "You haven't met this boy. He's mean spirited like no one's business."

"He wants out of your protection. If you kick them all out, what do you think will happen?"

Jedediah opened his mouth but she cut across him. "They'll kill more normals. Satellites will pick them up. People will photograph them. The secret will be *out*. A whole new war will begin against the Fey."

"Aren't you the one always telling me the normals are getting smarter?"

She smirked. "Aren't you the one always telling me we have to protect the normals and the Fey?"

"Then I'll get the High Tribe to order justice."

"Justice or punishment, Da? Can you even tell the difference right now?" Drake whined.

"Not you, too," Jedediah scowled.

Lanea smiled and rested a hand on his forearm. "Send a messenger to WaphRae or TherPriel. Tell them what has happened. Maybe it'll prod them to speed their enquiries. You gave them two moons, keep your word."

"You're a cursed hard-headed girl."

"Come by it naturally."

Jedediah nodded. "Elven trait."

"You don't want to go storming off into the woods with a duffel if Joe Franklin's watching anyway."

"Fine, but if anything else happens—"

"I'll sharpen pitchforks and prepare the torches," she said.

"What did the dewdrops see?"

Lanea fidgeted. "They must've gotten befuddled by the spell Treevoran hit the deputy with, but I managed to get something about brown uniformed normals with thunder iron."

"What about during the attack?"

She shrugged.

"You'll go to Fleet Hoof as messenger?"

She nodded.

"Take Drake. That'll get their attention."

She took his bag and set it aside. Taking his forearm, she led him downstairs. "It's been a long day. Let's settle you in with some food. I'll tune the mist into the 1960s and you can watch one of your westerns."

"Wrong time of day, girl."

She laughed, shaking her head. "You're bespelling the mist to pull their original airings forward in time, and you're fussing about a couple of hours difference?"

"Sometimes it's the principle that matters most."

CHAPTER THIRTEEN

New Festival, Old Flame

September became October and both ended without more bloodshed. Joe Franklin brought by more questions, but all civil. Deputies patrolling the adjacent highways waved when they saw Jedediah.

Drake and Jedediah attended the Cotton Picking Fair and Ossahatchee Indian Festival as planned. They ran into Alden at the latter, still chasing a criminal hiding out in such events. An Ossahatchee spirit elder swore a blood oath to his people's innocence.

The Winter Solstice celebration in Atlanta put Jedediah in good spirits. He enjoyed his October events, but not being renaissance fairs he left off playing a wizard.

Lanea attended, her nearly indecent costume summoning his scowl and too many drooling targets to hex them all.

The makeshift festival covered a parking lot and adjoining undeveloped land. The Georgia Renaissance Festival's permanent location dwarfed it, but free admission meant brisker business.

Jedediah strolled through opening day crowds, robes swishing around his ankles. Woven from metal threads finer than silk, the combat robes not meant for fairs remained among his most treasured possessions.

He scratched his beard. *Something's brewing.*

He drew to a stop near a gaggle of children, delighting them with some sleight of hand. Several adolescents joined the show. One pompous boy explained each trick to the girls with him.

Try explaining this, smartass.

Jedediah conjured a flurry of tiny faerie dragons, encouraging the mischievous constructs to tie the boy's shoelaces. He left the baffled teen in the dirt, a self-satisfied smirk on his lips.

He wound his way back to his booth, dazzling the crowds with prestidigitation. Drake sunbathed next to their stall, but hadn't re-extended his wings since Jedediah's last reprimand.

Jedediah eyed Drake, pushing up his sleeves to display his bare forearms.

Drake rolled his eyes.

A can of Cherry Coke slipped from his sleeve.

The dragon's head shot up, his tongue lolled out one side of his maw.

"It's him, Mom. It's him. The wizard with the dragon."

Jedediah whirled.

A boy of ten dragged an attractive mid-thirties woman through the crowd. Her chestnut hair framed fair skin sprinkled with cinnamon freckles and intelligent brown eyes.

Cold washed over Jedediah.

Elegant and tailored period clothing fit to her curves, as authentic as could be purchased—not a single item from a mismatched period. Even the deep blue and eggshell white matched medieval dyes.

He stared, and not just because of her bodice's plunging neckline. *No. It's not possible.*

Rain poured around them, making the rocky mountain pass slick and treacherous. Jedediah cursed the European style clothing soaked against him, wishing for the simple doeskin breeches of his people.

"Careful, Elsabeth," his hand stretched back to hers.

Invisible tears disappeared amidst rain down her fair cheeks. Auburn hair stuck against her face, softest waves the only testament of her curls. She stumbled again.

"We must stop, Jedediah," A soft Irish accent kissed her voice. "I cannae run further. Let me speak to me kinsmen to make peace, my love."

Dogs bayed in the distance: angry, frustrated, and frenzied. Rain washed his scent away, but they fled the only clear pass.

Jedediah helped her up. "Your father and brothers have sworn a blood hunt. No Peace Woman could persuade them to forsake such a warrior's vow."

Her legs shook visibly trying to support her weight. "I choose thee. I can make them understand that."

Jedediah smiled, scooped her into his arms and ran on. He struggled to draw strength from the earth. *Damn these thick-soled boots. Damn my own weak terramancy. Never again.*

A dozen strides later he kicked free the boots. Strength seeped into him, too slow to sustain him long. He shook frustrated tears from his sight. *I won't give up. I won't fail her.*

"Jedediah, please, you'll kill thyself like this. Release thy claim on the land. They'll let us go."

"It's sacred and cannot be theirs, Elsabeth. I've told you."

She smiled up into his face. "My heart cannae envision wonders such as thee describe."

"Bide and see them yourself."

"Thee taketh me to this protected paradise?"

"I'm not yet guardian. The Dutchman must grant you entrance, but then you'll witness it."

He stumbled, bringing both of them to the ground.

"We're lost," she cried.

Jedediah caressed her cheek and stood, shielding her with his body, arms +upstretched. "No."

Thunder snarled above Jedediah. A corona of light flickered around his set shoulders.

He glared down the path toward their pursuers. "Look away, beloved. You mustn't see."

A half-dozen lightning bolts arced above him.

Jedediah shook the memory from his thoughts. Many Fey—dryads, satyrs and whatnot—believed Mother rewarded good works with additional lives. *No. She can't be Elsabeth reincarnated. I won't believe it.*

She blushed but met his gaze firmly.

Not the timid maid I met so long ago. Jedediah shook himself once more. *How long have I stared like a fool adolescent?*

He coughed awkwardly and fumbled at his robes.

She pushed her hair from her face. "It's a bloodhound, Mason, not a dragon."

Mason? The boy from the Alabama Renaissance Fair who'd somehow seen through Drake's glamour?

Mason slipped from her distracted grip.

Jedediah's eyes drank in the woman before him. He realized the boy's intent at the last moment. "Mason!"

The boy's head snapped around. "Sir?"

"Sorry to startle you, youngster." Jedediah offered a gentle smile. He extended a hand to feel the boy's aura. "You don't want to charge Drake like that. He's old and a bit short tempered."

Drake slipped forward and wrapped his tongue around Mason's wrist. The boy's face exploded with glee. "It's okay. He likes me."

Jedediah scrutinized the dragonling. Drake's expression told Jedediah that he *did* like the kid. *Still, could be partly to spite me since I haven't handed over his soda.*

"I'm sorry about that. He's always going on about seeing this or that." She shrugged. "Healthy imagination."

The tiniest scent of ozone wafted up from the pair, distracting Jedediah. "What? No, that's all right."

She extended a hand. "I'm Mason's mother, Billie Jo Bartlett."

Jedediah took her hand with a flourish and bow. He kissed it. "Tis a great pleasure, milady. Allow me to present myself, humble peddler and prestidigitator: Jedediah Shine."

Billie Jo blushed. "Well, forsooth my heart is driven nearly to flutter by thy presence. Thee might claim the part of humble peddler, but in the sure light of day a gentleman of high court stands before me."

Mason made a face. "Mom!"

"Nay."

"Nay?" she asked.

Jedediah's eyes twinkled with mischief. "I'm no gentleman but a wizard. And thee?"

Billie Jo laughed. "A humble alchemist."

"She is not," Mason said. "She's a high school chemistry teacher."

Billie Jo's gaze didn't leave Jedediah's face. "Play with the dog, Mason."

"Dragon," Mason corrected.

"Whatever. Have we met?"

"Perchance. I frequent many a festival and fair."

"That explains it," Billie Jo almost whispered. She cleared her throat. "You seemed familiar."

"Drake and I love coming to these things. Guilty pleasure I guess."

She reddened. "Mine too. You're working at least."

"I don't always wear this getup. We might've met in my normal guise: shorter hair, trimmed beard," He grinned. "A little less Merlin."

Drake's beak swung his way.

"Yes...that must be it."

Mason and Drake watched with mixed expressions. Mason clambered onto his feet and stepped between them. "Do some magic."

"Mason, be polite to Mr. Shine."

"Jedediah, Ms. Bartlett."

"Miss," she said. "Billie Jo, please."

"Billie Jo."

"Please do some magic, Jedediah?" Mason asked.

"Mr. Shine," Billie Jo corrected.

Jedediah's attention remained on her. "I don't mind."

"I do," she said. "It isn't proper."

Jedediah shook himself and turned to find Mason's face supremely serious. "What would you like to see, Master Bartlett?"

The smile reappeared on Mason's face. "Anything."

Jedediah made the Cherry Coke disappear—much to Drake's dismay. His fingers twiddled through spell after spell. Billie Jo scrutinized his every gesture more intently than the earlier adolescent.

The private magic show quickly turned public.

Kids pushed their way into a half-circle around Jedediah, shoving Billie Jo to the rear with the rest of the parents. He checked a glare. *My own fault for using real magic to impress the boy.*

Jedediah finished with a bow and announced his next show time. They meandered off, some lingering to peruse his stall's wares.

"Very impressive," Billie Jo said.

"Thank you."

Mason tugged on his mother's skirts. "Mom, I'm hungry."

She offered Jedediah an apologetic smile. "Growing boys."

Jedediah nodded.

"Nice meeting you," she said. "Maybe we'll catch that next show."

Jedediah offered a conjured scroll. "I'll save you a seat."

Mason opened the scroll. Drake looked it over with a very undoglike stare.

Billie Jo raised her eyebrows. "How did you do that?"

Jedediah checked the fluid script added to his longtime prop. "Did I misspell your names?"

Drake openly gaped.

"No, but how did they get there?" She asked.

"Magic."

Mason dragged her away toward the food court. "I want a whole turkey leg this time. I don't want to share."

Jedediah watched them go. Sprites played rugby in his guts. Those few moments of banter had been like sunlight after a stormy winter. His breath froze in his chest.

Drake laid his head against Jedediah's leg. *<You're distracted, Master. Are you well?>*

"What?"

<Are you well?>

"What? Yes. O-of course. I'm just fine. The boy's keen-sighted?"

<Air kindred.>

Thought I scented ozone. Explains why she said he's always seeing things she doesn't believe are there. Jedediah looked down at Drake. *He saw through your glamour.*

Drake cringed.

"Is he strong enough to require watching or did you let your guard down?"

A woman's cackle drew Jedediah's attention. "First sign of madness, talking to animals like they're human. My cats don't count."

CHAPTER FOURTEEN

Changing Views

Lanea skipped around the fair's edge, enjoying the festive air and sipping the charged atmosphere like candied wine. Her outfit had provoked Jedediah as intended, but she'd been forced to insulate herself against the resultant cold.

"Damn it, come back."

She turned toward the voice to see a handsome sorrel trotting away from his handler. Sweat dampened trainer and horse, showing off spectacular flesh in both cases.

Lanea rushed into the horse's path.

"Stay back, he's not fully trained."

Lanea lifted a hand toward the horse's snout. The set of its eyes warned her a moment before it snapped its teeth where her fingers had been. She set them lightly on the horse's nose.

Calm yourself, friend. She hummed an elven tune.

The horse's tension washed from its stance.

"I'll be a son of a bitch."

She shifted her attention to him, running her eyes along the muscle tone broadcast by his sweaty t-shirt. Brown stubble outlined a thin beard along a square jaw.

Her brows rose appreciably. "Not the nicest way to talk about your mother, particularly considering all she's done for you."

"Sorry?"

"Nothing." Lanea stroked the horse. "He's not a bad horse. He just wants to run the wind."

"That sorrel's bitten or stomped on all the trainers. I'd have left him be if not for my own pulling a muscle."

"You're not a trainer?" she asked.

"Black and white knight, you?"

"Sorceress."

He chuckled. "Name's Dalton."

"Lanea."

"He likes you."

64 | MICHAEL J. ALLEN

The horse or... A blush rushed to her cheeks. Treevoran flickered through her mind, dusting guilt along his path. She shrugged. "I'm good with animals."

"Are you really a magician?" Dalton asked

She shrugged again.

"You live around here?"

"Asking me out?" Lanea asked.

"Yes and no."

One brow rose in unison with a corner of her mouth. "No?"

"Our druid's on maternity leave. If you're as good with pyrotechnics as animals, we could use someone around like you."

She studied him. *Dangerously cute, but job offers aren't a normal flirting technique.* "Why mention it?"

"You're cuter than the old man they got to replace her."

"You mean my Da?"

He colored. "I-I didn't know, really? Your father? He's so old."

She left him to flustered stammering while she considered what he'd offered. Jedediah wanted her as the next guardian, but it'd be centuries until he passed it on. She'd lived a tightrope life between the farm and her mother's elven city. She'd spent little time on her own. She'd only recently grown old enough to work with normals without her apparent agelessness giving her away. *Da's had my itching feet nailed solid for a long time. Maybe it's time for a little adventure.*

"Will you please say something so I can stop taste testing my foot?"

She opened her mouth with every intention of asking him out. The words froze in her mouth as Treevoran's face filled her thoughts. Ache speared her chest and the words refused to exit.

"I've got to take him back inside."

"I'll think about it," Lanea said.

"The job or the date?"

She stepped up to him and presented her phone. "Both. Give me your number."

He beamed.

Phone number stored, he led the sorrel back into the building. She watched him go, enjoying the way he did it. She smiled down at the number on her phone. A sudden urge to delete it flashed through her. She fought it. Treevoran sprang to mind.

No. A phone number isn't cheating. Besides, nothing lasts forever.

CHAPTER FIFTEEN

Never Again, Maybe

Jedediah turned toward the voice with a wide smile.

The woman before him resembled a strumpet version of Bewitched's Aunt Clara. She leered across the concourse—too far to have overheard. A sign just behind her labeled her stall as Mad Meadow March's Romance Concoctions.

"Good to see you, Meadow. Didn't notice you open up."

"Don't doubt it. Shame on you, grown man leering like a besotted jester. She wasn't even wearing my concoctions." Meadow gestured him over. "Mind?"

Jedediah checked his booth. Jenn and Karen each had a customer. Another waited for one of them to free up.

"Be over in a minute, Meadow."

Jedediah helped the waiting customer and another three that wandered in. He crossed to Meadow's stall once business slowed. A riot of colored liquids in exotic glass containers filled her small stand.

"Still pretending perfume and cologne are magical tinctures," Jedediah said.

"Aren't they? Have you smelled some people?"

He laughed.

"For the record, Jedediah, every word of my advertisements conforms to the spirit and letter of the law."

"I've no doubt."

"You should buy some. Bet she'd warm up to you faster if you didn't smell like a poor dirt farmer."

"So how's the law practice?"

"Spent last month in New York working on an industrial espionage case—data theft by corporate mole."

"Client's got you chasing spies?"

"I represented the mole."

Jedediah snorted with laughter.

She shrugged. "It's a hard life all around. I don't judge, just represent my client without prejudice and cash their checks."

Jedediah guffawed. "Speaking of judging, what happened?"

Meadow blushed and gestured at the booth. "Seems the constituents in my district didn't want an elected judge peddling perfume, but I'm not about to give it up. I have too much fun at these things playing the mad woman."

"Comes naturally."

She swatted him and threw a mock glare. "*You* never quit playing the rapscallion."

"You'll get elected sooner or later."

Meadow scoffed. "It'd mean a pay cut. I only ran as a favor to Justin."

Jedediah's eyes fell. "How is the old curmudgeon?"

"Wow," Meadow said. "Just wow. Worst pot and kettle offense I've seen in all my life."

Jedediah waited.

"He's tired," she said. "He took it hard when I lost, wanted me for his seat. Between us, I fear his mind's going. He spent my last visit regaling me with a tale of you two fighting World War I together."

Jedediah replied with a thin-lipped smile. "I really should go visit."

"You should."

"I've been busy, legal problems."

"You're supposed to share if you're growing marijuana in the back fields."

Jedediah related recent events.

Meadow frowned. "Purely circumstantial, you didn't even have to go with them for questioning. You need me to step in?"

"Not yet, but thought you should know just in case."

She hugged him. "You call. I'll come running."

Jedediah smirked. "In that?"

Meadow cackled. "I'll wear heels."

A young couple stopped to peruse her wares. She winked, switching from high-powered attorney to mad woman in a single, mad lascivious cackle.

Jedediah returned to Drake's reproachful expression. He pulled a carrot from one sleeve. Drake glared. Jedediah smirked and pointed.

Drake whirled. Six Cherry Coke peace offerings waited beside his tail.

Jedediah's evening performance exceeded anything the festival staff anticipated.

A twelve pack coerced Drake into "pretending" to be a fire-breathing dragon. Glamour transformed Drake into a cheesy, dragon-costumed bloodhound.

Billie Jo and Mason Bartlett sat in the front row. They'd oohed and aahed with the audience as wizard and dragon dazzled the crowds. Jedediah used mind touch to direct Drake through impromptu performance changes. The sometimes angsty dragon might've denied it, but he seemed to enjoy playing up for the crowd, especially singeing the seat of Jedediah's robe with an "accidental" sneeze that left the crowd in stitches.

The activities director wasted no time negotiating additional shows for the present and possible future festivals. Theophanie hung in the wings with Lanea. The gypsy's smile evaporated when the director offered Jedediah one of her show times.

He declined it with a wink to her that merely deflected all her ire at the director. She stormed after him the moment he tried to slip through the back.

Don't envy the earful he's going to get.

Mason magically won a prize voucher during the show, bringing him and his mother to meet Jedediah. Billie Jo held Mason back until all the other winners had claimed their prize.

"Amazing," Billie Jo said.

Over her shoulder, Lanea paled.

Jedediah bowed.

Mason skipped up to Drake and stroked his head. He gave his mother a look long ago perfected by too bright boys on the verge of adolescence. "A dragon. I told you so."

"So it seems."

Jedediah handed Mason the voucher. "Congratulations. Best hide it before Drake sneezes again."

Mason shoved the slip hastily into a pocket.

"Performance leave you hungry?" Billie Jo blurted.

"Mom!"

What do I say? What do I do? Elation and dread warred through him, leaving a frigid wasteland in their wake. *Stall.*

Jedediah pressed a hand to his chest. "My lady, I am stunned by your immodesty. What of your humility? Your virtue? You'll give the noblewomen of court a month's worth of fat to chew."

She blushed, not meeting his eyes.

Her awkward expression twisted his gut. "May I change first?"

She brightened, eyes caressing his robes. "Probably best. Any suggestions?"

"There's a salad buffet just up the highway. I'll tend Drake, change and meet you there in thirty minutes."

Jedediah finished with the crowd, got Drake to the hotel, teleported home, changed his age back to mid-thirties, selected an outfit and teleported back to his truck. It took forty-five minutes that hadn't won him points with the salad flanked Mason.

Her downcast expression brightened once she recognized him. "I thought you'd gotten lost."

Probably thought I stood you up. Great work, Mister Gentleman. He forced a smile. "Sorry, I simply couldn't summon a thing to wear."

She laughed.

Salads and soups, breads and pastas came and went. Jedediah and Billie Jo talked about everything and nothing. Conversations split through dozens of topics until Jedediah noticed Mason asleep and pointed looks from the sweeping restaurant staff.

"Might be best if we left," Jedediah said.

She woke Mason and led him to her van. The conversation resumed in the parking lot, continuing long after the restaurant's lights went out.

It had been a long time since Jedediah had enjoyed such a conversation and longer still since it had been with a normal woman.

He learned a thousand things about her. Despite her occupation as a high school chemistry teacher, Billie Jo proved an aficionado on all things medieval. She went to renaissance fairs and observed re-enactments whenever the opportunity arose. She'd never taken Mason to one, thinking him still too young, until her ex-husband forced things by taking him first.

His widower status left her unashamedly pleased. "That's rare to find a single wizard these days. Though I am sorry about your wife."

"Happened a very long time ago."

"You and your wife have any children?" she asked.

"None still living," Jedediah said.

"God, you're so young to have lost children. I don't know what I'd do if something happened to Mason."

She and Mason lived in northern Columbus, Georgia not far from where Jedediah shopped and put up with Joe Franklin's questions. He'd tried providing directions to the farm from Columbus proper, but she didn't recognize the roads.

She glanced at Mason, asleep in the backseat of their minivan.

"I guess I should get him home," she said.

"Been a real pleasure, Billie Jo."

"Maybe we'll run into each other again?"

"Maybe."

She fiddled with her keys, looking more at her feet then Jedediah. After a few minutes, she got in the van and drove away.

Jedediah climbed into the truck and stared at the steering wheel. *What just happened?*

He ran the night through his thoughts, pondering every sentence, every expression. It'd seemed so natural—too natural.

"How long are you going to stare at the dash, Da?"

Jedediah started, testament to the level of his distraction.

Lanea burst out laughing. "Oh my god, I caught you napping. *You*. I've *never* managed that."

Jedediah started the truck. "Practice is paying off."

"Don't give me that," Lanea said. "She distracted you—Elsabeth reinca—"

"Don't. That's not possible."

"Da? You okay?"

"I don't know."

She studied him. "Da?"

He didn't reply.

"No children, huh?" Lanea said.

"I didn't lie. You're not born of any wife. A half-elven daughter didn't seem like first-date conversation material."

Lanea frowned and looked out the window.

"I love you, girl. You know that, but—"

"But our lives are complicated enough, and it's best not to add greater danger by divulging my existence," she rattled off in a flat tone. "Maybe it'd be better if I left, gave you some space."

I shouldn't see her again. Jedediah didn't seem to hear Lanea. "I probably won't see her again."

Lanea offered him a sad smile before poking him in the side. "She wanted you to kiss her."

"Yup."

"You didn't want to?"

"Part of me did."

"Part of you believes, and that makes it weird, right?"

"I don't believe."

Lanea pursed her lips. "You waiting until it's all for her and not on account of your first wife who she isn't a reincarnation of?"

"Yup."

"But you probably won't see her again."

"Right."

"Do you want to see her again, Da?"

"Not sure, no, maybe."

They rode in silence for several minutes.

"You okay with that?" Jedediah asked.

A mischievous grin filled her face. "Well, I'd rather you picked one that came along with a sister."

"I'll see what I can do."

"Eww, Da. No, just no."

CHAPTER SIXTEEN

Twin Malevolence

One scanned the small wooden cabin's interior. Three rooms composed the building: living, kitchen and bedroom—assuming you didn't count the outhouse as a fourth.

Filthy, no, just hasn't been used in some time. He checked his phone. *Where are the others?*

His search of the outlying property provided a few good sniper positions, good cover against assault and an ideal weapon emplacement. Shine's fishing cabin would serve their needs exactly.

He'd have assigned a recon team to assess it, but Zero's instructions had been exacting.

It's as if he thinks Shine can raise an army on short notice.

He fetched wood from a covered pile, work distracting him from an uneasy feeling. When he could stall no longer, he removed his mask.

I just don't like this, and I hate surrendering control.

Shine's file teamed with warnings, superstitious nonsense against direct attack on the Shine family. The board's elaborate plan—dictated by Zero without room for discussion—insisted upon a face to face meeting.

The Namhaid enforced strict anonymity rules, protection from turncoats or surveillance. Zero insisted they all meet without masks.

Few have met Zero and survived. How many actually saw his face?

Someone knocked.

One donned his mask, adjusting its optics. "Who?"

A thick eastern European accent answered. "Muler."

One couldn't have picked out most of the Namhaid's operatives—unless he caught a glimpse of the killer in their eyes. Nondescript, ex-military types were almost interchangeable.

Muler wasn't.

Inheriting the deadly little weasel definitely isn't what I'd call a job perk. One opened the door to a short, thin man with a distinctive stance. "What?"

"A vehicle approaches. Shall we stop it?"

"No, let it through."

Muler clicked his boot heels, saluted and stepped away to radio his orders.

70

MURDER IN WIZARD'S WOOD | 71

One shook his head. *German mannerisms have got to be a disguise—file or no. What assassin wants to stand out?*

A dark SUV parked—window tinting illegally thick. No one got out.

"Set the perimeter further out. Anyone coming near the cabin without radioing first will be shot on sight."

Muler tilted his head slightly to one side.

"Then join us."

"Me, sir?"

"Yes."

Muler returned, glancing at the still SUV.

This is a really bad idea. One sighed. *Zero doesn't need theatrics to kill me.*

He removed his mask and ran a hand through his blond hair.

Muler's eyes widened. "Sir, your mask."

"Remove yours. Zero's orders."

Muler hesitated.

What's the weasel thinking?

He removed his mask, revealing a thin face neither bony nor angular. The thin, black mustache across his lip matched his short hair.

Doesn't look as greasy as he seems.

Three SUV doors opened.

Two mammoth, Samoan men—possibly twins—emerged. Tailored suits seemed wrong on deeply tanned men muscled like wrestlers. Buzzed black hair fit their predatory ursine movements.

A pale and sultry blonde emerged from behind the third door.

Whoa. That's Two?

A low cut, grey skirt-suit hugged her athletic build. Her boots, functional in the rough ground, projected the impression of heels. She flashed a burgundy smile. She strode forward just as confident as the Samoans, yet with a decidedly feminine air.

That is how she kills. Don't fall for it.

She extended her hand. "Mr. O'Steele, so good to make your acquaintance."

One took it. "Ms. Norway, trip satisfactory?"

"Quite," she said. "Shall we?"

One led them inside. "Muler, this is Two."

Two set her briefcase down and ran her eyes up and down the smaller man. "So you're he."

Muler smirked and folded his arms.

One cleared his throat. "This is Gordon and Flash, Zero's enforcers."

"I'm Flash," a Samoan corrected.

"Quite the dinner party, yes *fralein*?"

"Why is this miscreant here?" Two asked.

"I hoped you knew," One said.

Gordon spoke. "Zero."

"Why aren't we masked?" Muler asked.

"You fail," Flash said.

"You die," Gordon finished.

Two smiled. "We're to murder the sheriff here?"

"Once our preparations are complete," Gordon said.

"You get all the fun, Marc." She eyed Muler. "While I'm stuck in deep cover laying the next trap."

"Shine's predictable enough for that kind of trap?"

"Enough," she said.

"I dislike speaking up, but what're we discussing?" Muler asked.

One and Two outlined the plan.

Incredulity crept over Muler's face. "Daft, just shoot him."

"No direct engagement," Flash said.

Gordon loomed over Muler. "Obey Zero."

Muler's head bobbed back and forth. "Thanks, Dee, Dum, but we're professionals not sock puppets."

Two stepped between the Samoans.

"Muler, darling, I'd think twice about initiating unsanctioned engagements." She struck in a flash, pinning him to the ground, steadily increasing Muler's pain. "Not again. Not on *my* watch. Soldiers obey orders or people get hurt."

Gordon frowned. "Hurting people is a soldier's job."

"Right. Flash and Gordon, you're in the open, so cover each other. Muler, your tasks will necessitate stealth. Contact Two or me with updates and problems."

Two helped a glaring Muler up. "Understand, dear?"

Muler inclined his head at One. "He's the boss, *fralein*."

Two twisted Muler's arm behind his back. "Pardon?"

"Enough," One snapped.

She released Muler, batting her eyes. "Sorry, Marc."

One led them through a mission map. "Muler, next murders have to be witnessed around here."

"Pretty remote for a convenient redneck," Muler said.

"You'll manage," One said.

"One way or another," Two said.

"Driving by on the way to dinner, you know, Deputy?" Eldon Myers fidgeted with a ball cap, donning and removing it from his liver-spotted crown. "Looked like a scarecrow at first, you know? Except they don't attract crows."

John examined the body suspended spread eagle between old, crooked trees. Thin wounds consistent with arrowheads peppered all but a rectangle on the torso. Carved shapes filled the otherwise unwounded space.

"Thank you, sir," John said. "I've got your info if we need anything else."

Eldon smacked his lips, looking at the body. "You're sure? Headed to town for dinner. Don't want it now, though. I could help you get him down and all."

"Thanks, but the Sheriff will want to see this himself. Eddie, why don't you help Mr. Myers back to his truck?"

Eddie led Eldon away, listening to the old man defend his health all the way back to the road.

John circled the trees, snapping pictures. He ground his teeth. *What the hell, Shine? It's like you're thumbing our noses.*

Eddie returned.

"What're your thoughts, Ed?"

"Trees creep me out," Eddie swept a hand around them at the recently harvested fields. "Why would Shine leave trees blocking his access road? You remember seeing them here before?"

"I don't remember. That look like some kind of writing?"

"I suppose, Muslim maybe?" Eddie bent at a tree's roots following a ragged path with his eyes. "This doesn't make sense."

"Why should murder make sense?"

"No, look at these fields, ruler square, but this looks like someone ran a plow across fields and a few of access ways."

"Covers any tracks, doesn't it?" John asked.

Eddie scowled at his brother. "Migrants? Do it after harvest?"

"Looks fresh." John scratched his head. "Sheriff on his way?"

"Yeah, stopped by Judge Alcott's place, on poker night no less."

"I don't care if the warrant shows up on a pizza stained napkin, Ed. I want this guy."

Lanea sat cross-legged at pond's edge behind the greenhouses. Water arced off its surface, swirling smooth as glass at its apex. She bent the water lens, magnifying deputies, trees and another body.

She cursed and whirled a mist from the pond. *Da needs to know.*

She hesitated.

No, not yet. He might yell, but he'll still know sooner than he might otherwise. If I can figure this out before telling him maybe he'll finally treat me like an adult.

She dismissed the water lens, wrapping mist and water around the pond in a camouflaging glamour. She whispered a tune. The water's surface broke, two mottled green and brown heads rose weed-tangled from the bottom. Long whiskers protruded from their faces. More heads joined the first two, necks undulating like a charmed cobra until their combined body rose to the surface.

Lanea let her song end. Five catfish-like heads peered at her. "Sorry to interrupt your rest."

One head gulped a passing insect. Two blinked at her while another slipped towards the water. The last yawned.

Lanea pointed. "Wise sludge hydra, have you knowledge of what goes on there?"

All five heads turned. They spoke almost at once. "Normals."

Individual heads added other words. "Stupid." "Too far." "Boring." "Dead."

"Yes, the dead one. Did you see what happened?" Lanea asked.

All of the heads started nodding, only to shift to wagging back and forth. Her hopes fell. "None of you noticed what took that man's life?"

"Woodwise." "Beyond." "Forest Child." "Mule." "Seek." "Burden." "Ianyss." "Hedge priest."

Lanea frowned.

The heads slipped toward the water.

"Someone killed him elsewhere?"

Two heads nodded. Two slipped underwater. The last scooped a water strider from the pond's surface.

"Beyond the treeline?"

The chewing head nodded, following the others into the water.

"Probably just spouting random words so I'll leave it alone."

Water striders skipped over the last fading ripples, landing here and there. She studied them. *This ought to be interesting. Da's always saying you don't know until you try.*

She sang to the insects. They flitted from the water circling her round and round, eventually settling onto her skin. She imparted her desire, using the song to deliver both magic and will. Her song ended.

Water striders shot in all direction.

Hopefully seeking out all the nearby water dwellers. Guilt churned her stomach. *And not getting swallowed on my errand.*

Some of the insects returned, lighting on her skin once more. Try as she might, she couldn't figure out a way to learn what news they'd brought.

Lanea camouflaged herself. Neither deputy turned her way. She smiled.

Normally, she'd have stuck to the access roads. *Da can be unreasonable, but the fields are empty and I need a closer look.*

She crossed the fields, heading into the far woods. She veered close as she dared, eyeing the awful murder scene.

She found Ianyss lying supine in the fading afternoon sun.

Ianyss spoke first. "Something amiss, forest child?"

"Someone has killed a normal," Lanea said.

Ianyss lay seemingly unconcerned. "Did its life blood feed Mother?"

"He's hung between trees where no trees stood before."

Ianyss raised her head.

"Knew that'd get your notice. Did you bid your flock to do this?"

Ianyss rose. "Show me."

"We may have to wait until the normals are gone."

Ianyss touched Lanea's head. "No need."

Lanea's observations flashed through her mind. Ianyss shook her head, Spanish moss waving around her shoulders. "Those aren't of my flock."

"How can you tell from here?" Lanea asked.

"I've no Fey trees in my herd and no idea from whence they came."

"Rootwalkers?"

Even Ianyss's disgusted expression looked beautiful.

Hate that about her.

"Barkbiters."

Ianyss resumed her sunbathing. Lanea considered asking her for help, but while the dryad might act against barkbiters in her wood, these occupied Jedediah's fields instead.

Deputies and a coroner took the body away after sundown. She approached the barkbiters. In the moonlight, bodily fluids turned the earth at their roots into a blackish-looking mud.

Hands on hips, she eyed the two trees. Up close they represented living examples of dark or demon trees found in fictional nightmare. "Well? You want to tell me what you are doing on our property?"

Rips in the bark pattern expended on both trees, giving both their faces a jagged scowl. Leafless limbs creaked toward her as each barkbiter twisted to face her full on.

The rightmost's voice sounded like a rope bridge creaking in a storm. "Ours now, fleshling."

Her head tilted. "Really, now?"

"Bugger off, bent ear," the other said.

Lanea scowled at Lefty and Righty. "What if I intend to evict you?"

"You'll rot first," Lefty said. "Can't move us. Can't burn us."

Lanea frowned. *Da could do it, but I'm not running to daddy because of some bully.*

She studied them, chewing her lip. Lanea stomped on the ground. *Come.*

A rune-decorated quarterstaff, constructed of driftwood, jumped out of the ground into her hand. She leaned on the staff and thrust it into the earth.

"Little brat thinks she'd a dryad," Righty said. "How is planting a tree going to make us move, missy?"

They laughed.

Trusted sister, remember life. Thirsty sister, drink your fill.

Their laughter slowed.

Lefty stopped laughing.

"Stop that," Righty snarled. He leaned forward, but even the slight movement filled the air with creaking and cracking wood. "Give that back."

Brow wrinkled in concentration, Lanea let a gloating smile curl her lips. Branches budded on her driftwood staff, small leaves unfurling. The moisture and bodily fluid around her soaked into her staff, feeding growth.

Rapidly dried ground cracked.

"You're an elf. Life's sacred. Stop, you can't," Righty said. "We'll die."

Lanea maintained her focus, drawing water from their soil. Her hands tightened white-knuckled around her staff "Where'd you come from? Why did you have that man? Who killed him?"

"We ain't telling you dung," Lefty said. "We'll just move."

Lanea forced more water away. Pain throbbed in her temples. Each heartbeat labored harder. The stolen water rose into a thick frozen briar around the tableau, thickening layer by layer. A spark appeared between them, growing slowly into a flaming sphere.

"Fire's so erratic, so hard to control." Lanea spoke through gritted teeth. "It hungers. Where, oh, where am I going to put this rejected heat?"

Lefty and Righty wrenched their roots from the earth with a sound like a collapsing house. They shambled separate ways, crashing into the ice wall. It held.

The flame darted after them, a pup nipping at their heels. Smoke rose from roots where it bit.

Sweat trickled down Lanea's back. Even with her wizard's staff for focus, juggling so many forces took monumental effort.

My wellspring dwindles. She scowled. "Fire won't stay leashed. I won't ask again."

The barkbiters combined forces, unintentionally easing her burden by letting her focus on a single wall section.

Their roots smoldered. The flaming sphere dwarfed her. It's touch heated by the moment.

"All right," Lefty cried. "The centaur, offered us blood and fertile soil to hold his corpse."

"Which centaur?" Lanea asked.

"Don't know his name," Lefty said. "Chestnut male."

Lanea exhaled, rebalancing the elements.

Righty smashed a limb into Lefty's face. "What'd you tell her that for?"

"She meant to burn us to ash," Lefty returned the blow.

"She's an elf, you dumb stump," Righty hit Lefty again, smashing him through the ice wall. "She wouldn't have burned us up."

Lefty smashed Righty. "You overgrown weed, she's half human. They don't give a twig about trees."

Lanea watched while heat seeped back into the water and water refreshed the ground. "He's right."

Righty and Lefty turned to her in unison. "Who's right?"

"Figure it out, and get off our land."

Muler watched the old country highway, positioned to see as much approaching road as possible. A thermos passed hand to hand. *Come on. I've better things to do.*

One wanted another body. Zero wanted it here. *I really want to shoot someone.*

It'd taken a week to determine how best to murder someone with a witness on the sparsely traveled back road—import a body and create a witness.

An unconscious man hung from a spike driven through his sleeves into a tree trunk. Muler wore the same atrocious shirt and jeans. A Namhaid gunman—roughly Jedediah's size and dressed like the farmer—sat against a tree playing Angry Birds. His shotgun leaned against the trunk within easy reach.

A minivan rounded the far curve.

Muler signaled, splashing a thermos of blood over his shirt.

He stumbled into the road, screaming and waving his arms. He paused mid-road—too far for the minivan driver to get a precise view. Muler dashed into the opposite woods and dove low for a wooden rod.

The other gunman stepped onto the shoulder in plain view. He raised the long-barreled shotgun and fired at their prisoner.

The minivan slammed on its brakes. Muler yanked the spike free by a five hundred pound test line. Screams erupted behind him as he belly crawled far enough into the wood to run.

CHAPTER SEVENTEEN

The Other Horseshoe

Jedediah sat in his plaid Barcalounger opposite Lanea. Fingers dug into its arms. Sparks flickered around him.

"So, John kicked in the front lock. Had my hands full glamouring the boneyard or I would've called. Then the bees alerted me to a buzz up at the country market about another death off highway twenty-five," Lanea added.

"Joe Franklin?"

"Hunting you, but not like John."

"They see you?"

"No, Da."

"Need to visit Fleet Hoof before he sinks his teeth into me."

"What're you going to do, Da?"

He lurched to his feet, sparking. "What it takes."

Lanea chewed her lip. "You should employ reason, you know, be wise?"

"If cracking skulls don't work."

"You'd tell me to think this through."

"Yup, and I'm riled, girl, but I'm weighing things. Fast thinking's part of wizarding, but I don't want them knowing that. They've baited me. Maybe they'll gloat, let things slip. If not, I'll invoke fear. Maybe it pushes them off balance."

"Sure you don't just like intimidating people?"

"That's fun, too."

Jedediah glanced at the empty bow rack over the mantle. He chuckled. *Hope you're enjoying the replica, Joe Franklin.*

Pictures swamping the mantle caught his breath. He memorized the assorted faces once more, then turned to the glass display cases on either side of the fireplace. They matched the gun cabinet—stain, cut and molding. The two contained nineteen hand-crafted wooden clocks. Each differed in carving and ornament. Gay colors, horses, a baseball glove and bat decorated one. Another featured a horse and buggy before a church. Sailing ships—sails and rigging captured in perfect detail—dominated another.

One and only one ran. A tiny mantle clock, cane and rocking chair adorned it.

Jedediah reached over one cabinet's crown and brought back a clockwork key. He inserted the key into the church and buggy clock. He wound it up. Its hands sprang to life, second hand on the other freezing in place.

Jedediah replaced the key with a trembling, wrinkled hand. A brief cry escaped him.

"Da?"

He doubled over, fingers tightening on the thick mantle.

Jedediah gritted his teeth, waving her off. His hair shortened. Paprika replaced its grey. His shoulders and chest filled out. Muscles bulged. His waist slimmed. Skin smoothed. Ears and nose shrank. Another cry escaped a thin beard and mustache matching his hair.

A mid-twenties Jedediah straightened, eyes glowing like hundred-watt bulbs.

"Damn, those big shifts sting," Jedediah rasped.

"You don't make learning that spell attractive."

"You ever want to share a lifetime with someone, you'll be glad you did."

She eyed a simple, dark wood clock carved with twin hourglasses. Hair hid her face. "What if you'd misjudged?"

"I didn't."

"What if?"

He studied her, cupping her cheek. "You'll feel your connection fading first."

He snatched up his suitcase, climbed the stairs, touched the portraits and entered his bedroom. Drake stretched out on the four-post bed. Jedediah entered the closet.

Drake slipped to the floor, stretching out forelimbs as he did so. His back talons clicked onto the wood floor, and the dragonling stretched his back legs as he stepped into the closet doorway.

Jedediah stripped and pulled on a pair of buckskin breeches. He stuffed an old leather satchel with sundries, gear, fresh clothes and lastly his boots. He draped it across his bare chest.

Drake pressed against him. *<Fleeing?>*

Jedediah snorted. "Planning ahead."

<May I come?>

Jedediah's mouth twisted. "Of course you're coming. Ain't shedding lessons that easy. Packing anything from your horde? Plenty of space."

Drake shook his head.

Jedediah rummaged through the satchel, withdrawing an ornamental spear. Small beads and bones hung beneath a long, leaf-shaped spearhead.

He marched barefoot into the night.

Lanea studied the moon. "Going like that, Da?"

"Just like my warrior youth." He fingered the satchel. "Bit better equipped."

"You've already decided to seek *Mythela 'Raemyn.*"

"Decided, no, but well prepared. You should come."

Lanea chewed her lip. "I, uh, can't."

Jedediah's face darkened. "The elf?"

She didn't meet his gaze.

"Girl, what did I tell you?"

"To do my own thinking, make my own decisions."

Jedediah scowled. He opened his mouth, then shut it. "Yup."

"So, it's okay?"

"Think you're a damned fool, but I've said my piece."

Whatever nasty retort formed behind her eyes didn't escape.

He inclined his head. "Take care, if I ain't back tonight." Jedediah's teeth clinched. "Maybe go see your mother."

"Shouldn't I glamour myself to resemble you? Be your alibi?"

"Probably best if you didn't." Jedediah reconsidered. "Well, maybe at another property or off fishing, just not around here."

Jedediah hugged Lanea. "Ready, Drake?"

Drake wrapped a tongue around Lanea's wrist. She laughed and shooed him away.

Jedediah wove a mist walk. Sigils ignited silver along the spear's shaft. They strode into a silent, too still night.

Wood's inhabitants know I'm coming, know I'm riled, know to stay clear—even the shadowcats.

Jedediah released the spell at Fleet Hoof's border.

Therymn En'Prielar emerged from the shadows. Blood red tribal markings dappled the grey stallion's coat. Reddish tattoos painted inner forearm scars. He bowed, striking his chest with a fist in salute. "My honored foe returns to echo my defeat. You're welcome among us, *Lyanthen Ah Lah'Phriel.* I've watched many nights. Your patience grows."

They grasped forearms and held the embrace. "TherPriel, honored foe, wait you as warrior or friend?"

"Our grievances remain long behind." TherPriel released Jedediah. "I'm your shield, lest you bleed angry children."

Jedediah's brow rose.

The centaur chuckled. "You remain ever the impending storm. Youths whisper and beat chests, but they'll not cross a war leader—even retired."

"Respect for respect, knife brother. These young warriors do not understand the old way. Their prejudice and callous killing imperil all. I *will* see it ended."

"Ended only to rekindle, didn't I play the bloodthirsty fool?"

Jedediah smiled. "Wisdom quenched your thirst."

TherPriel extended his arms. "And pain."

"Sometimes, wisdom leaves a mark."

Both laughed.

TherPriel extended his forelimbs and bowed to Drake. "Forgive old foes beating chests, Elder Lord. You honor us, shall you also judge this matter?"

Drake glanced up at Jedediah.

"Drake is student and companion, he may witness but he'll not, I think, judge."

"It'll be the Rite of Knives then?" TherPriel asked.

Jedediah shivered unconsciously. "If wisdom and reason betray our trust, then parent shall lash spoiled children."

"Parent, not father?" TherPriel sucked in his breath. "You'll go that far?"

"Yup."

"So your youth isn't war's harbinger, but much worse."

"If they respect strength, they'll see strength. If I journey to the High Centaurs of *Mythela 'Raemyn*, my youth serves me."

"You'll not take your modern chariot?" TherPriel asked.

"I guard but one gate to the Sacred Valley. The Valley allows few approaches that won't cast you one side or another."

TherPriel nodded.

"I'd prefer no tempest between us, TherPriel."

TherPriel considered him. "Come, knife brother, the children await."

They wove through the camp. Warriors glared. Several cursed Jedediah. Most ignored Jedediah in favor of Drake. A murmur proceeded them between the tents.

A young palomino stepped from between tents to block Jedediah's path.

"Stand aside, Hynar Ah'Klach," TherPriel said.

"I, Hynar Ah'Klach, challenge this two-leg's right to enter."

TherPriel groaned.

"Accepted." Jedediah slammed his spear butt into the earth. A thunderous shockwave blasted his challenger off his hooves, through the air and into a tent some ten paces away.

A mare and two screaming fillies scrambled from the half-collapsed tent.

Jedediah bowed to them. "I offer my apologies. My quarrel is not with you; I meant neither injury nor offense. Are all well?"

The mare eyed Jedediah and then Drake. One of the fillies moved to voice a rebuke, but her mother restrained her. She inclined her head to Jedediah. "All are well. We take no offense and lay no blame. Go in peace."

"My gratitude, ladies."

"I'd say you've announced yourself," TherPriel said.

"Yup."

"Subtle."

Jedediah shrugged.

TherPriel stepped over Jedediah's challenger. "Foolish words, child."

The sorrel BauthEli, beautiful white WaphRae, and three other elders awaited them outside the pavilion. Four wore neutral masks.

Velith'Seravin glowered with undisguised contempt. "You dare return, disguised to play us false then attack our braves with your filthy magic?"

Jedediah smiled. "Would you avenge his failed challenge?"

TherPriel pushed Jedediah's spear arm gently back down. "*Lyanthen Ah Lah'Phriel* brings more grievances, his first yet unanswered. I beg the elders to hear him."

"Beg all you want, blood traitor. We won't hear him," VelSera said.

TherPriel's chest puffed up. "Do you realize who you're addressing, boy?"

"A defeated warrior and a two-legged trickster," Velith'Seravin said.

"Does VelSera speak for this council?" Jedediah asked.

"He is a member—" BauthEli said.

"But he does *not* speak for all of us," WaphRae said. "Your deeds are not forgotten, nor your grievance. No answer came because we remain undecided."

Jedediah pointed an accusing finger. "Four men and many animals have been murdered while you debate. A centaur coerced barkbiters into displaying this child's callous barbarism to the normals."

Outrage deformed VelSera's features. "You slander me, claim witnesses but do not present them. I could kill you for less."

"Challenge accepted," Jedediah said.

"Stop," BauthEli shouted. "The council does not challenge those heard for grievance."

"I maintain we do not hear this trickster," VelSera said.

TherPriel clucked his tongue. "Foolish."

"You will be silent, old nag," VelSera said.

Jedediah's tone lowered. "Insult my knife brother once more, boy, and I'll cut your tongue from your mouth."

"Stop this pointless bickering," WaphRae said. "We'd hear your new grievances."

Jedediah related events and Lanea's account, ignoring VelSera's derisive snorts. The other elders listened carefully.

BauthEli spoke first. "Things sound grave, but VelSera speaks truth. This isn't our affair."

"Your arrows started this," Jedediah said.

"You bring hearsay but no arrows, images but no bodies." BauthEli frowned. "What proof offer you centaur made these arrows and not elves?"

TherPriel snorted. "Elves haven't hooves."

"You're not a council elder, TherPriel. Be gone or be silent," VelSera said.

"This isn't the pavilion, boy. I've every right to stand here and defend my knife brother. Have you all forgotten his actions on our behalf?"

"With respect to TherPriel, perhaps we should take this discussion inside," WaphRae said.

"Inside or outside, this human is a liar. I vote we deny his petition and move we execute him for crimes against centaur," Velith'Seravin said. "Assuming he's too cowardly to claim the Rite of Knives in his defense."

"Without more evidence, I must deny his claim as well," BauthEli said.

"*Lyanthen Ah Lah'Phriel* has ever been our honorable friend. I weigh his words as truth," WaphRae turned toward the two thus far silent members of the council.

The older of the two, Phriel'Belshai, a venerable palomino mare cleared her throat. "WaphRae speaks rightly of the wizard's deeds and honor, but without proof, I'm unready to declare vote."

The last and largest council member folded dark-skinned arms across his massive chest, frowning at the tableau. His black coat faded to grey, foreleg to rear.

WaphRae turned to him. "What are your thoughts, Ena'Tharus Une Hashe?"

The black centaur's voice matched his powerful frame. "*Lyanthen Ah Lah'Phriel* rendered us aid. He healed my grandfather from musket balls. He cured many when sickness came amongst us in my boyhood. I honor him and trust his words. Yet, I too must defer his claim until proof stands among us."

VelSera laughed. "Then this matter is closed. Two votes to one."

"Actually," BauthEli said. "One speaks to find and discipline the culprit. Two claim no culprit to discover, and two others vote to search for yet more truth. By tradition, we must withhold decision and seek truth."

"Ridiculous," VelSera said.

"I agree," Jedediah said. "You want proof? I demand the Rite of Joined Dreams."

Only Ena'Tharus Une Hashe did not gasp.

"You've no right!" VelSera said.

"I am *Feihtor Ah Mythela'Raemyn*, centaur and brother to all tribes," Jedediah said. "As centaur, I've every right."

"You're *not* centaur, two-legger. You'll not pollute our minds with your own," VelSera said.

"VelSera's correct. Honorary brother, you remain human," WaphRae said. "The herd may gallop in the tribes' memories, but including so foreign a mind would endanger all."

Jedediah glowered. "My status is not honorary, nor is it mete for this council to question it. You're a spirit elder of the path, WaphRae. I demand you perform the Rite."

"He's threatening WaphRae," VelSera said. "Warriors, seize him."

Centaur warriors emerged around them, bows and spears at the ready.

Drake—quiet spectator to his teacher's audience—extended his wings and shifted to defend Jedediah's back.

"This council's wisdom died with Tharus A'Lyathin," Jedediah said. "You've lost your way and I my patience."

TherPriel stepped forward, placing himself between Jedediah and the closest warriors. "Jedediah, a storm never heals."

Jedediah met TherPriel's gaze. His eyes swept to WaphRae.

She wants to help, but she's afraid—maybe of the Rite itself. She's the spirit elder, if she won't initiate it then I must force her hand—unless the other walkers convince her first.

Jedediah addressed her. "Waphri Ah'Raemyn, seek your spirit walkers, call to your ancestors. I grant you one hour to consider my request."

"You grant?" VelSera's voice rose, "You grant? You have no rights here. Seize him. If the dragon interferes, kill it."

Ena'Tharus Une Hashe shielded Drake bodily. "Have you lost all sense, VelSera, threatening an Elder Lord?"

"That is the last straw," Jedediah thundered. "I've tried being reasonable. I've tried to grant time for wisdom's growth, but *no one* threatens my students."

Warriors tensed around the clearing.

"I am *Feihtor Ah Mythela'Raemyn*, judge among the tribes and I have witnessed enough." Jedediah drew a small burgundy and silver device from his satchel. He unfolded it, projecting overlapping holographic displays beneath Alden's face. "I'm calling in my favor."

CHAPTER EIGHTEEN

Cursed Chains

Jedediah agonized in the moments between his call and Alden's arrival. *I'm forced to wonder which is the greater crime, murders of innocents or to invoke an action that forces innocents to their greatest fears.*

"This is your wrath? Speaking into a box of illusions?" VelSera asked.

Jedediah scowled at him. *You're the reason I must do this, must cage a people born to run free. You've forced me to choose between charges.*

A vortex of lightning exploded in their midst. Alden stepped from within, blinking away light before turning to Jedediah.

"You summoned me to pay my debt, what boon do you desire, Two-Hawks?"

"Centaurs of this tribe make war upon innocents, a crime much like you enforce."

"The two-legger lies," VelSera said.

Alden raised a brow. "Jedediah Two-Hawks's honor is without question."

"Two-leggers sticking together," VelSera sneered. "Warriors take them both."

"Stop," WaphRae cried.

"How can you side with this thing, WaphRae?" VelSera said. "His kind stole from us the open prairie. They imprison us, forcing us to hide in tiny patches of land. Centaur, hiding while normals run free in the world. Were we not born first? Are we not elder Fey to the worthless normals, befitting of preference and privilege?"

Drake snorted. "Still smell like prey."

A smirk played at the edges of Jedediah's lips, but he forced it down. The irony of VelSera's words amused him, but his chosen course held only sorrow. "Alden, I must seek the High Tribe to judge between us, but to take that journey would be to leave the locals hunted without protection."

Alden turned to him. "What do you—?"

A warrior charged out of the crowd at Alden. He vanished, appearing behind the roan. Another two let fly arrows. Alden ceased to be in their path, blinking across the clearing to slice them from the air using a sword blade edged in circuitry.

Jedediah thrust his spear into an attacking centaur. He abandoned it, calling to his wizard staff. It arrived with a clap of thunder that threw four centaur to the clearing's edge. Silver-steel robes rippled down over Jedediah's bare chest.

Drake leapt toward a centaur, teeth and talons set to kill. Jedediah interposed himself, deflecting the dragonling's attack from a centaur warrior. "No, Drake. Stay impartial."

Alden and Jedediah moved like shards of wind. They struck, dodged, shifted and struck again with incredible speed. Their speed died in an instant. Centaur warriors lay in a haphazard ring, unconscious, bleeding but none critically injured.

"Speak," Alden panted.

"Imprison them."

Cries rose around them.

"Hold them impotent while I seek an impartial judge in this matter," Jedediah said.

"You can't," BauthEli said.

"You go too far, knife brother."

"Stop, let me seek the ancestors about the Rite you demand," WaphRae said.

"Just kill them both," VelSera said.

Jedediah straightened, beckoning with one hand. "Come try me."

Alden closed his eyes and whispered alien words. A dome of glowing force descended over the centaur camp.

Shouts and cries echoed off the dome's walls from all directions. Panicked centaurs raced toward the pavilion, crying out to the elders for answers.

"It is done," Alden said.

Jedediah nodded, head hung. "It saddens me beyond words to inflict this upon innocents, but the guilty have cowards' blood and cannot be left untethered."

"*Lyanthen Ah Lah'Phriel*, I beseech you. Do not do this," Ena'Tharus Une Hashe said. "Grant us more time to seek truth."

"It is done," Jedediah turned. "Waphri Ah'Raemyn, spirit elder, path strider, council eldress. You will accompany me, standing for your tribe before the High Elders."

"Wait, he can't," VelSera said. "They'll come here. They'll censure our council. Stop him."

"Dear Creator," WaphRae turned to VelSera. "What've you done?"

"Can you not see *Lyanthen Ah Lah'Phriel's* eyes, VelSera?" TharHa shook his head. "This burden rends his heart, but we've forced it upon him. May the truth be found and swiftly."

"Elder Lord," VelSera said. "You must stop him."

Drake snorted.

"I pray you haven't lied to us, VelSera," BauthEli said. "Or all our necks may bleed."

"I shall warden them until your return," Alden said. "None will suffer harm within this boundary. You have my word."

TherPriel supplied WaphRae while Jedediah and Drake awaited her at shield's edge. She arrived with saddle packs hung over her flanks and a dark glower. "You'll have no more honor here, not after this."

"If such is justice's price, I'll pay it," Jedediah said.

She glared.

Alden opened a doorway long enough for their exit. WaphRae regarded her kinsmen through the shimmering energy field. She shuddered.

"We're not meant for imprisonment," she said. "Have you no sympathy?"

"You know I do." Jedediah's thoughts unearthed long buried memories. He shuddered, images of his tribe, his people imprisoned in tiny rooms by those forcibly relocating them to lands no one wanted.

Bloody nightmares invaded his waking thoughts. *How many times did I get myself imprisoned? How many murders did freeing my kin cost? If I'd only known a gateway spell…no. There's no disease. They are walled but not chained, and Alden will not let them suffer hunger or thirst. He'll not torture them.*

I've done what must be done. Whatever my punishment, I will pay it as I have these many centuries.

Jedediah redoubled his pace. He addressed WaphRae after many miles. "We've a long journey by hoof and by foot. I'll work a mist walk if you'll permit me."

WaphRae glowered at him but didn't stop him from using the spell on her. Despite the tension, Drake glowed, literally, with anticipation. He bounded forward, only in sight by virtue of the light clinging to him.

Jedediah cupped his hands around his mouth. "Practice your stealth lessons, this isn't a holiday."

CHAPTER NINETEEN

Walking Among Briars

Their journey to *Mythela'Raemyn* began with sullen silences and resentful glares. The only real silver lining Jedediah could find traveling with WaphRae, once at least a friendly acquaintance if not a friend, proved her conservatism. *Isn't much, but I'd rather not have an unclothed woman scowling at me the whole trip.*

Over four centuries Jedediah had seen naked women. He'd acknowledge its wholesomeness. Human, centaur and Fey alike, nudity displayed the different beauties crafted on the Creator's easel.

Sure as shooting don't resemble Picasso's tortured recollections. Still unsure which Fey he ran afoul of.

Jedediah's mother married a Norse foreigner, bearing him a child. The scandal of mixing blood forced the Maykujay Peace Woman to redouble her priestly modesty and spirit walker's humility. Lesson and example beat the values into him. He'd questioned her teaching when adolescence aroused him to all possibilities female, but experience retaught her lessons in the most brutal way.

He glanced at WaphRae. *Still pointedly not looking my way.*

Assaults against tribeswomen reached from his mind's darkest recesses. He shuddered. Savage warriors and even more barbaric round-eyed invaders left horrifying wreckage in his past. Clothed tribeswomen suffered during raids too but provoked them less than naked breasts.

Jedediah turned his hands over, unwashable blood clinging red to his fingers. *Let my fury get the best of me a time or two, especially once I had daughters.*

Jedediah pushed his morbid recollections back into hiding. He checked their glamour. The Fey lived and breathed the magical camouflage. It cloaked centaurs in disguise or veritable invisibility among stronger Fey. It could push into unprotected minds and change their reality—sometimes with frighteningly permanent results.

Stubborn old mare argued with me when I ordered Drake to work her disguise—argued with a teacher, schooling his student. He shook his head. *Leastwise until Drake begged her for permission.*

Drake altered himself and Jedediah in addition to WaphRae's disguise as a horseback woman. Mist walk sped them across vast distances. Jedediah's anger

88

and WaphRae's resentment forced their march through their first night and following day without halt.

In her middle years, WaphRae's endurance flagged.

I should offer a stop. Probably just ignite another argument.

Drake bounded ahead, lit fire to a fallen tree and flopped down with all the grace of a newborn foal.

Jedediah frowned at him. *Lazy or wise? I'd thank him, but...*

He glanced at WaphRae. He shook his head and extinguished the flames.

Drake reignited the fire.

Jedediah reached for his magic.

"Thank you, Elder Lord. At least *someone* cares that I'm not a filly."

Drake shrugged one shoulder.

Damned unnatural on him. "Don't you forget the glamour in your sleep."

Drake looked up and groaned.

"Are you a bastard to everyone?" WaphRae asked.

Tingles shot along Jedediah's skin.

Drake shifted his tail, touching the centaur with its tip. Her head whipped toward him. She lowered her eyes. "Your student says I owe you an apology."

Jedediah waited.

A smile almost appeared. "You're a hard man."

"I've a debt to settle. His dame won't thank me for returning her son lazy and undisciplined." He glared at Drake. "Great lizard can't even mouth shape yet."

Drake snorted, turning his back on Jedediah.

Jedediah stifled a laugh. He planted his staff near the fire. Its runes danced with light, one then the other, alternating in a seemingly random manner.

"Won't that attract attention?" WaphRae asked.

"Yup."

Minutes passed.

Firefly lights glimmered around the camp's far edge. They collected behind brush and tree limb. Larger ones arrived. New colors appeared—mostly pastels with a few blazing reds and ember oranges mixed in.

His staff went dark.

They fled.

"I've got candy." Jedediah displayed a handful of cinnamon imperials.

Lights peeked through branches. They darted forward, a streaking army of kamikaze pixies.

Jedediah closed his hand.

High pitched voices tittered angrily. Some of the lights bolted away. One flew too near the dragon. Drake snapped grumpily at it but missed.

"Calm down, I ain't teasing you. Candy's payment in trade."

A pixie settled atop Jedediah's staff. Its angry red light faded, revealing the walnut-sized warrior. Bark armor clad its body. A triangular bark cap rested between its antennae. Its dragonfly-like wings kept moving, though too slowly for flight. It planted its pine needle spear and chirped.

Not even deigning to speak English, cheeky little snot.

"One each," Jedediah set a cinnamon imperial down atop the staff. "Paid sentry duty until the sun strikes dawn."

Its scowl became a face-covering grin. It hefted the candy under one arm, tapped spear tip to forehead just below an antenna and darted off.

Jedediah opened his palm.

The first few pixies approached hesitantly, but after they got their candies and escaped without injury, others swarmed.

"Hey," Jedediah snapped. A wind eddy swirled around a pastel green pixie. "One each."

WaphRae hid a smile.

The verdant pixie returned her second candy to his palm, offered a sheepish curtsey and darted away. They vanished. The scent of candied cinnamon filled the camp, wafted close by happy wings on feasting sentries.

Drake huffed.

"You want to sleep, glamour, and *guard.*"Jedediah sniffed the air. He smirked. "I don't think I smell any female dragonlings."

Drake raised his beak, sniffing the air.

Jedediah chuckled. "So who're you trying to impress then?"

Drake huffed smoke. He gave Jedediah an adolescent glare.

Jedediah laughed.

WaphRae shook her head. "You've a way about you."

Jedediah stretched out near the fire. "Sleep well, Eldress."

Alden poked at a campfire near the Fleet Hoof pavilion. Sullen and angry faces surrounded him interspaced with young, frightened or curious. They'd attacked him twice, once managing a surprise head blow that'd dazed him. He'd still blipped behind his assailant and laid him out flat.

Shanriel would've been pleased. Alden snorted. *Probably would've criticized my blip, strike and the resultant uniform wrinkles.*

He'd altered the shield, making it nearly invisible to comfort them. It flared in the distance. The controller reported assaults, bodily charges, even attempts to dig beneath the spherical barrier.

A beep from his chronometer predicted warned of the centaur's next attack. He rose wearily, addressing the soon-to pounce-warriors. "I've already told you, knocking me unconscious won't dismiss the shield. You can't remove it with the controller, it's voice encrypted."

A centaur stepped into view, opening his mouth. Alden cut across him. "Killing me will lock the shield in place until this planet no longer exists to fuel its power."

They charged anyway, slamming into the smaller sphere surrounding him. He shook his head. "Pointless."

TherPriel appeared. He eyed the shield flares with a wild expression before mastering himself. "Do you need food, warden?"

"Thank you, no."

He hesitated, apparently debating more strained conversation.

Hoof fall turned Alden's head. "Yes, councilman?"

"We're low on food," Velith'Seravin said. "No one foresaw us unjustly caged."

Alden smirked. "What would you like to eat?"

"We aren't your pets, two-legger. I've assembled a hunting party near the eastern tents."

Alden turned to TherPriel. "Can I entrust this to you? Your word to hunt and return with the party?"

"On my honor as war leader," TherPriel said.

They approached the eastern camp edge. The translucent force lines emitted a faint hum to forewarn of the edge, increasing in volume as they drew near.

Several centaur waited feet from a deep hole at the shield boundary. Sword-lances and bows bristled from them.

"You've no need of those," Alden said. "Bow, arrows and a knife are sufficient."

Sinesh Ena'Donishe, a dun-colored sorrel, trotted forward. "What's this, Elder?"

"Our warden doubts centaur honor and suggest he knows our hunting ways better than we. He sends this wizard-friend," VelSera gestured to TherPriel, "as your leader and nursemaid."

Glent Se'Lailos, a sleek black mare, stamped her hoof. "I object, SinDon. I'll not follow a kin traitor."

"Peace GlentLai," said VelSera. "We must hunt. Follow TherPriel this once."

"Alden, we use the sword-lances in hunting too," TherPriel said.

"Very well," Alden said.

GlentLai glowered, tail thrashing.

SinDon narrowed his gaze. "We hunt as you've commanded?"

VelSera nodded. "Let nothing stand in your way."

Alden opened passage and the hunters left.

The hunting party cantered through the woods for some distance, pausing every now and then to check for fresh game. On the third stop, SinDon frowned at the ground.

"Something amiss?" TherPriel asked.

"Yes, very vexing."

TherPriel leaned in, seeing nothing odd about the tracks. A sword-lance flashed in his peripheral vision, but he didn't react fast enough. It slid into his chest.

"I release you from the wizard's hex, honored one. Join the great hunt, assured your tribesmen hunt your betrayer." SinDon addressed the others. "We must catch this human and free our eldress."

"How will we catch him?" GlentLai asked. "The wizard has a day's lead."

"We are Fleet Hoof." SinDon reared, raising his bloodied weapon. "Embrace the wind. Kill the wizard."

The surrounding centaurs saluted. SinDon charged into the wood, weapon aloft, and the others hard on his tail.

Marc O'Steele finished his weapon sale and signed onto the coordination chat room.

The computer beeped:

```
ResourceSS03 has signed on.
One: Resource?
ResourceSS03: Done, sir.
One: Our asset?
ResourceSS03: He interfered. He eluded us, vanished into thin
air.
One: How do trained killers lose one green cop?
ResourceSS03: IDK, but something unhinged him. He's lost his
memory. All they can get out of his is rants about fairies or
some such. I infiltrated, met him eye to eye. He didn't know me,
so I let him live.
One: You left him? Qualms about killing a cop, resource?
ResourceSS03: No, sir. I felt killing him while under such
close scrutiny was the wrong move, for now at least.
One: I see. Get us a replacement asset.
ResourceSS03: Acknowledged
ResourceSS03 has signed out.
```

One waited and waited. His patience neared its end. *I hate tardiness.*
The computer beeped:

```
Muler has signed on.
Muler: One.
One: Where's Flash?
Muler: Not my problem.
Flash has signed on.
Flash: How'd the deal go?
```

One: 50 M16A2 rifles and 10,000 rounds, delivered by end of week.

Muler: :) Standard rate?

One: Almost twice that.

Flash: Cabin's prepared as ordered. More blood tightens the noose.

Muler: Why can't we just kill him?

One: Follow the Board's instructions.

Muler: People hire us to kill well-protected heads of state, and we can't kill one farmer we want dead? LOL

One: It isn't funny.

Muler: You're right.

One: Move the weapons and return for orders.

Muler: FINE.

Muler has signed off.

Flash: This one isn't pack.

One: Tell me about it, that's how we got him.

Flash: He'll ignore Zero's orders.

One: Probably. Speaking of problems, ResourcesSS03 left a compromised asset alive. Take care of them both and keep an eye on Muler.

Flash: Done and done.

Flash has signed off.

He shuddered. The way the Samoan twins talked, the way they moved unsettled him. *Like barely leashed animals.*

Marc scowled at Muler's chat on another monitor, setting up his delivery and running his mouth. Unaware of the invisible Number he badmouthed.

Better behave, Muler. I don't think the twins take prisoners. His scowl deepened. *Better have a chat with him. If he slips his leash, Zero might blame me.*

CHAPTER TWENTY

Gateway to Mythela'Raemyn

Jedediah searched the surrounding area until he found a young sapling. He unearthed it carefully and brought it to a magic circle lain before four interwoven trees that formed an arch. He set the sapling within a smaller circle drawn between the four elements of the greater circle. He explained as he worked, repeating the lesson exactly as he'd learned it.

"Aren't there only four wizard magics?" WaphRae said.

"The Dutchman assumed the fifth represented life or spirit—hence a fresh sapling," Jedediah said.

"Will the ritual kill the sapling?"

"No, I'll plant it in *Mythela'Raemyn*."

Jedediah invested four points around the circle with elemental simulacrum: fire, water, earth and air. Each focused upon the circle's center, seemingly locked in battle against an invisible foe. Jedediah danced the perimeter, alternately facing center and forest. He sang old words—harsh but melodic. He leapt on each fourth stride, landing hard on his right foot.

Drake cocked his head, tail thumping in time.

Air swirled like water in the archway. It rippled with each landing. The air cleared revealing a different wood beyond.

Jedediah retrieved the sapling and stepped beneath the arch. He faced Drake. "Rydari Phriel, I grant you passage within this corridor. Walk its halls softly."

Jedediah led them into a corridor that followed the Appalachians through yet more gateways. Surrounding forestland seemed part and not part of Earth.

"Not sure, mind, but I'm thinking this passage worms its way through different times," Jedediah said.

His beard itched.

He glanced behind them at the ancient twin arbors that served as the last gateway. No one entered the corridor without a guardian's permission and only at the origin arch.

"I thought you let Drake drop the glamour because no one could follow us."

"Yup. That's what I said."

"You don't look too convinced."

Jedediah scratched his beard. "Probably don't."

They camped near a rock outcropping. Jedediah didn't summon another swarm of pixies, not even to bribe for another light show. He leaned upon his staff and studied the rocks.

Drake loped up to his side, followed closely by WaphRae. *Glad she's warming up again.*

"What are you doing?" she asked.

Jedediah tilted his head. "What do you reckon, male or female?"

Shock colored WaphRae's cheeks. "Female, of course."

"Drake?" Jedediah touched the dragon.

"F-female," Drake stuttered.

Jedediah's eyebrow rose. "Female?"

Drake nodded.

Jedediah stifled a smile. "About time."

"J-jerk."

Jedediah roared with laughter. WaphRae's expression rekindled his laughter.

<Probably thinks you mad, Master.>

Should make you do this.

Drake cringed.

"Step back, Eldress," Jedediah raised his staff, chanting in a deep, gravelly baritone. The staff's runes glowed a muddy light unlike their normal silver.

The earth shifted, rumbling.

WaphRae shuffled backward, her footing unsteady.

The rocks groaned. Pebbles and dirt slid away from a shapely stone figure. She stretched her arms and yawned.

"Good evening, Mistress," Jedediah intoned in the same gravelly baritone. "Pardon me for waking you."

Her voice escaped smooth as river stone and soft as fresh-turned soil. "What century is it?"

"Twenty-first," Jedediah said.

An obsidian-sharp curse escaped her lips. She covered her mouth, her face suddenly rain darkened. "Pardon me."

WaphRae wore a maternal smile. "Problem?"

"I missed my symphonic performance of sedimentary percussion and strings," she sighed. "By a century."

"Dreadful sorry we didn't happen along sooner. Would've been something, I'm sure," Jedediah said. "This is Waphri Ah'Raemyn, that's Drake and I'm Jedediah."

"Kimberlite," she curtseyed.

"Might I enlist your protection for the night?"

"Just one night?"

"Yup. I don't suppose you like candy?"

Kimberlite shook her head. "It's not good for the figure."

Jedediah grinned. "Quite. Transfiguration? Maybe a lace of rose quartz?"

When Kimberlite smiled, the minerals in her teeth sparkled. "That'd be lovely, aeromancer."

Jedediah summoned a mirror mist. They conferred. Half an hour later she admired her new pink crystals in the mirror.

Jedediah leaned against a moss garbed boulder. "Sure this isn't a relation?"

"Sedentary."

Kimberlite planted herself directly behind them on the path. WaphRae folded her legs beneath her. She watched the vain stone elemental, her smile speaking volumes.

The night passed without event.

Jedediah stepped away from the camp, careful not to wake WaphRae. Drake watched him with one open eye, smoke and snores curling from his nostrils.

Jedediah twirled the morning mist into a passable mirror. "Lanea?"

Lanea appeared, still foggy from sleep. "What? Da?"

Jedediah chuckled softly. *Like her mother, tousle-haired and bleary-eyed, she glows like a sunrise.*

His smile rotted. He forced a replacement. "Good morning, girl."

"Morning, Da," she yawned.

"How're things?"

She stifled another yawn. "Al delivered your truck. The sheriff and his deputies are taking turns camping on the porch. They're pretty hot to chat."

"Didn't I tell you to make yourself scarce?"

"John keeps looking for the barkbiters and mumbling. Sheriff joins him once in a while."

"They suspicious?"

"John is, but you know humans, see what they want and shrug off the rest."

He glared.

"You know what I meant," Lanea chewed her lip. "Visited Fleet Hoof to find you."

"How are they?"

"It's almost like they're wilting, Da, if that makes any sense."

"Hoped they'd last longer, not being truly locked away. I'll have to hurry."

"Da, I found TherPriel dead outside the shield and tracks headed up your back trail," Lanea said. "They killed him."

Cold washed out the morning's warmth. His jaw tightened.

"Alden sent him out with a hunting party," she said

"Hunting me, not deer," Jedediah scowled. "Girl, clear out. Don't return to their camp."

"I can take care of myself."

Jedediah rolled his eyes. "You're all grown, can look after yourself, make your own choices. Why don't you pity your old Da and not add any more worries to my burden?"

"You're not old."

"Go somewhere safe, okay? Promise me?"

"Sure."

He watched her before dispelling the mirror.

"Everything all right?" WaphRae asked.

"They killed TherPriel."

"No."

Jedediah ground his teeth. "Yup."

"What of my people?"

"*Our* people. Believe it or not, I'm unhappier about jailing them then you are."

"You of all people know what caging them can do to them, Jedediah."

Jedediah looked away. "I remember."

"How are they?" she asked.

"Wilting. Only good fortune is the hunters are dead on my tail, so they *might* not murder any more normals."

"Can we mist walk?" she asked.

Jedediah chewed his lip. "Dangerous. There's a sort of resonance, a feedback echo, to magic used in the corridor."

"You transfigured her."

Jedediah glanced at Kimberlite. "Yup, slowly to minimize feedback. Mist walking here nearly killed me last time. It has to be recast in each gateway."

"You could ask your jailer to free them."

"More worried about those hunting us than Fleet Hoof's discomfort. Just the same I'll consider it since cat's already in the nip."

"Thank you."

"You won't thank me if they kill more normals," Jedediah said. "Let's go. Four more days to the grand stair."

They stopped between stone pillars at Appalachians' foot. They'd pushed hard, risen early and marched late—finishing in just over three days. They passed two centaur patrols where none should've been needed, substantiating the itch in Jedediah's beard.

Steps carved for centaur formed a grand stair. It wound its way up the mountainside.

"I never thought I'd see this place," WaphRae whispered.

"Still surprised you've never asked to come."

An exotic and lovely blush colored her weathered face. "No. My teachers insisted their training provided all I needed. I know, hardly wise."

Jedediah said nothing.

"As angry as I was—am—at you for what was done, I am glad for the chance to come."

"How mad were you?"

"Mad enough to vote against you right then and there."

"Feared as much. Wouldn't have mattered. This has gone beyond your council."

"Sure you haven't overstepped your authority?"

He shrugged. "It might not please you, but I spoke only truth. I'll enable you and the High Elders palaver with your council. I'll dismiss Alden then too."

She considered. "Thank you, but first we've a long climb."

Jedediah gazed up the stair he'd climbed many times—once with Elsabeth. "Just like life, Eldress, a long climb up a lonely road."

Drake watched them.

Jedediah's words struck a personal chord.

Stormfall went through a dozen wizards before forcing Jedediah to foster him. Unfamiliar with the deception's details, he knew his mother manufactured the circumstances that placed Jedediah in her debt.

I'd tell him if I didn't fear he'd cast me out. I never understood mother's desperation to divest herself of me, but I'm glad she brought me to Master's farm.

Sadness filled him.

Once his years of training ended. Long solitary decades stretched before him. Even if Jedediah remained a friend, he'd only do so until his life ended.

Times changed. Ages ended. Men died. Stone wore down. Through it all, his dwindling kind watched—a silent vigil from time's beginning to its end.

Drake loped to Jedediah and wrapped his tongue around the old man's wrist. *Come, Master, let's climb.*

Jedediah smiled down at him. "Lead on, you great lizard."

Drake bounded ahead with a smile. He savored the moment against a lonely future.

CHAPTER TWENTY-ONE

Road's End

The grand stair ended with a pillar-supported archway. Unlike the previous unadorned gateways, a detailed centaur history had been carved into the pillars. WaphRae gazed at the intricate stonework, tracing her fingers through history.

"This arch and I share a name," Jedediah said.

WaphRae whispered. *"Feihtor Ah Mythela 'Raemyn.* Few know how you came by such a prestigious title. Many doubt your claims."

"Skepticism is often wisdom's gateway," Jedediah said. "Mind your manners, Drake. Your mother won't take it kindly if you offend these people."

"Have they met Stormfall?" WaphRae asked.

Jedediah gestured to a sheer granite face on the far end of the valley. It looked as if cleaved in half by some great sword. Even at this distance, a carved arch crowded the sheered mountainside's edges—rivaling Saint Louis's.

"Gravid females bring their eggs, dipping them in the Dragon Spring to strengthen the dragonling. Stormfall brought Drake's egg twice." Jedediah led them to the archway's edge and gestured. "Welcome to *Mythela 'Raemyn*—gateway to magic's source."

Paradise stretched out before them. Small orchards and glens huddled in natural mountain alcoves. Wood and stone longhouses punctuated the tranquil scene. At the great arch's foot, twelve smaller, disparate archways surrounded a stepped, stone pyramid rising above the trees. Sunlight flashed off silver too far away to discern.

Three roan centaur galloped forward, bearing silver scimitars. Fine, silver breastplates and chainmail barding protected chests and flanks respectively.

Jedediah planted his staff and bowed to one knee like a knight of old. *"Feihtor Ah Mythela 'Raemyn* seeks the High Elders."

They inclined their heads in deference. The centermost mare spoke. "We've foreseen your arrival and are glad to receive you. I am Midall E'Cru, great granddaughter of Lelai Muen'Myn. She awaits your arrival."

Jedediah's face shot up. Blood fled it, rioting in his gut. "Lelai Muen'Myn yet lives?"

Midall E'Cru smiled. "She does, Honored Brother."

Another nudged her, whispering in her ear. All three extended forelegs and bowed before Drake.

Midall E'Cru flourished her hand, touching it to heart, lip and forehead. "Your presence honors us, Elder Lordling. We serve your whim and shall unseal the great arch if you desire it."

Drake glanced at Jedediah then inclined his head.

The centaur straightened up.

Jedediah rose and introduced Waphri Ah'Raemyn. The three greeted her in the high centaur tongue.

"Would you care to refresh yourself before we take you to Lelai Muen'Myn?" Midall E'Cru asked.

Jedediah glanced at WaphRae. "No, our audience cannot wait. Please bring us to the High Elders Council, Midall E'Cru."

"It would be my great honor if, *Feihtor Ah Mythela'Raemyn*, addressed me as MidCru," she said. "This way."

They followed MidCru while the other two centaurs rushed off in different directions.

"It'd be a great service to tongue and ear if you'd just call me Jedediah."

MidCru smiled. "I'm honored, Jedediah."

She led them to an open-sky amphitheater just beyond a shaded pool. Battle-garbed centaur statuary supported a stone ring, leaving twelve gaps into its center. Age discolored the rearing stone pillars, but their intricate carvings remained sharp.

Cherry blossom trees surrounded the amphitheater as they had centuries earlier at Jedediah's first visit. White blossoms tinged palest pink perfumed the air, and wide branches shaded the amphitheater except at high noon.

Eight aged centaurs flanked Lelai Muen'Myn. Wrinkled and ancient, her coat paled to silver. Moon-silver robes akin to Jedediah's garbed her from shoulder to crest to fetlock.

MidCru's former companions led four more elder centaur into the amphitheater.

Delight illuminated Lelai Muen'Myn's gaze. She reached almost reverently to caress Jedediah's arm. Her voice dropped to a mere whisper. "*Feihtor Ah Mythela'Raemyn*, returned at long last."

Pale, watery-eyed and unable to trust his voice, Jedediah inclined his head.

A sad smile reached her eyes. She touched his lips. "I know, Jedediah. Words for another time. First, declare why you've come."

Jedediah took a deep breath and told his tale. Discontent mutters arose when he reached imprisoning Fleet Hoof. The High Eldress's glance silenced them, allowing Jedediah to finish. "I'll order their release at the High Council's word. Permit me to join the fires, LelMyn."

She pursed her lips. "Proceed."

Jedediah stepped to the amphitheater's central fire. Few communication magics allowed discussion between *Mythela'Raemyn* and the outside world, but each tribe maintained a fire taken from valley to village. Jedediah reached his senses into the old flame. It flicked and sparked, cantankerous in its seniority and loath to take his commands. He mastered it. Smoke curled into an open window.

Alden rose, peering into the smoke. "Jedediah?"

"Our debt is settled," Jedediah said. "The High Tribe orders Fleet Hoof released on limited parole."

"Our debt is not paid," Alden hung his head. "I let their warriors hunt. They shed innocent blood I may not reverse."

Lelai Muen'Myn stepped forward. "Young one, I absolve you of their bloodletting. Justice will be levied."

Alden didn't meet her eye. "Call if you need me."

She turned to MidCru, scowl etched deep into her face. "We must have words with Fleet Hoof. Escort Jedediah and his honored protégé to their lodge. Waphri Ah'Raemyn, you will remain."

Jedediah ran a hand through Drake's frills. *Stay.*

<She dismissed me.>

She'd never eject you. I'm trusting you to be my witness.

Drake's chest swelled.

Little more subtle, you great lizard.

Drake reddened.

MidCru gestured. "A lodge to honor *Feihtor Ah Mythela'Raemyn* awaits this way."

"Yup." Jedediah led the way.

She fell into step and studied him. "You honor her greatly."

Jedediah smiled. "Even among such a great people, she's greater."

"Why do I sense sadness between you? A tragedy?"

"My fault." Jedediah's chest ached. "I was very young."

"Our worst mistakes populate our youth. I'm told my mother—fearing to see death before becoming High Spirit Elder—challenged Lelai Muen'Myn. She demanded great-grandmother step aside when no other would name her too old to serve."

He laughed. "How bad a mark did LelMyn leave on your mother?"

MidCru smiled ruefully. "Her regret yet haunts her. Some claimed building a lodge for the *Feihtor Ah Mythela'Raemyn* as folly. How many such guardians would ever live?"

"What did she tell them?"

"One guardian provided reason enough."

"Sounds like her."

They stopped outside the lodge.

"Will you rest here long?" Midall E'Cru asked.

"No. There're troubles afoot beneath the mountains."

MidCru extended a hand toward the lodge. "Your presence honors us. I'll return when you are summoned."

Jedediah watched her go then entered the lodge.

Crafted by centaur, its proportions made him feel small. A straw pallet lay beneath wide shuttered windows. A high table stood along under a large window. The high stool and massive brass bathing tub he'd added ages ago remained. The lodge crossbred medieval inn with a stable.

Not that I'd say so out loud.

Centaurs came, young and old. They brought deference and curiosity, fresh fruit and sharp cheese.

He bid them fill his tub. He heated the water, almost forgetting to rein his power so close to magic's core. A gesture bent steam into a solid fog curtain to protect his modesty. He sank into the water.

Eyes closed, he reviewed mistakes, past and present.

MidCru interrupted his reverie. "Pardon me. LelMyn requests your presence."

He levitated a towel into a makeshift privacy screen before rising from long-cold water. He donned his buckskins and followed her.

MidCru led him to a familiar sheltered glade to one side of the valley. LelMyn lay next to a dappled pool, shaded by another cherry blossom tree. A white blanket, fluffy like raw cotton, covered her.

"I am here," Jedediah smiled.

LelMyn studied him. "So beautiful. In your prime, like our first meeting."

"Time's granted me experience—maybe even wisdom. Though such years cannot diminish your beauty."

"Silver-tongued now as ever."

"I've put several miles of footprints on it," Jedediah said.

She laughed, but it wilted from her tongue. "I've not seen you since I sent you away. Not even when you returned with...with her."

"I served the High Tribe, protecting *Mythela'Raemyn* from those miners."

"No. I tasked you so I wouldn't have to look at you."

Jedediah frowned.

"So beautiful a man back then," she laughed wistfully, "Even for a human, no, especially for a human. So charming, so full of life. Such potential."

Jedediah's expression soured. "And so vulgar as to try to court a centaur, a walker, a seeker of Lah'Phriel."

"I feel I must explain."

Hardness bit into his voice. "You made yourself painfully clear then."

"I lied to you, Jedediah. I couldn't have both you and keep to my path, so I sent you away. It proved hard, harder than you know." She gazed into the distance. "I foresaw her, knew she'd steal your heart from me...then break it."

"Elsabeth never hurt me in life."

"In death," LelMyn said.

Jedediah turned away.

"I also foresaw her return."

Cold flame ignited in his chest. Jedediah spun, a snarl on his lips. "No. She bled not Fey. She's at rest."

A corner of LelMyn's mouth twisted up. "Explain then your heart's vehemence."

I can't.

"You're afraid of her, this new woman."

"Too similar, too easy," Jedediah's voice trailed off, "...like a succubus dragging me into hell's clutches."

"You're lying to yourself, Jedediah. You fear loving her only to lose her once more."

"Of course I do." His whispers haunted the glade. "I fell in a moment, into a trap crafted especially for me. If she's not a trap then an ill omen that I don't understand."

LelMyn laughed softly. "You never did take ignorance mildly."

He changed the subject. "Has the council decided?"

"Not yet. Your actions defy precedent. Fleet Hoof's council refutes your claims."

"I didn't act lightly nor am I wrong."

"Centaur blood on centaur spears," she sighed. "Unraveling this will take days. Rest while you can, Jedediah. Your premonitions may be truer than you know."

He scrutinized her. "You foresaw something else?"

"Perhaps I merely see you more clearly than you see yourself. You've hidden a long time. More and more, longer and longer, especially since Lirelaeli Ermyn'Phir ensorcelled you."

"Leave Lanea's mother out of this."

LelMyn placed a hand over Jedediah's heart. "I cannot remove something you carry with you."

He stomped out of her reach. "You've no idea how it felt having your dearest beliefs ripped away, having your very will stolen and used against you."

"True. I sent you away before you did it to me."

"It's not the same thing."

"You suffered a knife. I suffered a thorny rose." She inhaled, shuddering. "I'm weary. May we speak again later?"

Jedediah gave her a single nod and marched into darkness.

The High Elders deliberated several days. Drake watched Jedediah submitted to truth spells and rituals. His Master had balked at the insult, but LelMyn had assured them the spells would champion, not sully, his honor.

Finally, they summoned Jedediah back to the amphitheater.

"This trouble among the tribes bothers us," LelMyn looked at Jedediah. "Evidence from other tribes reveals blood and rebellion. True, rebellious voices are youth's language, perhaps our guiding hand has too long been absent. Perhaps we've been too remote, too wrapped up in our studies.

"Perhaps I'm to blame. I've been Eldress too long, leaving no room for new ideas while my roots and branches grew stiff and unyielding." She turned sad eyes upon Jedediah. "The moon rises and in time it sets. It brings love and magic. My moon sets this very day."

LelMyn gestured at WaphRae. "Here stands a daughter, an Eldress, who's never sheltered within *Mythela'Raemyn*. Her restless brethren strike out at humanity, endangering themselves in their fury. Guardians have long protected us. Before the new world, they protected our tribes in foreign lands, erecting barriers of magic or law. That centaur would attack our Guardians shames me."

WaphRae addressed her hooves. "What's to be done?"

"Folly roots here, a High Tribe too high and apart from its people," LelMyn said. "I decree remedy. As for *Feihtor Ah Mythela'Raemyn*, he is centaur despite his legs."

She gestured Jedediah into the center, placing a curled right hand on his chest. Her fingers twitched, uncurling in starts and shudders until splayed open over his heart. She whispered so low Drake had to strain in order to overhear. "There will be darkness, dear Jedediah, and great pain. You'll not understand what I invoke here, perhaps ever, but it's a gift for love I couldn't return before. Elder Lordling."

Drake started.

She smirked, raising her voice as she faced him. "Bear witness, Elder Lordling, long after Mother's reclaimed all here."

Drake straightened, displaying fierce dignity and solemnity.

LelMyn struggled with her robe's neck. MidCru rushed forward. LelMyn shooed her away. A silver pendant pulled free of LelMyn's robes. She offered it. "Waphri Ah'Raemyn, seeker of Lah'Phriel, take this and bear witness."

WaphRae swallowed, lowering her head to receive the gift. "Yes, Eldress."

"*Feihtor Ah Mythela'Raemyn*, I mark you as centaur with my last breath."

Jedediah's eyes burned hot. Words failed him.

Her hand glowed.

A breeze rose, galloping hooves audible upon it. The others looked around for the source, but Jedediah's eyes stayed locked with LelMyn's. Her skin, already translucent with age, faded still more. Her outline blurred.

A tiny, silver armored centaur galloped down her extended arm. It leapt from her flesh to Jedediah's. It settled upon his chest, galloping in place.

Lelai Muen'Myn shimmered—a faint glow like moonlight on water. Her robes fell through her vanishing echo. Her shadow fled and with it, her bracing hand. Jedediah collapsed.

MidCru raised a horn to her lips. A long mournful call filled the valley. Others sounded, one by one filling far corners with a sorrowful keen.

Drake nudged Jedediah over. *Master?*

The tiny centaur mark blew a soundless horn. A thought invaded his mind. *<Cry and behold, Lordling, a harbinger of great sorrows.>*

WaphRae knelt beside him. "We should take him to his lodge."

MidCru replaced her horn, unable to speak through sobs. She nodded.

CHAPTER TWENTY-TWO

Mounting Peril

Jedediah caressed the sacred stone's unmarred surface atop the pyramid. A shallow depression encircled it, worn down by centuries of hooves. A subtle, magical thrum met his fingertips. Jedediah's eyes rose to the great arch. He opened his connection to magic, adding trumpeted harmony to the stone's song.

Simple jeans and red flannel couldn't protect him from the chill LelMyn's loss left in him. He stared toward the sheered mountain. His vantage offered a clear view of large, ornate border carvings. Much smaller top-to-bottom runes flanked a doorway seam which didn't actually part.

Moon-silver shields hung on against each of the pyramid's tiers. The twelve arches surrounded the pyramid's foot.

Jedediah looked past it all, seeing beyond and behind.

Wives and lost loves paraded through his memories. Friends and honored foes lined the path behind. His heart ached for children stolen from his life. Fear iced his chest. Lanea's departure neared, life stealing her for its own purposes.

I hold her too tight. My grip will probably send her sooner rather than keeping her close, but I can't help it. Without her, I am but a lonely old man marking time on mantle clocks.

Tears threatened, but he sucked them inside to the dark knot that hid his pain from others and himself.

TherPriel is gone. I'll miss you, old foe. Heat flickered in his chest, but ice extinguished it before it raised oaths to his lips. *LelMyn departed before we could make peace.* He cast his gaze toward Drake, gnawing a deer haunch—bloodying *Mythela'Raemyn* as only a dragon would dare. *You'll be gone too one day. Will you look back through the millennia one day and count me among your treasured losses?*

The deer haunch lingered longer than most. *Does something deaden your appetite, young dragonling? Has your heart caught my troubles like a flu?*

WaphRae lingered with the other spirit elders elsewhere in the valley. They taught her lore recorded only behind the protections surrounding the sacred valley. She might even participate in the ritual to open the Great Arch for Drake's journey to the Dragon Springs.

I'd have counted you as friend, Waphri Ah'Raemyn, before at least. Are you now another enemy at my back? Has the High Tribe's declaration tempered your anger? Jedediah rubbed his chest absently. LelMyn had settled the matter of the Rite of Joined Dreams

106

in ways he still couldn't fathom. She'd marked his chest, written his title of *Feihtor Ah Mythela'Raemyn* upon his flesh.

The High Elders decreed him centaur. They'd censured Fleet Hoof and ordered her to perform the Rite upon their return—one reason for her additional instructions.

Will the mark stay with me when I alter my age? He scratched. *Will the damned thing ever stop its ticklish movement?*

He studied the arches surrounding him—smaller than the Great Arch but large enough to allow passage of a dragon in flight. Dwarven smiths had crafted no two alike despite originating from the same stone. They'd carved meaning, almost life into the rock, depicting each destination. Each offered tempting escape save the Atlantis gate—blocked after the last Dragon War.

A Guardian and his heirs protected exits for the eleven corridors: Cities of gold, Cibola, El Dorado, the Fountain of Youth, Shamballa, and so many more.

<You may thinketh me gate poor orphaned cousin against the Grand Twelve.> The Dutchman's thick accent repeated in his thoughts. *<Mark me, Two-Hawks, we guard the Golden Gate, a rough servant's corridor too small for full grown dragon. Afterthought though it be, it offers vital succor to the vast Fey communities against impending plunder by our normal cousins and their quenchless greed.>*

Jedediah scowled. *The Golden Gate—gold, a mistranslation that cost its Guardians, cost me so dearly. The truth, that magic's life rather than soft, yellow metal lay beyond cost us even more.*

He regarded Drake once more. *Will you join your forebears? Will you learn their greed and turn your power against us once more? Will you add to a lifetime's triple share of war, fighting and death just to horde its power to yourself?*

Jedediah shook dark memories from his thoughts. He'd held the Dutchman's gate for three centuries. He couldn't walk away, surely couldn't leave its plague to sweet Lanea. If he died without a designated heir—a real death rather than those Jedediah Shine periodically suffered—another Guardian's successor would have to take his gate.

Laughter bubbled from him. *Suit Velith'Seravin right if I walked away and let him have his run.*

His mirth shriveled on his lips. *How many Fey would my selfishness kill? How many dwindling kinds would I sacrifice to the final death? I couldn't just walk away anyway. Too few full Guardians remain. Their apprentices aren't ready...and I'd miss my farm.*

He snarled. "Stop wallowing and focus. People are dying."

Drake's beak snapped up.

"Not you," Jedediah said.

Drake's concerned gaze lingered.

Jedediah paced. Anger warmed him against recent loss. The itch in his beard lingered, but within *Mythela'Raemyn's* protected valley it couldn't mean attack. *Could it?*

He shook his head. The subconscious itch implied something more sinister than mere physical attack. Something about the murders didn't fit.

Centaurs didn't use rifles. Centaurs didn't slay animals outside a hunt, and they never ever left carcasses to rot.

His mother's tribe, like all those later called Indians, had lived and learned with the Fey—incorrectly recorded by near-sighted anthropologists as spirit guides or beings of worships.

Centaur tribes taught them to give thanks for a brother animal slain to feed the tribe. Nothing went wasted lest it dishonor the animal's sacrifice.

Velith'Seravin makes me want to chew nails, but I can't believe Fleet Hoof has fallen so far as to abandon that tenet.

Two of maybe six normals had been slain by centaurs. The Rite of Joined Dreams might add the others upon Velith'Seravin's account, but something nagged him about the deaths. They didn't feel centaur.

If not centaur, why're people dying on my land? What am I missing?

Fixing the problem remained essential, but left the blame. Joe Franklin couldn't be expected to ignore the mounting evidence—circumstantial or not. If bodies kept falling, they'd pile too high to overlook.

Dying's the easy answer. Jedediah scratched his chin. *Something about that feels off somehow.*

Jedediah descended the pyramid tier by tier, walking each counter clockwise. He touched the plaques of moon-silver, forged and engraved to honor a spirit elder. He paused at the newest one, forged in the two days since LelMyn's death, and bowed his head in silent farewell.

He turned.

Midall E'Cru studied him.

He forced a smile. "Need something, MidCru?"

"You've been atop the pyramid some time."

"Too many questions, and not enough answers."

"Is that why you linger?"

"Drake's waiting to see the Spring. Can't just leave my charge behind, can I?"

"I thought perhaps you awaited WaphRae's curiosity to wane."

"Imagine mountains wither to sand faster. She's needed to perform the Rite and settle things, but I don't command her."

"Didn't you command her to come?" MidCru asked.

"In that, I had authority to bring her for judgement. The High Elders ruled, but placed no deadline upon her departure."

"I see."

Jedediah examined her.

Centaur priests tended toward scholarly manners, but MidCru's face seemed so youthful, so earnest, he couldn't read her expression.

They studied one another.

She trotted away before the silence grew awkward.

Jedediah returned to his lodge, hoping another bath might wash away whatever obscured his troubles. He dozed. He awoke in cold water, ears tingling from a weak attempt at mist mirror communications.

He heated his bath with a swirling finger, bringing to life a layer of steam. He reshaped it upright but froze, spell on his lips.

What if it isn't just a weak sending? What if someone's spying? Jedediah cursed himself. *You're getting paranoid.*

Jedediah sent his will back along the web-fine sending, reinforcing the call. "Yup?"

Lanea's face appeared, pale and breathing hard. "Da?"

"What's the matter, girl?"

Lanea's face wrinkled with pain. A coughing fit bent her.

Cereal boxes lined a shelf behind her. Her image waved. Her spell unraveled. Young, yes, but inexperienced and weak didn't apply to Lanea.

A mist mirror shouldn't even make her blink.

He lent it more power, keeping the signal going. He went cold despite the hot water. "Lanea, what's wrong?"

Lanea turned pleading eyes toward him, blood staining her lips. "Help?"

Dead weight filled his stomach. He pushed more power her way.

Her eyelids drooped. The last few words fell away into whispers. "Someone shot me."

The mirror shattered.

CHAPTER TWENTY-THREE

Poisonous Relationship

Lanea leaned against Treevoran's door, unsure how she'd gotten there. She pounded with kitten-weak blows. The door opened.

Jedediah stood in the doorway.

"Da?"

The glamour flickered. Treevoran gaped. "You're covered in blood."

"Help."

Treevoran cradled her, helping her inside. "Maker, you're ruining the carpet."

"Sorry."

He lowered her onto his couch. Lanea tried to smile. She had fond memories of the couch. "Cold."

Treevoran grabbed the bloodied throw rug and draped it over her. His hands ran over her body. She felt the touch, but not the tingle that normally accompanied it.

"I've got to remove the bolt to perform a healing."

"Bullet," Lanea corrected.

He ripped her shirt away.

Wish I had time to do my hair.

Flickers of Jedediah echoed around Treevoran.

Fingers probed the -hot wound. Treevoran wore a focused expression mixing concern and disgust. She watched his bloody hands, pressing long delicate fingers into her flesh.

Ugly green veins shot up his gorgeous skin.

The glamour echo vanished.

Treevoran shrieked and stumbled backward. He beat at the hand, ugly veins spider-webbing across his flesh. They blossomed up his neck toward his face.

"Trevor?"

He convulsed against the chair, shrieking. "Get out! Get out!"

A sudden urge to leave pounded against her wandering thoughts. Green veins spread out from the wound. She stumbled unsure from the couch to the door. Blood and ugly veins ran down her naked chest. She stumbled over the threshold, tears wetted her cheeks. Her face splashed into a rain-rippled puddle.

"Da. Help."

CHAPTER TWENTY-FOUR

Life, Death & the Fight Between

Jedediah exploded from the water and forced jeans over wet skin. He hurtled outside barefoot, tripping on Drake laying outside the entrance.

"Blasted dragon, fetch WaphRae. We're leaving."

Drake glanced toward the Great Arch.

Electricity arced from Jedediah's skin. "Someone's shot Lanea."

Drake tore away, talons ripping turf.

Jedediah's hands blurred. His belongings rocketed from corners, shoving themselves into his satchel. He raced after Drake, letting the satchel catch up when it would.

<Stop and think, Two-Hawks. Panic costs lives.>

Jedediah stopped at the Dutchman's admonition. He inhaled, trying to organize thought. *Even running full out with a mist walk, we're a day from the exit.* His mind lost all sense of up and down. *What if the bullet contains iron?*

He sprinted into the lodge, passing his satchel headed the other way. He superheated the bath, cracking the tub. Steam drove him a step back. He marshaled it with will, framing it with soft wind.

Who can help? Old Mauve? Justin? Mama Yamai?

Mauve knew Lanea. She could teleport but made horrifying mistakes every time she dealt with normals—a necessary evil if Lanea ended up in a hospital.

Mama Yamai didn't know Lanea and compared to Mauve, her people skills offered full blown disaster even when she deigned to put clothes on. She'd have to take corridors too and likely wouldn't leave her African tribesmen in any case.

Justin's condition left him too frail to teleport. He lived two very long hours away without Atlanta traffic.

He ran through the other Guardians. They'd help, but none knew the area enough to help fast enough.

Three people leapt to mind. He eliminated Treevoran outright. The egocentric elf wouldn't play the hero without gain.

Never trust him with Lanea's life in any case.

Lanea's mother, Lirelaeli Ermyn'Phir, was twice as bad. Opening a direct link to her offered her a second opportunity to enslave Jedediah's mind. His panic-distracted mind wouldn't keep her out if she tried. Lanea's life should've outweighed enslaving him once more, but elf capriciousness defied prediction.

Leave her for last.

Jedediah adjusting a spell on the fly, using sheer willpower to overcome technological issues. A ringing tone emanated from within the mist mirror.

"Joe Franklin."

"It's Jedediah—"

"Where the hell are you?"

"Shut up, my da-farmhand's been shot in some grocery store, I don't know where. Please. You have to help her."

"Witnesses claimed *you* got shot. We're at the Piggly Wiggly now."

"Me?" Jedediah adapted. "Bullet hit her instead. You have to find her."

"You're in shock, Jedediah, delirious from blood loss."

"What're you blathering about, you've got to help her."

"I'm watching the video right now. There's no farmhand. Where are you? I'll send an ambulance."

Jedediah swore and hung up. *Damn the consequences.*

He reached for Lirelaeli. The spell searched and searched without success.

She's been shot at the Piggly Wiggly. Treevoran had an apartment nearby. Jedediah framed the spell.

Terror hit Jedediah the moment their mind's connected. Pain and revulsion drove into him, ejecting him from the elf's mind.

Jedediah screamed. Lightning split the tub in half. Hot water scorched his feet. Breath rampaged from his lungs, fleeing the hazy red rage surrounding him.

Jedediah raced outside.

WaphRae's gallop skidded to a stop. Drake landed a clumsy glide behind her.

Jedediah opened his connection to magic all the way. So close to the source, Harmonics screamed in his ears. Power flooded him, emanating outward in physical waves.

Cords of electricity as thick as his wrist surrounded him. Grass and the nearby lodge smoldered. He raised a hand skyward and another down. His staff whirled around him. Thunderheads swirled into existence. Magma bubbled up before his feet.

Fury, focus and strain bent his expression. He pushed against centuries of protections.

He brought both hands together onto the staff, halting its spin. A supernova of power carried him upward on a stroke of lightning.

It slammed him back into the ground. He struggled to his feet. Lightning launched him skyward once more. It slammed against the earth once more.

Sobs wracked him. Blood drew lines from his ears. He reached into the power once more and catapulted himself against the valley's shield, intent to bash his way through.

It slammed him into the growing blast crater once more.

"Dear Creator, Jedediah stop. You're killing yourself."

"Back," he snarled, spitting blood.

He launched himself against the shield a fourth time. When he hit the ground once more, Drake leapt atop of him.

<Stay down, Master. You can't help her this way.>

"Get off me, you worthless lizard. She's dying. I have to get to her."

Drake sank talons into Jedediah's body. *<You will stop.>*

Jedediah fought, worsening the rips in his flesh.

Drake pressed his serrated teeth to Jedediah's throat. *<I command you to stop.>*

Cooling energy rushed over Jedediah, balming his wounds and calming his mind. WaphRae touched his forehead. He hadn't even noticed WaphRae's approach.

"All right, Drake. Let me up."

Drake's thoughts pushed into his, unskilled but incredibly strong. He lowered his defenses, letting the dragonling satisfy himself regarding Jedediah's mental state.

<Apologies, Master.> Drake climbed off.

"Come on," WaphRae said. "We'll run."

Jedediah nodded and ran to the Golden Gate's entrance. He incanted the spell and sprinted down the stairway, thankful for wide centaur-sized steps.

Jedediah pushed them relentlessly through the night and all the next day. His magic reverberated back at him, vibrating his teeth and bloodying his nose. Drake led the way, letting Jedediah constantly rebalance the spell to limit the damage inflicted upon him. The feedback forced slower progress than he'd anticipated.

He fell into exhausted sleep that night half way to the exit. Their gateway to gateway race resumed before dawn.

They didn't talk.

They didn't waste breath.

Jedediah's jaw remained set the whole way.

Waphri Ah'Raemyn watched the wizard. Her own talents let her see the waves of magic crashing against him. He refused to bow before it. *Though for how long? I'm surprised he hasn't collapsed under the pressure.*

They passed Kimberlite, still camped out on the path, without a word.

Jedediah quickened their pace.

She glimpsed a shift in his energies. Jedediah stopped deflecting the energy and drew it into himself, down one arm and into his staff until full-fledged lightning danced up and down it.

They stepped through the last gateway. A heretofore unnoticed pressure vanished from them.

Jedediah spun toward them. "Gather around for a telepo—"

Arrows rained down upon Jedediah. Two arrows struck Jedediah in the leg, one stuck in his shoulder and another pierced his lung. He stumbled and fell, gasping and gurgling for breath.

Battle cries filled the wood. SinDon and another sorrel charge Jedediah, sword-lances leveled.

WaphRae raised her hands. "Stop. I command you to stop."

Drake roared.

He leapt between Jedediah and their attackers. A fiery ribbon seared SinDon, driving him sideways. The others reared in panic. Drake shredded the centaur's exposed underbelly, unleashing a cascade of gore.

WaphRae interposed herself between them, waving her arms and crying for them to stop. Arrows riddled her flanks.

SinDon staggered, blinded by smoke and pain. Drake launched himself at the wounded warrior, spraying arrows with flame. He wrapped jaws around SinDon's neck, but Jedediah's insistent, rasping summons beckoned urgently.

Drake left SinDon's neck whole and leapt to the others. He roared once more and spat flame.

Jedediah slapped his staff against the ground. A lightning tempest engulfed them.

They vanished, reappearing in a seemingly different reality—a peaceful farmhouse, a police cruiser, and Joe Franklin.

"Merciful God." Joe Franklin ducked a plume of dragon fire.

He rushed toward them, mind unable to rationalize the scene. He tended the woman first, knowing the injured horse might crush her if it panicked. Jedediah's bloodhound spread wings and snarled flame, barring his way.

"Drake," Jedediah gasped. "Red. Jug."

Drake bolted into the farmhouse.

How's the woman fused to her horse? Joe Franklin shook his head, keying his radio. "Get an ambulance to the Shine place, now."

Questions filled his radio.

"Just move." He approached the woman.

"See to the wizard," She said.

Joe Franklin blinked. *Wizard? Jedediah?*

"Help him," she insisted.

Joe Franklin propped Jedediah's head on his lap, trying to relieve the gurgling noises accompanying Jedediah's breathing. Jedediah faded in and out of consciousness.

He opened his mouth to ask the woman a question, but Drake rocketed around the corner with a jug in his mouth. He dropped the jug into Jedediah's lap. Red liquid dribbled down its fang-punctured sides

"Help him drink."

Joe Franklin stared at the hound dog. He'd witnessed many strange things. He'd seen people attempt the dumbest things a human being could do. He'd seen mind-boggling dare or drink related injuries.

Jedediah, perpetrator of many mysteries Joe Franklin had chosen to ignore, lay in his lap peppered by honest to God arrows. A similarly injured woman somehow fused to a horse, lay bleeding next to them.

His mind struggled to handle the situation, but it flat out refused to deal with a winged, bloodhound verbally ordering him to help Jedediah drink red punch.

Drake nudged the jug. "Help him drink."

"How the hell's fruit punch going to help?"

Drake growled.

"Okay, okay," Joe Franklin unscrewed the cap. Raspberry aroma filled the air. "We're drinking the punch."

He trickled some into Jedediah's mouth.

A faint glow crossed Jedediah's lips. They moved ever so slightly.

"More."

Joe Franklin complied. The glow spread, worming down Jedediah's huge frame.

Drake's head darted forward like a striking asp. He snatched an arrow out.

"Don't he'll bleed—" Joe Franklin stared. The glow reached the wound. The flesh closed itself.

The dog snatched arrows away, leaving only the one near his heart.

"Her," Drake said.

Joe Franklin passed the jug.

"Thank you, Sheriff," she drank deeply.

Drake nudged her, making her spill. "Master."

WaphRae handed it back. Joe Franklin drizzled more into Jedediah's mouth. The jug passed back and forth. Jedediah's gurgling ebbed, but his breathing remained labored.

Sirens sped nearer.

WaphRae struggled to her hooves and turned toward the forest.

"Stay right there."

"I must go, my people's injuries require assistance," WaphRae said.

Joe Franklin wrestled his gun out of its holster. "Not until you explain this."

Drake growled.

Terror unlike anything he'd ever experienced drowned Joe Franklin. It disappeared, but with it so had the woman.

Drake snatched the jug and bolted around the house.

The sheriff raised his revolver. He lowered the gun.

Ambulance tires crunched up the gravel driveway.

CHAPTER TWENTY-FIVE

Unwelcome Realities

Jedediah awoke to stubborn darkness and a sore throat. A rhythmic beep chirped in time with his head's throbbing. Something foreign filled his windpipe. His eyelids wouldn't open. He reached up to wipe them but found his arms restrained. His stomach bemoaned extended neglect.

He strained to open his eyes, blinking until bleariness and gummy strings revealed a dim room. Pastel people busied themselves beyond a bright window.

A pink one entered.

Pink. Girl, have to find Lanea. He gurgled a choked rasp.

"Be still, Mr. Shine," she fiddled with an IV. "Don't try to talk."

He gurgled desperate pleas for release.

She patted his hand. Darkness usurped his eyes. The world came and went. Time eluded Jedediah's grasp. Green and handsome replaced pink and pretty, followed by daisies, dinosaurs and blood red. They flitted pixie-quick through waking glimpses, elusive as tumblebees.

Jedediah's eyes opened. His tubeless throat ached. Smaller intrusions besieged his nose. He swallowed, trading soreness for burning. He reached up and rubbed his throat.

"Water, wizard?" Joe Franklin asked.

Jedediah turned, summoning more pain.

The sheriff sat beside drawn window blinds. He pried himself from between chair arms and poured water from a bedside pitcher into a ready cup complete with bendy straw.

Jedediah reached.

"IV, Jedediah."

Jedediah took the cup cross body, sipping cool water. "Thanks."

Joe Franklin settled back into the too small chair.

"Find my farmhand?"

Joe Franklin held back a tsunami staged upon the tip of his tongue. He shook his head.

They shared silence.

Jedediah sipped water. *I need to find Lanea, but there's no quick escape here.*

"How long?"

"Three weeks."

Jedediah tried to bolt upright. Pain and tubes tore at him with fierce little claws.

Joe Franklin pushed him back down.

Three weeks?! He'd lain bedridden three weeks since Fleet Hoof's bloody reception. *If they've cost me my daughter, I'll slaughter them.*

Jedediah sipped from a shaking cup.

"We need to talk, Jedediah."

"About?"

"Are you kidding me?" Joe Franklin pinched the bridge of his nose. "Witnesses and video show you shot. Doctors found no bullets, only an arrow left by your winged hound. After that the list gets peculiar: red punch, a half-horse woman, you dropped onto your porch by a lightning storm on a cloudless day."

Jedediah opened his mouth, but Joe Franklin held up a hand.

"Let me finish, *wizard.* Had time to think waiting by your bed, about your lack of age, six murders, an attempted assassination, and a dozen weird things I let go over the years." Joe Franklin gestured at the pitcher. "Throat tubes are hell on the voice, so I'm demanding nothing now, but by God, you owe me answers—honest ones if you honor our friendship."

Jedediah nodded.

Joe Franklin heaved up. "Good. Boys are guarding your door. We'll start our chat tomorrow."

"Think they could stop me?" Jedediah whispered.

Joe Franklin halted. "I'm counting on enough mutual respect that you pretend they can."

Jedediah watched him leave. *Won't be the first time I've had this conversation. I could avoid it, befuddle his memory with permanent glamour—about as precise as nuking an anthill. Anything more precise requires rituals unavailable while I'm bedridden.*

An attractive doctor's entrance interrupted his ruminations. She offered her hand. "Good afternoon, Mr. Shine. I'm Doctor Weslin."

Jedediah shook it. "Doc."

"How are you feeling?"

Jedediah rubbed his throat. "Frisky as a spring colt."

"Mm-hmm," she studied her clipboard. "Know where and why you're here?"

"Kissed the wrong side of an arrow."

"Indeed. Few people shake off severe direct pneumothorax so quickly. Your lung puckered around the shaft as if it'd had time to heal around it. Saved your life, but complicated removal."

The straw gurgled in his empty cup. "When can I leave?"

"Chest tube's out, but I'd prefer you remain immobile and under observation for several weeks."

Jedediah reached over himself for the pitcher. The attempt tangled his tubes and pained his IV arm. "Would you, Doc?"

She glanced up. "Hmm? Oh, certainly."

She filled his cup and set the pitcher in easy reach.

"Thanks. What about something to eat?"

The clipboard absorbed her attention. "We'll start you on today's soft menu—soups and gelatin."

He nodded.

She fixed him with her whole attention. "I have a question about your tattoo."

"What about it?"

Her eyes bored into him. "Where should it be?"

An answer half formed in his mouth. He hesitated, took a long, slow breath, and listened to his skin for a faint tickle.

"My back."

She frowned. "All right. Try to sleep. I'll check in later."

Jedediah stared at blind-concealed day. *Where are you, girl?*

A mousy brunette in white scrubs with harp-playing cherubs replaced the doctor. She smiled and adjusted wire-framed spectacles. "Feeling well yet?"

"I'd appreciate a steaming cup of tea—for my throat."

"Honey and lemon?" she asked.

"Please."

"Up for visitors?" she asked.

Jedediah brightened, but just as quickly sobered.

She smiled. "Deputies checked him out if you're worried."

Little I can do until my tea arrives. He nodded assent.

"I'll send him in."

A male copy replaced her. Slightly taller, dressed in a suit rather than scrubs, the mousy, bespectacled man carried a manila folder under one arm.

What've you got there?

"Good afternoon, Mr. Shine. I trust I'm not disturbing you."

"You are?"

He fidgeted. "Francis Keaton, a, uh, hospital administrator."

Understanding dropped by to nudge Jedediah. "A bookkeeper."

"Accountant. If I'm bothering you, I can come back later."

"Bet your bosses prefer alacrity."

Francis had the good graces to look embarrassed. "True. You've been here quite a, well they didn't find an insurance card, and we couldn't find a record of previous treatment," A nervous chuckle escaped his lips, "leastwise not for a century."

Memories froze Jedediah's response. *That'd been a dreadful day.*

Francis paled. "Are you all right, Mr. Shine? Should I get a nurse?"

"Man facing me, hat in hand, calling in a debt should call me Jedediah."

Francis cocked his head. "Sheriff said you might be somewhere between thirty and sixty."

Jedediah forced a rakish grin. "Do I look like an old man to you?"

"N-no, but the sheriff said he'd known you at least thirty years."

Jedediah smiled. "Clean living."

"Immaculate," Francis chuckled. "Um, about the bill. Insurance?"

"Haven't got any."

Francis frowned. "No?"

"No."

"Do you know your credit score?" Francis asked.

"Never used it. Cash is king."

"No credit score."

"Don't fret. I'll pay in cash."

Francis fidgeted, glancing inside the folder. "It's a substantial sum."

Jedediah reached out. Francis handed him the folder. Jedediah flipped to the end.

"Of course, that's as of this morning," Francis said.

"This today, the rest when I leave?"

Francis reclaimed the file. "Oh. No, sir, Jedediah, when you leave is fine, it's just—"

"Huge tabs unnerve your boss, particularly with no dime on the bar."

Francis offered an apologetic shrug.

"I'll take care of it."

The young man's body language nearly screamed relief.

Hospital admin must be riding the boy pretty hard.

"Need anything else?" Jedediah asked.

The mousy nurse offered Jedediah's tea.

"Thank you, ma'am."

Francis fled with a small wave, twin on his tail.

Jedediah concentrated on his cup. He built energy cautiously. The steam thickened, solidified and then formed the reflective surface of a mist mirror.

Power suffused his voice. "Drake."

Mirrored surface rippled, but Drake didn't appear. Jedediah pushed a little harder. The harder he pushed the more the mist acted like a sinkhole. Sweat beaded on Jedediah's lip.

Could be asleep, typically that feels different, though. He released the seeking spell.

Jedediah took a moment. *Drake's my best source of information. He'd have sought Lanea. No matter her condition, he should be able to report.*

He squared his metaphysical shoulders and prepared himself for the worst. Dread and hope teetered on the next connection.

"Lanea."

Jedediah reached out through the mirror, feeling for his daughter. He evoked memories to strengthen the search: long years of mud covered mischief, teaching her magic, and watching her inch toward the woman she'd become. They warmed him, but cold dread blossomed faster.

He felt nothing, as if no one remained to answer.

He reached deeper, pushing until his limbs shook. He bent the mirror into a looking glass, seeking her broken or otherwise. No image resolved to loosen the cold, boney fingers clenched around his heart.

He closed his eyes, breathed slowly and reviewed people he might call upon. Any ally he might summon would either be ill-equipped to find her among normals and less capable of finding her magically than he who knew her so well.

I've no choice but search by magic until I can leave.

Jedediah held the mist together by will long after his tea had gone cold. Exhaustion ambushed him at spell's release.

I'm weaker than I thought. A little sleep will set me right. Tomorrow I'll find a new tack.

Jedediah's morning tea arrived with Joe Franklin, so he drank it.

"Morning, Jedediah."

"Morning."

"You good enough to talk?"

"If I said no, would it make any difference?"

Joe Franklin licked his lips. "We should make something of a start, even if only yes and no questions."

"You're a good man, Joe Franklin, and I like you so I'll be both blunt and honest."

"I'd expect no less."

"I don't want to tell you one damned thing."

A bark of laughter filled the room. "All right, Ronnie Gerald. Did you kill him?"

"No."

"How about the other three boys and their dogs."

"Nope."

Joe Franklin offered some pictures. "You kill these boys?"

Jedediah studied them. "No."

Both men stared unblinking into the other's gaze. The sheriff looked away first, sucking on his teeth. "Don't look good. All these boys, all on your property, what's your part?"

Jedediah watched him.

"Arrows kill Ronnie Gerald?"

"You know that."

"The same arrows pulled out of you?"

Jedediah smirked. "Probably not the exact same."

"But from the same people?"

Jedediah gave an affirming nod.

"You know Greek Mythology?" Joe Franklin asked.

"Well enough."

"I liked Greek Mythology back in high school, recalled something last night about a half-horse race."

"Centaur," Jedediah said.

"Recall they fancied bows and arrows."

"I imagine they might."

Joe Franklin studied his fingers. "The woman I saw?"

"WaphRae's a centaur."

Joe Franklin's agitation expressed itself in twitches and fidgets. "She had arrows in her, too."

"That a question?"

"The same people shoot her as you?"

"Yup."

"They trying to kill her, too?" Joe Franklin asked.

"No, she got in the way saving my neck."

A nurse came in wearing orange sherbet scrubs.

Joe Franklin scowled. "I'm conducting an interview here, miss."

She pursed her lips. "I've got a job to do Sheriff, same as you. Give me two minutes then no one will bother you."

"Fine," Joe Franklin rose, parting the blinds.

The door closed behind her.

"No need to be surly."

"This isn't a pleasant situation, Jedediah."

"Nice or not," Jedediah said. "Most folks remain ignorant about reality. Happier that way. You wanted truth, ain't her fault you don't care for the taste."

Distress and disgust warred for Joe Franklin's expression. "You going to tell me about wizard schools and kids with super powers running about?"

Jedediah's laughter turned to choking. "Not exactly."

"Your farm houses a pack of centaurs?" Joe Franklin asked.

"More precisely, my properties serve as a sanctuary for countless Fey, including several centaur tribes," Jedediah said. "I think one of them killed Ronnie Gerald for encroaching upon their territory."

"Which is on your land. That why you're such a bastard about trespassing?"

"Anyone without my token risks attack. Plain and simple, many Fey have a grudge against normals."

"The whistle you gave the three boys with the dogs?"

Jedediah sighed. "Gave that to Ronnie."

"You lied to my boys."

"No, Joe Franklin. Ronnie knew not carrying the token constituted trespassing. He didn't have it on him. Told your boys the truth."

"How'd the other three get Ronnie's token."

"That's one of the things I've been trying to figure out."

"Which is what got you shot."

Jedediah chuckled. "Actually, jailing some of the centaurs got me shot."

"So you're some sort of sheriff wizard?"

"Sort of?"

"You're *really* a wizard."

"And four centuries old."

Joe Franklin threw up his hands and stared at the wall.

"You said you wanted to talk about my age."

"Hoped you'd tell me you've got a plastic surgeon."

Jedediah chuckled. "Humans prefer ignorance and flimsy excuses to truth. I've taken advantage of that more often than I can remember."

"Drake's not a bloodhound, is he?"

"Dragonling."

Joe Franklin whipped around red-faced. "As in baby dragon?"

"Yup."

"How do you hide that?"

"It's called glamour. Most Fey have it."

"The hurt woman looks like what with this glamour?"

"Woman on horseback most likely."

"How the hell's a man supposed to trust his eyes?"

Jedediah smiled. "Learn to see true."

Joe Franklin scowled. "Red punch?"

"A healing draught. Alchemically distilled natural magic."

"Why's it red?" Joe Franklin asked.

"I mix in raspberries, a lot of them—otherwise it tastes like gym socks."

"Why not strawberries? They're cheaper and more common."

"I'm allergic," Jedediah said.

"You're a wizard, can't you fix that?" Joe Franklin asked.

"Magic can't fix everything. I am, as it happens, a wizard who's allergic to strawberries," Jedediah laughed. "Better than being lactose intolerant, imagine centuries without butter pecan ice cream."

Joe Franklin dropped back into the chair. Both groaned. "You're really four hundred years old."

"Four hundred and eleven last summer."

"Why does your age go up and down?"

"I alter my physical age by borrowing days from different periods of my life— stored and accessed through a series of magical constructs. It's extremely complicated. Think about it this way. I get about ten years at twenty-one, so I lived one of them and stored the other nine."

Joe Franklin cradled his head in his hands.

"Anything else you want to know?"

"I don't think I could take any more."

Jedediah waited.

Joe Franklin asked the question he knew had to come. "I can't bring these centaurs in for murder, can I?"

"No."

The sheriff shook his head. "I can't just let them get away with killing."

Jedediah's frame crackled. "They're not getting away with a damned thing, Joe Franklin. I got a judgment to use special magic that'll force them to reveal who did what."

"Then what?"

"Justice, and not the liberal kind."

Joe Franklin shook his head. "I can't, this just can't be real. I'm a practical man, Jedediah. There can't be people outside the law, people I can't police. I just don't—"

"Want to believe it?" Jedediah asked.

"Don't deserve any of this."

Jedediah chuckled.

"It ain't funny," Joe Franklin said. "Healing punch fix your bullet wound?"

"No one shot me, with a gun leastwise."

"A dozen witnesses saw it."

Jedediah tightened his fists until white-knuckled. Sparks reappeared around his body.

Joe Franklin shied away. "What else aren't you telling me?"

"Someone shot my daughter. Someone who'll shortly be very, very sorry."

"What daughter? No, the witnesses said..." Joe Franklin hesitated. "Glamour?"

"I told her to get out of town."

"Your daughter, the farmhand?"

"Yup."

"So you don't know what happened to her."

Jedediah looked away. "No, not yet."

CHAPTER TWENTY-SIX

Look to the Trees

Jedediah called a Florida money management firm the next morning. An armed courier delivered bags of cash. He acquired another cup of tea. Fruitless searches consumed its warmth until he wanted to rip the hospital down. A nurse stepped in to take his vitals.

"I'm discharging myself today."

She opened her mouth but left without objection.

Fifteen minutes later, Dr. Weslin entered with Joe Franklin.

"Mr. Shine, you need several week's rest and observation," Doctor Weslin said.

"Might be best if you stayed," Joe Franklin said. "All things considered."

Jedediah struggled to dress. "Bill's paid. I've got things to do."

Further arguments failed to dissuade him.

Joe Franklin drove Jedediah home, watched him disrobe and chug red punch. Red glow suffused Jedediah's body. Bruises faded. His chest healed, pink and healthy.

Jedediah wound a different clock, returning to his mid-forties. Joe Franklin's green-tinged, hasty exit spoke volumes.

Maybe I've lingered too long. Perhaps the Shines need to die for a while. He checked the centaur mark. It remained, but had aged—matured not faded.

I'll experiment later.

Joe Franklin returned outwardly shaken. "You're your father, right? He didn't die."

"Gives new meaning to southern stereotypes, doesn't it?"

"I-I need to go," Joe Franklin said.

Jedediah escorted him out.

Horse and incense tickled his nose. The cruiser disappeared down the drive.

"Why've you come?" Jedediah asked.

"We must settle things," WaphRae said. "Have you learned Lanea's fate?"

"Not yet."

"Anger runs rampant within the tribe—casting you as villain. We can't wait the Rite much longer."

"I'll kill any who attack me."

"If in defense, then we take no offense and lay no blame," she said.
"Attackers will receive defense, but I levee blame upon their instigators."

Lanea and Drake shared complicated existences. It'd drawn them together.

Lanea's had been hard to watch, harder before Drake arrived. She'd aged too slowly for public school and normal friends, but too fast for the glacial pace of elven lessons. Adulthood's approach meant acceptance among elven adults, her lingering immaturity a match for their capriciousness.

Much as I hate it, I should probably send her traveling. She's got to be feeling elven wanderlust by now.

Constant travel across the world would season and enrich her without exposing her apparent agelessness. She could choose to age normally, storing life as he had. She'd never fully understood his stated reasons, and he'd thought her too young for others.

Drake's life had been even more sheltered.

Word among the Guardians reached him about Drake's journey to his doorstep. Wizards worldwide had rejected Stormfall's attempts to foist her hatchling off far too early.

Her condescending, arrogant demands hadn't helped, but her killing several had effectively censured Drake.

Dragonling rarity dwarfed that of elf children or even half-elf. Dragons never fostered their young with other hatchlings. Jedediah suspected dragon parents didn't want young dragons banding together to threaten their hordes. Unfortunately for wizard brethren, Stormfall campaigned for a remedy to the dwindling dragon population—possibly only to manipulate Drake's elitist sire into a mating.

Not that dragons aren't horrid parents to begin with, but Drake's dame takes the bakery.

Emperors in their own minds, they didn't love. They didn't couple. They didn't share. Dragons mated sporadically, choosing mates as trophies of power, prestige, and status. They tolerated hatchlings until old enough to foster several decades with a wizard tolerant of the distraction.

So I've got two missing loners and no idea where to find them. Guilt roiled his stomach. *I should've been here.*

Jedediah paced his study. He invoked his Risk board, tapping the Southern United States card for a dynamic local map. Central America rested atop the deck.

Would you contact Old Mauve, girl? He shook his head. *Called me first and even with help, she couldn't hold it.*

He glared at the board. He tossed one red and one green wooden square onto the board.

"Show me Lanea. Show me Drake."

They reformed, assuming representative shapes that milled about uncertainly.

Jedediah considered. Few things might block the specialized bloodhound spell. Death corrupted smell, confusing the seeking spell.

I'm not casting a death seeker until I've exhausted everything else.

Protective barriers might block it. Places external to the natural world like *Mythela'Raemyn* might also foul the spell.

I should check the still—if it hasn't wandered back to Romania. Jedediah scratched his beard. *No, still's fully stocked with healing potions same as the farmhouse. If she'd gone there, she wouldn't be missing.*

He set the green figure where Lanea'd been shot and the red atop the farmhouse. *Drake's the key.*

He nudged the still dragon. "Where'd you go, Drake?"

Can't mist mirror yet, but if he found her he'd have brought her back...unless he couldn't. What could hide Drake and stop him from returning?

Jedediah marched outside and around the barn. Three interconnected greenhouses formed a u-shape behind it. A thrum reached his ears before he reached the far section. Jedediah strode into a protected section housing thousands of happy worker bees. He didn't bother with a beekeeper's mask, a smoke kettle or any other such paraphernalia.

His arrival excited them further but didn't stop the work. Four exits allowed them either outside or into the other two greenhouses. Swarms darted into and out three of these, avoiding the greenhouse containing Jedediah's new carnivorous plants.

Jedediah sat, closed his eyes and felt the air. Few aeromancers learned to talk with bees. It'd taken decades to learn the trick.

He focused until he could differentiate miniscule winds along his skin hair. Hums and vibrations tickled them, each one voice of the hive's thousand minds. They landed atop him, close wings raising their respective voice. They chattered, sharing gossip, cares and local news.

Jedediah tightened his focus to manipulate the tiniest wisp of air, creating kindred vibrations with his finest hairs.

"Good to see you well, too."

Conversation played out along his own sympathetic hairs. He nodded, chuckled then nodded again.

"Wonderful, truly. Have you any news of Drake or Lanea?"

The tone changed, no longer the hum of happy hives. They happily hadn't seen Drake.

"I'll talk to him about stealing honey."

The surrounding noise altered. A baby boom pushed the hives to bursting. They needed more room but remained reluctant for their princess to brave the world outside Jedediah's greenhouses.

"We can fix that, but I'll need some honeycomb in return."

The happy thrum returned.

Jedediah obtained his honeycomb where they designated. He collected all of his saucers, teacups and soup dishes from the kitchen. They lined the porch filled with milk, fresh honeycomb, cinnamon imperials and the last of his imported German candies. Next, he emptied the barn's rat traps, arranging their victims among the queer buffet.

He planted his staff and dropped into an old wooden rocker. His staff cycled through signals, each summoning a different Fey group. Gangly, long-nosed brownies in tattered burlap garments arrived first. Mole-like star noses led their fine-furred bodies. Long-clawed fingers made them resemble cat-sized Freddy Kruger's. They sipped the milk, protruding eyes on the wizard.

Iridescent fairies and their smaller pixie cousins showed next. They fell on the sweets with shameless abandon, not bothering to question Jedediah's largess. Pixies settled along the eaves with laps mounded with candy, munching deliriously. Skipper doll sized fairies gossiped around the honeycomb. Antennae tips, fingers, toes and intricate wing designs glowed a psychedelic light show.

Jedediah eyed the shadows outside his porch light's edges. A shadow shifted. Fairies scattered in a rushed flurry up to porch beams. Two more shadows appeared moments later. When the sixth arrived, bobcats of swirling smoke sauntered onto the porch, glaring at porch lamps until they dimmed. They turned hungry gazes at the fairies.

Jedediah cleared his throat.

The cats each settled down next to a rat.

"Good evening."

Silence greeted him.

Jedediah frowned. "Good evening."

Fey replied, each in their own language. He engaged each in turn, asking after gossip to test the waters.

He swept them with his aura, letting its power draw every eye. "Thank you for coming. Y'all witness different parts of the world. Talents might overlap, but your abilities reign superior."

The cats groomed themselves with smug satisfaction. Brownies stood straighter. Pixies glowed and fairies straightened pastel locks and dress hems.

"I ask you to lend me those abilities. This little tea party is a token gesture. You'll have my full gratitude if you locate Drake or Lanea."

The rats dissolved with their owners. Eyes and fangs lingered like an afterimage. The other Fey watched Jedediah.

He gestured toward the dishes. "Waste not, want not."

Brownies slurped their remaining milk, wiped their mouths and departed with a short bow. Sparkling wings swarmed the remaining sweets, streaking neon, giggling colors into the night.

Maybe I should summon more.

The next morning, Jedediah experimented with several seeking spells. None found Lanea or Drake.

Maybe I should call Stormfall. She'll have a dame bond she could find Drake with—of course, she's as likely to attack me as help.

A brownie tugged on his overall leg, grumbled up at him, shrugged and departed.

Jedediah sighed. *It's going to be a long day.*

Pixies and fairies fluttered up to him all day, the last arriving after sunset. They tittered their exploits in minutest detail. Ianyss reported a dryad had seen Drake weeks prior, but couldn't locate him. The Fey rededicated themselves before departure, some not even begging candy. One particular fairy insisted her victory celebration be catered by a specific Atlanta chocolatier.

The first shadowcat appeared just before dawn, lingering just outside the porch light. The moment Jedediah noticed it, it flirted its tail and sauntered into the night.

Subtle.

It appeared and disappeared, melding into dark pools of shadow and appearing farther ahead from different shadows altogether.

Its rapid gait, not to be confused with haste, forced him to mist walk. Eerie silence went before and after it, typical of darker Fey.

Jedediah's heartbeat thundered in the quiet. The path wound through wood, crossed highways, followed roads and cut through backyards. They crossed the Chattahoochee, following its twisted path.

Jedediah's jaw itched. A dreadful portrait painted his instincts in broad strokes. Their destination fit. Desperate as his search had been, old anguish had rationalized the elven wood as the wrong direction. The farmhouse provided closer potions bereft of guilt trips and drama.

Dawn trickled into the wood. His guide stepped gingerly around dappled light shafts touching the forest floor. When several sunbeams ambushed the shadowcat together, it glowered at Jedediah.

"You chose to show up so near dawn."

A growl escaped its throat.

Jedediah gestured. "The elves, right?"

It showed pointed white teeth and melted into darkness.

"Damn drama queens." Jedediah chuckled darkly. "Reward will be waiting at the farm once verified."

Like so many other places around the United States where humans discovered profound beauty and peacefulness, state parkland surrounded the elven wood. The ground, the trees, even the sky, soaked up the elven magic. Normals felt it. They didn't understand, but they *needed* to protect it.

Of course, lawmakers who'd never stepped onto the land called selling off chunks progress. Guardians, like Jedediah, bought it up for those who originally owned it. The elven wood existed partly on parkland, the rest within Jedediah's holdings.

He'd spent plenty of time within its borders half a century before. He loved its tall old arbors, its gentle streams, and its fragrant blossoms. They'd balmed long-burning wounds. He encountered an artist of brush and melody whose works quickened healing of those hurts until she tore them wide open by force.

Things began well. Lirelaeli Ermyn'Phir's talents eased Jewel's murder. It softened the accidental loss of Esme and Jocelynn—the sisters' mother. It filled an emptiness.

Old, deep cuts rekindled. Heat edged in to haze his vision as he felt the knife twist all over again.

She'd betrayed him for his own good.

At least that's how the amoral bitch saw it.

In hindsight, she hadn't started with betrayal. The capricious, self-absorbed sorceress had grown impatient with his queer human sentiments.

She regarded his objections, beliefs, his free will as unimportant. She wouldn't be denied her heroic gesture's success.

He wouldn't feel alone, for she'd fill his every thought. He wouldn't miss stolen love, for fulfilling her every desire would satisfy him as opportunity to prove himself worthy of her adoration. He wouldn't mourn lost children, for she'd give him the only child he need remember—Lanea.

A mist mirror, a simple air magic, had been turned against him as a gateway to force an overwhelming, permanent love glamour into his mind.

Owning him had eventually bored her. Inattention weakened the spell. He'd broken most of it, though wisps still lingered. They whispered accusations. They decried his ungratefulness. They declared him villain rather than victim. He'd squandered eternal love by being unworthy.

I'll be rid of their guilt-mongering yet.

He loved her, hated her, but mostly he feared Lirelaeli might desire him once more and forge wisps into new chains.

Jedediah quickened his pace reflexively, clipping a tree and nearly falling. His ears warmed.

How many elves witnessed my mistake?

His stomach knotted tighter with each stride. His steps quickened once more, trying to outrace discomfort.

Without the faintest whispered warning, Lirelaeli stood in his path. A conspiratorial shaft of sunlight illuminated gorgeous skin and sultry curves. Her still grace tantalized ear, eye and mind like fluid music. An ivory gown of thinnest Fey silk danced with the slightest breeze. Honeysuckle and raspberry enticed his nostrils.

My favorite scents. Jedediah cursed inwardly in whispers, lest she hear them. *I should've dressed better, maybe de-aged to something young—what the hell?*

His magic rose without being called. He fought it, but formal moon-silver robes materialized in place of his overalls.

Snap out of it!

His body executed the deep flourish of a formal elven bow. Words tumbled honey sweet from a mouth despite rising bile. "*Iy'Fre Saulth, Felwithe A'Phir, Lirelaeli Ermyn'Phir.* Lirelaeli Ermyn'Phir, goddess of the wood, I give you my greetings."

She laughed, an exquisitely musical sound that despite the perfectly executed gesture left him feeling adolescent.

"Oh, Jedediah, I've missed you so."

Jedediah pictured Ronnie Gerald. He forced Joe Franklin's pictures to mind. Gruesome death offered little reprieve. He envisioned Elsabeth, getting Billie Jo instead. The dual shock unraveled her glamour. He called sparks across his skin, singeing body hair and overwhelming perfume with ozone. Nails cut into his palms.

"If you don't dial back the glamour I swear on the Dragon Spring I'll summon a Fallen into your pretty city borders for a rampage starting with you."

"You're so adorable when you're miffed."

Jedediah called an Infernal Tome to memory, flipping through mental pages for an Arch Demon with a taste for elf flesh. Power not commonly invoked by arcane practitioners dimmed her convenient moonlight.

Her smiled faltered. "Your daughter would die too."

The incantation froze in his thoughts. Whether infernal power or Lirelaeli's actions, glamour no longer battered his consciousness.

"She's here then?"

"*E'Noa Lah,* would you have really—"

"In a heartbeat."

"You've changed."

"Yup." He gazed upward through glamour concealing an elven city of graceful arches. "Take me to my daughter."

Flowered walks and fluid lines enhanced the forest's natural beauty while proclaiming its own.

"Still as you remember?" she asked.

Jedediah grunted assent.

She leaned in, laughing, and kissed him on the cheek. "Oh, I have so missed you."

"Don't. Push. Me."

Scowling, she led him to her bedroom. Sight of the door evoked anxiety. He glanced at her frown.

Cowed for now. Lanea's in there—she better be anyway.

Drake curled up next to Lanea on the acorn-shaped bed. His head lay on her stomach, one eye open toward the door. Three rapid steps brought Jedediah to

Lanea's side. He settled onto oak-cradled Fey-silk and down softness. Lanea's skin out paled moonlight, but her breast rose and fell with steady determination.

He bit his lip. Glancing back at Lirelaeli. Elves tended to be immodest. *Don't much like the idea of seeing her topless, but I've got to check her wounds.*

He removed her covers. Two angry punctures puckered her chest. Grey veins spider-webbed around red, semi-healed bullet wounds.

Jedediah replaced the down comforter. "Why haven't you healed her?"

Even anger looked good on Lirelaeli. "Of course, we have. Our best healers, magical and otherwise."

"Then why?" Jedediah asked.

Lirelaeli gestured.

Jedediah overturned a fluted crystal glass into his palm. Brown blood clung to the twin, tapered grey slugs. *Iron.*

"Treevoran nearly died trying to remove them. His heroics deserve reward, maybe Lanea's hand."

Jedediah gritted his teeth. "I'll let him live."

He returned his attention to the unfamiliar bullet. Lanea's mixed blood had saved her from its poisons. Even so, the iron would've hindered her magic and prevented even a healing draught from offering a lasting cure.

"I glimpsed Treevoran's mind," Jedediah said. "How'd she get here?"

"Dewdrops."

His brows rose.

"They occupied the rain where she collapsed. Some puddle skipping game."

"They brought her here? To you?"

"I'm her mother and well respected among the Fey," Lirelaeli said.

A gossamer thin sound escaped Lanea. "Da?"

Jedediah pocketed the slugs, taking her hand. "My Fey lily."

"Haven't called me that in ages," a weak smile lit her face. "Where've you been?"

"Drake didn't tell you?" Jedediah glowered at Drake. "He sure as hell didn't tell me where to find you."

Drake cringed.

Jedediah put his fingertips over her mouth. "Don't worry about your old Da. Everything's fine now."

"What happened?" She gasped as the encounter and Jedediah's injuries flickered from Drake's thoughts into those touching him. "Oh, Da."

Drake's cringe deepened.

"Everything's right as rain." He searched her face. "Do some good, you gormless lizard. Show me."

Her pain bit first, her chest burning like napalm had in Vietnam. Sorrow and guilt, worry and love meandered through her weak thoughtscape.

"How touching," Lirelaeli said.

Their recent interaction flashed through Jedediah's thoughts.

"Mother," Lanea's weak scold turned to sympathy. "No need to feel guilty, Da, you had to check." Horrified wonder tinged her thoughts. "A Fallen?"

Jedediah pushed the Tome's pages deeper into memory. "Everything's settled, Fey Lily. Think of the attack, please."

Lanea remembered for him.

Tears collected around his eyes and his fingernails dug into his palms. What she remembered, the lancing pain, her fear of failing him, tormented Jedediah almost as much as the absence of her attacker's identity. Someone had attacked Jedediah, inflicting a greater wound than intended.

Magma seared his chest.

Jedediah removed his touch. He held back tears, but he couldn't keep them entirely from his voice. "You just rest. I'll take care of everything else."

He realized Lirelaeli's hands upon his shoulder. That she'd shared their thoughts filled him with rancid vinegar. *When did she enter the memories?*

"Don't touch me."

She removed her hand slowly.

"Watch her, I've got work to do."

Lirelaeli inclined her head.

"Come along, Drake."

Lanea opened her mouth.

"I'll return your guardian after a little chat."

Drake cringed. He returned later resembling a beaten dog.

Jedediah touched lips to Lanea's forehead. "Remember, Drake. If anyone dares harm her, there are no rules, no limits, you destroy them."

Drake growled, flaring his wings.

Good.

Jedediah marched from Lirelaeli's home. He didn't pause to speak to her. He didn't descend to the forest floor. He drove power through his staff, reckless and unrestrained, taking satisfaction in the way it seared his flesh. He rapped his staff on the smooth wooden catwalk and vanished in a fury of lightning.

CHAPTER TWENTY-SEVEN

Schism

A peal of thunder announced Jedediah's arrival outside Fleet Hoof's pavilion. A shroud of heat and raw power distorted his view of dozens of responding warriors. He clasped his hands around his staff, waited and seethed.

Four tribal elders arrived at a gallop. Velith'Seravin arrived later surrounded by an armed war party.

"You know why I come," Jedediah said.

Others came—in fear or anger, for curiosity or justice.

Velith'Seravin strode forward, but the large, dark-skinned elder, Ena'Tharus Une Hashe, forestalled him.

"*Feihtor Ah Mythela 'Raemyn* has proven his right, we will join hands," TharHa said.

"We will not," VelSera sneered. "He is not centaur."

Magic never before experienced overtook Jedediah before he could speak. Skin tingled as if body and limbs remained asleep. A maddening itch plagued his skin, but his arms refused command to scratch. Vision blurred, sharpened and blurred again. Centaur gasps thundered in his ears.

Many retreated. Foals ducked behind parents' flanks. Fear clouded every face.

His stomach knotted, but felt cavernous. Muscles bunched, twinged, but still refused to move. His toes felt crushed, as if forced into shoes many sizes too small. Blackness swelled in the corners of his vision, and a pixie parade of colorful spots exploded before his eyes. His lungs strained against breath yet held for mere instants. His perceptions sharpened beyond aeromancy augmented sight and hearing. Green tinged his vision.

The fit ceased.

Ravenous hunger remained his only discomfort.

"It seems he *is* centaur," TharHa said.

Jedediah looked down at a centaur body. He shuffled back and forth on four legs, and his tail swished of its own accord.

He bit back a curse.

WaphRae took Jedediah's hand and reached toward her nearest kinsman. "We join hands."

Velith'Seravin moved his war party from her, but spirit walkers in solidarity with the tribe's mares refused to part.

"We will not participate in this farce, no matter what tricks the two-legger conjures," Velith'Seravin said.

Jedediah lifted his staff.

WaphRae pushed it back down. "The High Elders have decreed that *all* Fleet Hoof will obey. Any refusing suffer immediate summary execution by Fleet Hoof's spirit walkers."

A murmur ran the crowd. The female perimeter tightened, shoving Velith'Seravin toward its center.

Waphri Ah'Raemyn led the Rite of Shared Dreams. The ritual started simply, much the same and yet not as the mental union Jedediah'd experienced earlier.

Elation and joy filled Jedediah. *It's like running as one with a mustang herd.*

They galloped as one, turning in unison through minds and memories. Spirit walkers turned the edges, preventing strays. A mental nudge summoned related memories. Jedediah couldn't discern one mind from another.

<You're here as witness only, Feihtor Ah Mythela'Raemyn.> WaphRae chastised.

One particular mind focused upon retribution against Jedediah to the exclusion of all else.

Jedediah chuckled. *An unschooled wall of focus meant to shield against invasion.*

<School your thoughts, Jedediah.>

Jedediah thought his apologies then pictured Ronnie Gerald. Memories flashed like leaping salmon. Bright pride lit the dark tableau. Warriors relived their victorious torture of the invading two-legger, reveling in it all over again—self-righteous and self-incriminating. Outrage and recriminations flickered images of their jailing. Tempers rose. Centaur minds bucked and stomped.

WaphRae turned the herd to Joe Franklin's pictures, laid upon Jedediah's memories of an interrogation room table.

Dead dogs intensified their outrage, but no murderous recollections entered their shared dream. Gloating minds hung another two-legger from barkbiters manipulated by their crafty leader—Velith'Seravin. Pictures from the hospital flickered into minds, but no new guilt entered the thoughtscape.

Jedediah interjected a vehement and powerful memory of a time when Therymn En'Prielar led a similar conflict over human encroachment. His friend's murder flooded the joint recollection.

The herd snarled and stomped hooves, demanding justice for kin slaying at least.

Lanea's memories flashed through him, but no centaur added to the memory.

<It is witnessed,> TharHa thought. *<We are guilty, but not for all.>*

Time flowed on its own throughout the Rite of Shared Dreams—the participants oblivious to its course. Despite the short duration, the herd's unity transformed to peril. WaphRae directed the other spirit walkers, peeling each identity away from the whole one by one like sheepdogs.

I know myself. I'll not be lost.

<You'll wait your turn,> WaphRae cautioned.

He didn't argue.

BauthEli spoke first among the elders. "These evils are not our way. This council must right them."

BauthEli, TharHa and the venerable palomino mare Phriel'Belshai entered the pavilion. Velith'Seravin raked Jedediah with smug menace before following.

Gloat all you want. I'll have blood for my knife brother.

"Innocence and dire guilt met us in the Rite." WaphRae frowned at him. "Horrors will be righted, but for the rest, you must seek elsewhere."

Jedediah followed her into the pavilion. *There's more to these murders. Mismatched pieces and misdirection, either ill-timed or perfectly.*

"What is *it* doing here?" VelSera asked. "This is a closed council meeting."

Jedediah met him chest to chest. "I am *Feihtor Ah Mythela'Raemyn*, Judge of the High Tribe. It's my right to oversee this ruling."

"Have we lost all sanity?" VelSera said. "Will we allow this abomination to treat us like naughty children?"

"He's proven our guilt," Phriel'Belshai said.

"I'll not stand for this," VelSera said.

"Try something. You'll not lance my back like TherPriel," Jedediah said.

"This doesn't help, *Feihtor Ah Mythela'Raemyn*," BauthEli said. "Nor your tantrums, VelSera. Haven't we enough to answer for?"

"We've nothing to answer for. We protected what's ours. And you insult me, accuse me of childish tantrums?" Velith'Seravin said.

"You ordered the murder of an honored war leader," BauthEli said.

VelSera drew a knife from his belt. Jedediah tensed, expecting a challenge. Instead, VelSera threw the knife into the pavilion's fire. VelSera stormed from the pavilion, blowing a complicated series from his horn.

The elders stared at the fire, but Jedediah followed Velith'Seravin.

Hooves shook the ground, a fifth of Fleet Hoof assembling to his call. Young males dominated with a handful of younger mares accompanied by their colts, fillies and foals.

"As I foretold," VelSera said. "The elder's betrayal leaves us no choice."

TharHa's deep rumble proceeded him from the pavilion. "What're you doing?"

VelSera's summoned cast their knives into the fire. They arrayed themselves in solidarity.

"We reject Fleet Hoof. We defy the human jailers." VelSera fixed a triumphant, murderous glare on Jedediah. "We are Wizard's Bane, no longer answerable to the High Tribe."

"Please, reconsider," WaphRae pleaded.

VelSera puffed up his chest. "It's done. We'll allow no peace while filth of his kind yet breathes."

A feral smile filled Jedediah's face. "You want to try your luck unprotected, boy? Give it a go, but mark me. Wizard's Bane isn't under Guardian protection."

"Good riddance."

"Any centaur endangering our protected Fey will be executed." Jedediah licked his lips. "In deference to those you've bamboozled, I grant you clemency until sunrise to get off my land peaceably."

"And if we do not recognize your land?" VelSera demanded.

Jedediah's lip curled. "Then we'll mark my borders with your blood."

"We're not afraid of you, old man."

A sardonic chuckle rumbled from TharHa. Such dark laughter from the thoughtful, slow-to-speak elder made hooves shuffle. "Only fools do not fear wizards. Only the suicidal dismiss *Lyanthen Ah Lah'Phriel*."

Velith'Seravin snorted. "Your threats are meaningless."

An uneasy current swept his followers.

"I suggest you beg your elders' forgiveness," Jedediah said.

"Never." VelSera turned to go. "Gather your things, we're leaving."

"Have you forgotten something?" Jedediah asked.

VelSera rolled his eyes.

"Three murders, three souls dead on my lands at your hands."

"Oh, boo-hoo." VelSera sneered. "I tremble upon my hooves."

"Choose."

VelSera blinked.

"Choose *leader*, which three of your followers die for these souls?" Jedediah asked.

"Jedediah, wait," WaphRae said.

TharHa restrained her. "They're outside our protection, WaphRae. Justice remains unbalanced."

Centaurs, rogue and tribesmen alike, watched in frightened silence.

"I tire of your games, wizard. My people aren't subject to your whims, and I'd never sacrifice them to you." VelSera puffed out his chest. "Slay me if you must, one scalp for the old savage."

Jedediah's hands flashed out. Lightning slashed four charred centaur across his left breast.

"For Wizard's Bane's crimes, three followers close to your heart shall suffer and die. When the last falls and one mark remains your own life becomes forfeit." Jedediah eyed the crowd. "VelSera led you to folly. Embrace his venom at risk of your life. Now get the hell off of my land."

Returning to human shape required enormous effort. Lingering rage shook already wobbly legs—not improving his footing. Breathe seethed in his chest.

Exiling his followers, declaring open war on his protectors...that takes a special kind of stupid right there.

Worldwide, centaur outnumbered wizards, but Wizard's Bane didn't number enough to challenge their apprentices.

Lanea could drown them in blood all by herself.

Loose organization offered wizard kind's only true disadvantage. He contacted other Guardians and dispatched elemental messengers. Responses from those that bothered at all varied from incredulous to outright mirth.

```
Muler has signed on.
Muler: You wanted me?
One: You took matters into your own hands.
Muler: What about it?
One: You've complicated my operation.
Muler: I nailed him twice in the chest.
One: He's alive and now wary.
Muler: Luck.
One: Luck's the scapegoat of the incompetent.
Muler: incompetent?!
One: Competent marksman kill their targets.
Muler: Screw you.
Muler has signed off.
One: You see?
Two has signed on.
Two: Yes.
One: Put a team on him.
Two: If he steps out of line again?
One: Be competent.
Two: Always.
One: The board's agreed with my proposal.
Two: Then we lay off Shine a while, let him relax.
```

CHAPTER TWENTY-EIGHT

Trouble, Trouble, Boil and Bubble

With Lanea safe and Wizard's Bane off his property, Jedediah went to town for groceries. He called Billie Jo on the market's pay phone and returned home.

Ronnie's tearful widow and extended family surrounded Eddie's cruiser, a small mob backing them up. They noticed him. Beer bottles smashed against his pickup.

Jedediah unlocked his door.

Eddie triggered a shrill megaphone blast. "Move through, Mr. Shine."

A local newspaperman photographed Jedediah driving through the crowd. They let him through reluctantly, jostling the truck until they surrounded it.

Ronnie's widow slapped his passenger window. "Why? Why?"

They fell upon him, a pack against escaping prey. Mob mentality fed upon itself. Rocks smashed his back window. A baseball bat spider-webbed his windshield.

Jedediah knew their grief, felt it. *They need to act, to make things right in some small fashion. That's why I donated the fake life insurance check to Ronnie's widow.*

Eddie shouted himself hoarse within the mix, shoved back and forth in the press. His eyes tracked threats, finding more threatening the deputy than himself. He summoned an aquamantic charm to quietly defend poor Eddie.

The sense of a lazy summer day filled him, bathing the crowd with onto an impression floating downstream a cool, soothing river. It spread outward, slowly dousing anger if not curing actual hurts. His truck eased out of the lulled mob and up the drive to where Joe Franklin waited.

The sheriff circled the truck, examining damage and shaking his head. "Bad business, Jedediah."

"Your deputy could use some help," Jedediah said. "Marines, maybe."

Joe Franklin frowned. "Kept a lid on things best I could. Have you found the culprits?"

"Centaurs guilty are dealt with, though after seeing this perhaps too gently. Unfortunately, we've got more killers." Jedediah related events to the sheriff.

"Bad, bad business." Joe Franklin shook his head. His head came up. "Can you travel, you know with magic?"

"Yup."

"How fast?"

"Want lunch in China?"

"This ain't a joke, people are angry and rightfully so."

"I agree."

"D.A.'s got an eye witness."

"Need me to volunteer for one of those line up things?"

"Might settle things a bit." Despite the cool day, Joe Franklin wiped his forehead with a handkerchief. "Witch hunts ain't rational—no offense—but until you're cleared things will stay bad."

"You've had your warrant, searched my place. You've got nothing."

"Got an eye witness, if she cleared you, this ought to settle." Joe Franklin squirmed. "I'd rather not damage our friendship pushing this."

"Anyone else, I wouldn't even consider it."

How high is Meadow going to kick my ass if I agree? Agreeing won't salve the family's wounds, just take me off their hit list—and free Joe Franklin from D.A. scrutiny so he can concentrate elsewhere.

"All right, I'll come down peaceable for a line-up."

The sheriff's cruiser led Jedediah's pickup through the gate past Eddie and two reinforcements. The district attorney's teal Mercedes awaited them in the station parking lot.

A deputy grouped Jedediah with four similar men and led him into a room, settling him under a painted number four. Jedediah sharpened his hearing and bespelled his eyes to see through the one-way mirror.

Joe Franklin and the D.A. flanked a mid-thirties black woman in a darkened room. She wore professional clothes, hairstyle and a Synovus security badge.

"Now, just take your time," Jedediah disliked the D.A.'s whiny, self-satisfied voice. "No rush—they can't see you."

"You're sure?" she asked.

Jedediah restrained a chuckle.

She stared at each in turn. At Jedediah, her mouth twitched to one side. She continued to the last man before returning to him.

"Number four looks the most like the guy I saw."

Jedediah's stomach writhed.

Joe Franklin glanced toward Jedediah. "We need you to be sure, ma'am. We need a positive identification, not who looks the most like the killer."

The D.A. frowned at Joe Franklin.

"Well, I mean he looks kind of...it was pretty far." She studied Jedediah.

I need this nonsense settled so Joe Franklin and I can be about finding the murderer. Jedediah cursed inwardly. He studied her, eyes narrowed. *I don't think she's lying. It'd be wrong, but glamouring her could well save lives.*

She fidgeted. "You're sure he can't see me?"

"Impossible," the D.A. said.

I might feel guilty they died on my land, but I didn't kill those men. I know I'm innocent, maybe just a little nudge,

Jedediah met her gaze, focused his will and sent a burst of glamour into her mind. Two tiny lights flickered off the mirror.

Joe Franklin stiffened.

"No, it isn't him. Similar, but definitely not the guy."

"You're sure?" Joe Franklin asked.

"I'm certain."

Joe Franklin escorted Jedediah out. He scowled, something sour stuck in his craw. Jedediah let it be. He put the truck into gear.

"You magicked her."

Jedediah sighed. "You know I'm innocent."

"Thought I did, but do I know you're innocent because you magicked me?"

"That makes sense, muddled with your mind, but left you aware of the magical world."

"Damn it, you tampered with a witness," Joe Franklin said.

Jedediah took a deep breath. "Prove it."

Several months passed by in a pleasant, murderless blur. Still physically and mentally drained by iron poisoning, Lanea left the elves to putter around the farm. Simple spells tired her, but her loss of confidence troubled Jedediah most.

She'll regain her strength, but we need shod of this victim mentality.

He sent her on a shopping spree for half-priced Valentine's Day candy and asked her help in throwing a massive feast to thank the Fey. Jedediah did a credible Pied Piper imitation, benefiting his neighbors and fattening the local shadowcats.

"Da?"

Jedediah turned from the massive candy bowl set between him and contingents of pixies, sprites and fairies. "Girl?"

"You can stop mothering me, the Fey have their own lives," Lanea said.

One sprite darted into the bowl, scooped up a jelly bean and hugged it to his chest, squeaking admonitions at her.

"Just bartering a bit of border patrol," Jedediah said. "Nothing to do with you."

She folded her arms. "I'm capable of defending myself. Your barrier is holding just fine."

Jedediah chuckled. VelSera had led one raid against the farm. Lanea'd helped Jedediah transfer a mist mirror of two dozen warriors slamming face-first into the barrier onto Blu-ray.

Should feel bad for those VelSera's bamboozled. He cracked up. *It's just so damned funny. I'll watch that again before Maverick.*

"Are you listening to me?" Lanea asked.

Jedediah smirked. "Just thinking about that video."

She rolled her eyes, fighting a grin. "I can take care of myself. I want—"

Jedediah darkened. "Stay away from the boy."

"He tried to help me."

"Stupid idiot nearly killed you both. Stay on the farm and leave him be." She stormed off.

Jedediah turned back. Assembled female Fey tapped feet midair, arms crossed and their smiles vanished.

Drake's control and speaking ability experienced a burst of progress related to Lanea's attack, but with her safe Drake relaxed. *He's losing momentum. Got to get him going again somehow.*

Jedediah scratched his centaur mark. *You're one to talk. Haven't managed centaur shape since the Rite. Too distracted by*—A jolt went through his system. He flipped open his pocket watch. *Crap, I'm late.*

Air Fey shot his candy-laden retreat nasty looks. "Sorry, got to go. We'll continue this later."

He rushed into the house, wrapping a cloud layer around his body. Clothes teleported away, replaced by a hot, soapy thunderstorm. He skipped touching the portraits on the second landing so as not to get them wet, guilt churning his stomach. A warm whirlwind dismissed cloud and storm. He stepped into his closet clean and dry.

Hells, what am I going to wear?

He dressed in business casual attire and ran for his truck. He'd have teleported, but that would've left him without a vehicle to pick up Billie Jo in.

Need to buy a house near hers so I can keep one in town.

Deputies patrolled the highways, but they didn't see Jedediah rocket by— even if their devices alarmed at nothing. He pulled up to find the driveway blocked and Billie Jo in full blown argument with her attractive, impoverished ex-husband dressed in designer clothes.

She glanced up at his arrival, shoving a stray hair back into place. Her ex's jaw tightened, and his eyes narrowed. Mason, apparent center of the argument, smiled and jogged up to the truck.

"Everything okay?" Jedediah exited his truck.

Mason rolled his eyes. "Same as always. Did you bring Drake?"

"Sorry, thought you were off gallivanting with your dad this weekend."

Mason's face fell. "Yeah, but he got a call..."

"Right," Jedediah clapped Mason's shoulder, feeling the telltale tingle of another aeromancer. "Why don't you come along with us then or we can drop you at the movies."

"Mom's not going to let me go to the movies alone," Mason said.

Jedediah scoffed. "Why not? You're ten, that's almost a man."

"Almost eleven," Mason said.

"There you go."

"Move this junker so I can leave," Marcus said.

Billie Jo reddened.

Jedediah twirled a finger. An air cushion embraced Mason's ears. The boy moved his jaw.

"Thanks for bringing Mason back early. We know what a burden fatherhood is on you. I figured we'd catch a movie whenever you copped out."

Billie Jo shot a scandalized glance at Mason. He wiggled a finger in his ear, trying to clear his hearing.

Marcus darkened. "What did you say to me?"

"Thank you for being a deadbeat?"

"Step out of the car and say that," Marcus said.

"Didn't you still want me to move it first?"

"Marcus, you are not fighting Jedediah in front of our son," Billie Jo shot Jedediah a withering glare. "Whether or not his behavior in front of Mason is totally inappropriate or not."

Crap, stupid, pompous idiot. I was so set to bait the man I forgot Billie Jo has no idea I clogged Mason's hearing, and there's no way to explain it.

Jedediah sighed. "You're right. I apologize."

"Better watch it, old man," Marcus said. "You don't want to be on my bad side."

"There's another?"

"Jedediah!"

Jedediah backed the truck out of the drive and got out.

Marcus ruffled Mason's hair. "Sorry, bud, I've got to go."

Mason shouted. "What?"

Marcus frowned.

Jedediah dismissed the air.

"I said I've got to go," Marcus repeated.

Mason nodded. "Okay, Dad."

Marcus drove away.

Billie Jo searched Mason.

Probably looking for bruised feelings. Kids are tougher than people assume these days—not that Marcus should've abandoned him on their weekend together.

"Couldn't hear anything, Mom, like on an airplane, but I couldn't get my ears to pop. So weird."

She glanced at Jedediah. "Just as well, we'll get you an appointment with the doctor next week to have them checked."

"Jedediah said I can come with you guys, so you won't have to cancel your date," Mason said.

"Maybe I should anyway," she frowned at Jedediah.

"Come on, mom, you can drop me at the movies so I'm not in the way."

"I certainly will not. You're never in the way, Mason. I can't believe Jedediah would say something like that to you."

Jedediah opened his mouth.

"He didn't say that, but I mean Dad…well, I know you guys mostly date when I'm with him," Mason said.

"You know, I haven't been to the pictures in a long time," Jedediah said. "How about you pick for us, Mason?"

"Cool, there's this great new fantasy out about this epic cool wizard," Mason launched into a description.

Wizard, huh? Jedediah chuckled. "You like magic?"

Mason beamed.

Billie Jo frowned at the truck. "We'll take my car, it has seatbelts and airbags."

Jedediah smirked. "Whatever makes you happy."

"I'm telling you, I have no idea what's gotten into the girl," Billie Jo said.

Mason stared out the windows, ignoring his still agitated mother's latest tirade.

"Father needs to take a firm hand with the girl," Jedediah said. "Knock some sense into her."

"She doesn't have one, I told you she's in foster care, and besides you're not allowed to hit your kids anymore," Billie Jo said.

"Which is why we have problem children like this girl," Jedediah said.

"Mason's not like that, and I don't hit him," Billie Jo said.

"Worse," Mason said. "She confiscates my power cords."

Jedediah chuckled.

"She's very intelligent, Jedediah. She could be so much, but she's always pulling these weird pranks."

Jedediah nodded, keeping half an ear while thinking about the recent murders.

"Like yesterday. I gave them a test, and I'd swear she never left her seat, but all kinds of stuff started falling off the counters around the room, distracting the class. I had to cancel the test so we could clean up all the glass."

Jedediah zoned back in. "Wait, no one anywhere near the stuff? How can you blame her?"

Billie Jo fidgeted. "Okay, I don't *know* she did it, but the other teachers who have her talk about weird stuff like that happening when she's in their class."

"Not when she's absent?"

"No. The way I hear it, she kept losing foster families for the same nonsense. I just wish someone would talk some sense into her."

"How old?" Jedediah asked.

"Sixteen or seventeen, she's a junior."

"Mom! Can we *please* do something fun?"

CHAPTER TWENTY-NINE

Secret Mission

Their date conversation stuck with Jedediah on the drive home. He considered using his clocks to investigate the girl, but Lanea needed restored belief in herself.

He found them lounging by the pond. "I've got a job for you."

Drake huffed and rolled onto his back to sun his belly.

"Date didn't go well?" Lanea asked

"Billie Jo's got a problem child in one of her classes. I want you two to investigate."

"Do I look like Scooby Doo?" Drake asked without flipping back over.

"You can barely pass for a bloodhound, let alone a handsome one," Jedediah said.

Lanea laughed.

Drake growled.

"Moreover, you look like my student, and this is a lesson."

"For your *girlfriend*," Drake said.

"Starting to wish you hadn't learned mouth shaping."

Drake shrugged upside down.

"No stress, pack your things. I'll send Lanea alone."

Drake flipped back to his talons. "Master, no."

"If you don't want to obey me, then you've no place on this farm," Jedediah said.

Lanea stroked Drake's frills. "You can't just send him away."

"I've a duty. If the girl Billie Jo's having trouble with is just a hoodlum, we let her deal with it. If the weird things are an emerging magical talent..."

"We have a duty to train her," Lanea repeated. "For her safety and others."

Jedediah smiled. "Nice to see you remember."

"I'll go," Drake said.

"Thought you might."

<Lanea, why are we sneaking in at night?>
Simple, sneaking into the school with students here is harder.
He rolled his eyes.

I want a look at the classroom without having to glamour us.

<I can glamour myself.>

Like your bloodhound imitation? She gestured to the door and stepped away from him. "Earn your keep."

Drake growled. "I hate feromancy."

She smirked. "Probably why Da insisted you handle all the locks."

Drake huffed. He stepped forward and extended his wings. Lanea smothered his magic with a watery damper three times, preventing the door's destruction. She glanced around.

"Look, I'll do this one to get us out of the open. Then they're yours."

"Thank you."

"You can thank me by practicing finer control," Lanea said.

"Sound like, Master," Drake grumbled.

She brightened. "Thanks."

Lanea cupped the lock in one hand, filling both with summoned water. Heat seeped from her hand to the rest of her as the water chilled. She commanded the sluggish element into exploring the lock's mechanism. Heat ebbed out of it until it found the right shape. She froze it there and unlocked the door.

"You didn't use feromancy."

"Nope," Lanea smiled.

They stepped into the high school corridor. Drake wrinkled his beak. "Smells like gym socks and mating."

Glad I can't smell that well. "All right, Scoobs, nose to the ground. Let's find Billie Jo's troublemaker."

"Don't I get a pre-search snack to bolster my courage?" Drake asked.

"Are you afraid?"

Drake stiffened. He shook his head.

They followed Drake's nose down corridors and past lockers. Longing plagued Lanea. *I could've gone to school if I weren't elven.*

Drake's head came up. "Why do you smell sour?"

Hands planted onto her hips. "I beg your pardon."

Drake cringed. "Did something make you unhappy?"

"It's nothing. Let's find the classroom."

Linoleum halls smelled of disinfectant at war with body odor, even to her. Club banners and event posters draped on every wall, intensifying Lanea's loneliness. She stroked Drake's frills. *Thank you for coming with me.*

<Anything for you.> He turned left. *<That one. I smell magic.>*

Lanea exhaled. "Guess we're going to get a new friend."

She watched as he worked the door. *What's she like? Will I like her? Da said she's been kicked from a lot of foster homes. She'll probably end up an entitled brat, worse after learning magic.*

The door clicked. Drake pulled it open.

Lanea stepped to a nearby water fountain and filled her hand with water. She splashed it into her face, ignoring the smell. Two blinks and a push of aquamancy form-fitted her new lenses to her eyes. She turned to the open classroom door and gasped.

Oh, hell...serious brat material.

They entered the chemistry classroom. Lab tables filled the central space, occupied by various alchemical paraphernalia. Counters and cabinets lined the outer walls. Golden magic stained them in thick streaks. Spokes of fading power stretched over floor and ceiling, concentrated at one station in particular.

"Something smells," Drake inhaled. "*Really* good."

Lanea sniffed. "All I'm getting is chemicals and unwashed teen."

Drake breathed deeply through his beak. "Familiar too."

Aeromancy. The girl's yet another aeromancer. Even Drake—a dragon—aligned as an air kindred. Why do I have to be the only oddball?

"You smell sour again."

Lanea threw up her hands. "Why don't you go raid a Coke machine if you're not going to be any help."

Drake sulked from the room.

Lanea took a deep calming breath. *I shouldn't have snapped at him. It's not his fault Da's going to squeeze me out for another star pupil.*

She neared the magical residue, rubbing fingers across it. A layer of charged dust came away on her fingertips.

You'd think janitors would keep the counters clean.

She rubbed them together and brought them to her nose for a sniff. *Ozone— air magic...and fairy?*

Lanea shifted one water lens off of her eye. A line cut through fairy dust she'd thought part of the counter's design. She checked another table, finding only the lightest dusting compared to the magic radiating station.

"Excuse me?"

Lanea whipped around. Nothing filled the doorway.

"Excuse me, Guardian?"

Lanea followed the voice to the floor. A tiny brown-skinned Smurf fidgeted with her hat, fingers stained charcoal. Black hair fell around her cherubic face and round glasses. A workman's jumpsuit bulged with her miniscule figure and tiny tools.

"I'm not a Guardian," Lanea said.

"Oh," she squeaked, southern drawl thick in her voice. "Sorry, I knew a Guardian fostered a dragon hereabouts. I saw a dragon at the soda machines. I just assumed he sought..."

"Drake's our scaly Cherry Coke addict. I'm Lanea. My Da's the Guardian."

"Oooh, you're an apprentice, just like me."

"What's your name?" Lanea asked.

"Tilde, like the mark," Tilde said.

Oh, she's a book gnome. Lanea smiled. "How can I help you?"

"Well, um, I don't want to bother you, but a Guardian, we hoped you could help us," Tilde said.

"With what?"

Tilde's expression blackened. "The Destroyer."

Lanea's brows rose.

"Teenagers are bad enough, terribly hard on our flock, but the Destroyer—we can't keep up with all the damage...and he's *burning* some of them."

"Is the destroyer a fairy?"

"Yes and he's got such a dreadful mouth on him," Tilde said.

"He curses?"

"That too, but gnome one can understand his thick accent," Tilde said.

Lanea barely resisted laughing.

He chuckled, unfurled his wings and focused his magic. A can of Cherry Coke thumped into the receiver.

Master should be proud, I'm practicing feromancy.

He snagged it from the tray with his tongue and sank fangs into the can. Sweet fruit and cola filled his maw. Sugar tingled along his tongue as carbonation sizzled down his throat, delivering a euphoric rush of caffeine. He sucked the can dry, crunching the aluminum a few times before swallowing it. He summoned another, then another.

He pushed magic at the machine once more. A can fell to the receiver bereft of its usual clunk-clunk. He picked it up with his tongue to find it empty.

He magicked four more empties from the machine.

Drake scowled at the empty Cherry Coke can laying between his talons with four brothers. He sniffed the can, a familiar aroma filled his nostrils.

I don't like this smell anymore.

Drake shifted his attention to the next dispenser chute. Coke's flavor didn't compare, but it delivered comparable euphoria. A Coke can dropped heavily to the tray. Light burst around it, dazzling Drake. He blinked away blindness to find the Coke can vanished.

Drake growled. *Someone's stealing the Coke before I can.*

"Come on, Drake, that's enough," Lanea called.

He glared back at the machine, lip curled.

"Enough already, leave some for the students."

Drake snarled in warning. He'd be back, and the thief had better leave him some Cherry Coke.

Lanea met the rest of Northside High School's book gnome caretakers. Each gnome's name matched a punctuation mark, like Tilde, or another bookish term.

The master book gnome Amp—short for ampersand—rattled on and on, connecting wildly different conversations in an endless train. He talked so long the early arrival of the school librarian nearly caught her unaware.

She nudged Drake. "Wake up, school's starting."

<Just five more minutes.>

"Drake!"

He bolted upright, nostril's streaming smoke. "I'm up. Where's the centaur? I'll rip him to shreds."

"Could you move the dragon a bit further from our flock, Miss?" Amp asked.

"Calm down, Drake," Lanea said. "It's morning. We need to get out of here before we're seen."

Drake's image wavered, a bloodhound stood in his place.

"Not bad, but can you do this?" Glamour cloaked Lanea.

"You look like one of the students," Tilde said.

"Hateful creatures, horribly hard on books." Her brother Colon grumbled.

Drake fumbled with his glamour, trying to mimic a student. The illusion ended surly and morose much to Tilde's praise.

"One problem, Drake, you take up more room than most normals," Lanea said.

Drake intensified his sulk.

Lanea laughed. "That might just be enough to keep everyone at arm's length. Come on, let's get out—"

The librarian entered. "What're you kids doing in here? You know the library doesn't open for another hour."

"Sorry," Lanea scurried for the exit.

"I better not find out you've been doing things you shouldn't," she scolded, "or I'm calling your parents."

Drake glowered his way past. He headed down the hall toward the entrance, early morning students giving him a wide birth.

Lanea stopped outside the chemistry class, a mischievous smile on her lips. Drake looked back at her.

"Go on, I'll be along in a little bit." She stepped into the classroom. Lanea sucked in breath.

Billie Jo looked up from her desk. "Can I help you?"

You could stop looking like Elsabeth for one.

Lanea smiled. "I'm new."

"I didn't get a notice for a new student," Billie Jo said.

"They're still working out my schedule," Lanea said. "I'm, uh, Mary Ann Duke."

"Welcome to Northside. Settle in while I go over my lesson plans, ok?"

"Sure."

Lanea sat at the fairy dust-plagued station.

"Um, you might not want to sit there," Billie Jo said.

"Why not?"

Billie Jo reddened. "Faye's very bright, but she doesn't get on well with others."

Lanea shrugged. "I'll chance it."

Billie Jo shrugged and returned to her lessons.

A fairy glared up at her from Faye's seat. Beer bottle caps and tabs formed its plated armor vaguely resembling some movie samurai. A New Jersey accent garbled its words. "This is my dame's desk, water witch, move along."

The door opened to admit other students. When Lanea turned back, the fairy had vanished, leaving a fading beer bottle brown glow atop its liberal fairy dusting.

A girl flopped down into the vacated seat. A black walnut chopstick pinned her hair into a soot-black pile. Acid green highlighted its tips, matching eye shadow glaring at Lanea from a few inches taller.

"Hi," Lanea smiled.

The girl scowled and rummaged through her bag. "Find another seat, Bubbles."

Shock distracted Lanea from the girl's intricately detailed jeans. "Bubbles?"

"Look, perky, bubbles, whatever your name is. I don't do cheerful. I don't do besties. Just get lost," Faye said.

"Faye—"

Faye shot her a murderous look. "It's Jordan. Not Faye, not Jerdan like most these idiots pronounce it."

"Fine, Jordan—"

"Just go away," Jordan said.

Lanea scrutinized her. Her façade remained rock hard, but something lingered behind her eyes. She turned away before Lanea could look too deeply. Lanea set a hand on her arm. "Jordan—"

Earth magic coursed off of Jordan's skin, combining with Lanea's in an earthy wave like a thin mud bath. *Terramancer.*

Jordan snatched her arm away. "And I *don't* do girls."

Lanea smiled. *I like her.*

Drake shook his head back and forth. <*No. No, no, no.*>

Drake, please.

<*We have to tell Master.*>

We'll tell Da. We found the disturbance, the fairy—though why an air Fey is protecting a terramancer, I can't imagine. He'll send us back to catch the thing, if only for the book gnomes. Mission accomplished.

<*Master said he had a duty—*>

We have a duty, we includes me. I'm going to teach her.

Drake goggled. <*What?*>

I've been helping you, haven't I?

He drew the word out in his thoughts. <*Yes.*>

There's no way she's going to learn from someone like Da, and with her attitude, he's going to ride her worse than he ever did you. I think I can reach her.

<*Bad idea, really horrible atrocious idea.*>

But you'll do it? Please? For me?

Drake growled. <*Fine, but you owe me Cherry Coke, a lot of it.*>

CHAPTER THIRTY

Running

Jordan finished dressing out, a tingle of excitement in her stomach. Georgia heat, bad accents, the weirdly too-friendly people bothered her—nothing like the New Jersey sanity she'd somehow lost. Running, though, that remained the same even if the muggy air smelled funny.

She stretched against the locker room wall, leaving her sitting stretches for the grass outside. She still couldn't fathom how the foster system had exiled her to Georgia.

It's not like I got kicked out of every foster family in Jersey—there had to be more.

Bright sunlight blinded her, a wall of thick wet-heat ambushing her. She blinked back sight and turned to sit where she regularly stretched.

She groaned. *What the hell is Bubbles doing here?*

Lithe, cute and cheerful, the girl really needed to be punched in the nose.

She tossed brown hair over her shoulder. It glinted silver red in the sunlight. She waved. "Hi."

Twice, definitely punched twice.

"So, cross-country, huh?" Mary Ann asked. "Mind if I join you?"

"Yes."

An atrociously musical laugh escaped Mary Ann's face.

Jordan examined Mary Ann's thin legs. *No need wasting my energy being mean, she'll never keep up anyway.*

Jordan finished her stretching, leapt up and started at a slow jog. Mary Ann bounced into pace beside her.

"So how long have you gone to school here?" Mary Ann asked.

"Two fosters."

Mary Ann frowned.

"Two foster jailers." Jordan managed her breathing. "Different school with my first Georgia wardens."

"So you're not from around here?" Mary Ann drawled.

"Obviously." Jordan sped up.

Mary Ann didn't lag behind. "Where'd you live before?"

151

"North." Jordan increased the pace. Sweat beaded down her forehead. She hadn't sweated like this back in Jersey, something about the humidity seemed to suck it out of her.

"What's the foster system like? Is it rough making friends?"

"Don't need nobody." Jordan eyed Mary Ann in glances. She breathed normally despite the run or the conversation slowly taking its toll on Jordan's air. No sweat dampened her perky appearance.

All right, Bubbles, let's see what you've got.

Jordan pushed herself faster. The pace was leaving cross-country and headed toward foot race, but she could maintain it a good quarter mile at least.

Mary Ann sped to match, turning around and running it backward. "Everybody needs somebody, especially when you're different—or is that why you push people away?"

"How're...you...doing...that?"

"Doing what?"

"You're...not...sweating...not...breathing...hard."

Mary Ann shrugged. "Magic. You could do it too, or something similar."

Great, a psychopath's latched onto me. Jordan eased the pace. "Go away."

Mary Ann's smile verged on apologetic. "Can't."

Jordan stopped over a dozen strides, sucking in deep breaths. "I can make you."

Mary Ann snorted. "No, you can't. I've got to teach you first."

"Magic?" Jordan asked.

"Yup."

Jordan's fists tightened. She relaxed them. "This isn't some movie. Life's not filled with elves and fairies and pretty princesses. I don't want into your perky cult, or coven or whatever."

Mary Ann shrugged.

"Look, Mary Ann—"

"Actually, my name's Lanea."

Jordan frowned. "Ms. Bartlett called you Mary Ann."

"She calls you Faye."

Jordan's jaw tightened. "I hate that name."

"It's actually kind of fitting, seeing as your magic originated with the Fey."

Jordan glared at her. "Now I'm some sort of fairy?"

"No," Lanea chewed her lip. "At least, I don't think so. All magic originated with the Fey—the first evolutionary young, i.e. the dragons."

"I don't believe in magic."

"Why not?"

Jordan stared at the girl. *How can she ask such a stupid question? Just look at the world, magic genuinely existing would make everything better. My parents would still be alive. I wouldn't be in this Southern hell.*

"Well?" Lanea asked.

Jordan folded her arms over her chest. "Lots of reasons."

"Okay."

"What do you mean, okay?" Jordan asked.

Lanea shrugged. "You don't believe. That's okay—mind it'll slow down your progress, but we can start with the basics."

"I don't want to learn magic."

Lanea beamed. "Think of me as your friend then, one with weird interests. If nothing else it'll be an excuse to get out of the house."

"My foster jailers' are never going to let me hang out with some crazy girl, it took my case worker threatening their check to get them to let me compete cross country."

"I'll convince them."

"With magic?" Jordan asked.

"Something like that." Lanea smiled. "Maybe I'll sick a dragon on them."

CHAPTER THIRTY-ONE

Spring Changes

Jedediah strolled into the boneyard. Old toilets and truck carcasses spread out in artfully untidy rows. Faces poked up here and there, mostly smaller Fey without sufficient numbers to fend off predators.

A toilet seat slammed shut, leaving Jedediah only a partial glimpse of dark fur and star-shaped nose.

He chuckled. *Or those that just don't get along with others.*

Deep in the boneyard, refrigerators joined the redneck landscaping. Little old ladies and other busybodies had shoved petitions down his throat about removing their doors. The doors stayed and with good reason. Despite the apparent disarray, he positioned each with mathematical precision.

He glanced around, raising his voice. "Boneyard's about to get a shift, clear out or enjoy the ride."

Flickers of movement shot away from the yard's center. Younger Fey darted in from the edges, mounting toilets and other debris with eager grins.

Jedediah snorted. He closed his eyes, reaching out to every item with a windborne touch. He stretched his consciousness sideways, selecting another refrigerator from the pile of old ones saved for this purpose.

He ran through his mental map, double-checking the proportions and calculations for adding the new house off Weems Road.

A grumpy voice growled from his shins. "You're not going to blast that new age music, are you?"

Jedediah glanced down at the curmudgeonly brownie. "You think this is the ballet?"

"Don't cotton to that new music."

"This spell doesn't involve sound," Jedediah said.

"Especially that airy stuff you use at planting."

Jedediah smiled. "One more helpful suggestion and I'll accompany the spell with some Elvis or Queen."

The brownie shot him an ugly glare. It trudged away grumbling, its star-nose shaking back and forth.

Jedediah reviewed his spacing once more. A twist of his closed eyes saw the magic connecting each object. Thick taproots interwove below the ground while

154

connection branches stretched into the horizon in thick colors. He lifted his hands and the boneyard's contents rose with them.

They spun a lazy DoSaDo. Miscellaneous objects wove in and out to new positions mandated by the refrigerators' new configuration. He set the boneyard down once more.

"Again, again," a clapping pixie called.

Jedediah chuckled and walked the boneyard, double-checking every connection. He nodded to himself and stopped in front of the new fridge. Dirty, dented and too small for anyone his size, the old Kelvinator made a perfect addition.

As part of the boneyard's master spell, a taproot grew slowly downward into the network powering the yard. Jedediah stepped behind it to where the absorbed power spread across the unit's refrigeration coils. He pulled a screwdriver from his overalls and removed a single bracket screw.

I'll stop by the realtor on my way to Billie Jo, still don't understand why the paperwork's taking so long. I paid the seller what they wanted, cash on the barrel.

Billie Jo and Jedediah went out several more times over the next few weeks. Some dates included Mason, while others had been romantic dinners, moonlit walks or more adult movies. Considering Mason's fondness for Drake, Jedediah'd tried to convince Lanea to babysit. She claimed attempts to trap the fairy terrorist monopolized her time. He considered stepping in, but the project kept her engaged and entertained.

One fairy can't cause that much damage.

He and Billie Jo argued on occasion: child rearing, corporal punishment, law, money and occasionally religion. Minor disagreements arose over one or two fine points. Contradictions in her religious beliefs baffled him. She found no fault with his stage magic or renaissance festivals. Fantasy magic skated the line. Blatantly fictitious magic presented no problem, but anything suggesting sorcery as real represented devil-spawned witchcraft. The longer they dated, the more it seemed revealing his magic would end their relationship—something Jedediah couldn't decide as good or bad.

Jedediah whistled through the house, packing for the spring Renaissance Festival in Atlanta that weekend. Several weeks playing the wizard would be improved by Billie Jo and Mason's visits—affordable for the poor teacher thanks to vendor passes and a strategically found Circle K gift card.

Drake's recent molting provided fresh dragon hide aplenty for custom orders or tinkering.

He paused before twin freestanding mirrors. He might end up with a different stall year to year—even if a rarity. Neither Lanea nor Drake could manage a teleport's drain. The mirrors offered them easy escape from booth to farmhouse.

A pre-prepared boneyard portal linked to a storage facility near his hotel. Placing on mirror within it allowed a quick gateway back to safety from the fair.

Jedediah scratched his chin.

They'd heard little from Wizard's Bane, but outside his protective borders, anything remained possible.

He'd arranged to keep the stall well-staffed to compensate for any hasty exit. The arrangement delighted Jenn and Theophanie's other gypsies. Their presence would definitely enhance the festive experience.

Jedediah found Lanea seated in his study, nose pressed into some new novel she refused to put down.

Have to grab it when she finishes. Jedediah cleared his throat. "Sure you won't come?"

She laughed. "I'll be just fine, Da."

"I'd enjoy your company is all."

"Stall's full of company."

He chuckled and turned to his shelf.

"Thought you'd take the truck."

"Just thinking I might want more muscle."

Lanea laughed. "Armored car or a tank?"

His expression increased her laughter.

"Think it's possible to make a tank street legal? Rubberized treads? Tail lights?"

Lanea choked with laughter. "Oh, yeah, I can picture you cruising town in a candy-apple red Sherman."

He laughed.

Lanea regained her breath. "Got anything else that'd carry the mirror?"

"You know object size is always negotiable."

She frowned. "Even with a fixed portal?"

Jedediah took down an old Dodge Charger. "If you're careful."

"That's too small," she said. "New Chargers are bigger, or a minivan."

He replaced it on the shelf and glowered. "I look like a well-cushioned soccer mom to you?"

Lanea scrutinized him over her novel.

Jedediah folded arms across his chest.

"More of an evil Uncle Jesse."

"Ought to tan your hide for that," Jedediah said.

"Yup," she mimicked. "*Evil* Uncle Jesse."

Jedediah attacked, tickling her out of breath. Her squeals drew Drake, flame curling from his nostrils. He eyed them both and huffed.

"Ready?" Jedediah asked.

"Bark," Drake said.

"Smart ass."

Lanea dissolved into giggles.

Jedediah's attempts to open his stall would've failed entirely if not for the gypsies. Merchants, performers and others he didn't know stopped by with questions both blatant and subtle. Their interest in the murders and associated rumors indicated many had been interviewed by the police.

"Off the suspect list," Jedediah forced a chuckle. "Or at the bottom at least."

Jordan ran along the old railway line to the river landing. It'd shocked her when Lanea managed to get her last jailers to let her out, but then Lanea had talked the halfway house Gestapo into letting her go. *Just unbelievable. Maybe I should try perky...nah, couldn't stomach it.*

Lanea awaited her on the 15th Avenue bridgeway between Georgia and Alabama, talking with an absolutely gorgeous man with waist-length golden hair.

It took Jordan half the bridge to realize them deep in an argument. She stopped short, but he turned toward her. "Who's this?"

"None of your business," Lanea snapped.

He strolled over. "Come now, Lanea. You've made your feelings clear, why not introduce me to your lovely friend?"

"Because I like her."

He pressed a delicate hand to his silk shirt. "You wound me—your hero."

Lanea shoved him from behind. "You threw me out—while I bled to death."

Cold welled up in Jordan. She eyed the pretty man. She wouldn't go so far as to call Lanea a friend, but any guy that'd throw his girlfriend bleeding into the street was real scum.

He spun gracefully in a way no longer as attractive. "I tried to help you."

"You call selfish and stupid help? You panicked when I needed you most," Lanea said. "Get lost."

He winked at Jordan.

She glowered.

He sauntered off, a lilt in his step.

"Who's he?" Jordan asked.

"Bad news."

"Wow. You're pissed. Must've really liked him," Jordan said.

Lanea scowled at his very nice retreating backside, her expression softening to include regret.

"Someone shot you?"

Lanea sighed. "Yeah."

"Gang fight?" Jordan asked.

"Misunderstanding with an assassin." Lanea turned up the bridge into the nearby park. "So, we've covered the basics."

Jordan rolled her eyes. "Yes, the x, y, z's of magic types, hurrah."

Lanea laughed.

I still hate how musical that sounds.

"You still don't believe me."

"Of course I don't. I mean it sounds great, and I really do appreciate you springing me all the time, but if magic genuinely exists why doesn't everyone have it?"

"They don't know how to listen," Lanea said.

Like people ignoring you telling them to buzz off? "I don't understand."

"You ever try to tune one of those old radios?"

"Sure, we never get digital goodies."

"Some days you can get your station in perfectly, others even if you didn't move the tuner, it doesn't come in very well. Magic works kind of like that," Lanea said. "Some people, like my Da, get the signal perfect all the time. I get it pretty solid most days, though it comes and goes. It's gotten easier with practice of course."

"So why can't everyone tune in?"

Lanea snorted. "Their tuners are broke?"

Jordan laughed, but cut it off.

"Some people can barely hear the signal even when they've got it set just right. Others can't get their tuner lined up," Lanea shrugged. "It's not a perfect analogy, but you get the gist, right?"

"I suppose. I must be one of those who can barely hear it even when tuned because I can't feel anything."

"Belief comes into play too."

"Good, then we're done with magic," Jordan said. "Let's see a movie."

Lanea sighed, mumbling under her breath. "I'll never give any teacher a hard time again."

Billie Jo and Mason arrived opening day and often after that until the fair thoroughly bored Mason. Billie Jo delighted in displaying a wide array of costumes, most handmade considering her finances. She and Jedediah whispered in the stall under gypsy smirks.

Mason sighed for the fifth time.

"Why not let him explore?" Jedediah asked. "Drake can keep an eye on him."

"Something might happen."

A little mischief, nothing untoward for a boy his age. Jedediah winked at Theophanie. She nodded and whisked from the stall. He whispered into Billie Jo's ear. "Let him go, then I'll explain."

Mason beamed.

She frowned at him.

Jedediah nodded.

"Fine," she frowned at Mason. "You'll be good, stay safe?"

Mason rolled his eyes, hugged her and bolted before she could change her mind.

Billie Jo inhaled. "This better be good."

"I sent word ahead. Merchants, performers and plenty of gypsies will keep an eye on him."

"Gypsies?"

"It'll be fine."

"So, remember Faye Jordan? The girl in my class?"

"Yes?"

"I'm at wit's end. Thought things would improve when she befriended Mary Ann—such a sweet girl, but she's constantly getting into trouble. Faye says the mischief isn't her doing, but no one believes her."

It isn't. He sighed. *Maybe I should help Lanea after all.*

"She's lost *another* foster family. Most do it for the check. They don't want a troublemaker. She's back in state housing."

"Children need a firm hand."

"Within limits."

He smirked and shook his head, unwilling to start another argument. "What a waste."

"She's not a waste. She's a smart girl." Billie Jo slipped her hand into his. "She just needs someone who actually cares to reach her."

"We can hope."

"You could do more than hope."

Ice water rushed through his veins. "Oh, no, Billie Jo, I ain't—"

"You've got plenty of room. Farm work, fresh air, wholesome environment, what could be better?"

Jedediah looked away. *I'd like to help, on principle in addition to making Billie Jo happy, but...*

He couldn't expose the girl to his life. He had no business fostering a normal child into a secret magical world filled with warring centaurs and assassination attempts—to say nothing of his half-elf daughter or dragonling apprentice.

"I don't know."

"Please? At least meet her? I'll bring her up here. You don't have to do anything."

Jedediah shook his head. "A teenage girl with an old man like me. Probably wouldn't even consider me."

"You're not that old. Besides, it's easy to become a foster parent. Take a few classes, a medical examination, do a few interviews. Oh..." Billie Jo trailed off.

His brow rose.

"They cleared you as a suspect, so a criminal background check won't be a problem, right?" She didn't let him answer. "Everybody seems to know you, always volunteering, helping people out. People respect you, even if you do pretend to be grumpy."

Jedediah groaned. "No good deed goes unpunished."

She cuddled against him. "You'll meet her? Please?"

"Yes."

She squealed and kissed him.

What harm could it do?

CHAPTER THIRTY-TWO

Luck, Fate or a Cruel Joke

Jedediah wanted to meet the girl after the festival.

"No, next weekend before the school year ends," Billie Jo said. "We'll take the fostering class this week."

"We?"

"We'll call it a date so you don't forget."

"Shouldn't rush things like this. And what happened to me not having to do anything but meet the girl?"

Billie Jo, woman on a mission, wouldn't listen. She arranged a lunch interview with Angesa Cooper, Faye's case worker. She sweet talked Joe Franklin into joining the three of them for dinner, substantiating Jedediah as free and clear of any charges.

Jedediah hoped Angesa would find him unacceptable. Failing through no fault of his own would've been best. *It's going to crush Billie Jo for me to say no after all this.*

"You look nervous," Jenn said.

"Guess so, not sure about meeting this foster girl."

Jenn smiled. "Doing it for a woman isn't a good reason for making big decisions."

Jedediah shot her a look.

"She's not exactly quiet," Jenn stepped over to a customer.

Billie Jo, Mason, Miss Cooper and a girl made their way through the crowd toward him. Angesa Cooper looked a frazzled mid-thirties bleach-blonde despite being an intelligent, Catholic schoolmarm packing a ready ruler. She dressed all business.

"Hang back, Drake."

Drake nodded.

The girl, whatever her name, stood two hands shorter than Jedediah—taller than Angesa or Billie Jo. She wore neither goth nor punk, something closer to the newest teen rebellion, Elmo or whatnot. Paint, glue and glitter spattered her jeans. Meticulous fairy images hid between careless splotches. Their disgruntled expressions conflicted with the vain, often-ditzy creatures.

Look at the skill and detail she's put into her "screw off" appearance. He shook his head.

Soot-black hair with acid green highlights piled atop her head, pinned there by black walnut chopsticks. A baggy, faded black concert t-shirt disguised her gender. A lightning storm spelled *Djinn Storm* above and below the shirt's pentacle.

He snorted. *Billie Jo's innocent girl has a thing for a half-elf rock band—nice boys though they are.*

Billie Jo frowned at him.

Drake loped up to Jedediah's heel, head cocked.

The girl stared at Jedediah too, though in lazy, nonchalant passes.

What do you think, Drake?

<I'm in so much trouble.>

Jedediah's head shot down. *What?*

Mason dashed to Drake and hugged the dragon. "How're you doing, boy?"

Drake cringed, tail wagging nervously. Their stage gambit had convinced Mason his mother saw through Drake's extremely convincing dragon costume, and Jedediah'd lectured Drake extensively on thought shielding.

A crowd of German shutterbugs cut between him and the approaching women. A young boy and girl, each sporting the same tow-headed mop, gaped at Jedediah and his old wizard costume.

"*Guten Tag, meine Damen und Herren,*" Jedediah greeted them theatrically. He conjured two sparkling pinwheels on wooden sticks to their amazement.

"*Für Sie,*" Jedediah handed them one each.

They raced delightedly after their family.

Angesa's expression indicated a shift in attitude from the child doting caseworker.

The girl scowled at him.

"Jedediah Shine, this is Faye Jerdan."

"Jordan, *just* Jordan," she snapped.

Jedediah chuckled. He'd known the arrogant, slave owning Jordan family. When they changed their name's pronunciation to separate themselves from their former slaves, he'd called them insufferable toss pots and refused to use the changed pronunciation.

"Pleasure to see you again, Ms. Cooper. Please, forgive the costuming, it's all part of the show."

"Odd hobby for a man of your years."

"What's a farmer to do between crops?" Jedediah chuckled. "Gossip all the time?"

Angesa laughed.

"He donates half what he makes on his leather goods to our schools," Billie Jo added.

"Does he?" Angesa asked.

Jedediah extended a hand to the girl.

She didn't take it.

"Faye," Billie Jo's accent thickened. "Please, show Mr. Shine some respect."

Billie Jo's nervous too. He tightened the cloak of power threatening to spark around his frame and wished for some mint.

The girl rolled her eyes and petted Drake's head. "Hello, Drake. Where's Lanea?"

Drake cringed.

"Drake?" Jedediah asked.

The dragon shrunk as low to the ground as he could manage, beak on Jedediah's boot. *<She made me. Lanea's to blame.>*

The girl shoved him. "Don't be mean to Drake."

A tiny spark jumped between them. Power coursing through Jedediah drained to nothing. "Ah, hell."

Billie Jo and Angesa shared a shocked look.

The girl's mouth twitched. "Something wrong, Mr. Shine?"

"Forgot the hand sanitizer. Nasty dirty creature, Drake. Should kennel him for retraining."

Drake whined.

She scowled.

"Let's step over there, Angesa," Billie Jo said. "Give them time to get to know one another."

Angesa frowned. She addressed the girl. "You won't try to run again, will you?"

Mischief twinkled her eyes. "No, of course not."

"She won't, Ms. Cooper." Jedediah locked her gaze. "My word on it."

Gauntlet's down, little terramancer, best we settle the pecking order here and now.

Billie Jo pulled on Angesa's arm. "Come on, Mason."

"I want to play with Drake," Mason said.

Jedediah smiled. "I'll keep these three out of trouble."

The girl lowered her voice. "Think so?"

"Absolutely, Faye."

Mason watched the coming storm, Drake cringing beneath his petting.

"*Don't* call me Faye, hillbilly. My name's Jordan."

Jedediah shrugged. "Pronounce or mispronounce your name as you like."

"You got a problem with my name?" Jordan asked.

"Met Lanea, have you?"

Drake slunk backward, toppling Mason who'd been leaning against him.

"It's wrong to dress an animal in all that garbage," Jordan said.

"He's kind of attached to it. How *exactly* do you know Lanea?"

Jordan threw out her chin, her tone snide. "She's teaching me *witchcraft.*"

"That so?"

Jordan smirked. "Oh, yeah. Satan worship, blood sacrifice, the whole shebang."

"Hard to believe, considering Lanea's an aquamancer without a bit of witch talent."

"Pardon?"

"Witches and Satanists are different, but we'll get to that in your lessons."

Jordan paled. "What are you talking about?"

"Once you're fostered, of course."

She frowned, staring down at her fingers. "I've been kicked out of everywhere I've ever been fostered."

"So I heard."

"I'm a troublemaker. Way more effort than getting into Ms. Bartlett's panties is probably worth."

Jedediah darkened. *Guess you need another demonstration.*

He handed Mason several bills. "Mason, get your Ma's permission to fetch us some ice cream. You want ice cream, Jordan?"

Her eyes narrowed. "You can't buy me, old man."

Mason tore across the thoroughfare.

Jedediah gazed into the clouds. An airy yet ominous tone escaped him. "If I had a mind, I could buy you: flesh, spirit and soul."

The crowd aligned just the way Jordan wanted. Quick as a cheetah, her leg muscles tensed to bolt. Her hips pivoted. Her feet, however, seemed welded to the ground.

Jedediah smirked. "Problem, *Faye?*"

She tried to hop. "What the hell?"

Angesa stepped toward them.

Jedediah remaining outside arm's reach, held a hand toward Angesa.

"Give them a chance," Billie Jo assured her. "Isn't that why we're here?"

Angesa inclined her head.

Jordan struggled to move her feet, face pale and heartbeat thundering loud enough for Jedediah to hear.

"Earth magic, terramancy, not my specialty but I manage," Jedediah said.

"Let me go."

"Drake," Jedediah growled.

The dragonling slunk forward.

"Glamour. Sight and sound, smell too just in case."

Drake's wings extended. Several of Jordan's hairs stood. A soft wind whirled around them, absorbing sound. Inside Drake's newly extended glamour disguise, his reality crystallized. Ancestral fear doubled her terror.

Jedediah held hands up, lightning arched between them.

Jordan shrieked bloody murder.

No one noticed.

Jedediah stepped closer. "I'm guessing Lanea didn't give you the whole show, probably trying to ease you into it—typical of aquamancers teaching their first students. Let's cut the crap. I'm a wizard—a no-bullshit fire-juggling, lightning-throwing arch magus. I could incinerate you here and now while giving them an illusion of you running away," Jedediah's smile portended a disaster beyond Hollywood special effect science. "I'd have to apologize for not keeping my word, but they'd never guess your fate."

The defiant scowl remained, but most fled her voice. "What'd I do to you?"

"If you *ever* say anything like that panties crack again, particularly in front of Mason, I'll dust what's left of you off my boots, clear?"

"Yes." Jordan squeaked.

"Bad news time, we're stuck with one another. I can't let an earth talent like you run wild. You ain't ever getting kicked out either, but I can make your life hell without anyone else being the wiser, can't I Drake?"

"Yes, Master. I'm sorry, Master. Lanea made me—"

Jordan stared dumbfounded.

"We'll discuss this later," Jedediah said.

"None of this is real, it can't be," Jordan said.

"Stubborn as your element."

"No, I'm not, I, you're a gorram liar."

Jedediah looked at Drake. "Gorram?"

The dragon shrugged.

"It's a fake curse word off TV." A mischievous grin crept into her features. "Means god damned, but isn't a real curse word."

"I understand, all too well." He scowled. "We've got a lot of work ahead."

"What if I don't want to go with you?" she asked.

"Not your decision anymore."

"And if I tell them you're a raving lunatic?" Jordan asked.

"Think they'll take your word for it?" Jedediah asked.

"I could tell them—"

Jedediah snapped his fingers. Her mouth snapped shut. "Work with me, and I'll show you wonders. Work against me, and you'll regret it."

Jordan glared.

Mason scrambled around another crowd.

"Drake."

The wind died.

Mason slid to a stop. "Here's your ice cream."

CHAPTER THIRTY-THREE

Complications

Billie Jo gave Jordan and Angesa a tour, leaving Mason with Jedediah. He reminded Jedediah of Erik, his first son—a mixed blessing. He's had few sons among many daughters. Erik had been Jedediah's greatest pride, greatest hope and greatest failure.

Mason regarded Jedediah with the supremely serious expression only the young manage. *Very Erik-like.*

"Jedediah, sir?"

"Thought your Ma didn't want you calling me Jedediah."

Mason hesitated. He squared himself. "Men should talk eye to eye—talk plain."

Jedediah beamed. "True enough, speak your mind."

"What Jordan said...."

I'll bury that girl in chores first thing.

The ten-year-old chewed his words until he picked some that tasted right. He went beet red. "I know about sex."

"Yeah?"

"Mom's taught me how a boy's not supposed to you know unless married. He's not supposed to like lie or trick a girl into it."

"Sounds about right."

"Are you tricking my mom for sex?"

Jedediah sat, offering Mason a seat side by side. He searched Mason's earnest expression. *How do I allay his fears?*

"That's a question fit for your grandfather's mouth. It feels queer coming from a face without its first whisker."

Mason's face fell.

"Don't hear me wrong. Times change, Mason, not always in a good way. She might get riled, but I'm going to speak straight with the man of your house."

"Me?"

"You." Jedediah chewed his words, unsure how far to go. "I like your Ma. That's as far as I've thought things, but I can tell you I ain't a liar and I don't play people false as a rule, understand?"

Mason nodded.

166

"My Ma was a peace woman, kind of like an ambassador. A strong, smart woman. Ma's people treated women like equals, different but just as good. Some people have forgotten that. I'm not one."

"But what Jordan said?" Mason asked.

"Girl and I have already had words on the matter. She won't speak that lie again."

"Your Ma taught that boys don't have sex until married, well my Ma taught that if a man bedded a woman they *became* married—even without a preacher to say the words." Jedediah studied Mason's grave expression. *What's the world come to that I should see a man's eyes in a ten-year-old?*

"So, you're going to have sex, so you're married?" Mason asked.

"No."

"But you like Mom."

"I do things just to see your ma smile, like see a girl movie or try some new food, but I haven't decided to court her or not."

"Court?"

"Right, that word's too old for you. Courting's like sharing the road to marriage, figuring out if you're suited travel companions for the rest of your life."

He nodded.

"To court a woman, a man has to have permission from the woman and the man of the house. If I decide to court your ma, I'll come for your permission. That square us? Man to man?"

Mason offered his hand.

Jedediah shook it.

"We're square, sir."

Jedediah smiled.

"One question, though," Mason said.

"Go ahead, son."

"Do I have to give you dowel rods then?"

"I don't understand."

"I saw it on a *Bonanza* rerun. Girl's dad gave a dowel rod to the guy marrying his daughter."

Jedediah roared with laughter. "No, no dowry needed."

"Good," Mason said. "I don't get much allowance."

"There's chores about the farm worth a dollar or two."

"Really?"

"Sure thing. You ever seen *Gunsmoke?*"

Jedediah and Drake drove the pickup down the back highways toward the hotel. The dragon set his tail up against Jedediah's side.

<*So where does this leave me?*> Drake asked.

"In trouble, especially for being too lazy to mouth shape."

"If you take her on as an apprentice. What happens to me?" Drake asked.

Jedediah laughed. "You're not leaving until your training's done, and done right."

"Jordan, Lanea, Mason and myself—should build a schoolhouse."

"One of you'd burn it down."

"Not Mason, he's a minor talent at best."

Jedediah chuckled. "You'd know better than me, rolling around in the mud with him like a clutch mate."

"Having a little brother's new to me."

"So is talking to me like you're an equal," Jedediah said.

Drake laughed. "You're the one not equal, Master. I'm Elder Fey."

"Knew taking you the *Mythela'Raemyn* would haunt me," Jedediah mumbled.

"I'm dragon, and it's time everyone treated me with the respect I'm due."

"So, teenage arrogance has finally raised its scaly head. Next will be infinite intelligence and unfathomable wisdom." Jedediah lowered his voice. "Let me tell you something, mister Elder Fey, I'd watch where you throw that weight around."

"Is that so?" Drake asked.

"Yup."

"Why should I?" Drake asked.

"How about we take a little drive over to Savannah. A cousin of yours over there thought he could throw his weight around too, slaughtered whole tribes. Druids imprisoned him in an endless rotting state."

Drake bristled.

Jedediah's arm hair rose. "Costly spell work, but he deserves every moment."

The road wound to the left. A semi rounded the corner wide, a dozen lights blinding Jedediah. He swerved. All four tires blew. They careened into the trees.

Jedediah blurted magical phrases, invoking raw air and force energy as a cushion. The truck struck something, flipping end over end through a swath of young growth forest.

Time slowed around them as if Jedediah'd inadvertently invoked chronomancy. Sounds exploded into focus, silence to concert roar in a moment. Branches tore the truck. Glass shattered, and rending metal shrieked. Behind them, the semi screeched to a halt.

Drake screamed and snarled all at once.

Glass pixie dust floated in moonlit flight.

Time and gravity reasserted themselves with something to prove. Center in the protection spell, Jedediah skipped like a river stone to an eventual stop.

Drake, partially outside the spell, careened like a lost pinwheel with a broken wing. He yelped, slamming a tree with an audible crunch, thump, and whine.

Jedediah eased himself upright, cautious about possible broken limbs.

A flashlight shined his direction. The semi's driver shouted after them. "Hey, you all right?"

A tree trunk helped Jedediah to his feet.

"God, what happened to your dog?" The unshaven man wore a black knit cap, red flannel shirt and jeans.

Jedediah's brain regained cognitive speed. He searched for Drake.

Drake's body wrapped a thick trunk, bent and broken. Dizziness hampered Jedediah's forward rush. Jedediah cringed. Blood painted everything.

"I need a first aid kit."

Red beams flashed through the trees, their color unregistered in Jedediah's sluggish thoughts. The driver reached for his belt.

This idiot so accident prone he carries a first aid kit?

"You helping or not?" Jedediah snarled.

The driver raised his gun. "Not."

Jedediah didn't understand why. How remained hazy, but what represented an assault on him, not an accident. Thin red beams swept toward him, leaving no time for elegance.

Jedediah flung himself defensively over Drake, threw open his connection to magic and screamed power. Concussive energy blasted outward in an omnidirectional wave. It catapulted the driver through several tree limbs, continuing unabated through the assault team. Fingers convulsed around triggers, discharging weapons in staccato bursts. Some rounds exploded inside magazines. The sphere reached nearly to the road before Jedediah's reserves gave out.

All clamor stilled.

Jedediah shielded Drake. He gasped breath, surrounded by trees flattened outward like spokes.

Gunman at the wave's outer edges recovered their feet and weapons. Flashlight beams swung back toward his direction.

Jedediah sucked in power once more. Furious wind lashed the area. Lightning haloed him in wrist-thick chords. He unleashed it with a primal roar.

"Stupid. Mortals." Jedediah snarled. "You. Hurt. My. Dragon."

Lightning and terror arched from man to man. Several got off short bursts before the lightning turned them into blackened corpses.

Bullets tore through Jedediah's body, but none penetrated his rage. Survivors of his lightning onslaught took cover beneath the semi. Jedediah slammed power into it, hurling it entirely airborne into the trees behind.

The men scrambled into the woods, firing on the run.

Jedediah called his staff, but the lightning struck wood didn't shoot into his hand. He swept his anger through the earth, raising a wall of molten rock. It swallowed bullets and rolled after the men like a slow motion tsunami.

"Furnaris toldent solari."

The wave parted, shaping into four, fiery wolfish forms. They gave chase, trailing scorched glowing earth.

Jedediah stumbled to the pickup, scouring the ground. He tripped on the first remaining length of his shattered staff. His curses would've wilted the dead, ravaged wood from tree top to grass blade. He squeezed into the truck, retrieving a half-demolished first aid kit.

He knelt next to Drake. *Maker, where do I start?*

Wounds outnumbered available bandages. One wing lacked an intact inch of unshattered bone. Drake's other wing wrapped around in a horrifying manner. None of this terrified Jedediah as much as the unnatural bend just above Drake's hips. Drake's rear legs twitched pathetically.

I need help.

A weak, magic-fueled whistle escaped his lips.

A squirrel-like Fey peeked its silver whiskers around the nearest whole tree.

"I cannot pay you now, but Jedediah Shine's word. Do my bidding, and I'll shower you with riches."

The diddle's face darted to the tree's opposite side. Another peaked out a head lower, followed by others.

A fortunate fate, fast as wind and almost as smart.

"Carry me a message..." Jedediah's head jerked up. *How long did I lose?* He found the fairy diddles still waiting. *Not long.* "Tell Ianyss, Lanea, and Lirelaeli Ermyn'Phir, tell them Stormfall's son will die without help."

Jedediah blinked.

He straightened out of his slouched position, cold tingled his limbs. Thirst dried his mouth. The diddles had gone.

Drake?

The dragon wheezed breath in and out.

Jedediah's connection to the Dragon Spring slipped in and out of his grip, returning nothing. He crawled over to the nearest tree, tottering to one side barely within reach. "Forgive me."

Jedediah absorbed the tree's life, extending most to lift the whimpering dragon from the ground. He staggered toward mayhem's edge, dragging the floating dragon. He collapsed at the tree line, one hand upon a tall, sturdy tree.

I hope you host no dryad.

He touched Drake's head.

Emerald energy trickled along Jedediah's arms. He kept barely enough to close wounds and maintain consciousness. A green aura suffused Drake. The tree's bark whitened and split. It released a canopy of dead leaves to the ground. One limb snapped, falling rotten near them.

"Please, Rydari Phriel, hang on."

Across the road, Muler ignored the fresh urine smell, unsure if it belonged to him or the body atop him. His fallen log cover partially obscured Jedediah Shine. What he saw couldn't be real.

I'm in a nightmare, but can't wake.

One man had wiped out an entire assault squad *after* being run off the road. Lava wolves had pursued his last living gunmen. Lava wolves.

I'm alive. I've got to tell One. He stifled a nervous chuckle. *If I'm not heavily medicated in some looney bin, he'll put me in one.*

He hoped another witness survived to corroborate the mad encounter.

The old man drowsed again.

I should kill him now.

Muler'd lost his gun. The body held a melted rifle. A scan found no surviving firearms.

Shine jolted awake.

I might make it. Wait for him to drop off. Cross the road and smoldering wasteland to the remaining trees. Circle them and strangle him. Unless he wakes at the wrong moment. Muler shuddered. *Or those things return. Screw this, Zero told me, I just didn't believe. I'm leaving before cops or worse show up.*

CHAPTER THIRTY-FOUR

Bad to Worse

A hand on his arm awoke Jedediah. Lanea's worried expression softened. She smiled.

"You all there, Da?"

"Check Drake," he rasped.

"Elves took him to the village."

"How is he?"

"The worse for knowing you," Lirelaeli said.

He turned. She gleamed, an erotic fury in cold moonlight, freezing his retort. Ianyss directed trees behind her. Roots slithered and shuffled wherever Ianyss instructed. A vine archway pulsed amber light in the distance.

Lirelaeli sashayed toward him, caressing his chin. "What've you been up to?"

"Nothing."

Lirelaeli frowned. "That mortal woman's brought undesirable elements into your life."

"Ma."

"Billie Jo's got no part in this." His voice turned acidic. "If you consider putting me first undesirable, age befuddled your mind."

"Da!"

"This is no coincidence," Lirelaeli said.

"My only concern right this moment besides Drake is aspirin," Jedediah said.

"Still blind to the long view," Lirelaeli said

"Ma's got a point," Lanea said. "The murders, the stolen shotgun, now this? Centaur don't use machine guns."

Jedediah glanced down. Someone had healed him further.

"Share a season with us, Jedediah. Dally away from the mortal world a few years."

"Done that. Still got the chains."

"Been many decades since we enjoyed time together," Lirelaeli said.

"Five or so since you enslaved me to stud you."

Lanea blushed scarlet, fleeing toward Ianyss.

"How will you explain all this?" Lirelaeli said.

172

The dryad took turns glowering at Jedediah and herding trees to camouflage the damaged area.

"Lover, come sojourn with us. Bring your apprentices."

"And Billie Jo?" Jedediah asked.

Lirelaeli covered a scowl with a smile. "I wouldn't dream of asking you to leave her behind in harm's way."

Jedediah snorted. "I can only imagine how you'd protect her."

Color tinted Lirelaeli's features. "I don't know what you mean."

"I suppose you don't."

"She's *mortal*. What in the Maker's wood can she offer that I can't?"

Jedediah scratched his beard. "Marriage? Home? Family? A partnership? Love? Freedom?"

"I gave you Lanea."

"I love her more than you could ever know, but it doesn't change facts. You *took* Lanea."

"What I did, I did for you, for the best."

"No, you did it for yourself despite what it did to me."

Lirelaeli spun and marched through the arch.

Flashing lights and sirens approached in the distance.

Jedediah sighed. "Time to pay the piper. Again."

Jedediah sat on an ER table, bandaged head in his hands. A hospital gown replaced his bloodied clothes. Jedediah endured triage, an interminable wait, a cursory examination by a harried nurse, another wait, and another examination by a doctor at the tail end of a thirty-hour shift. They confined him to a second-floor room for 24-hour observation.

A local detective bullied his way in as soon as a doctor cleared Jedediah from immediate danger.

"For the hundredth and last time, Detective Rade, I don't know what happened to the damned driver. The truck swung into my lane. I swerved, blew a tire and wrecked. I woke up just before your people arrived."

"Explain the shells we found." The plain-clothes detective had dark curly hair and matching bushman eyebrows in need of thinning. He made more notes on his cell phone.

Lirelaeli probably convinced Ianyss to leave the casings.

"It's rabbit season?"

Rade scowled.

"Duck season?" Jedediah asked.

Rade folded tanned hands behind his back and glared. "This isn't a joking matter, Mr. Shine."

"Does it look like I'm dancing a jig covered in bells?" Jedediah asked.

The detective frowned. "Pardon?"

"Forget it."

"What happened to the truck?" Rade asked.

"I got ran off the road."

"The semi," Rade said.

"I can't say."

A buxom tavern harlot with a six thousand dollar Italian briefcase entered. She glowered at Rade. "I'm Ms. March, Mr. Shine's attorney. Are you charging my client?"

Gratitude drowned Jedediah's voice. "Meadow."

She flashed him a smile. "Just sit there and be quiet. This won't take a minute."

"We're questioning him about the accident and some peculiar evidence found at the scene. Surely as a good citizen with nothing to hide, he's happy to help."

Meadow pursed her lips and gave him an oh-I've-never-heard-that-garbage-before glower. "How long have you been being a good citizen, Jedediah?"

"Hours? I might have a concussion," Jedediah said.

She pointed an accusing finger at Rade.

The sight of mad Aunt Clara scolding the taller detective overwhelmed his control. Jedediah giggled

She shot Jedediah a concerned glance.

He quieted.

"Fifteen more minutes as a courtesy," Meadow said. "In exchange, you agree to provide Mr. Shine with full immunity."

"Immunity? For what?"

"Whatever." Meadow smiled sweetly. "Mr. Shine has been the victim of a tragic traffic accident. If you've got no charges, why object?"

"I'm not offering immunity until we determine what the hell happened."

"Mr. Shine's tired. He'll answer through me for clarity, fifteen minutes and we're done."

A woman in police blues entered, passing a folder to Detective Rade. He glanced through it. "No bodies, but we've evidence of an intense explosion. Semi trailer's empty begging the question what you hauled?"

Jedediah whispered to Meadow. She nodded.

The lie tasted bitter. "Few cans of black power and two one-gallon gas cans."

"Black powder?" Rade asked.

"Added pyrotechnics to my show recently," Jedediah said.

Rade smiled. "Does your client have a permit?"

"The Renaissance Festival has a blanket policy on file." Meadow said.

"Your client's paperwork listed his occupation as farmer," Rade said. "Is he certified to handle explosives?"

Jedediah and Meadow exchanged words.

"Under controlled conditions. I'm not at my best in a tumbling pickup truck."

The detective radiated dour disapproval. "How did you obtain these items?"

Meadow answered. "They're commonly available at farm supply stores or your local home improvement store."

"He mixes himself?" Rade asked. "Where'd he learn?"

"My Da learned demolitions in Vietnam."

"Why would he teach you such things?" Rade asked.

"Stubborn tree stumps?"

Rade typed into his phone.

"Any anti-American leanings, Mr. Shine?"

Jedediah reddened. Meadow restrained him. "My client is more American than the President."

"The attending noted bullet holes in your clothes, but not in you, explain."

"Sparks burns?" Jedediah said.

"And all the blood?" Rade asked.

"Head wounds bleed a lot," Meadow said.

Rade shook his head. "Too much, unless he had a terrorist accomplice."

Jedediah shrugged and shook his head.

"No one accompanied him," she said.

"Have you received any threats recently?" Rade asked.

"I'm assuming assassination attempts count."

"One of your tires blew?" Rade asked.

"Yup."

Rade glanced at the report "There are fist-sized holes on the interior sidewall of all four tires? Do you recall hearing the others blow?"

"Sorry, no."

"Do you have evidence attributing this accident as some kind of attack on my client?" Meadow asked.

"Inconclusive, I hoped your client could clarify the evidence," Rade said.

"I do not recall more than one tire going. I also don't recall running over anything," Jedediah said.

Rade's phone chirped. He took a moment to read the new message. "Where's your father?"

"Gone," Jedediah said.

"Where?" Rade said.

"Born on the farm, ended on the farm," Jedediah said.

"What did he die of?" Rade asked.

"Shame."

"Shame?" Rade asked.

Jedediah met Rade's eye with a hard glare. Acid edged Jedediah's response. "The Jedediah Shine that served in the Vietnam War proved himself a hero. Twice awarded the Bronze Star, once the Silver Star and a Congressional Medal of Honor. He came home to find himself reviled by idiots that hadn't lived a tenth of what he had."

Rade looked away. "That wasn't right."

"Is that all, Detective?" Meadow asked. "My client needs his rest."

"We're going to need a list of the chemicals your client claims to have been transporting," Rade said.

"Asked and answered," she said. "Black power and gasoline."

"I'll need him to provide that in writing," Rade said. "After which there's no immediate reason to charge Mr. Shine. Though we may need to talk to him in future."

"His admission form lists a home address," Meadow said.

Rade nodded, pulled a pocket notebook and pen from his jacket, ripped out a few sheets and passed both the sheets and a pen over to Jedediah. He left the room.

Pyromancy didn't require flash pots and gunpowder, but they offered a convenient way to explain away the explosions and fire. It also eliminated more entanglements with the police. He wrote both down even though he'd already listed them to the detective.

Meadow smiled. "What now?"

Jedediah hugged her hard. She escaped the embrace breathless and blushing furiously. "Jedediah! What would Billie Jo say?"

He adopted a falsetto. "Thank you for saving the big idiot."

"My pleasure."

"Make sure to send me a bill," Jedediah said.

She scoffed. "We're friends."

"Charge me to guarantee privilege."

"Damn, I liked you owing me a favor," Meadow said. "Be all right here tonight?"

"I'm leaving," Jedediah said.

Meadow frowned. "You need to stay where the doctors can look after you."

"Drawing innocents into the crossfire? No."

"So, an attack? Really?"

"Yup."

She shook her head. "Why didn't you tell them?"

"Between you and me, whatever's going on, it's too big for the police."

"I don't want you going vigilante. I know Justin wouldn't approve."

"He'd understand better than you know," Jedediah said.

"I can't talk you into staying?" Meadow asked.

Jedediah shook his head. "Not giving them another chance. I'm checking out of here and my hotel. At home I can see them coming."

"I don't like this," she said.

"That's why I didn't ask you for a ride," Jedediah said.

"How are you going to get back home without your truck?" she asked.

"There'll be a car for me at the hotel in an hour or so."

Her pensive expression released a single nod. "I'll take you to the hotel."

"You're the best, Meadow."

She led him to an obvious rental—too plain for the vibrant woman. She stuck to the interstates, running at least thirty miles above the posted speed limit.

"Tickets?" Jedediah asked.

She smiled. "Good attorney. I didn't know that about your dad."

Jedediah shrugged. "It never came up."

"What really happened?"

"Pretty much like I said. Sometimes I think he had the right of it."

"What do you mean?"

"World might be better off once I'm gone," Jedediah said.

"Don't let Billie Jo hear you say anything like that," Meadow scolded. "That woman's got it seriously bad for you."

"Without a drop of your perfume."

She laughed and pulled into the hotel parking lot.

Jedediah kissed Meadow on the cheek. "Thanks again."

She touched her cheek. "Should've had a detective harass you years ago."

Jedediah chuckled and strolled into the hotel lobby. A cooperative wind held his hospital gown perfectly shut.

Bitter medicine, but Lirelaeli's accusations hit too close to the mark. He'd spotted the inconsistencies in *Mythela'Raemyn*. The Rite left him with plenty of loose threads, but in his arrogance, he'd never considered the attacks directed at him.

Wouldn't anyone who wanted to strike me personally know what I really am? Wouldn't they attack magically? Either they didn't know before or aren't powerful enough for it to matter.

A sense of unease crept into him. For the first time since Vietnam, he felt a sniper's sight between his shoulder blades.

Where would some random crazy get military rounds to shoot Lanea?

Magical or normal, someone had organized a vendetta against him. They'd hurt his loved ones.

I haven't crossed anyone in years...except Lirelaeli, and she'd never shoot Drake or Lanea.

He wanted to kick himself. *Stupid, arrogant, idiot. Lanea nearly died for your arrogance, now Drake.*

Heat built up in his chest. He'd be ready if they dared attack him prepared and aware. He pictured the truck driver. *If they don't come after me, I'll go after them.*

An attractive blonde behind the counter greeted him. "Morning, Sir."

She wore a standard hotel uniform, black slacks and a white, buttoned top. A nametag declared her: Kaci, Assistant Manager.

He stopped midway to the elevator and approached the desk.

Kaci offered a disturbingly eager smile considering the hour. "How can I help you?"

"I'd like to check out of room 212."

She typed into the computer. "Do you have your key?"

"Yup. I'm heading up to grab my things. Can you have my bill ready by time I get back?"

She flashed a lovely smile over the lobby. "Good idea, the three a.m. checkout rush is just crazy."

He laughed and headed for his room. The hotel dresser held Jedediah's neatly folded clothes. Already ironed clothes hung in the closet. The bathroom counter supported soldierly lines of toiletries. Donning clothes and packing everything but a case-protected model took moments. Model under one arm and suitcase under another, he returned to Kaci.

He checked the bill, handing over keys and cash.

Kaci smiled. "Thank you for staying with us, Mr. Shine. Have a good morning."

"You too," Jedediah said.

She picked up a phone as Jedediah strolled out.

Who would she call at this hour?

He walked down the sidewalk until well out of sight. He removed the old, burnt-orange Dodge Charger model from the display box and set it onto the road. A burst of magic restored it to full size and weight. Minutes later he drove for home.

"Hello?" Marc said.

"One? Two. Check secure?"

"Secure," he said.

"It's time." She scratched the itchy polyester hotel slacks absently.

"I'll send Flash," Marc said.

"Acknowledged." Bianca hung up.

A dark shadow blocked the moon not fifteen miles down the interstate. Hair stood up along his neck. He accelerated until the feeling receded.

Slowing returned pursuit. The moon dimmed again. Jedediah cast a vision spell, cut off headlights and stomped on the gas.

He got thirty seconds of moonlight before a great black shadow blotted out the sky. Ember-like glows flickered just above him. Fear pummeled his conscious mind.

Jedediah swallowed hard. *Damn it, I hoped it'd take her until morning to arrive.*

He pulled off the highway, parked in a vacant strip mall and stepped out of the car.

Stormfall landed in front of him amid wind and brimstone stench. Her bulk filled the parking lot, sending several light poles crashing to the cement. Smoldering eyes glared at Jedediah.

Jedediah bowed to one knee. "Stormfall."

Her voice, usually soft and feminine, careened around Jedediah's head like a wrecking ball in a massive pinball machine. *<I've heard from Lirelaeli Ermyn'Phir. I will now hear from you, wizard.>*

Bitch. Jedediah thought, then immediately added. *Not you, I swear it.*

Stormfall's house-sized maw lowered, showing off teeth larger than Jedediah. Vibrant, velvet red lined her mouth. *<I've no time for mortal squabbles. Tell me of my son.>*

Her use of mortal, akin to his own hours before, unnerved Jedediah. Ice skated up and down his spine. *I entrusted Drake to Lirelaeli and her healers. I don't know his condition.*

<I know his condition, pray it improves.>

Jedediah offered a single grim nod. *Someone attacked us, Revered One. I know not their instigator, but I punished the perpetrators.*

Her mind shoved into his, digging the details from his memory. *<You gave my son's attackers too quick a death, their passing deserved far greater suffering.>*

Jedediah cringed despite himself. *My priority had to be Drake.*

<NOT DRAKE! Rydari Phriel! Speak it with terror and respect.>

If I find others guilty for the attack upon Rydari Phriel, I'll not repeat that mistake.

<When, wizard. You owe me for your life, twice now for I spare you again this very moment.>

You can't hold this against me. I've no part in this attack.

<You own blame, wizard. Find them. Bring me their leader. Let him cower between my talons before my son leaves this world or you'll take his place.>

I shall deliver him with concerted alacrity, though I'm unsure where to begin.

<Question the dead.>

The ice skater doing tricks along his spine split into an ice hockey team. *Lirelaeli took them.*

< I care nothing for your excuses!> His eyes crossed under the assault. *<My son lies broken by humanity's hand.>*

I'll find a way.

Stormfall leapt to air, creating much more wind than her initial landing. She circled above him. *<See that you do, wizard. Next time remember your place. Mortals do not mind speak with their betters.>*

"Bitch," Jedediah mumbled once her shape diminished sufficiently.

A huge Samoan strolled into Kaci's hotel, wheeling a suitcase behind him.

Kaci inclined her head. "Morning, Flash."

He didn't stop until he reached room 212. He donned rubber gloves, dug a Ziploc baggie from his jacket, and donned the rubber gloves inside it atop the first. He unlocked the door and locked it once inside. He opened the suitcase atop the horrible orange bedspread and withdrew another baggie of photographs. He fanned them atop a dresser and frowned. The day maid had taken meticulous pictures of drawers, closet, and bathroom each day.

He withdrew a tape measure and replicated the item layouts exactly.

Flash rolled an empty suitcase out of the hotel, dropping a baggie of cash onto the front desk with a word, "Two."

Kaci deposited the bills in the hotel register, then turned to update the reservations computer as he stepped from the lobby.

He returned with a seemingly unconscious child over each shoulder, barely adolescents. The morning desk clerk glanced from Kaci to the big man.

He smiled at them. "Poor tykes are worn out, dead to the world."

Kaci laughed, leading the clerk into the office.

Flash laid out the two dead runaways in room 212, positioned exactly as instructed. He scowled at his perfect work, placed a Do Not Disturb sign on the door and departed the hotel.

He flipped open a cell phone and thumbed speed-dial number one.

"Yes?"

"It's done. Day clerk looks unlucky, the type to suffer accidents."

"We'll add it to his tab. Replace Gordon to improve your alibi."

Flash snapped the phone shut.

CHAPTER THIRTY-FIVE

Death of the Party

Jedediah returned to the farm shortly after sunrise. He climbed upstairs and fell into his massive bed. Disjointed dreams plagued him. He wandered through crowded renaissance fairs, glimpsing feral shadowcat-like grins but never catching faces. Faces dear to him ghosted in and out—pained and accusatory.

Someone pounded on his door.

Jedediah bolted upright. Exhaustion played to his advantage: dressed, if rumpled, he opened the bedroom door.

"What is it?" Jedediah asked.

Lanea's terrified face hadn't a shred of color. "Stormfall's outside."

His stomach plummeted. "Drake?"

"Fine, well, not dead."

Maker, what does she want now? Jedediah felt like crying. He did indulge in such things, but he hated feeling powerless. "Stay inside."

"But, Da."

"Stay. I don't want you seeing whatever happens."

Lanea paled further. Jedediah squeezed her hand.

Stormfall waited in the drive. Sunlight caught her charcoal scales, flashing crimson along their edges. If anything, daylight made her more intimidating.

Jedediah glanced over his shoulder. Upstairs curtains shifted back into place.

Jedediah bowed to one knee. "Stormfall, I didn't expect you so soon."

<I would know your progress.>

Jedediah stood. He locked her gaze, jaw clenched. "None."

Stormfall snarled. Hot air blasted Jedediah backward. *<You doubt my threats?>*

Jedediah glared back. "I doubt nothing, but last night remains this morning. As you pointed out, I'm mortal. I exhausted myself protecting Rydari Phriel. The dead bow only to strength. I had no choice but to rest."

<This is not sufficient.>

Jedediah folded his arms and raised his chin. "Then rip out my throat and find them yourself."

Stormfall glared.

"Decide, Revered One," Jedediah said. "You're not the only one worried about Drake—"

181

<I commanded you to use his proper name.>

Jedediah altered his usual phrasing, making a point as the dragon's Name rolled off his tongue. "I care about *Rydari Phriel* too."

She bristled.

"There've been enough mistakes. If you want my service, let me do things as I see fit. Otherwise, enslave yourself a thrall."

<Better I merely enslave you.>

"I'll destroy us both first."

<You could never destroy me.>

Jedediah snorted.

"You think Rydari Phriel is the only true name I've collected over the years? Need I invoke another to remind you what a wizard can do with one?" Jedediah held his mental shields for all they were worth. He hadn't lied, but hers wasn't among the Names he had at his disposal despite considerable effort. "Decide, let me work or fight."

She launched herself skyward.

Jedediah watched her go. Even shaking with fury, he admired her beauty.

Lanea slipped her hand into his.

"It's okay, girl."

Sobs broke her voice. "It's not okay. She wants to kill you."

"There's a queue."

"Dragons don't wait in line, Da," Lanea rasped.

"Neither do wizards. Inform your mother Stormfall demands last night's dead bodies."

"Demands?"

"Yup, she summoned Stormfall. She can share in the dragon's displeasure."

"Why would she do that?"

Jedediah looked at his daughter. "You ain't dense, girl."

"But, Da, that's so...petty."

Jedediah shrugged. "Since I'm up, best be about things. Get her that message, then we'll discuss Jordan."

Lanea blanched. "Who?"

"Your pupil and new foster sister."

Lanea opened her mouth.

"Go, Lanea. We've little time."

Jedediah changed into fresh overalls and planted himself in front of his bathroom mirror. Steam rose from the tap. He focused a moment. "Mauve."

A woman appeared—a lithe, ultra-sexy Morticia Addams with honey-brown hair instead of black. Delight filled her eyes. Ruby lips parted in a predatory smile.

"Hello, handsome. Find Lanea?"

"Yup," Jedediah said. "Thank you."

"Do your thanks include a few days luxuriating together in Acapulco?"

"I'm dating someone, Mauve," Jedediah said.

Mauve's lips twisted into a pout. "Always Frankenstein's bridesmaid."

Jedediah chuckled and outlined the situation.

Mauve cursed. "Elf loves to make things worse."

"When it suits her. I need you here."

Mauve smirked. "Girlfriend not taking care of you?"

"You know firsthand I don't dally outside marriage."

"Proof positive no one's perfect." Mischief curled her lips. "You know being a necromancer brings new options to death do us part."

"Mauve."

She shrugged. "I'll be over this afternoon."

"Need a gate?"

"No."

Jedediah closed off the communication. *I hope I haven't complicated things worse. Still, with Stormfall hovering, I need the best.*

Boneyard to storage unit, storage to renaissance festival, Jedediah appeared in his booth. Theophanie's friend Tina jumped, pressing a hand to her chest.

"Sorry," she said. "You startled me."

Jedediah nodded. "Something's come up. You girls handle the stall or should I close up?"

Panic flashed across her eyes. "I thought you'd only be gone today."

Jedediah frowned. "Who told you that?"

"Lanea, something about a family picnic," Tina said. "I really need the work, most of us do. We can handle things if given the chance."

Jedediah dipped a hand into his overalls and produced a folded wad of money. "This will take care of y'all for the rest of the fair, with a bonus for doing without me."

She hugged him. "Oh, thank you."

He stepped from her embrace and crossed the thoroughfare to Mad Meadow March. Meadow pitched her wares to a plumping redhead. A tall, blond man's profile beside her seemed familiar. He recognized Marc O'Steele the moment he turned.

Marc whispered into his girlfriend's ear and stepped toward Jedediah. She glanced after him, but Meadow drew her attention back in moments.

"Mr. Shine, right?" Marc asked.

"Marc O'Steele. Enjoying the fair?"

"Annie loves it." Marc flashed a guilty smile and leaned in conspiratorially. "Not my thing, but what guy wouldn't suffer for the right girl?"

"Suppose so."

"You got an Annie?" Marc asked.

Meadow led Annie over, the girl tucked a small bag into an oversized purse. She curled around Marc's arm, and he gave Jedediah a knowing smile.

Meadow rolled her eyes behind their backs. "Where's your Miss Right, Jedediah? Run her off with your misadventures?"

Marc's gaze sharpened.

"Misadventures?" Annie asked.

"Nothing happened," Jedediah said.

Meadow laughed. "Nothing? A semi ran poor Jedediah off the road last night. Had to pry him out of that detective's clutches."

"Why'd the cops want you?" Marc asked.

"Wanted me to confess to terrorism." Jedediah shrugged. "Guess they win steak-knives for nabbing enough terrorists."

Marc laughed. "You?"

Annie smacked his shoulder.

"No offense," Marc said.

"Nice seeing you again. Meadow, I need a word?" Jedediah took Meadow aside. "Could you keep an eye on my stall?"

"Not sticking around?" Meadow asked.

"Had enough excitement. Theophanie will handle everything, just make sure there's no trouble."

"You've got my number right?" She grimaced. "Just in case?"

"Yup."

"I want a cut of your profits."

"Ten percent after cost?" Jedediah asked. "Assuming you're okay stealing books from school children.

She swatted him. "You know I meant it as a joke."

Jedediah smiled and left in search of Theophanie. He explained the situation, leading her to the activities director.

"But your show generates substantial repeat business, Mr. Shine."

"Can't be helped," Jedediah said. "Theophanie's troupe is happy to assume my show times."

Jedediah returned home to a front porch piled with bodies.

He carried them behind the farmhouse to his old icehouse, cursing Lirelaeli and elves in general. As an afterthought, he added a disguise spell to prevent casual search.

Be just my luck if some patrolman stumbled down the stairs into my house of corpses.

Lanea stepped out of thin air. Jedediah narrowed his eyes, seeing through her glamour veil. A pavilion rested near the old well. Tables supported stacked pizza boxes and several pitchers of sweet tea. Pepsi and beer swam in ice filled washtubs. She'd lit his fire pit grill.

"Family picnic isn't going to distract me from you lying."

"I didn't lie to you."

"You told me a fairy caused Billie Jo all that mischief."

"He is."

Jedediah's brow arched.

Lanea beamed. "While investigating, I discovered Jordan's talent. I had a duty to see her trained."

"So you took it upon yourself instead of bringing her to me."

Lanea folded her arms. "I'm not an apprentice anymore."

Jedediah frowned and scratched his beard. "Girl, I've got corpses on ice, killers trying to bury me, a dragon ready to help, cops sniffing around and a necromancer flying in. What makes you think this is a good idea?"

"You're right."

"Glad to hear it, about what?" Jedediah asked.

"Most elves are too capricious and too disconnected from current events," Lanea said. "But they're right about celebrating every day, sunrise to moonrise and into the night."

"So nothing about our current situation strikes you as good enough reason not to throw a barbeque?" Jedediah asked.

"We're celebrating Drake's recovery. Anyway, Ms. Cooper's letter insisted on more supervised activity before deciding on the fosterage."

"So, rather than magicking Jordan out of their care, you throw a party."

Lanea kissed his cheek. "Yup. Girlfriend's here, you should change."

A minivan pulled up the gravel drive.

Lanea laid steak and chicken halves on the grill with a grin. Mason threw open the door and bolted out, searching for Drake. Billie Jo proceeded Angesa and her ever-present clipboard. Jordan brought up a reluctant rear, employing her usual disinterested scrutiny.

Lanea bounced up to them. "I'm so glad you could all make it. I'm Lanea—"

"Lanea?" Billie Jo glanced at Jordan who refused to meet her eye. "Is Mary Ann your sister? You sound exactly alike."

Jordan scowled. "She's right, you do."

Lanea shot a nervous glance at Jedediah and forged on, her voice pitched higher. "Make yourself at home, we're waiting on a few more guests."

Billie Jo rushed to his side. "My God, Jedediah. What happened to you?"

Jedediah had left his injuries unhealed because of the police. He'd forgotten about Billie Jo. "It's nothing, just a little car accident."

"I told you. That old truck's unsafe. It doesn't even have seatbelts, let alone airbags. You could've been killed."

"There's nothing wrong with my truck."

Lanea rested a hand on Billie Jo's arm. "Don't fret. It didn't survive the crash."

Billie Jo blanched.

Jedediah folded his arms. "I'm sure I can fix it."

"Where's Drake?" Mason asked.

"Being looked after," Jedediah said. "Accident hurt him too."

"You wouldn't put him down, would you?" Mason asked.

186 | MICHAEL J. ALLEN

"Not if my life depended on it."

Mason smiled.

"Anyone else get hurt?" Angesa said.

"No one that mattered," Jedediah ignored her puzzled glance.

"You drink Pepsi," Jordan announced. "That's awful. I won't touch it."

"Always the charmer," Lanea said.

Jordan closed the distance, lowering her voice. "You're not Lanea, what gives? Where is she?"

"Remember that whole glamour thing?" Lanea asked.

Angesa and Billie Jo edged closer.

Jedediah cut the conversation off. "Pepsi is the perfection Coca-Cola can only mimic and poorly at that. It's like gold around here."

Lanea snorted.

Billie Jo led Jordan to the pavilion, heading off a possible argument. "Look, Jordan. They've got tea."

"And beer," Jordan said.

"Not for you," three adults said together.

Jedediah approached the drink table. Something flashed in his peripheral vision. He stilled. Nothing moved. Jedediah reached for a Pepsi. Another movement flash.

Our mysterious fairy's arrived.

He grabbed a soda and popped the top. It exploded all over his shirt. Jordan, Mason and Lanea laughed. Billie Jo smiled sympathetically, offering him a few disposable napkins.

"Lanea," Jedediah growled.

"Sorry, it amused me," she chuckled.

"About as funny as ruined books."

Lanea stiffened, glancing around. Joe Franklin's cruiser pulled up the drive.

"Why's he here?"

"You've been friends a long time," she whispered. "Past time you put this mess behind you."

"Considering all we've got on ice, it's hardly a good idea."

"Your beer's illegal?" Jordan asked. "Where'd you import it from?"

Several tense moments later Joe Franklin and a young woman got out of the car.

"Are we late?" Joe Franklin fixed his eyes on Jedediah's shirt. "Drinking problem I need to know about?"

"Funny," Jedediah's ears reddened.

"Got one of the grandkid's bibs in the trunk," Joe Franklin added with a grin.

Jedediah turned toward Lanea and mumbled, "The comedian you invited is here."

"Play nice, Da."

Jedediah shook Joe Franklin's hand. "Joe Franklin, this is Billie Jo Bartlett, her son Mason, Faye Jordan a teen I'm considering fostering, and her caseworker Angesa Cooper—whom you've met. You know my, uh, farmhand Lanea. I haven't met your lady friend."

The woman with Joe Franklin giggled. "Lady friend. That sounds so funny."

"This is Nancy," Joe Franklin said.

Jedediah extended a hand. "Nice to meet you."

Angesa looked around. "Quite the party. If everything works out, Mr. Shine's farmhand can show you the ropes, Faye."

"Jordan," Jordan snapped.

Billie Jo bustled over, leading Nancy into a conclave of women. Jedediah and Joe Franklin shared a glance chronicled in the unwritten annals of maledom.

Lanea shoved a wooden box into Joe Franklin's hands. "Horseshoes at ten paces, gentlemen."

"This everyone?" Jedediah darkened. "You didn't invite that boy Trevor, did you?"

Lanea's happy expression faded. "Everyone I invited."

The final guest appeared with the party well underway. The gorgeous woman did exactly that: appeared. If jealousy at young Nancy's youthful attractiveness sent Billie Jo's running for an interception, Mauve hurled her into sudden death. Old Mauve's extremely minimal black gown suited a formal to-do rather than a backyard barbeque.

She sashayed up to Jedediah and French kissed him, wrapping entirely around his body. Life energy flooded Jedediah, washing over him like a soothing mint somehow both warm and chill.

Billie Jo's expression turned mortified. The other women mixed embarrassment, astonishment and irritation.

Breathless and dizzy, Jedediah forcibly peeled Mauve from around him. "Mauve, Lanea said you declined her invitation. Allow me to introduce my *lady friend*, Billie Jo?"

Mauve's accent approximated silky cream. It sounded vaguely Russian. "Oh, dearest Jedediah, *so* delightful to see you. Absolutely no one compares to you where I live."

Jedediah shot her a frigid look. Mauve's smile blossomed. He turned her by an elbow, marching her away amidst hushed whispers.

Lanea whispered to Billie Jo. "It's all fake."

"Plastic surgery?" Billie Jo asked.

Lanea smiled. "The kiss."

"Didn't look fake."

"She can't help herself. She craves attention, women jealous or scandalized, men panting."

"Is she an old girlfriend?"

Lanea offered a reassuring smile. "They attended school together. She's tried, um, dating him, but he's too old fashioned for her."

Billie Jo scrutinized Lanea. "How old are you?"

"Fifty-three."

Billie Jo stared.

Lanea's giggle drew laughter from her. An uncertain frown replaced it shortly thereafter as she watched Jedediah.

Jedediah marched up to Billie Jo. "I'm truly sorry about that. We've had words. She won't try another stunt like that."

"I should hope not," Billie Jo said.

"She's journeyed a long way, and I'd rather not insult an old friend, but if you want, I'll send her way."

"You went to school with her?" Billie Jo asked. "Nothing else?"

"Nothing."

Billie Jo examined the beautiful woman, clearly unconvinced.

CHAPTER THIRTY-SIX

Dead Memories

Jordan wandered away from the crowd, glad to be alone. She strolled into the farmhouse, wandering room to room. The old man kept a tidy, lived in house.

Probably had Lanea One or Lanea Two do all the work.

She scanned his books, glanced at models and paused to examine the wooden clocks. The old television gave her pause.

Jesus, there's no computer, hell there isn't even a DVD player. How can anyone live without electronics? An urban fantasy she'd read at one halfway houses occurred to her. *Shit, if they believe they've really got magic, does that mean no electronics out here? Ever?*

Magic. Lanea had taught her about magic. Jordan hadn't believed any of it. You tolerated it like having a foster jailer addicted to reality TV—putting up with their stupid bought you something.

The old man's light show freaked her out, but she'd worked out how the charlatan managed most of his little tricks. She'd attended the picnic to get a closer look at the strange dog and snoop through the house.

Anyone who claims they can do magic—let alone I can—has neon, blinking skeletons that'll save me from his creepy, nut-ball fingers.

She glanced at the mantle pictures without really seeing them. She meandered upstairs. A long hall of pictures, portraits and rooms waited at the top. Closed doors offered prime snooping opportunity.

A portrait caught her eye—hand painted, not some mass-produced print sold in mega marts. The pictured woman wore a medieval white gown. She couldn't have been Ms. Bartlett's twin, but easily a sister or cousin.

"Uncanny, isn't it?" Lanea asked.

"Yes," Jordan looked up to find Lanea One. Her appearance shimmered, resolving into Lanea Two. "What the hell?"

"Glamour," Lanea said. "This is my normal disguise."

"What do you really look like? Some horror, freak show?"

Lanea shimmered again. Her appearance altered only slightly—ears pointing, face sharpening, hair turning lustrous.

Great, she's a gorgeous, fairy tale princess. Jordan shook her head. *Horror show would've been better.*

Lanea reddened and hid her face behind silky cascades. She gestured. "The resemblance is what caught Da's eye."

"Aren't you just a farmhand?"

Lanea shrugged. "Just one more secret to keep, like your magic."

"I don't have magic. Magic isn't real," Jordan said.

Lanea offered an apologetic smile. "Denial doesn't alter reality. You're a terramancer."

Jordan rubbed her face. *They're insane.*

"You'll learn the other disciplines too. Da forbade me water magic entirely until I mastered the others."

She'd never experienced a game like theirs, but every foster family had one. She'd figure it out. Her hands itched. She tightened them, resisting punching her with all she had. "Will you please stop? This isn't funny."

"I'm sorry. Look, Billie Jo sent me to check on you."

"What is it with you people? Why does she even care?"

"Some people just care, Jordan. We protect people." Lanea looked at the closed doors. "Even some we barely know."

Jordan fidgeted with her hands.

"Look, most people don't believe in magic, coming face to face with it can be a bit scary." Lanea chewed her lip. "I'm sorry I didn't do a better job, but there's a wondrous magical world in store for you."

Jordan shook her head. *What do I say to this kind of bullshit?*

'Speaking of teachers, be nicer to Billie Jo, Da's fond of her."

"She's going to kick him to the curb after what he did with that little slut."

"We'll see."

"She will if she's smart. Men aren't worth those kinds of games. You know that after pretty boy."

Hurt edged Lanea's reply. "You're right, most aren't."

Lanea crossed to the stairs. A blur flashed between her ankles on the second step. She turned the stumble into an inelegant slide down to the landing.

Jordan hurried after her. "Are you all right?"

Lanea grimaced. "Yeah. I've had about enough of your little prankster."

Jordan felt her cheeks burn. "I didn't trip you."

Lanea's hands flashed too fast to see. She brought back a small fairy encased in a water cage. Beer bottle caps and tabs formed vaguely oriental armor.

Jordan leaned in. "What the hell?"

It saluted. "Hello, my dame. Let me out so I can teach this water witch a lesson—Jersey style, ya know?"

Jordan gaped, thoughts sprinting too fast to make any sense.

Lanea blew a short breath into the fairy's face, causing it to pass out within the cage. "Guessing you didn't know about your magical stalker."

The party went long into evening, long enough that Jedediah started checking the skies for a reappearance of Stormfall.

She won't stay away just because I've got normal guests. Probably try to gobble them up as a peace offering—force us to kill her.

Horseshoes allowed him to make an uneasy peace with Joe Franklin.

Mauve approached Billie Jo. "My dear, I'm terribly sorry about our little misunderstanding earlier. I'd have apologized earlier, but in your place might've done something unladylike without cool down time."

Billie Jo didn't reply.

Mauve leaned in. "I'm jealous—you've succeeded where I failed."

The silence dragged into awkwardness.

Lanea cleared her throat. "Mauve, why don't I take you to your hotel?"

"Yes, of course, dear," Mauve said. "Good night, all."

Billie Jo watched Mauve drive away, stiff and distant.

Jedediah cleared his throat. *Not what else I can do to convince her who I fancy, I've blatantly declared my preference for her all day.*

"Perhaps we should go," Angesa said. "It's very late."

"We should go too," Nancy said. "Don't you agree, Joe Franklin?"

The sheriff heaved himself out of a garden chair.

"Night all, thank you for coming." Jedediah loaded a sleeping Mason into their minivan. He kissed Billie Jo goodnight with enough feeling to leave her breathless. A smile flickered, beaten down by her frown.

He watched them go and heaved a sigh. "Nice illusion, girl. Let's go inside."

Lanea and Mauve got out of the still parked truck and followed into the den. Lanea lit the hearth and served Napoleon brandy in crystal glasses.

Mauve sipped hers, pinky in the air. "That woman's supremely jealous." Mauve tossed her hair. "Not that I blame her."

"I don't appreciate you thumb-screwing her insecurities," Jedediah said.

Mauve scoffed, turning to Lanea. "You're looking quite grown up these days. How long has it been?"

"Ten years," Lanea said.

"I rather miss having you around," Mauve said.

Lanea smiled.

"Five years without doing the dishes would spoil a lesser woman." Mauve sipped brandy. "Perhaps I need a new apprentice."

"I've got spares," Jedediah said.

"Why can't you help your poor father, darling? Don't you remember my lessons?" Mauve asked.

Lanea blushed. "I remember. I'm just no good with the dead."

"There's no good or bad with the dead, my dear. You order, they obey— command and presence."

"Dead things creep me out," Lanea said. "They don't obey those afraid of them."

Mauve leaned forward and patted her hand. "You're lovely, dear, that excuses most shortcomings."

Jedediah and Lanea shared long-suffering glances.

"That new girl's going to be a handful," Mauve said. "She didn't utter a single polite comment all night."

"We've laid a lot on her," Jedediah turned to Lanea. "Where's her fairy?"

Mischief lit Lanea's face. "In the West greenhouse. He'll have ready answers by time we get to him."

"Won't he escape?" Mauve asked.

"He's between gorgon vines and a weretree." Lanea smiled. "Doubt he'll chance it."

"So where's that incontinent flying badger? I figured we'd have to fight her off and wipe the normals."

Jedediah sighed. "Overdue."

Mauve rose, smile perched on her lips. "Then let's be about your favor. Dead won't dally forever, places to go after all."

Lanea folded her arms. "Where?"

"Ladies, we haven't time for a row."

"Into their next incarnation," Mauve said.

Jedediah scowled.

"Still don't believe?" Mauve asked. "Looked close at your tootsie?"

A final tone set Jedediah's opinion in stone. "She's not Elsabeth."

He led her to the ice house, opened its doors and descended.

Mauve frowned down the dark stair. "How're your glamours these days, Lanea?"

"Mauve?" Jedediah called from below.

"I can trod a normal's toes unnoticed," Lanea said.

"Summon one, would you?" Mauve asked.

"Why?" Lanea said.

Mauve's nose wrinkled. "I'm not much for dark and dank."

"You're a necromancer," Lanea said.

"Doesn't require lurking in crypts, dear. The dead and I are quite happy lounging on the beach."

"Which beach?" Lanea asked.

Mauve's face lit up. "Still the clever girl after all."

Jedediah came up the stair. "Well?"

A dead body tapped Jedediah on the shoulder, making him jump.

"Pardon me," it squeezed by him.

Others followed. A motley procession of dead presented their varied states of repair. Dirt clung to them from wherever the elves had unearthed them. The last in line glanced down the stairs before taking his place.

Mauve winked at Lanea. "Dead's no excuse for lying about. Butt up here. Now."

The last corpse hurried up the stair and into line, mumbling apologies with a broken mouth.

Mauve gestured. "All yours."

"As you wish." Jedediah turned to the dead. "I'm Jedediah Shine, hear my voice and obey."

A chorus of mumbling, interrupted by side conversation, reached a general consensus. One corpse finally shrugged. "Sure."

Mauve stomped her foot. "You've been given an order."

All bodies snapped to attention. Slurred and mumbled voices spoke as one. "Yes, Mistress. Yes, Master."

"See," Mauve shot a snide look at Jedediah. "Presence."

Jedediah's jaw tightened

"Da."

"Right," Jedediah said. "Did someone send you to kill me?"

"Yes," the lead corpse said.

"Why'd you want to kill me?" Jedediah asked.

Several dead snickered. They rolled eyes or jabbed thumbs Jedediah's direction. The lead corpse volunteered as spokescorpse. "Money."

"No other reason?" Jedediah asked.

"Nope," it said.

"Who hired you?" Lanea asked.

"None of your business," it said.

Jedediah glared. "Answer her questions as if mine."

"Muler," it replied.

"Why does this Muler want me dead?"

"The Board wants you removed," it said. "Muler wants to be promoted within the Namhaid. He opted for a quick kill."

"As opposed to?" Lanea asked.

The dead discussed this question. After a few minutes, their spokescorpse said, "Subtlety."

"What is the Namhaid?" Jedediah asked.

"Mercenaries mostly," it said.

"Who is Muler?" Jedediah asked. "Is Muler a codename?"

It shrugged. "Muler is Muler."

Jedediah glanced at Mauve. She busied herself filing her nails.

"Is Muler dead?" Jedediah asked.

"No."

"He the one driving?"

"Yes."

"How do I find him?"

"Place a kill order? We have a website."

Jedediah blinked.

Lanea chuckled.

Wizard or linguist Jedediah might be, but technologically Jedediah remained in the Dark Ages.

Jedediah cursed. "Drake's telepathy would be a boon right now. Describe Muler."

Corpses spit teeth and facts at Jedediah.

"Stop," Jedediah pointed at the spokescorpse. "Describe him."

"Average height. Dark brown hair. Caucasian. Nordic ancestry. German accent. Often unshaven. German special forces tattoo on his left shoulder."

Jedediah sighed, stepped forward and touched the spokescorpse's forehead. The clammy skin slid nauseatingly under his fingertips. He pushed his mind forward, mumbling a spell, until his consciousness sank into the rotting quagmire of the corpse's mind. Once severed from a soul's anchor, thought and memory rotted far faster than flesh. Mauve had forced souls back into bodies. Rotting halted, but damage remained.

Jedediah mumbled Muler over and over, trying to sift through erratic memory flashes for enough of an image to serve his need. He moved down the line, finding only squad leaders and a single gunmen cooperating with Muler on a more public reconnaissance mission had met with him face to face.

Jedediah stepped back and wiped his hands with a handkerchief.

"Where does Muler live?" Jedediah asked.

It shrugged. "Hotels mostly. We all stay on the move. Those dumb enough to have an actual home or worse, family, don't survive long."

Jedediah shoved a pinch of shredded mint into his cheek. "I don't know what else to ask. I doubt this Namhaid has a headquarters."

Mauve sighed. "What does the Namhaid do?"

"Weapon sales, criminal enterprise and mercenary contracts," it said.

"What's their interest in Jedediah?" Mauve asked.

Jedediah opened his mouth to object, but she held up a hand forestalling him.

"Destruction of the Shine line," it said.

"I asked that," Jedediah said.

"No," Mauve said. "You asked why Muler wanted you dead."

"They want the whole line dead? Why?" Lanea asked.

"Retribution."

"For what?" Lanea asked.

It shrugged.

Jedediah shook his head. "This isn't going to satisfy Stormfall. She wants blood."

"I'm with her on that," Lanea's expression darkened so far it seemed fitting alongside the dead. She rubbed her chest. "Wait, is the Namhaid responsible for the other shootings and murders plaguing us?"

"Everything but shooting him at the grocery store was part of the plan."

"Do you know the whole plan?" Jedediah asked.

"No, only what's been executed," it said. "Agents in charge of the plan handle the setup, handing out orders to the rest of us just before we act."

Jedediah sighed. "We do it the hard way then."

"Are you done with them?" Mauve asked.

"Yup."

"You sure?" Mauve asked.

"I can't think of any more questions," Jedediah said. "Lanea?"

Lanea shook her head.

"Any of you hydrophobic?" Mauve asked the dead. "No? Good. Walk that way until you reach the river. Swim to the bottom and follow it into the ocean. Once fifteen miles out you're released."

The dead walked out of their lives.

CHAPTER THIRTY-SEVEN

Family

The sound of a car on the gravel drive drew Jedediah's attention. He stepped out of his workshop. A tiny pink sprite rocketed up to him.

"I hear them," Jedediah said.

Her face fell.

Jedediah extracted a box of candy. "All right, but last freebie."

She darted forward, hugged his nose, snatched the candy and sped away.

Billie Jo's minivan rolled into view. His stomach flipped. He glanced down at his paint-splattered jumpsuit, sighed and waited at the porch's foot.

Billie Jo leapt from the driver's seat, embraced Jedediah and kissed him. She leaned back without letting go. "You got her."

"Jordan?" Jedediah asked.

"Angesa picked her up. I overheard something about a situation at the halfway house and her telling Jordan to pack." She frowned. "I'd have called, but...how do you live without a phone?"

"Who'd want to talk to me?"

She rolled her eyes. "Angesa's bringing her over tonight...what're you wearing? You paint?"

"I ain't fast, but I like to keep my hand in."

She frowned at her paint-splotched clothes.

Jedediah offered an apologetic smile. "Buy you a new one?"

His offer made her smile. "You don't have to do that."

"Oh, speaking of which, you headed back up to the renfest?"

"Why would I without a certain peddler there?" she said.

He took her hand and led her into the house, seating her in the den. "Stay here, and close your eyes."

She did.

"Keep your eyes closed now." He levitated a dressmaker's dummy down in front of her. "All right, open them."

She opened her eyes.

The dummy held a single-piece gown with stomacher nearly four centuries old. Delicate whirls of deep blue elaborately patterned its soft blue silk.

Her face exploded with delight then drained of color. "Dear God, Jedediah, that's a *Mantua*—silk rather than satin. Where did you get a copy? There are only a few surviving examples."

"It's not a copy. A lady I knew wore it to the New Year's Eve Ball at White Hall in 1662."

"And how did you get it from her?" Billie Jo asked. "Charm it off of her?"

"Yup."

She leapt toward the gown. He intercepted her before she got paint on it. A queer smile filled her reddening face.

His hands hadn't landed where he'd intended. His ears turned scarlet. He dropped his hands to both sides. "Sorry, I only meant to protect the gown."

She gave him a wry smile. "I don't mind."

"I do."

"You know if I got these clothes into the washer we could probably get the paint off before it's ruined."

"Got a change with you?" Jedediah asked.

She smiled sweetly. "No."

Quick, change the topic. Jedediah turned toward the stair. "I should have a dressing gown that'd fit."

She stopped him. "That's not what I had in mind."

Jedediah met her steamy gaze. "I realize that."

She ran fingers across his chest from paint splotch to paint splotch. She chided him. "Jedediah, we've been dating for months. It's not like we're a couple of virgin kids."

Jedediah took her hands in his. "I realize that, but this isn't the way I want things to happen."

Her frown turned back to a smile. "They won't be here for a while. I haven't since Marcus, and I started birth control shortly after we started dating, so we wouldn't need to worry about protection."

Jedediah's frown grew into a fully-fledged scowl. "Billie Jo. You're a very desirable woman, but we're not married."

"You're *so* old-fashioned," she said. "I love that about you, but really there's no reason we can't—"

He wanted her, he knew he did, but it all happened too fast, too soon. "How is it you believe all magic is witchcraft because the Bible says it, but sex outside marriage isn't a problem?"

She frowned. "Because love is from God. Our bodies are from God. Magic isn't."

"Because God didn't make it?"

"God made everything," Billie Jo said.

"Then how is it evil?"

"Lucifer gives it to his followers to perpetrate evil."

"So God let the devil take *all* the magic?"

She opened her mouth but shut it in a firm line. She pressed up against him, fingers pushing the boundaries of his willpower. "Look, we're alone. There's no need to argue about things outside our life together. Make love to me."

For a moment, he considered it. *It's not right, besides I gave my word.*

"Not unless we're married."

"Why not?"

One answer occurred to him guaranteed to shut her down. "I promised Mason."

An ice water bath couldn't have done better. She folded her arms and almost out-scowled him. Her eyes flashed. He'd been attracted by her inner flame, her strength of spirit, but now it blazed perilous danger. "What *exactly* possessed you to discuss such things with my ten-year-old?"

"He approached me after Jordan said I'd only foster her to get into your panties."

She snarled. "That girl tempts my beliefs about spanking."

"Mason asked to talk man to man. You should be proud."

"And you promised Mason you wouldn't have sex with me?" Her tone rose. "Just who gave you the right to do such a thing?"

"Had to allay his fears."

"By teaching him menfolk make decisions and womenfolk do as their told?"

Jedediah's blood warmed. "I told him nothing of the sort."

"You don't get to treat my wants and desires as if they didn't exist, as if they don't matter...as if *I* don't matter."

"I would never."

Tears lined her cheeks. "That's it, isn't it? I don't matter because you don't want me."

Jedediah reached out to take her hand, but she slapped him away.

"I *do* want you."

"Prove it then."

"No."

"No? That's it, no?"

Jedediah hesitated. *Probably won't be a better opportunity to end this relationship, give her a reason to leave before she truly hurts me.*

He shook his head. "You don't understand. Ma raised me with different beliefs. To me, such an act would be a marriage in itself."

"Bull...spit! You're not much older than I am," she said.

"I'm four hundred years old," Jedediah snapped.

She gaped at him, eyes flashing but nothing to tell him what went on behind her widened eyes.

He lowered his head and whispered. "I'm not ready."

She watched him in silence.

Truth he hadn't fully realized tumbled from him in whispers. "It still hurts. We've got something too valuable to cheapen. I promised Mason not to share relations outside marriage, but the truth is, serious as we've gotten, we're not ready for this. I'm not ready for this."

Tears brimmed from her eyes. She collapsed into his arms. "You're too good for me."

Jedediah shook his head. "That, my love, is merely an illusion."

"You really are a magician."

"Yup."

An approaching vehicle interrupted their embrace. She looked down. "Heavens, I'm such a mess."

He ushered her toward the bathroom. "Go on and clean up a bit. I'll fetch you a shirt and go meet our guests."

Jedediah retrieved a flannel shirt and handed it through the bathroom door. He rushed outside. Angesa Cooper stood beside a white sedan. Jordan pulled a suitcase from the back seat.

"Ms. Cooper," Jedediah inclined his head and lifted a Xerox paper box from the back seat then took the suitcase. He set both on the porch.

"You're not surprised to see us. I called your town house. You didn't answer, so we came out here."

Billie Jo stepped out onto the porch. "That's my fault. I overheard and couldn't keep it to myself."

"Normally we'd wait until the school year ended, but—not disclosing anything inappropriate—it'd be safer for Faye to stay here," Angesa said.

Jedediah studied Jordan. "She's agreed to this?"

"Yes. There's some final paperwork, but otherwise, we're entrusting her care to you until she's placed elsewhere, adopted or she turns eighteen in two years."

"You've my watch and warrant you won't find a better place for her on this earth." The depth of his sincerity drew Jordan's gaze to his. "We're truly blessed to have her join our family."

"We?" Angesa frowned.

"Me and Drake," Jedediah said.

Angesa displayed a form to him upon her clipboard. "I need to confirm she'll reside at this address in town at least weekdays next school year?"

"Yup. Property even sits in her current school's district."

Billie Jo's hand shot to her mouth. She dug out a cell phone and cursed. "Jedediah, I forgot Mason at little league. My blouse is in your washer. Didn't know if you needed other clothes washed and I'd rather not waste water. Please get it washed before that paint dries."

"I'll take care of it. You and Mason will come back for dinner?"

"Laundry's taken care of, Mr. Shine," Lanea appeared from around the house.

"Lanea, take Jordan's bags upstairs, please," Jedediah said.

"Yes, sir," Lanea said.

Jedediah led them into the formal dining room. An exquisite hardwood dining table gleamed beneath a candle chandelier. Ten matching chairs surrounded it, flanked only by twin china cabinets. It all matched cabinets elsewhere in the house.

Jedediah pulled out a chair for Angesa and moved to get Jordan's. She seated herself. Lanea entered with a pitcher of tea.

Angesa cleared her throat. "I've been meaning to ask Mr. Shine, but since you're here, Miss...?" Angesa trailed off, waiting for Lanea to finish.

"Fey," Lanea said. "F. E. Y."

Angesa tittered at Jordan. "No relation I imagine."

"No," Jordan said.

"Our paperwork's geared toward households rather than farms. Do you live here?" Angesa asked.

"No," Lanea said. "Just had a bad breakup, so I'm staying with a friend and her fiancé while I find my own place."

Angesa nodded.

Jedediah excused himself long enough to change. Lanea came and went on farm business, occasionally refilling the pitcher. They finished and cleared away the paperwork.

Lanea returned with a linen tablecloth. "Staying for dinner, Ms. Cooper? Do you like lamb?"

"*You* eat lamb?" Jordan asked. "You're not a vegetarian?"

Lanea laughed. "Lamb is delicious. Why miss out on partaking of all the elements designed by Mother Nature for use in the Circle?"

"You're joining us, Lanea?" Jedediah said.

"Of course, sir."

Lanea set six places. Mason and Billie Jo arrived as she set the last covered dish upon the table. Jedediah pulled out the far end chair for Billie Jo, pushed it in then pulled out Lanea's.

They lingered over dinner in pleasant conversation.

"I don't mean to be rude," Jedediah rose. "But I should see Jordan settled. She needs a good night's sleep for school tomorrow."

Angesa rose. Billie Jo kissed him, and Jedediah carried Mason out. Both cars disappeared down the drive.

Jedediah turned to Jordan. "Let's talk."

"What happened to getting me settled?" she asked.

"Few things need to be settled first," Jedediah said. "Angesa told me you agreed to this, is that so?"

"Yeah," Jordan shrugged. "Lesser evil."

Jedediah frowned. "You're here for two reasons. First, we want you in a good home. Second, you've got to learn magic."

"What if I don't want to learn magic?" Jordan asked.

"You don't have a choice. You've a heap of natural talent, kiddo. You're too dangerous untrained," Jedediah sighed. "If you really can't stand things here, other accommodations can be made, but they'll all include magical training."

"Besides, chores without magic take *forever*," Lanea said. "You're just lucky this isn't a conventional farm."

Jedediah smirked. "State made me your acting Da. I don't expect you'll call me that. Apprentices address their teachers as master, but sir or Mr. Shine will do too."

An incredulous expression filled Jordan's face. "Master?"

"We'll settle the apprenticeship contract later, right now a few warnings," Jedediah said.

He and Lanea covered the various dangers around the farm, the centaur threat, the murders and murder attempts. Jedediah enumerated his expectations for Jordan as foster-daughter, resident, and student.

"Now, I realize we've pushed a lot down your throat in a short while," Jedediah said. "I recall being a teen. Authority figures are the enemy. In your place, I'd be planning rebellion or running."

Jordan watched him.

"You'll be suspicious of what I say, so I've left the nicer parts to Lanea," Jedediah said. "Do what you're told and you'll enjoy many freedoms you've probably never had before."

Jedediah pulled a wallet from his overalls, a chain dangling free from it.

"Shouldn't that be anchored to something?" Jordan asked.

"It is," Jedediah pulled a silver plastic card from his wallet. A Visa hologram reflected from its surface. He handed it to her. "This debit card will take care of your essentials."

Jordan's eyes widened. She turned the card over in her hands. It already had her name on it.

"There's effectively no limit on it, but anything you buy that ain't a living essential comes out of your chore allowance," Jedediah said.

"Which means you work it off," Lanea added. "And he doesn't pay union rates."

"Do you know how to drive?" Jedediah asked.

"Mostly," Jordan said.

Jedediah frowned, putting a pinch of mint in his cheek. "We'll take care of that too. Okay, go ahead and get her settled."

Lanea extended a hand. "Come on. I'll show to your real room."

Jordan refused the hand.

CHAPTER THIRTY-EIGHT

Uncertain Possibilities

They made their way upstairs. Lanea gestured to the right. "That's Da's room. Other side's mine. Yours is the next on the left. Bath's there on the end."

"What did you mean by my *real* room?" Jordan asked.

"You were paying attention." Lanea grinned. "We're going to be thick as thieves as Da would say."

Jordan waited for an answer. Lanea pushed the bedroom door open. A spacious room contained a big four post bed, decked out in an old, age-faded pink quilt and white sheets.

Jordan's nose wrinkled. "He's kidding, right?"

Lanea shot a glance down the hall. "This room belonged to Esme. No one's been in it since, well it's a long story. Go ahead and redecorate, but don't throw anything out."

"Why'd you look down the hall?" Jordan asked.

Lanea lowered her voice. "An accident killed Esme and her mother Jocelynn long before my birth. I'll tell you what I know, but where he can't overhear."

"Why?" Jordan asked.

"He still blames himself for the accident," Lanea said. "You're expected to keep your room tidy, but don't fret too much. Your town bedroom has to stay spotless, but you won't spend much time there anyway."

"My other room?" Jordan asked. "You know, I'm starting to feel like a parrot. Couldn't you just spit it all out at once?"

Lanea laughed. "We're trying not to overload you."

Jordan gestured to the barren room. "You grew up like this?"

"Mostly," Lanea said. "He's strict, but never cruel—not that I don't get my hide tanned now and then."

"He spanks you?" Jordan objected.

Lanea shook her head. "He uses a hickory switch."

"I'd report him to child services," Jordan said. "They'd never stand for that."

Lanea frowned. "He's four centuries old, not one child born after 1960. Regardless, no bureaucrat or new age guru's going to tell him how to raise a child."

"I hate it here already."

Lanea chewed her lip. "He isn't as bad as it sounds. Take that Visa debit card. He knows you'll overspend at first and he'll let that slide."

She lowered her voice.

"Look, Jordan, he's testing you. If you're planning a tantrum, he wants it over with before you get ahold of some magic. He's tough. He expects a lot, but he'll help mold you into the best you, you wish to be."

"Why would he want to help me?" Derisions filled her voice. "I'll figure out what your game is, like I believe this friendly little advice session isn't all a sham."

Lanea's image shimmered a moment, but beneath the calm image, her voice broke slightly. "I'll be down the hall."

Jedediah picked up Jordan from school the next day in the old Charger. He drove them a short distance into a subdivision. She managed to keep up with the turns. She had a knack for finding her way once she'd been somewhere and always seemed to know which way was North. He pulled into the driveway of a blue-grey house.

"We visiting someone?" Jordan asked.

"This is your official residence, keeps you in the same school," Jedediah said. "Obviously, they know you'll spend time out on the farm too."

Decades-old television and furnishings coexisted with modern carpet. Next to the fireplace a yellow-painted spiral stair spun its way up to a princess loft. Jedediah climbed the stair with Jordan in tow.

"This is your room. There is plenty of room here for a bed, desk, whatever. The closet is a bit small, but the clothes you keep here will be mostly for show. You can expand it once you learn the knack."

The room dwarfed any place she'd ever been given. "Do I have to share it?"

"No."

"What about food, a phone, cable, internet?" Jordan asked.

"Phone's already set up. Number's tacked to the cork board near the door. We'll get whatever you need, but you won't have much leisure time until you earn it."

"You always this grumpy?" Jordan asked.

Jedediah chuckled. "Girl, at this moment, I'm about as tickled pink as I get. Time for shopping. You prefer going with me or Lanea?"

"I get a choice?"

"This ain't a prison. We're not exactly family, but we're not enemies either. Ain't seen you drive or you could fly solo."

"Really. You'd let me go on my own?" Jordan asked.

Jedediah cupped her cheek.

She slapped his hand away. "Is that your game, you're some kind of freak?"

Jedediah's hurt expression didn't fool her.

"Just trying to show you some affection, girl," he said. "With what I've seen about foster kids, I don't figure you've had much. I wanted to show you, not just tell you, that we care what happens to you."

"Right, whatever you say, warden," Jordan said.

Jedediah's face reddened. "You're of adult age. You choose how you get treated, adult or child."

She folded her arms and glared. *Does he really think I'm buying this?*

Jedediah descended the stair. He placed keys on a breakfast bar between kitchen and dining room and stomped down the hall. "Lanea will arrive in a few minutes. Enjoy your shopping."

Jordan heard a door open deeper in the house. She followed him, poking her head into the other three bedrooms and the bathrooms.

"Warden?"

No one answered. She checked the front window. The old Charger sat in the drive

Bottomless credit card, a car with keys and no one to stop me? This is some kind of trick.

She'd checked the card out on the school computers. She could pull a lot of cash off of it before they locked it down. A license plate change or two and she could elude chase and make a new life without the government looking over her shoulder.

She scooped up the keys and got into the car. She put the key in the ignition. *Watch, it won't start.*

It roared to life.

Tank's even full, what's his game?

Lanea exited the house and approached the driver's side.

Jordan rolled down the window.

"Waiting for me or running?"

"Where did you come from?" Jordan asked.

"Da asked me to come shopping with you. It took me a minute to dress and get here," she said. "So, running?"

"I knew he wanted me to run," Jordan snapped. "What's the deal? Cops down the block?"

Lanea folded her arms. "Nope."

"Then what's the deal?" Jordan demanded.

Lanea glared. "You hurt him, me too truth be told. If this is how you're going to be, then leave. We won't stop you."

"Thought I couldn't be kicked out."

"We're not getting rid of you, just not stopping you. Make a choice, Jordan. You're the one who'll live with the consequences."

"Thought someone had to teach me."

"He'll put the word out. Someone will find you eventually. He'll probably let you try it solo for about a year, though."

"Then what? Back to Shine Federal Penitentiary?" Jordan asked.

Lanea shook her head. "Just go, Jordan. Have a nice life."

The Charger bolted backward out of the driveway. Jordan watched her.

She proved she's a wizard. So why isn't she doing something?

Jordan stepped down on the accelerator. She made it three blocks, no cops. She pulled onto the highway, no one to stop her. She turned onto the interstate, still no pursuit.

Everyone wanted something. Everyone had an angle. Rich daddies didn't take in orphans. Annie never escaped the gutter.

I'm right. They don't care. They want something. No one cares, ever.

A few showed minor concern. Miss Cooper had been more attentive than any other case worker. She'd offered Jordan a chance to reject Shine. Miss Bartlett put a lot of effort into getting her fostered.

There's no magic. There're no miracles. He just wants into her pants.

Her vision blurred. Tears ran her cheeks. She slammed on the brakes. The Charger fishtailed, but stopped more or less in its lane. Only moderately traveled, the highway served as a huge onramp to bigger and better interstates. She pulled the Charger to the side.

What if I'm wrong? What if hurting them before they hurt me isn't the right choice this time?

A highway patrol car rolled to a stop behind her. The patrolman stayed in the car a moment, probably checking the tag for a stolen vehicle report.

He studied the tire marks on the concrete highway before approaching her window. "Car trouble, miss?"

She looked up at him. "No."

"You all right?" he scanned her tear-streaked face.

"Yes," she sniffed. "Thank you."

He glanced at the tire marks again. "May I see your identification?"

Jordan nodded, took her false ID out of her purse and handed it over. He scanned it a moment, then handed it back.

"You sure you don't need any help?"

Jordan wiped her eyes. "Yeah."

"Parking on the shoulder is only for emergencies," he said. "I'd appreciate it if you moved along."

"Okay, thank you."

He returned to his car and waited for her to move. She started the car and pulled out slowly, unsure where she'd go and even less certain it didn't matter.

CHAPTER THIRTY-NINE

Sights & Sisters

Jordan pulled the Charger up the farm drive. Jedediah and Lanea sat together on the porch talking. They stopped talking to watch her park.

Lanca glowered over a model car in her hands.

Jedediah inclined his head and gave her a smile. "Nice drive?"

Jordan nodded.

He pulled a pocket watch from his overalls. "If you're feeling better, there's still time for shopping."

Jordan, unable to trust her voice, nodded again.

"Me, Lanea, both, neither?"

"Lanea, if she'll go with me."

Lanea glanced down at the model car. "Sure."

Jordan looked at the new model.

Jedediah extended his hand for it. "Well, let's see it."

Lanea handed over a glossy black model of the new Dodge Charger. Jedediah turned it over in his hands, scrutinizing every inch. He handed it back with a nod.

Lanea strolled down the driveway and set it down behind the old Charger. She invoked a spell. The Charger grew to full size.

Jordan couldn't believe her eyes. "It's real?"

Jedediah shrugged, looking pleased with himself, and strolled into the house.

"Yes," Lanea said.

"Are they all real?" Jordan asked. "Even the plane?"

Jedediah exited the house, an assault rifle propped against his shoulder. "Yup. But you keep out of my plane."

He pointed the rifle at the Charger.

Jordan started forward. "No! Not the car!"

Jedediah opened fire. Smoke wafted away on a summoned breeze, revealing the unscratched Charger resting in the driveway.

Jedediah smiled at Lanea. "First rate enchantment. You girls have fun."

Jordan looked at her hands. "Um, so, second-hand store?"

"If you want," Lanea said reluctantly. "Pretty cool retro stuff there, but Da wants us to get essentials. I'm heading for the mall."

Lanea drove. She didn't volunteer much, but she answered Jordan's questions.

After so many years in the foster system as a commodity rather than a person, Jordan knew to remain detached. She didn't know why she gave up her chance to run.

There's just something different here. She frowned at Lanea. *But that means mending fences.*

"I'm sorry," Jordan said.

Lanea pulled into the mall without comment. She maintained a stubborn silence, but her shopping zeal cracked her bristly façade. Lanea transformed into surprisingly good company. They talked about everything: music, computers, movies and boys. The pretty boy remained a sensitive subject, but otherwise, they shared more interests than Jordan would've guessed.

The newest iPod caught Jordan's eye. She tore herself away. Lanea bought it and handed it over.

"But that's not an essential," Jordan said.

"Says you," Lanea replied. "Farmhouse can be pretty boring. Anyway, *I* bought that as a replacement."

Jordan's brows wrinkled. "But you gave it to me."

Lanea winked. "Da can't tell them apart. Don't really want to transfer my music, but you can have my old one if you'd rather."

New cell phones featured next on their shopping agenda. They bought Jordan a top of the line model, and the simplest phone they could find.

"Tell Billie Jo you got it so she can call Da."

Previous foster home shopping focused on second-hand stores, making do with ill-fitting clothes. Bags of every color in the mall spectrum filled the Charger's trunk and back seat.

Jordan lounged, the seat reclined further than the driver's side. They'd gone all out, not bought the minimum model. Music—good music—from Lanea's iPod pushed an incredible sound system.

With Lanea's permissions, Jordan browsed Lanea's song lists. It almost could've been Jordan's list. It included some she'd never heard of and Jordan's favorite underground band, Djinn Storm.

How can this be real?

No matter how many angles she tried, she couldn't make sense of all this. Finally, she opened her mouth.

"I still don't understand why you're both being so nice," Jordan said. "Particularly after earlier."

Lanea shrugged.

"Look at all this stuff, you barely know me."

Lanea sighed. "Being a foster kid can't be easy. Probably like being half-elf in a way. We're letting you get to know us. Maybe you'll return the favor."

"But," Jordan looked back at Mount Shopping.

"Don't worry about the money. Stay or go, we're happy to take care of your needs. It isn't like we can't afford it."

"Because he's a wizard?" Jordan said. "Lead to gold, that sort of thing?"

Lanea smiled. "Sort of."

"Can you turn lead into gold?" Jordan asked.

"Not personally and not lead, but Da can create gold when he's of a mind," Lanea said. "Anyway, he made a fortune as a moonshiner, bootlegging during Prohibition. The long lived have plenty of ways to make money."

"Like?" Jordan asked.

"Da's a pack rat. He takes good care of his things. That old biplane is one of seven genuine working relics—collector would pay a fortune for it."

Jordan thought about it. "So he's got old stuff hidden away like the guy in Highlander."

"Yeah, great movie, too." Lanea beamed. "I know it's late, but would you mind me checking on Drake?"

"Where is he?" Jordan asked.

"Ma's looking after him—attack nearly killed him."

"Attack?"

"Don't worry, you're probably not in any danger." Lanea rubbed her chest. "Unless you disguise yourself as Da."

Lanea turned the Charger onto a northbound highway. They entered a state park after sundown. The locked gates opened at Lanea's command.

"So elves live in a state park?" Jordan said dazedly.

"No, I took you shopping just to chop you up in the woods," Lanea parked, glanced over at Jordan and frowned.

"What?" Jordan asked.

Lanea chewed her lip. "Maybe I'd better warn you. Ma isn't exactly happy with Da at the moment, so you'd best be really polite—quiet's probably best, though you'll have to talk a little. There's going to be glamour too, lots of it. After a while, you get so you can see through it, but you haven't had that kind of time to practice. Just stick with me, okay?"

"Maybe I should wait in the car."

"Nah, don't you trust me?" Lanea asked.

Jordan looked down at her hands. "I want to, but—"

"No problem, stay here. I'll return soon."

Lanea got out and headed for the trees.

Damn it, after what I pulled today I probably owe her a little trust. She jumped out of the car. "Lanea?"

Lanea appeared. "Yes?"

"Wait up," Jordan said.

Lanea beamed and held out a hand.

They ran hand in hand into the trees. They had only gone a few paces when the car alarm went off. Lanea motioned for Jordan to stay and vanished Cheshire style. She reappeared, shrugged and took Jordan's hand once more.

Holding hands felt awkward, Lanea's hand a bit sticky. *Probably just leading me to the path.*

No visible path emerged from the wood.

"I'm transferring sight to you by touch—night vision and clearer sight through glamour."

"What if we get separated?" Jordan asked.

Lanea chewed her lip and scoured the forest floor. A smile lit her face. "You're not afraid of mannequins or puppets or anything like that, right?"

Jordan drew out the word. "No."

Lanea bolted over to a massive tangle of roots and snatched up a twig. She held it out to Jordan by two fingers.

Jesus, it's moving. Jordan looked closer. The tiny wooden creature struggled in Lanea's fingers, trying to sink sharp teeth into her. A rapid clicking escaped it.

Oh, hell no, she's not putting that thing on me.

Jordan stepped backward.

"Hold out your hand," Lanea said.

"And get bitten?"

"Trust me."

Lanea dropped the little thing onto Jordan's palm, it whirled, teeth barred and little twig claws outstretched. Tiny eyes widened in its face. It placed a hand across its chest, bowed to one knee and clicked several times.

"What the frak?" Jordan asked.

"Oakmite," Lanea said. "It's earth Fey."

Jordan's forehead scrunched together. "I'm missing something."

Lanea chuckled. "It takes a lot of explaining, but simply it's on your team."

Jordan frowned at the bowing twig. It clicked at her. She raised a brow.

"Oh, sorry, I'm an idiot." Lanea reddened. She muttered something. A blue shimmering mask exited her face to splash cool and refreshing on Jordan's. "She understands you now."

"Earth sister, may I slaughter this water witch in your name?" the oakmite asked.

Jordan looked at Lanea. "Why did you give me this thing?"

"He'll help you."

"By slaughtering you?" Jordan asked.

Lanea shrugged. "He'll guide you if we get separated."

"Great, I've got Tour Guide Twiggy."

Jordan liked competing in cross country but loved running through actual woods. Most foster jailers hadn't allowed it.

Lanea set a casual pace, running slow enough for conversation, if only in short bursts. A faint silver halo edged the world around Jordan. Animals stepped from cover to watch them pass apparently unafraid of Lanea and by association Jordan. Cool blue colored their auras rather than silver. A doe with a yearling ran with them so close Jordan could've touched them.

They leapt over roots, dodged trees and ran. Lanea glowed, expression and aura.

One more love we share.

Another shape appeared ahead. Violet edged it, so dark it nearly remained invisible—a cat of some sort, a big one. It slid from her vision. Another appeared in a well of shadows farther along their path. Another appeared, then another.

They're pacing us, maybe two of them somehow jumping shadow to shadow?

"What're they?" Jordan asked between breaths.

"Shadowcat," Lanea said. "Won't bother us together."

"If I'm alone?"

"These might not."

"Why?" Jordan asked.

"They're working for the elves—as much as any cat works for anyone."

"If they didn't?"

Lanea's expression spoke volumes.

Check, shadowcats are dangerous.

Their run seemed longer than necessary, especially for a direct route. *How deep in are we going?*

Like a glowing alien ship landing in the movies, a light peaked between trees high and ahead. It grew more beautiful. Even without details, it stole her breath.

She stared, no longer watching her feet. A root caught one foot, sending her tumbling. Her hand slipped from Lanea's, and she plunged into sudden absolute darkness.

"Lanea?" She climbed to her feet, using the tree whose root had ambushed her. She favored her leg. "Lanea? Oakmite?"

Something skittered down her back. Glowing dust sprayed into the air, bringing the world back into view. The oakmite ducked under another mushroom, scooping spoors from under its cap. It raised cupped hands to its mouth and blew another fountain of glowing motes.

They fell onto Lanea. She extended her hand. Jordan took it. Lanea's glow returned, the dazzling city lit behind her.

Jordan reddened. "Scary."

"You okay?" Lanea asked. "We could walk the rest of the way."

"Thanks," Jordan turned to the oakmite. "Thank you, too."

It smiled, bolted too fast to see across the distance separating them and up her clothes to her shoulder.

Lanea led them to the base of the city. A spiral stair wrapped around a massive tree.

Lanea released her hand. "You should be fine now. We're inside the spell. If things get too weird, speak up."

Jordan swallowed. "Weirder than this?"

"Glamour can be taken to extremes. You might encounter literally anything. Speak up, and we'll hold hands again."

"Magic's supposed to be wondrous, not leave me feeling like a frightened three-year-old."

Lanea smiled. "Relax. You've got two of us looking out for you."

"You only need one," the oakmite grumbled. "Still think we should slaughter the witch."

They ascended wooden steps, polished smooth by countless years of feet. Steps and ornate railing flashed silver in torchlight. Vine roses wound around the railing, heavenly fragrance drifting from their full blooms.

They climbed past several elves. Each greeted Lanea and then Jordan. Gorgeous elven men left her desperate for makeup, a hairbrush and a mirror. The need disintegrated with a young elven woman. Cold inadequacy filled Jordan. She'd felt homely compared to Lanea's exotic beauty, but Lanea couldn't compete with the homeliest elf girl.

Wonder if they make her feel ugly too.

As if in her thoughts, Lanea whispered, "Don't let it bother you. Rotten fish wrapped in gold still isn't fit for dinner."

Jordan tried but didn't succeed feeling at less self-conscious.

Lanea stepped through an ivy arch atop the stair. White lilies laced trough it glowed silver. She followed, glancing up to see white petals shimmer.

A corner of Lanea's mouth twitched up. She shook her head. "Da and his riddles. He said 'Faye' fit you."

Jordan frowned. *What is it with everyone and that stupid name?*

Lanea led her deeper. Jordan tried not to gawk at the unbelievable city like a yokel. She failed. Grown more than crafted, the city contained no metal except glowing bits of silver.

Wonderful, maybe the most fantastic place on the planet.

A tall, imposing woman in a cerulean gown blocked their path. Terrible, glowing beauty scowled down at Jordan with overwhelming disapproval. Her lips parted, revealing pointed, blood-coated teeth. Terror hit Jordan.

I'm dead. She's going to suck away my blood and complain about the taste. Jordan whimpered.

"Mother!" Lanea snatched up Jordan's hand.

The elf woman remained frightening and beautiful. White even teeth replaced the other, and her height dwindled beneath Jordan's. Her forbidding expression

212 | MICHAEL J. ALLEN

still managed to look down upon Jordan, but in an unpleasable fairytale stepmother way.

Jordan's terror eased but didn't abate.

"Ma," Lanea said. "This is my friend, Jordan."

"The street flotsam your father succored to seduce the mortal?" Lirelaeli regarded Jordan like a plague-infested rat.

Malice and mischief played across Lanea's face. She raised her voice so others around overheard. "Mother, I'm ashamed of you."

Lirelaeli darkened. "How dare you speak to me like that, child?"

"How dare you scorn the rules of hospitality allotted kin?"

Eyes everywhere turned their direction.

Now Lirelaeli's voice dripped venom. "She's no kin to me."

Jordan shrank, voice tiny. "Lanea, please, you don't have to—"

Lirelaeli's furious expression stole the words from her throat.

"How dare you attack another elf with glamour, Mother?"

Lirelaeli opened her mouth. She narrowed her gaze. "There's no elf blood apparent in this normal."

Lanea smiled. "The guardian vines don't agree."

Lirelaeli marched them back to the entrance and demanded Jordan pass beneath the arch. It shimmered. Disapproving expressions settled on Lirelaeli.

I don't know what Lanea's game is, but publically humiliating this woman can't be a good idea.

Lirelaeli assessed the disapproving crowd. She bowed. "Forgive me, cousin, my intolerable rudeness cannot be forgiven. I must make amends."

Lirelaeli produced a long thin dagger from her bodice. "With this token, I pledge unto you the protection of my household, my house is your house, kindred."

Jordan turned the dagger over in her hands.

"Now we're sisters." Lanea embraced her.

What the hell?

They reached Drake's bedside before she's dealt with the whirlwind of sights and experiences. Drake curled upon an acorn-shaped bed, surrounded by elves on three sides. His head lay on a down pillow, surrounded by oak-cradled Fey-silk.

The elves seemed oblivious to their entrance.

"Healer's trance," Lanea explained.

Drake's eye opened at Lanea's voice. Jordan shied away, but Lanea rushed to his side and touched his beak. Expressions passed over their faces, but neither said a word. After a few minutes, Lanea remembered her.

"Come here," Lanea said. "He's hurt, so be gentle, but touch him anywhere."

Jordan reached out hesitantly and placed a fingertip on the end of Drake's tail. His and Lanea's thoughts filled her head.

<*Good to see you again, Jordan.*> The voice in her thoughts had to be Drake. Masculine and deep, it still reminded her of how Mason spoke.

<*Yeah, he's a lot like a little brother.*> Lanea thought. <*But better.*>

"This is unreal," Jordan said.

<*Don't speak. Just think.*> Lanea thought.

"How do I hear your thoughts too?" Jordan hurriedly focused on thinking. *Oh, sorry.*

<*Simpler to let us hear each other than separate us.*> Lanea said. <*He's still weak.*>

<*I understand, Jordan.*> Drake thought. <*Hard for me to speak and not think.*>

Lanea frowned. <*We shouldn't keep him up. I just wanted to check on his progress and introduce you to the little pest properly.*>

Drake seemed to think a smile her direction.

Jordan smiled back. "Get better, I've got a thousand questions."

Lirelaeli drew Lanea away. Jordan rose, but Lanea waved her off. She glanced at Drake. He strained. His tail flopped over against her side.

<*I've better hearing.*> Drake thought.

Jordan heard them arguing through Drake.

"You tricked me, humiliated me before the others."

"Serves you right, Ma," Lanea said. "Treating her poorly because you're jealous. She isn't even related to Billie Jo."

"I am *not* jealous of a *mortal* woman."

"You're a rotten liar, Ma. You breached hospitality law, and you made your bed with Da too."

"You're a horrible child," Lirelaeli said.

A flippant tone struck from Lanea's tongue. "Wonder where I learned that?" Lanea stormed back into the room.

"Come on, Jordan." She stopped in the doorway and crossed to stroke Drake's frills. "Get better soon? Or learn to project thought to us at the farm so we needn't worry."

Drake responded with a thought that Jordan translated into a probable laugh. <*I have to be able to see you.*>

"Try the visualization techniques Da taught you for mist mirrors," Lanea said. "I'd rather not have to visit you here."

An elven healer corrected Jordan's leg. They wasted no time getting home.

CHAPTER FORTY

Danger at the Walls

Marc O'Steele climbed the long stairway entrance to the Chattanooga Aquarium. His sports coat, shirt and slacks didn't quite stand out amongst the thronging tourists.

The man standing by the shark petting pools did.

Tall and fit, he dressed in a charcoal pinstripe suit far too good for an aquarium. The red of his dress shirt nearly glowed on either side of a thin black tie. Dark red shoulder-length hair complimented the flame of his shirt. Silver threaded his wavy locks.

Zero.

Marc approached cautiously, checking the crowd for telltales of surveillance or trouble. Zero watched young sharks entertain school children.

He didn't look up. "Marc."

"Sir, would you mind identifying yourself?" Marc asked.

"You tell me who I am."

"No. You could merely assume that identity," Marc said.

Zero studied Marc with a blue-eyed gaze through oval wire-rimmed spectacles. Zero's eyes dropped slightly in their corners, adding a sorrowful aspect to his expression. He smiled. "Splendid. The Board values caution in its lieutenants. I'm Zero."

"What can I do for you, sir?"

"Explain to me why Shine isn't incarcerated and on his way to prison?"

"Our deputy says the Sheriff keeps clearing Shine. Nothing's sticking. An unfortunate incident brought Shine to the attention of Atlanta law enforcement."

"Muler's assault," Zero said. "Were you cognizant of this attack?"

"No. He did not include me in his idiocy."

"It aroused Shine's awareness. That is dangerous."

"I put things on hold with the Board's approval, hoping he'll relax. What else would you have me do?"

"Yes, a good move but one that complicates the hotel setup." Zero removed a sealed envelope from within his jacket and handed it to Marc. "This details locations spanning multiple states where bodies are buried on Shine's lands. Have

Two report the hotel deaths as soon as news of these breaks. Federal law enforcement will assume the investigation."

Marc nodded.

"Before that bring Shine and the sheriff to legal odds once more," Zero said.

"To what end?"

"Joe Franklin's been a nuisance. His death will not only lay heavy on Shine, but it'll also lay at his feet."

"Muler?"

Zero scowled. "Employ him a bit more before we end him. He won't attack Shine directly again."

Sweeping wind broken by a leather wing flap reached his ears. He sighed, set his palette down before the portrait in progress, and exited his workshop. He shoved mint into his cheek and folded his arms.

Stormfall landed gracefully, leaving huge talon marks gouging the earth.

"As if I'm not fending off enough mortal questions," he grumbled.

<I command a report.>

"Drake rallies. I'm using what we gleaned from the dead to prepare a tracking spell focused on the attack's leader," Jedediah said.

Her tail whipped forward over his head. It struck his back, knocking him between her front talons. She planted one upon his back.

Her presence bulled into his thoughts. Her mind ransacked his memories, taking no care to be gentle.

The unexpected assault left Jedediah scrambling for his defenses. Memories seared his mind in lightning fast flashes.

He marshaled his will, struggling but succeeding to erect barriers ahead of her mental rampage. *Get out.*

Stormfall ignored him.

Get. Out.

Wind exploded beneath her wings, forcing her off of him. He lashed out with his thoughts. Stormfall's head snapped backward by the force of his mental ejection. She pushed at his mind, but he ignored the pain and refused her.

He spoke through gritted teeth. "You've no right—none. I pay my debts, but I don't belong to you."

Stormfall raised a talon.

"Do it," Jedediah spat. "Attack me. You'd better kill me outright or what's left of you can raise your son because I warrant no other wizard will."

Her lip curled, displaying gargantuan teeth. Her mind pummeled at his.

"Speak. You'll not gain free access to my mind again today, but if you want Drake's attackers found, you'll give me space to do it."

Stormfall roared.

"Throw down or be gone," Jedediah said.

Fire shot from her maw onto the farmhouse. Intense heat singed his arms and eyebrows before his defensive barrier rose. She leapt to wing without a backward glance, unaware her petty attack hadn't even cracked the farmhouse's paint.

He watched her climb but didn't lower his guard. The threat that he held her Name prevented his death almost as much as her vanity and laziness. Raising a dragonling threatening her leisure, but worse he'd threatened her precious status too. If he forced her to personally raise Drake, she'd be the laughingstock of her peers.

Status trumped all, for now.

He returned to his painting.

A taxi dropped Jordan off at the farmhouse angry enough to tear down brick walls with her bare hands.

Trouble started when Ms. Bartlett treated her differently in chemistry. By lunch time the school knew she lived with her teacher's boyfriend. They broke into her locker, stole her gym clothes, and filled it with cutout hearts and lips.

She confronted Sandy Topp about it. The argument devolved into shoving. In the midst of it, Sandy's blouse strings came undone.

"You yanked the strings," Sandy said.

"I did not."

The argument escalated to blows.

Jordan rubbed sore knuckles. Sandy sucker punched Jordan. She threw a right, but a teacher's yell distracted her enough for Sandy to dodge. Her fist hit the lockers. She'd been dragged to the principal's office. The principal called Angesa instead of Jedediah. She headed off Jordan's expulsion then dropped Jordan off at the Weems house.

"You tell Mr. Shine he's to meet with me and Principal Jacobson tomorrow."

Jordan paid the cabbie and stormed into the West greenhouse. The fairy's cage gaped empty. A gorgon vine slid up her shoulder. She slapped it away, but a barb caught and ripped her new denim jacket.

She stormed out, slamming the greenhouse door.

A long chore list hung from her bedroom door. She ripped it down before slamming the door shut. She snatched up her iPod off the charger and thrust earbuds into place. She touched the screen.

Nothing happened.

She tried it again—still nothing.

A quick check found the charger's plug kicked loose from the wall.

She screamed.

She didn't care if she brought half the household running. Farm living offered possibly only one benefit, far off neighbors that never complained of noise. Heat filled her chest. She needed to release her pent anger before she exploded.

I need to run.

The elf park sat on the far side of Columbus. Make out spots and drug markets dominated the closer parks.

The elf park felt safe. I'll take the Charger.

Jedediah and his truck were nowhere to be seen. The old Charger rested on the study shelf under plastic.

Fine, I'm stuck here, but here has plenty of wild lands. He's already going to be pissed, might as well add undone chores to the list.

Jordan changed clothes and jogged out the back door into the boneyard. Machinery scents gave way to woodland. A breeze built against her face. Fey filled the woods ahead. Lanea warned some of the wilder ones might be dangerous until they knew her.

Doesn't matter. I can handle myself.

Every footfall chipped at her anger. The rhythmic motion of each stride— broken occasionally by necessary accommodation to the rough terrain—made music all its own. Trees stood sentinel around her. Brush grabbed at her. Fallen branches and rocks blocked her way. None of them could stop her.

I'm free.

On the run, she became only Jordan. Only she and the run mattered. No one held her back. No one failed her. No one to abandon her. She pushed herself. Rhythm mattered, not speed.

She broke out of the woods onto gently rolling grassland. No crops filled the open fields.

I'm probably off his property now. It's just me and nature...and a centaur. Jordan stopped short. *I know only grass lay that direction a moment ago.*

A centaur watched her in profile. Tan sorrel for a lower half, a bare, muscular torso of all maleness stole her breath.

He turned fully toward her.

She cringed.

Half his body had been melted, deformed into horrifying dark ridges. They twisted his smile into something menacing. He reached up.

Sorry bud, flipping your long sandy locks isn't going to make me forget the ick.

He lazily pulled an arrow from a quiver peaking over his shoulder.

Jordan put up her hands. "Whoa, I'm sorry I flinched."

SinDon fit the arrow to his bowstring. "Last thing you'll do, wizardling."

"I'm not a wizard," Jordan snapped reflexively.

He raised his head, scenting the air. "I know wizard blood when I smell it."

The escaped fairy darted between Jordan and SinDon—still dressed in its bottle-cap samurai armor. It held Excalibur letter openers in each hand.

"Get back, my dame." The fairy ordered in a thick New Jersey accent.

The fairy charged the centaur, swords a blur. The centaur slapped him contemptuously from the air. SinDon raised his massive hoof to stomp it.

"No!" Jordan cried.

The hoof came down, deflected by an energy barrier. SinDon cursed.

The fairy rose drunkenly from the ground, doing a much more creative job of cursing. "I'll chop ya into glue-chunks for that, ya old mule."

The fairy's charge ended the same as his first.

"Leave him alone," Jordan rushed forward between fairy and centaur, close enough to smell a mixture of sweat and horse.

The centaur's mouth twisted. He raised the bow. "Stand still, two-legger, I'll send you both on with a single shaft."

The fairy launched itself against her, pushing against totally inappropriate places. "Run, my dame. Save yourself."

She slapped his hands away, sending him into a spin. "Watch the hands."

"Yes, run, wizardling," SinDon said. "Attempt to outrun death on the wing."

What do I do? Fairy's been more trouble than I deserve, but I can't just run away and let it die.

The fairy sped past her. "Run, my dame."

Jordan ran.

The centaur bellowed.

Glowing ripples faded where his arrow impacted against the barrier. "VelSera be damned, I'll have my revenge, and I'll have it now."

He slammed his body into the barrier, trying to muscle his way through. Light built up around him.

My god, he's pushing through.

The energy hit critical mass and catapulted the centaur backward end over end.

"Serves you right, you old nag. Hope you broke a forelock!"

Jordan ran toward the farm, turned about and desperate to find Jedediah or Lanea. She spotted cultivated fields at twilight. She sprinted to the farmhouse to find the drive still empty.

She put her hands behind her head and walked around, catching her breath.

The fairy bobbed around her. "You're all right, my dame?"

"Why do you keep calling me that?" Jordan asked.

"You rather I call you my broad?"

"Go away," Jordan said. "Unless you can find Lanea or Jedediah for me."

"Leave it to ol'Paulie. I'll find yer pops." He sped away.

"Fine. Good. Thanks."

CHAPTER FORTY-ONE

Farming by Moonlight

A flatbed semi-truck arrived at the farm late Saturday morning loaded with seed bags. The driver and his two passengers were handsome, strong and probably weren't drinking age. Jedediah showed Jordan where to stack each type of seed. Organization in place, he bent back and carried sacks to match what they hauled combined.

Does he typically help, or only to keep handsome deliverymen from us?

"Don't farmers keep seeds from the previous season's crops?" Jordan said.

Jedediah wiped sweat from his brow. "Mauve mentioned a few impending shortages—drought, famine, that sort of thing. I ordered to suit."

Jedediah retreated into the house before unloading finished. He reappeared with a washtub of iced beer.

Deliverymen attentions rose like bloodhound snouts.

"You boys heading right off?" he asked. "We're having ourselves a drink then moving the sacks out to the fields."

"We're in no hurry, Mr. Shine," their driver said.

"I'd offer you and your boys a drink, Jeffrey, but Joe Franklin would have my hide if you went driving right after," Jedediah said.

Jeffrey eyed his companions. "If we haven't outstayed our welcome, we sure could go for a drink—in exchange for helping the ladies move seed out to the fields."

"Mighty neighborly of you," Jedediah said. "If you helped my girls, the least I can do is provide a drink or two. Got some leftover burgers in the kitchen too. You hungry?"

"Sure, we could eat." Jeffrey passed beer around.

Jedediah disappeared into the house.

Jordan glanced Lanea.

The half-elf shrugged, head to one side and eyes narrowed at the washtub.

Jordan approached the washtub with motions sure to gain deliveryman attention. She smiled at Jeffrey and reached for a beer. Something cracked against the back of her hand.

Jesus, Catholic school all over.

219

Jedediah appeared with a tray of burgers. He kept his attention on the deliverymen, but her stinging hand suggested he knew she'd try.

Jordan found Lanea struggling not to laugh.

"Something going on, girls?"

"No, Da. Something just struck me funny."

"No showing off in front of the boys now," he said.

He exchanged a few significant looks with the three deliverymen.

Great, beer and burgers are fine. She glared at Jedediah. *But he's removed dating from the menu.*

Food and drink disappeared. The sacks found their way to the fields and deliverymen departed down the gravel road.

Jordan cornered Lanea "What the frak just happened?"

"Frak?"

"Fake f-word. What did you find so gorram funny?"

"Da bespelled the washtub so we couldn't take a beer. Took me a moment to figure out the spell."

"Yet, you didn't warn me."

Lanea smirked. "You moved too fast."

"No way those guys are old enough to drink either," Jordan said.

Lanea held up four fingers. "Four centuries old, remember? Let's just say double standards die hard."

Jordan wanted to kick something. "You put up with this?"

"He's strict, but a good Da."

"Fine, so what now? Plow? Tractor?" Jordan asked.

"Nah, farm machinery's just for show."

Color drained from Jordan's face. "Please tell me we're not planting by hand."

Lanea let the question linger until she couldn't restrain her smile. "Yes and no."

Lanea headed into the house. "Come on, nap time. Billie Jo and Mason are coming up for supper. It's going to be a long night."

Jordan tried to nap, but sleep just wouldn't come. She laid atop her new black comforter in silence. When silence overwhelmed her, she shoved headphones in and listened to music.

She didn't hear Jedediah knock.

A globe of light appeared above the bed. She bolted upright and ripped out the ear buds. The floating ball rang like an old fashioned alarm clock.

"Yes?" Jordan said.

"Can I come in?"

A parent that doesn't just barge in? That's a first. "Come in. I'm dressed."

Jedediah stepped inside, hat in his hands and mint bulging his cheek. He scanned the now prevalent acid green and black décor. Posters proven to induce apoplexy in foster parents covered the walls.

He nodded once. "Djinn Storm, nice boys. Couldn't sleep?"

Jordan shook her head.

"How're things going otherwise?" he asked.

"What do you mean? You pissed about what happened at school?"

"Nothing wrong with standing up for yourself," Jedediah said. "New house. New family. Centaur attacks. Magic. You've had a lot thrown at you. How're you handling it all?"

Jordan considered and rejected a snarky remark. "I guess I'm okay."

"I know you didn't believe anything I said that first night, but I do care. I'm here if you want to talk."

Jordan looked at her fingers. "Thanks."

Jedediah rose and put his hat back on. "Up for a little more weirdness?"

Jordan gave him a crooked grin. "Weirdness is my life."

Jedediah led Jordan into the West greenhouse—the one he'd warned her to avoid.

"Keep back from the gorgon vines there, and don't walk under the weretree." He addressed the bizarre-looking plants. "You behave yourselves now."

"I've been in here before."

"Well, we've got something new in here."

The plants watched them pass. One of them inclined its buds at her. A pig pen took up a greenhouse corner. Mounds of mud filled it.

A mound moved.

Jordan looked closer. All but the biggest pile moved. She squinted, tilting her head to one side.

Sow and piglets?

Jedediah motioned for Jordan to follow him over the fence. He crouched, reached down and tugged gently on a stubby tail.

That's not a pig tail.

The tail's owner padded over to him, tail wagging.

"These are mudpuppies. Go ahead, let it sniff you."

A puppy of living mud licked her hand. It stood on its hind legs, trying to lick her face.

Jedediah smiled. "Figured they'd like you."

"What are mudpuppies? They're not real dogs are they?"

Jedediah smiled approvingly. "Nope. Earth elemental spirits. I've known Sarah there for years. She came by to whelp this litter a week and a half ago—probably because of you."

"What do you mean?" Jordan asked.

"Could be a new danger around her den, but I think your magic called her."

The pup chewed Jordan's fingers. Another joined it, turning her hand into the object of tug of war.

Jedediah chuckled.

"I don't know what to believe anymore."

He nodded. "I figured. Let's test your magic. You're a runner, right?"

Jordan narrowed her eyes. "Someone tell you that?"

"Nah, most Terra's like running. Can't say why," Jedediah pointed into a corner of the pen. "You see that area there?"

"You mean where the mud's all kind of lumpy?" she asked.

"That's where the pups are doing their business. Left untended, it'll be a real mess. Clean it up."

Disgust wrinkled her nose.

"*Girls.*" Jedediah rolled his eyes. "Use magic not your hands. Churn the mud, fresh mud to the surface and waste underneath."

"How?" she asked.

"Well, that's a rock and a hard place. First, you've got to find the source. You can use your own energy of course, but it's dangerous until you know what you're doing."

"Lanea described it like tuning a radio."

"Yup, imagine there is a harmonic to it. Aquamancers are good with sound waves. For a terra, though, not sure how you'd tune in. Magic's very personal. I could tell you how I do it, but odds are even my way wouldn't work for you. Chose this because it's easy, and other than making a mess of yourself, there's no damage you can do."

"I don't know where to start."

"Start with running. There's a place you go when you dig out a last burst of speed. Reach in there and will the mud to churn."

"You're not staying?"

"Heck no. I'm wise enough not to stay in muck range of your first experiments. Besides, you don't need stage fright gumming up the works. Get me when you're done."

Jedediah left.

Bored with chewing on fingers not fighting back, the mudpuppies returned to eating or curled up to sleep. Jordan examined the lumpy corner.

She felt stupid. This whole thing felt stupid. *How am I supposed to make mud move by thinking at it?*

She knew the place Jedediah meant. She dug deep as if about to sprint and glared at the mud.

Nothing happened.

She tried again. Each failure grew her frustration. She glared. "Churn gorram you."

One of the mudpuppies, the first one she'd met looked at her. It shambled over to her target spot and started digging.

Great, it's adding more crap I can't move. Stupidity reddened her cheeks. *Cats bury scat, not dogs.*

Other pups joined the first, digging in the corner.

"No. You'll get filthy."

She rolled her eyes. *How stupid am I, they're made of filth.*

The puppies stopped, staring at her.

She gaped. *Did they just obey me?*

"Go over there with your mom, okay?"

They did.

"Sit."

They did.

No way. They're too young to be obedience trained. How do I test this? An idea hit her. "You three go there, you two here and you right there."

They did.

"Okay, I can talk to mud. This isn't weird."

The mudpuppies blinked up at her.

"Oh, um, you're free to whatever."

Three of them started wrestling. The pup sitting by itself shambled over and asked to be petted. The remaining pair curled up together in the corner. She petted the one and shooed him toward his mother. She leaned closer to the mess and thought at the mud as hard as she could.

"Take off your shoes," Lanea said.

Jordan whipped around.

"Trust me," Lanea said.

Jordan slipped out of her shoes, putting her feet down in the mud. It squished between her toes, feeling oddly good. She's always liked going barefoot. *Is that because I'm a terramancer?*

She pulled from the inner point and glared at the mud.

It bubbled.

She pulled harder, feeling at once full and ravenous.

The mud rippled.

Giggles bubbled from her.

It's moving!

Mud turned itself over like a spoon folding whipped cream into eggnog.

She glanced up at Lanea. "Why?"

Lanea's eyes rose, as if searching for something inside her head. "Earth's kind of touch oriented. It likes to be connected. Da would say that's what makes bricks or adobe so strong. The earth wants to be together."

"Do I have to go barefoot all the time?"

"Maybe at first, or use your fingers," Lanea said. "Think pup training is neat? Try pottery or sculpture."

Jordan's dinner proved excellent if a little uncomfortable. Billie Jo watched her intently.

"Wuh?" Jordan asked through stuffed cheeks.

Billie Jo tittered. "Probably a growth spurt."

Jedediah pushed a bowl of greens toward Jordan. "A good day's work."

Mason appeared with Jedediah's Risk game. "Can we play?"

Jedediah took it from him gingerly. "Next time, Mason, but not with this old copy."

Bit over protective?

The Bartlett minivan disappeared down the drive.

Jedediah clapped his hands and rubbed them together. "All right, let's be about it."

"We're planting now?" Jordan checked her phone. "It's almost midnight."

The other two smiled at her.

"Come on, isn't it like three months too late for planting season?" Jordan asked.

Jedediah chuckled. "Nothing wrong between your ears. We're not a conventional farm, so we don't have to plant so early."

"Why farm at all? Aren't you rich?" Jordan asked.

"It's honest, and I enjoy doing it, even if we shortcut a thing or two," Jedediah said. "Then there's the revenuers. They're mighty suspicious of folks with lots of money but no obvious source."

"He means IRS, right, Lanea?"

"IRS, DEA, pretty much any three letters you can cram together," Lanea said.

Jedediah led them to the closest field. "Lanea, would you please?"

Lanea turned on a spicket with an old hose connected. She raised the hose to her lips.

"Don't drink out of that," Jordan said.

Lanea looked up. "Why not?"

"Drinking out of hoses isn't healthy, there've been studies," Jordan said.

Jedediah snorted. "Nonsense people believe these days."

Lanea sipped, smiled and took a deep breath. She blew into the stream. Water fanned out into the air, twisting and turning but not falling. A musical symphony rose from the water, liquid harp strings stroked by Lanea's breath. Flutes and horns came next followed by more string instruments—all from the water Lanea blew into as if an instrument.

Then it hit Jordan. *Aquamancer. Water is Lanea's instrument.*

Jedediah glowed with pride. Scores of tiny lights around him helped with the glowing part. Fairies joined the pixies, listening to Lanea's performance.

Other than the oakmite, she'd never seen one of the tiny Fey—not for real. She stared at the nearest fairy. It stuck a tongue out at her.

Jedediah chuckled. "It's not polite to stare."

Jordan stuck her tongue out at him.

Sarah and her litter appeared around Jordan's legs. More adult mudpuppies appearing every moment. They congregated around Jordan like pixies and fairies swarming Jedediah.

A small knot of women approached along the path. All sultry curves and smooth bark, they made Jordan feel ugly. Mosses of different colors and types served as scanty clothing or hung from their heads in various hairstyles. Living wood challenged elven beauty.

Ianyss regarded Jordan. "Greeting, Jordan. I am Ianyss, and these are my sisters. Your presence gladdens us."

"Why?" Jordan asked.

Ianyss gestured first to Jedediah then to Lanea. "Lightning strikes down our trees and brings fire. Floods wash the nutrients from our roots, but earth loves and sustains us. We take joy and strength from both it and you."

Jedediah glared at Ianyss.

What's between those two?

"That's enough, girl."

Lanea took in a long breath. Her water instrument splashed to the ground.

Ianyss bowed before Jedediah. "We come to honor our bargain, deserving or not, whichever you be."

Jedediah glowered. "Look, Ianyss, I apologized already. I did what I had to in order to save Drake."

"Behave, Da, so Jordan can see how we work *together*."

Jedediah bowed his head. "We thank the Fey for their generous aid which they exchange for protection from the normals."

"Da."

"Thank you," Jedediah said.

Lanea sidled closer to Jordan. "We wanted you introduced to the Fey this way rather a tour through their communities. This way's supposed to help you understand how all things tie together, why we have all this land, why your magical studies are so important. Without us to protect them from humanity, all of these Fey might die.

"Guardians have held such preserves in trust for centuries. The struggle to protect them against human expansion has always been hard, but it's worsened every year since the industrial revolution. Few understand the whole nature of the symbiosis between the assorted Fey and the Earth, but the Guardians know enough to understand the danger to us all if even one Fey species went extinct."

"Why not tell everyone? It's not the middle ages anymore. Surely, the world's populace could help," Jordan said.

"If humanity knew about the Fey, they'd become a new resource to exploit, nothing more," Lanea said. "The Fey know humans would exploit them, that's why we have the problem with the centaurs. They assume Da's enslaving or exploiting them by not letting them roam free outside the protected borders."

"So he does all this to protect them, and they hate him for it," Jordan said absently.

Jedediah stepped up behind them. "Kind of like raising a teenager."

Jordan would remember what followed for the rest of her life. No fairytale motion picture could've dreamed of such beauty in motion. Jedediah produced a fiddle from midair. His foot tapped three times, and his bow flew into "The Devil Went Down to Georgia."

Work began.

Full grown mudpuppies dove into the field. They swam downfield in parallel like a pod of dolphins bobbing in and out of the earth. They left neat furrows in their wake. The pups tried to help. Sarah pulled them from the field, set them at Jordan's feet and with one look charged Jordan with their care.

Jedediah released his fiddle, sawing fast-paced country-rock midair. The foot tapping music seemed custom made for the work at hand. Brownies scampered down rows, rolling rocks away in some kind of race. Fairies dusted the rows with fairy dust and delivered seeds, lining the night with sparkling colors. Pixies hopped after them in threes. Their peculiar game of leap frog involved driving a seed into the ground with both feet.

A fine mist followed the pixies downfield, dampening rows.

The fiddle changed tunes.

Dryads danced like ballerinas down the rows. Plants sprouted from the ground mere seconds after they passed.

The ensemble moved to the second field before Jordan knew it. She kept pups from underfoot and watched.

"Da," Lanea said.

Amazing how many things she can say with one word.

He snatched a fairy out from the air by one wing. He scooped seeds from the soil and held them before its nose. "What is this?"

The blushing fairy shrugged.

"Uh huh," Jedediah said. "Get those elderberry seeds out of the ground and plant what I gave you."

Field after field, the Fey plowed, seeded and sprouted the crops. Modern machinery made the task possible in mere days. Magic completed it before the moon ducked her head over the horizon. Hundreds of acres planted, sowed with multiple crops, and sprouted all by the light of a single moon.

CHAPTER FORTY-TWO

Jeopardized Harmony

Jedediah's blue pickup—a blue twin to the one Muler destroyed—crept up to the farmhouse. A levitation spell suspended a mattress in its bed, ropes tying it to four corners. An invisibility spell concealed the dragon laying with his face leaned into the wind and tongue lolling.

Jordan waited on the porch railing. Lanea rocked Jedediah's rocker. They leapt up simultaneously.

Jedediah laughed. *Took fifty years, but Lanea's surly twin has finally arrived.*

They rushed the truck as it rolled to a stop, loosening ropes to extract the mattress. Drake rolled his eyes, gathered himself on the ever-shifting mattress and leapt to the ground.

Girlish delight braced Jedediah's glower. "Healers told you to take it slow. You'll exercise each day, eat healthy—no magic, no junk food, including Cherry Coke."

Drake groaned.

Jedediah gestured to a newly erected paddock filled with fluffy white lambs. "We've got you some sheep for a bland diet."

"He's going to *eat* those lambs?" Jordan said.

"Yup. Nice, tender meal sized for Drake to gnaw on, but don't you worry, you'll get your fill too."

"They're babies," Jordan said.

Jedediah smirked. "Hence tender."

Lanea placed a hand on Jordan's arm. "You're not going to win this one."

Jordan glared and stomped over to the penned lambs.

"Da."

"No lectures. It's best for Drake. When've you known me to be cruel?"

Lanea opened her mouth.

"Outside when it's deserved."

Lanea smiled.

Jedediah lowered his voice. "How's she doing else wise?"

"Slow, stubborn, suspicious, guess that's why you started my lessons so young."

"Makes for a lot of changes in how she thinks about things. Work with her more. You're more like to explain things at her level."

An ancient telephone bell erupted from his pocket. He dug the cell phone from his overalls. He flipped open the cell phone enlarged to payphone size, eyes twinkling.

"Tell Billie Jo I said hi," Lanea said.

Jedediah nodded and strolled over to his rocker. Drake slipped off somewhere, uninterested in the lambs. Lanea followed Jordan.

Jordan climbed into the pen, hand feeding lambs. Lamb tongues tickled her to laughter.

"Not quite the same girl I met."

Jordan flashed her a guilty expression. "Sorry about that."

Lanea climbed onto the rail. "Want to catch a movie or something tonight?"

"He wants me to practice. Figure I'll run to focus my mind first. You're welcome to come."

"No, I'd distract you."

Jedediah leaned over the porch rail, phone to one ear and a smirk on his lips. "Hey, stop playing with your dinner."

An explosion rocked the house. Fire and concussive force blew out the windows, sending Jedediah hurling over the porch rail. Heat and glass showered everyone.

Lanea and Jordan spoke simultaneously. "Drake."

They bolted for the house, brought up short next to Jedediah. He waved them on, shaking his head like a dog dislodging water. Power shimmered around Lanea ahead of her. Jordan fell behind, cautious not to sprint into heat or fire. An unburnt den brought her up short.

What the hell?

She pushed it from her thoughts and bolted after Lanea. Drake cringed at the blown out refrigerator's foot. A soft aura flickered around his outspread wings. A charred can of Cherry Coke smoked in his beak.

"Is he all right?" Jordan asked.

Jedediah stepped in the back door. "Shielded himself. Heard something before the blast?"

Drake shrugged, dropping the can to the linoleum.

"Wow, he protected the whole house?" Jordan asked.

"What do you mean?" Jedediah asked.

"Nothing's damaged but the windows. No fires, nothing burnt, Drake did that?" Jordan asked.

Jedediah snorted. "This lazy lizard? Not hardly. I've had enough dragons and apprentices burn the place down that I've got precautions in place." Jedediah glared. "Keeps stupid from damaging anything important."

Drake cringed. "I know, no Cherry Coke."

"And no magic, Drake," Lanea scolded. "Telepathy only."

Jordan gaped at Jedediah. "You blew up the house to keep him from a Cherry Coke?"

"Can't say that's not a good idea with this one around, particularly with how bad Coke is for you."

"You drink Pepsi," Jordan said. "Same difference."

"I beg to differ," Jedediah folded his arms. "Pepsi is a delicious and healthful beverage originally designed to aid in digestion—not addict its drinkers."

"You know a lot of sodas started like that right?" Jordan asked.

Lanea headed off their argument. "Namhaid again, Da?"

"Yup and the inconsiderate jackasses blew up Billie Jo's dinner."

Lanea snickered, and Jordan couldn't help but laugh.

"No telling how long the bomb's been here. Probably had no idea only Drake drank that garbage."

"What're you going to do about it?" Jordan asked.

Jedediah scratched his beard. "First, we're taking this old fridge out to the boneyard. I'll add the finishing touches to my portrait so it can dry. I guess we're stuck unveiling Lanea's birthday surprise a bit early."

Lanea lit up. "Surprise?"

Jedediah glowered at Drake. "Go to your nest and stay there. Lanea, call Billie Jo, tell her I'll call her with new dinner instructions in a bit."

"If she asks why?" Lanea asked.

He smirked. "Tell her Drake blew up the kitchen."

Lanea stepped into the tool shed, glancing behind her. Neither Drake nor Jordan had followed. "Da?"

Jedediah picked up a shelf of paint cans knocked over atop an old hand truck. "Here."

"This is serious you know." Lanea chewed her lip, face paler than normal.

"Yup." He shoved mint into his cheek and resumed stacking the cans. "Barrier doesn't keep out normals. You and Jordan could've been hurt. Drake's death would've brought Stormfall down on all of us."

"Normals are trying to kill you."

"Yup."

Lanea colored. "Don't you care at all?"

Jedediah set the last can on the shelf. "What should I do? Panic? Race around cursing? That girl's under enough stress. We've got her on a tightrope. We need her to learn abilities she doesn't really believe in without being terrified for her life. The calmer we keep her, the more her ingrained humanity rationalizes the hard-to-swallow fantastic away.

"Normals are after me, but we only know about one in the whole world. I don't have his hair, his blood or his bones. I've never touched him. I've never sensed his aura. He's got no magical signature to track. I've got a partial, probably false name and partial images from several decaying minds."

"All right," Lanea said. "You've made your point."

"I don't think I have. We're stuck. We can't just bolt to Sanctuary Hole. Centaurs attacked Jordan once already."

"What? When?"

"Billie Jo's convinced magic is evil. Between murder and taking Jordan in, government's breathing down our necks." Anger rose in Jedediah's voice. "Billie Jo and Mason have to be on the Namhaid's radar by now. So you tell me, how do I teleport us all to safety without exposing our secrets and alienating our loved ones in the worst ways?"

Lanea chewed her lip. "I don't know."

"Then we're stuck right here, where the Namhaid can attack me instead of them. I've already got Fey watching them all. I can't wall off the property without diverting the target onto Billie Jo. Closing off the through highways shores up our defenses."

"Yeah, that'd go unnoticed."

"See? What then, corridor spells? The energy requirements would all but cripple the protections we have now." Jedediah knocked the cans back down. "I'm already employing all my strength to keep Stormfall from destroying me or my mind."

"What do we do?" Fear filled her expression.

"Finish the painting and hope to hell this new tracking spell finds Muler and the answers we need," Jedediah said.

"Drake's strong, but I doubt he heard that bomb," Lanea narrowed her eyes. "You shielded him, didn't you?"

A reluctant smile flickered across his face. "I'm maintaining a ward around Drake and Jordan."

"But not me, right?" Lanea asked. "You know I can protect myself."

"Right," Jedediah said.

She folded her arms. "Da, don't waste energy on me. You need it."

He hugged her.

"Please, girl, just act normal. Help me throw you a party like everything's all right. Can you do that? For everyone else's sake if not for me?"

Lanea nodded.

"Good, let's take Jordan's mind off things."

"How're you going to do that?"

"By harassing my apprentice."

Jedediah wheeled a hand truck into the kitchen. He unplugged the destroyed refrigerator and stepped back, looking at Jordan.

"What?" she asked.

"Well? Get moving."

"You're not going to move it?"

Jedediah chuckled. "Equal rights too much for you?"

She glared, yanked the hand truck away and shoved it under the refrigerator. She grabbed its top and leaned both toward her. It tipped part way and stopped. She tugged and pulled, using her weight to lever the appliance out. It only tipped so far.

Thanks for the help, old man.

Jordan looked over. Jedediah's eyes twinkled.

"What's so gorram funny?"

"Temper helping? Stubbornness your asset?" Jedediah asked.

"What are you on about?"

He folded his arms. "Nothing."

Jordan attacked it again, throwing everything she had at it.

Lanea entered. "Billie Jo said okay. What're you doing, Jordan?"

Her response escaped gritted teeth. "Moving the fridge for lazy bones."

"It's never going to clear the lip if you don't pull it out first."

Blood drained from Jordan's face. She let the fridge down and peeked over the top. Cabinets blocked her efforts. She closed her eyes and counted to ten.

Jedediah roared with laughter.

"Shut. Up," Jordan snapped, face scarlet.

"Da set you up, but you're to blame for letting him. Ordered you to move it in some aggravating way, right? Shoved women's rights in your face if you complained?"

"How'd you know?"

"Same mistake I made," Lanea admitted. "Apprentices do dirty work to pay for learning, but most times the work comes with a lesson."

Jedediah caught his breath. "What is today's lesson, Jordan?"

"Don't let your temper get in the way?" Jordan asked.

"All right, what else then?" Jedediah asked.

"Don't be too prideful?" Jordan said.

"Sure," Jedediah said.

Lanea nodded encouragement.

Jordan wracked her mind. Finally, she shrugged. "I don't know."

Lanea sucked in a breath.

Jedediah narrowed his gaze. "No. 'I don't know' isn't an acceptable answer in this house."

Lanea tapped at her forehead.

"Saw that," Jedediah snapped.

232 | MICHAEL J. ALLEN

Lanea whipped her hands behind her back, feigning innocence.

"Um, think?" Jordan said.

"Good start," Jedediah said.

Lanea made chugging motions with her arms. Jedediah whipped around and pointed. "Out."

"Da!"

"You heard me," Jedediah said.

"Think before you run...no, act?" Jordan ventured.

Lanea fled with a smile.

Jedediah raised his voice. "I'd be happier if you'd thought that up on your own."

Jordan looked at her feet. "I'm sorry."

"Lanea knows better than to interfere with someone's lessons," Jedediah said.

"But isn't she my teacher too?" Jordan said.

"She's got a point," Lanea's voice came from the other room.

Jedediah spun toward the doorway. "Out farther!"

Lanea's laughter retreated.

Jedediah caught Jordan's sly smile when he turned around. "You two are going to drive me to drink. Go on then, let's move this fridge out to the boneyard."

Jordan pulled the fridge out. Jedediah helped her tip it. He held the back door for her but stood back when she reached the back stairs. Jordan set the fridge down and looked at the stairs. Not very broad, the steps dropped a good distance to the next.

Even money the fridge and I fall. So, how do I do this? She glanced around.

Several boards lay stacked down the porch. Jordan snatched up some and laid them against the stair. They slid out of position before Jordan could return to the fridge.

Jordan frowned.

A hammer and nails lay with the remaining boards.

I can almost hear the lecture if I nail the boards into place permanently. She smirked. *Could tell him someone his age needs a wheelchair ramp...no, it's way too steep.*

<Chores without magic take forever.>

Okay, Lanea, what kind of magic helps here?

She knelt next to the stairs. She pressed one hand into the dirt and held the boards with the other. She closed her eyes and listened.

Nothing.

She strained to hear the signal, tune into the magic.

Nothing.

How did I manage with the mudpuppies?

She stood back up, shaking her limbs out and jogging in place like preparing for a long run. She resumed her former position. She pictured what she wanted to happen and dug deep for a burst of speed.

Her stomach rumbled. *That didn't come from my stomach, I just ate.*

The rumble crept from her center, like the feeling of shuddering even though her limbs didn't move. The rumble slid glacially slow down the fingers shoved into the earth.

Tiny pebbles shivered then shifted. They jostled back and forth. They started to roll. Others joined them, dirt and sand rolling along behind. Slowly the tiny pieces built a ramp beneath the boards, helped occasionally be a larger stone.

The earth eventually settled itself into place. Jordan shivered, cold filled the rumble's wake. Her head spun. She grabbed the railing, hauled herself up and stepped onto the boards. It slipped from beneath her. She fell. Her grip prevented knocking her forehead on the porch.

Shaking hands pulled up one board. She frowned at the ramp of loose earth. *Not solid enough for the hand truck.* She examined her construction. *Wood, dirt and rocks. Could I make the earth hard as concrete?*

She shook her head. *I'd need water or heat. How do I make it stable?*

Jordan glanced up at Jedediah. He watched her, a slight glow to his intent eyes. *He's watching me and the magic. He hasn't objected, so I'm doing something right—not that I have any idea what.* She resisted throwing her hands in the air. *This is stupid, I'm just supposed to grow some sort of ramp?*

Grow... She eyed the old boards. *It's magic, right? Magic can do anything.*

Jordan replaced the board and knelt. She placed both hands on the wood. She found the rumble and whispered to the wood. "Wake up. You were trees once, mighty and majestic. You're pieces of the same forest, maybe even the same tree."

"You expecting it to talk back?" Jedediah asked.

She pushed him from her thoughts, whispered her encouraging litany and searched for the life in the boards. She pushed the rumble into the wood, willing the wood to reach for soil, water, life.

Verdant magic lit a single cell.

The rumble grew louder. Magic spread cell by cell up the boards, into the stairs and porch. Tiny roots grew downward, grafting into each other and growing ever downward. They anchored into the earth ramp.

The rumble just stopped, sudden silence deafening.

Jordan collapsed backward. Sweat soaked her shirt and dripped from her hair. She looked up.

Jedediah beamed. He grabbed the hand truck and eased the fridge down her ramp. "Come along then."

She struggled to rise, but her legs wouldn't lift her. Her stomach rumbled. He waited, one hand extended and the other holding the fridge tipped. He hefted her up and rolled the fridge forward slower than necessary.

"You did good," Jedediah said. "Thought it out, worked around the obstacles and kept trying."

"I'd feel better about it if passing out didn't feel like a real possibility."

He chuckled. "Patience, girl. Power's a redwood. Takes its time growing, but grows broad and tall with enough nourishment."

They rolled the fridge into the boneyard. He stopped studying the yard.

"Organize your junk in alphabetical order?" Jordan thought she caught movement several times. *Just near-exhaustion hallucinations.*

"Nope, just deciding if I need to rearrange again."

"Can we please just dump this somewhere so I can collapse?"

He chuckled and pushed the refrigerator to a stack. A wind lifted it from the hand truck and settled it down on the pile like cordwood.

"It's dangerous to leave the doors on all these old fridges."

"Why's that?"

"Some kid might play in them and get stuck inside."

He shook his head. "Wouldn't happen."

"It could," Jordan said. "There've been studies. I could take them all off for you if you want."

"Leave them be, girl. Else someone might really get hurt."

CHAPTER FORTY-THREE

Relationship Issues

Lanea hurried from the farmhouse while Jordan struggled with the refrigerator. Drake followed.

"Go back, Drake."

He cocked his head.

"This is none of your business. Anyway, Da sent you to your nest."

He slunk off, looking dejected.

Deal with that later.

Using the greenhouses to block Jedediah's view, she extended her hand over the pond. "Come to me."

A shaft of driftwood leapt from the water. Dark cerulean runes glowed along its surface. She planted one end in the mud and marked out a circle around the pond. The sludge hydra raised a single head, snapped a water strider and sank back into its depths.

Lanea stepped into the circle. Cool air hit her as if she'd entered air conditioning. She folded her legs beneath her next to the pond, laid her staff across her lap and leaned forward until her hands dipped into the water.

She opened herself to magic and poured the torrent into the walled space. A fine mist wafted off the pond's surface, thickening as she concentrated more and more magic.

Come on. Come on, he's going to notice.

Tiny geysers lifted her from the shore and floated her to the pond's center. Water spouted upward, flowing into a crystalline series of three-dimensional lattice rings. They spun around her like a carnival gyroscope ride.

Faster, I have to do this before he stops me.

Water's calm helped her forge a cease-fire with the emotional turmoil at war with her focus. Liquid syllables escaped her lips, glowing characters attaching themselves to the circling rings.

The last symbol escaped her. She held her breath. It wobbled in the air, too slow to catch the spinning lattice. She pushed power at it. It darted upward, snapping into place on the rings.

The farm vanished.

Stone walls vaulted above her. Elation and exhaustion filled her. *I did it. Da's spell chamber.*

Lanea rose, leaning on her staff. She wobbled toward one of the four elemental resonance crystals humming at room's edge. She touched the water crystal and borrowed from the power stored there.

She crossed the chamber in steady if rushed steps.

I have to finish before he finds me out.

A solid silver table shaped like a pentagon rested at chamber's center. Five unique tokens hovered above its surface.

Which one?

She reached into the crackling energy, careful not to disturb the others. She slid a small, fairy doll from the field and laid it on the table outside the spell.

Da needs all his strength. I can look after myself. She bounced on her feet into his study. *A quick trip through the hearth and I'm back in time for my surprise.*

Drake sulked. *It's not fair.*

His return from convalescence had included the proper attention, but Jordan had it all now. He'd been the one almost killed. He'd been almost blown up in the kitchen. If it hadn't been for the shield that appeared around him.

Apparently, she's the favorite apprentice now—because she's human.

He huffed smoke from his nostrils.

Not that she's bad, but she isn't Elder Fey. Lirelaeli made it quite clear that I wasn't being treated with the respect I'm due, even before Jordan usurped my place.

His gaze turned toward Lanea, working some spell near the pond.

Even Lanea doesn't want anything to do with me now that's she's got a new sister—as if her company's better than mine.

Jedediah'd restricted him from wandering, from magic, even from chasing the occasional car on the highway. He sulked into the greenhouse, curling a lip at the weretree. The other plants let him pass unmolested into the hives.

He flopped down in the midst of the adoring buzz, huffing smoke to their lazy delight.

It's just not fair.

Lanea parked the new Charger in Weems Road's driveway. Billie Jo exited the house.

She's got keys?

Mason bounced up and down behind her. Jordan seemed equally bemused beside her. Jedediah's smug expression waited in the rear view mirror.

Mason grabbed her before she'd closed the car door. "Come on, you've got to see this."

Billie Jo leveled a warning tone. "Mason."

He flushed and let go. He bounced around her like a ricocheting cartoon character. She smiled at Jordan and went inside. A full sized billiards table met her entrance. Blue felt offsetting its polished cherry body.

"Oh, Da!" Lanea rushed forward.

Her headlong rush came up short. Eyes traveled the living room, but words refused to leave her.

Jordan gasped behind her. "Frak me, I'm in heaven."

"Jordan," Billie Jo scolded.

Jordan adopted an innocent expression. "If Lanea doesn't want it, I'll take it."

"Guess we should send it all back," Jedediah said.

Lanea found mischievous light twinkling his eyes. She hugged him as hard as she could.

Speakers peeked from behind theater-style chairs and couches. Movies and games covered two walls, separated by a carnival popcorn cart and a four flavor soda fountain.

Several televisions had been fitted into a massive single screen on the last wall.

"Da, how did you? You can barely spell electronics."

He adopted a hurt expression.

Keys. Her gaze darted to Billie Jo. "You helped?"

"A little. I spent Jedediah's money anyway." Billie Jo pointed at Mason.

Mason nearly burst with pride. "The TV's are 3D. A friend told me farmers are all dirt poor, but Mr. Shine said everything had to be the best available."

"Just like my girls."

Jordan's head whipped around.

Billie Jo wrapped herself around Jedediah.

"Look, look," Mason said, "I got us *everything*."

"Some of it might need a firmness upgrade," Jedediah said.

Lanea didn't bother correcting him.

Mason adopted a singsong voice, waving a wrapped package, "There's something for Jor-dan."

Jordan chased him. Surprisingly quick, Mason eluded her, but she dove over the couch and tackled him. Jordan snatched the package and ripped it open.

Jordan lobbed it to Lanea and embraced Jedediah. "Thank you. I've been dying to see it."

"Put it in," Mason said. "Put it in."

"Lanea, dear, could you wait until we're gone? That's too mature for Mason."

Lanea frowned at the copy of *Serenity*.

Mason whined. "But, Mom, it's Lanea's birthday!"

"But it's not yours, mister. I'll not have you watching violent movies."

"It's only PG-13," Mason said.

"You're only ten."

"Dad lets me watch PG-13 all the time."

Billie Jo darkened. She opened her mouth.

Jedediah cleared his throat. "Seems I heard tell there's supposed to be some sort of show that comes before that movie."

Jordan smiled. "Yeah, fourteen episodes."

He smiled at Billie Jo. "Be a shame to spoil them."

"Jedediah," Billie Jo snapped. "Come help me with dinner."

Why's she angry? Da headed off the argument.

"Pick something," Jedediah said. "There're *plenty*."

"More than a video store." Billie Jo grumbled. "I'd like a private word with you before you spoil my son like you do your daughter."

Jedediah paled.

All eyes fixed on Billie Jo.

"What? I'm stupid? How many times has she called you Da in my presence?" Billie Jo asked.

"Lanea is Jedediah's daughter?" Mason asked.

"You know what, Mason. We'll get dinner on the way home. Enjoy your birthday, dear." Billie Jo marched out the door.

Mason's mouth moved, but his feet didn't.

Jedediah followed her out.

"You're mad."

"Darned right I'm mad. You lied to me," She pointed into the house. "Then you undermined me with my son."

"I stopped you before you did something stupid."

Her face purpled. "Pardon me?"

"Marcus intentionally lets Mason do things you wouldn't to start *exactly* those kinds of arguments—making *you* the bad guy."

"What do you know about divorce? Your wife *died*."

Jedediah's eyes narrowed.

She took a breath. "I'm sorry. You didn't deserve that."

"When did you figure out about Lanea?"

She turned her back on him.

Ah, that explains the two weeks of silence. She runs when mad. He set a hand on her shoulder. "Billie Jo…"

She swept it from her. Tears broke her voice. "You lied to me. Everything seemed so perfect, you seemed almost cut from an old story, but you lied to me from the start."

"You're mistaken."

"You told me none of the children from your marriage survived."

"That's true."

Billie Jo whirled, wet cheeks flushed. "Proof's right in there. You're a liar."

"Then why'd you come back around?"

"No one wants a single mother. Oh, sure they'll take you to bed if you let them, but they don't take your son along on dates. You're so sweet and smart, and you spent time with Mason. He needed a good role model like you."

Jedediah smirked. "So you did all this for Mason."

She shook her head. "You listened. Hell, you even refused to sleep with me. What kind of guy does that?"

"Why would you want a liar bedding you?"

She opened her mouth, closed it, opened it once more. "I don't know. Why didn't you sleep with me, really?"

"I told you."

"There's another reason," Billie Jo said. "Am I fat? Too old? Unattractive?"

"No, you're wonderful."

"What kind of guy won't sleep with a woman because she's wonderful?"

"An old fashioned one."

She sniffed. "Why did you lie? I have to know."

"I didn't. Lanea was born out of wedlock."

Billie Jo darkened. "You won't sleep with me, but you'll knock up some random floozy?"

"My mother's an amoral sociopath." Lanea's voice wavered. "I'm the product of rape."

"Girl," Jedediah said.

"I know daughters don't often get along with their mothers, but don't say mean spirited things about her." Billie Jo said. "I don't know what lies your father told you, but a man can't be raped."

"Ask Jordan if you don't' believe me. She's met her. Ma drugged Da and forced him to impregnate her."

Billie Jo narrowed her eyes. "Tell me she's lying."

Jedediah turned his back. "We're not discussing this."

"You didn't lie?" Billie Jo asked.

He shook his head.

"You swear?" Billie Jo shifted her gaze to Lanea. "You swear this is the truth? On the Bible?"

"It's the truth," Lanea said.

Billie Jo watched them for several minutes. She nodded to herself. "Just so long as there aren't any more big secrets."

Lanea watched Jedediah, breath held.

"So, how old are you, Lanea?" Billie Jo asked.

Lanea smiled. "Fifty-four."

Billie Jo chuckled. "Oh, right. You wear it well."

Lanea raised her brows.

Jedediah shook his head.

Lanea slipped up behind Jedediah in the kitchen. "You should tell her."

"Not yet."

"Waiting isn't going to make it easier, Da."

Jedediah stared out the dark kitchen window. "Longer I wait, longer she stays."

"Really think she'll leave you?"

"Magic is evil. Besides, everyone else has."

"Not me."

Jedediah hugged her. "No, not you."

"Incredible movie," Lanea said.

Jordan smiled. "Figured you'd enjoy it."

Jordan glanced around. Mason slept on the floor. Jedediah and Billie Jo talked on the deck outside.

"You know," Jordan said. "There's a sort of convention up in Atlanta in the fall. The actors might be there."

"Really?"

"It's pretty expensive. I've never actually gotten to go."

"If things calm down I'll talk Da into letting us go."

Jordan gave Lanea a sheepish grin. "Could we like go as elves?"

Lanea stared.

"No, really, everyone dresses up. I thought dressing up would be kind of neat."

A smile crept over Lanea's face. "Yeah, that would be a lark."

"Lark?" Jordan poked Lanea in the side. "You've *got* to stop hanging out with your dad so much."

Lanea blushed. "He's not so bad."

A faraway expression veiled Jordan's face. "Yeah, he is kind of cool."

"You okay?"

Tears glistened in Jordan's eyes. "No?"

Lanea hugged Jordan.

A knock interrupted Jedediah's concentration. He inhaled, set his paintbrush on an easel, and counted to ten.

"Yes?"

Jordan stepped through the door. Two mudpuppies bound inside, nipping her heels. "Um, I'm sorry to interrupt."

Jedediah wiped his hands. "It's fine. What do you need?"

"You asked us to remind you. Billie Jo will be here in thirty minutes," Jordan said.

Jedediah frowned. "All right, be inside in a minute."

She peered at the easel. "You paint?"

"Yup."

"Did you paint the one up in the hall? The woman in white that resembles Billie Jo?"

A stomach flutter surprised him. "Yup."

"It's really good. She someone you knew?"

"Elsabeth," Jedediah's tone caressed the name. "My first wife."

"It's a beautiful picture."

Jedediah turned away. "A beautiful woman—especially that day."

Jordan shooed the puppies and slid around the clutter. "Wedding day?"

"My present to her. They didn't have cameras back then."

Jordan smiled. "Sweet of you."

Jedediah looked away.

Jordan examined the easel again. "Who's this then?"

Anger flooded his voice. "The man who tried to kill Lanea and Drake."

Jordan snorted.

He glowered.

She cleared her throat. "Sorry, just seems a funny thing to do, making a portrait for a killer."

"It's for a spell."

Jordan reached inside for the rumble. She raised it to her eyes like Lanea showed her. Power pulsed along each brushstroke's edge. She stared harder, revealing another layer of lines and symbols. "What'll it do?"

Jedediah gave a smile any shark would have envied. "It'll bring us together."

Jedediah stood inside his closet, shirt in either hand. He glared at one shirt, then the other. Neither looked good enough, increasing his baffled frustration.

A soft knock sounded. "Da?"

"What do you want?" Jedediah snapped.

Lanea poked her head in and smirked. She took both shirts, replacing them with a dark red one.

Perfect. He smiled. "Thanks."

"Billie Jo's coming up the drive," she said. "The pixie wants a gummy instead of cinnamon imperials."

"That candy's nearly bigger than she is."

Lanea shrugged.

"She told you before you sensed the car?"

"Yes, Da."

He shrugged. "Pay her then. You girls will be all right with Mason?"

She rolled her eyes.

Jedediah fumbled with the buttons. "I wanted to talk to you."

She grinned. "What did I do now?"

He met her grin and raised an eyebrow. "Why don't you tell me what you did?"

She laughed. "No, sir, I stopped randomly confessing twenty years ago. Specifics, old man, or you get nothing."

"Worth a try." He shrugged.

"What's up?"

"Jordan has been giving us glimpses of the real her, not many, but I'm proud of you. Whatever you've done, it's working."

"I haven't done anything special."

"Special or not, don't stop," he said.

"You're as much to blame for her attitude as I am."

"Blame, huh?" Jedediah's fingers flexed and eyes twinkled.

"You're already late for your date, Da," Lanea warned. "Attacking is only going to ruin your outfit."

"I can get you without wrinkling the shirt."

She wagged her eyebrows and held both hands glistening soft blue. "How about water spots?"

Jedediah and Billie Jo drove into Atlanta to an excellent restaurant. The conversation went well all through the drive and long into dinner. On their way back, Billie Jo leaned against his shoulder while they talked.

"So, in this old-fashioned world of yours. Does a girl have to wait for the proposal or can she act?"

"Not sure we've found enough common ground to marry."

"I'm happy."

"I'm fond of you too, but we've still got a few differing perspectives."

"Well unless you're planning on getting me pregnant, I don't see any we can't work around."

"Pregnant?"

"I won't agree to you spanking a child."

He chuckled and stared out the window. *That's a big one, but not THE big one.*

They found Mason out cold on Jedediah's couch, one leg draped over its back. Billie Jo stifled a laugh.

"I hate to wake him," she said.

"Then don't," Jedediah draped a blanket over the boy. "You can stay tonight..."

Billie Jo's eyes lit up.

"...in the guest room."

Disappointment marred her face. "This is stupid, Jedediah."

"It's not stupid to me."

Concern tiptoed into her expression. "Don't you want me?"

"Thought we settled this."

"You saying it's so doesn't settle a discussion," Billie Jo scowled.

He crossed his arms. "I won't be forced."

Billie Jo opened her mouth. Tears welled in her eyes. She woke Mason and led him out to the minivan without a word.

Jedediah watched them drive away.

Something hit him on the shoulder. His head whipped around. Jordan glared at him, her fist still balled. "Jerk."

She stormed away, squeezing by Lanea in the doorway.

Lanea scowled. "Real slick, Da."

"What?"

She shook her head and walked away.

CHAPTER FORTY-FOUR

Portrait of a Killer

Muler paced the Mall of Georgia food court, guzzling his fifth bourbon-enhanced, designer coffee. He turned, checked behind him. He cursed. He turned, checked again and cursed. He turned and cursed once more—a litany of profanity to make any sailor proud.

He went to a shop, said the right thing. The response sent him to another shop. He bought the right thing. The receipt directed him to another shop. He insulted the wrong customer, but found another and insulted them.

Who'd have thought there'd be two obese women in leopard muumuus?

He went through the motions. Move and countermove. Convoluted cloak and dagger precautions taking far too long.

What the hell is wrong with One? Marked this as urgent.

He found a short-range, secure headset left in a department store changing room.

"Go for Muler."

"You're lucky to be alive."

"One?" Muler asked.

"Did we or did we not warn you about direct action?"

"I didn't believe you. That's changed."

"Report."

Muler told him.

"He threw lightning, *schwöre bei Gott* lightning." Muler's tone evidenced pending breakdown. "Wolves made of lava ate my squad. He pointed and blasted the truck a hundred meters. Pointed!"

"Have you been drinking?" Marc asked.

"Yes, but no matter how much it won't go away," Muler licked his lips and ranted on. "The reports. The warnings. It makes sense now. He's a demon."

"Where's the squad?"

"I don't know. I barely escaped." Muler looked into the mirror. His reflection looked crazed. He turned his back to it. "And his dog—it's no dog."

"What is it?"

"A dragon. I swear it's a dragon," Muler said. "What the hell is going on?"

One didn't reply immediately. "I'll admit something's not kosher. Shine's slipped charges he shouldn't have. I don't like not understanding."

"Leave them alone. Whatever they did or have, it isn't worth the risk."

"You're missing the big picture," Marc said. "I've a job for you."

"As long as it takes me far from that demon," Muler said.

"Steal an inconspicuous SUV from the airport. Abduct Joe Franklin from his girlfriend's during his after quickie nap. Let her leave first. Retrieve instructions from the drop box. Don't screw this up," Marc said.

"Look, One, I know you think I've lost my mind. I'm right there with you, but believe me. We've got to leave Shine alone."

"Maybe another witness survived. Don't leave any traces behind."

The headset went dead.

Muler exited the dressing room, sweat beaded his forehead. He re-entered the mall.

SUV, sheriff, drop box—need one of my stashes.

Jedediah set down the wand and gazed at the portrait. Mist obscured road, truck, forest but not Muler.

Jedediah removed the utility jumper, revealing casual clothes underneath. He approached his workbench without losing sight of the portrait. He released a wooden sword-cane from the vice holding it. Bronze sigils etched its walnut length. A small, bronze Drake capped it.

Fog swam the portrait's background, obscuring the semi-truck.

Jedediah leaned on the cane and waited.

Mist shrouded the background. Muler's clothes changed. The man's image faded into focus. He strolled through a weekend sale in a mall somewhere.

Jedediah licked his lips.

Muler's image sharpened by the second. He became real.

Jedediah touched the four bronze caps on the canvas's corners. Workshop and portrait vanished. Mall surrounded him. He cushioned his foot falls with air, caught up and grabbed Muler's shoulder.

Muler whipped around. His angry retort died, drained away with his color. He bolted.

Muler bulled into the crowd, shoving shoppers this way and that. Knots of angry people slowed Jedediah's pursuit.

I won't lose him now.

A wedge of air carved Jedediah a path.

Muler sprinted around a corner.

A guard shouted at Muler from a kiosk. "Hey, slow down."

Muler skidded to a stop and pointed at Jedediah. "Help me, he's armed and trying to kill me."

The mall rent-a-cops puffed up their chests. "We'll take care of it."

Muler ran on.

Three guards blocked Jedediah's way. One placed a hand on his shoulder. "Just a minute there, old man."

Jedediah glanced around them, tracking Muler's fleeing form. A resonant chord lay underpinned Jedediah's voice. "Get out of my way."

Two guards stepped blank-faced from his path. The third blinked, hesitated then frowned. "Are you carrying a weapon, sir?"

"I am a weapon, son."

A guard watching from the kiosk spoke into his radio. "We're going to need the police to the west end."

Jedediah raised his cane and slammed it into the ground. A shockwave blasted everything backward. Jedediah sprinted through the opening. People screamed and panicked around him. Previous incidents flashed through his mind.

Maker, I hate mob instinct.

"Get out of my way," Jedediah sprinted toward Muler, gaining ground with every stride. Muler spun, facing Jedediah.

"You and I are going to talk, Muler."

Muler lobbed the gun to Jedediah.

"Gun!" Muler pointed at Jedediah "Gun! Run for your lives!"

Muler bolted into the panicked crowd.

Security reinforcements saw the gun. They dove into cover and pulled Tasers in a rough perimeter.

"Put it down, sir," a guard said. "There's no reason for violence."

Muler disappeared with the crowd.

Jedediah eyed the gun then the guards. He swore.

Police arrived. "Lower your weapon. Place it slowly on the ground."

Jedediah obeyed with exaggerated slowness. He summoned power with each inch, focusing energy and will into layered spells. An invisible wind whipped out toward police and guards. It swirled around them into their lungs.

Sorry, boys.

They collapsed.

He pocketed the gun, turned down a bathroom corridor and disappeared. He reappeared inside Weems Road. The old Charger took him to the sheriff's office.

Jedediah set the gun onto the counter. "Where's Joe Franklin? Think the sons of bitches who murdered those hunters dropped this."

Eddie strolled out from the back. He spied Jedediah, the gun, and the young deputy's horrified expression. "Mr. Shine?"

"Joe Franklin here?"

"No, why do you have a gun?"

"Think this belongs to whomever killed those hunters."

Eddie blanched. "Why didn't you call us? You can't just move evidence."

Jedediah frowned. "Joe Franklin said to bring him anything I found right away."

"That's not what he meant. Your prints are going to be all over it."

"Didn't eject the magazine or fiddle with the bullets. When will the Sheriff be back?"

"He got a call that pushed back his lunch with Nancy. Afterward, he needed to check something out. I don't know when he'll return."

Jedediah reached for the gun.

"No," Eddie snatched up random paperwork and thrust it between Jedediah's hand and the weapon. "I've got it, okay. Simpson, fetch an evidence bag."

"Sorry, Eddie," Jedediah seated himself across from the desk under the watchful lens of a camera. "I'll sit right here and wait."

While I'm waiting, life being what it is lately, might as well work out a spell for removing select fingerprints.

Nancy pulled out of her garage and drove away. Muler pressed the button on his signal catcher, opening the garage door once more. He parked inside, cursing One, fall heat and his ski mask. The inner door proved unlocked.

Arts and crafts dominated interior surfaces. Scrapbooks and future contents covered a coffee table. Muler followed game show sounds on light feet into a hall. He checked his safety off, bolted down the straight hall into an empty bedroom.

I'm cursed. Can anything else go wrong today?

Running water drew Muler to a mostly closed door. The old sheriff's silhouette hid behind steam, frosted glass and a poorly hummed college fight song.

Muler positioned himself and waited. Steam intensified his discomfort, making the mask unbearable. He removed it.

Joe Franklin stepped out, turning toward the towels. Muler struck. He dragged the unconscious body to the bed and snatched up discarded clothes.

"Good news, bad news, baby," Nancy's voice entered a moment before her. "Car broke down a few blocks down. I called in—who're you? My God, what've you done?"

Muler lunged, but missed. He pursued the screaming woman into the living room, around the furniture. She snatched her phone off its charging pad. Muler tackled her, clipping the table with his shin. She struggled, gouging his face with pink nails. He knocked her out, cursing viciously. He ripped her shirt free and pressed it to his face, searching the floor for blood. He found none.

Finally, some good luck.

He tied and gagged them. He loaded them and their immediate possessions into the SUV, grabbing an extra shirt for the little bitch.

A muffled squelch escaped the passenger seat floorboards. "Joe Franklin?"

Muler glanced into the rear view mirror, tilted to observe his prisoners.

Love new model SUV's, seats fold into the floor for convenient abduction. His chuckle emerged half-hearted. Fear and doubt ate at him. *There has to be a way to survive this.*

He resumed his Atlanta to Columbus evaluation of current dire straits.

One, pissed and probably under pressure from the Board, assigned him a menial abduction.

Shit work, but I can deal with that.

Moments later Shine showed up and neatly pinched him.

How's he back on his feet? Hell, how'd he find me? He barely leaves his farm, and I've only gone to that mall twice.

"Sheriff?"

Muler searched for the radio in glimpses. *Leave it. I've no idea which deputy's on the payroll anyway.*

Muler'd narrowly escaped two tickets racing there to abduct the sheriff. One'd be pissed if he knew Muler chanced the tickets in a stolen car, but his cell leaders already seemed people–about–to–die furious.

One needed this playing card for his elaborate house. Without it, the plan might collapse. Muler either delivered or died.

I'll tell him she ripped my mask off. He'll understand. Leaving her body would have fouled his plan. Muler groaned. *Who am I kidding? I've no idea what's going on. All I know is simple strategies work, and this one isn't simple.*

One confessed confusion about Shine getting cleared for the killings. Muler didn't like the elaborate shadow game, particularly without all the pieces.

Muler checked his face for bleeding. *The why is painfully obvious now.*

Taking on Shine directly had sent his life into a downward spiral. He'd racked his brains for a way to kill Shine anyway. Without that particular feather, One and the Namhaid would leave him in an unmarked grave.

He parked in the Britt David sports complex. Joggers and dog walkers patrolled the park. He checked his prisoners' bonds and covered them with a blanket. He withdrew a plastic crabbing ruler from his duffel. He hurried to a Coca-Cola machine in the snack bar area. An out of order sign had been taped over the bill feeder. Muler pressed the c-shaped ruler into two buttons at once.

The machine whirred. A can thunked into the dispenser tray.

Muler retrieved the envelope wrapped can. He scanned the enclosed instructions. He absently popped the Cherry Coke top and raised it to his mouth. It stopped an inch from his lips.

Muler lowered the can. *Doubt he'd end me while I'm carrying his package, but no more risks. Plenty of places to buy a drink on the long drive.*

He threw it out and drove away.

CHAPTER FORTY-FIVE

Alibis & Epiphanies

Jedediah waited in the Sheriff's station until midnight thinned his patience. *I have to stay where they can see me. Where the hell is Joe Franklin? Damned blue pills.* Frustrated, he opened the newly discovered solitaire game on his phone. *Swear the damned thing cheats.*

Deputies congregated in groups, whispering concerns Jedediah heard clearly. He made them nervous, but not as nervous as Joe Franklin's absence.

Jedediah stood.

Every eye turned toward the motion.

"John?" Jedediah said.

"Yeah?" John asked.

"Any idea what's keeping the sheriff?"

John's jaw tightened. "No."

"Any more questions?"

"No. We'll be in contact."

Jedediah stared directly into the camera before departing. He drove to the farmhouse, lost in thought. He barely paid attention to the road, having used the wagon route since long before it'd been paved. He pulled up to the house.

Jordan rose up off Jedediah's rocking chair.

Lanea bound off the porch. "Where've you been?"

"Sheriff's office."

"They let you go already?" Lanea asked.

He strolled inside and into the kitchen. "No, they didn't let me go."

"You escaped?" Jordan asked.

"What're you girls on about?" Jedediah asked.

"They showed you on TV," Jordan said. "Security camera footage from Mall of Georgia."

Jedediah snorted. His stomach growled. "Couldn't have been there. Been sitting in the sheriff's office since lunch—smack dab in security camera view. You girls make dinner?"

Lanea scrutinized him.

"There's pizza in the dining room," Jordan said.

"Three cheese with sausage and tomato?" he asked.

Jordan nodded.

Jedediah opened the box, frowned, and closed it. He passed a hand over it and opened it again. Warm, tantalizing aroma wafted from it. He took a bite and chewed with lazy relish.

Lanea smirked. "You old fox."

"He's done that before," Jordan said.

"No, not the pizza. He knew the mall cameras would record him, so he teleported to the sheriff's office and sat in front of their camera. He used the police as his alibi."

"Yup."

"But he can't be in two places at once," Jordan's gaze narrowed. "Can you?"

"Nope. Couldn't have been in North Atlanta then in the local sheriff's department a few minutes later either."

"Lanea said...aren't you like technologically ignorant?" Jordan said.

Jedediah eyed Lanea. "Did she now? Might be I'm slower than others to latch onto new fads like this internet thing—usually better waiting for them to pass rather than make a fuss over keeping up."

"Internet's not a fad," Jordan said.

"We'll see. My point is, I might be slower about it, but I'm not too old to pick up a thing or two." He took a huge bite, barely chewing as he shoveled down several pieces. "Gorram, I needed that."

"He just say gorram?" Jordan asked.

"Space western—see, not totally oblivious after all." Jedediah shrugged. "It's a good show, looking forward to season two."

Lanea and Jordan exchanged looks.

Jedediah scowled at Muler's portrait.

Something about that's damned familiar, but I can't seem to figure out what.

Tactical gear and mask covered Muler in head–to–toe black inside some kind of cabin. Masked or not, Muler's portrait would always show its subject. Muler stood with at least six others next to an unconscious Joe Franklin tied to a chair. The image faded out again. He pushed more power into the tracking spell. It came and went.

Something's interfering. That shouldn't be possible.

A black-clad fist flashed into view. Blood trickled down Joe Franklin's face.

Heat rose in Jedediah's gut. *Time to teach some boys respect for their elders.*

Jedediah worked terramancy, strengthening limbs and toughening skin. He sank into wind's speed, winding up his reflexes. More aeromancy enhanced vision, smell and hearing.

The heady scent of jungle filled his senses. Hot, humid air sending phantom sweat down his back. Jedediah pushed the memory away.

Jedediah cracked his knuckles, then his back. A wave of electricity rolled up and down his skin. He snatched up his cane and set the teleport spell. He touched the painting's corners and tapped his cane.

The briefest glimpse of cabin flashed across his eyes before a massive power feedback threw him backward. He exploded into the workshop, careening through the wall into the dirt outside. His head slapped against the ground, and all went black.

Jedediah awoke. His head felt as if he'd used it to ring all of Notre Dame. Clothes smoldering, he cursed to wither plants around him.

Damn good thing the girls are out. I'm a twice-damned arrogant fool. Someone's magical defense just handed me my ass.

He limped into the kitchen, raising a gallon jug of red punch to his lips. A tiny hint of gym sock slithered from beneath the sugary fruit flavor.

Not enough raspberries in this batch.

Magic coursed down his body, easing wounds and dulling the throb in his head. When the refrigerator joined with its twin into a single appliance, he returned to the workshop and the smoking remnants of Muler's portrait.

He cursed.

It'll be fine. I saw the place... His head throbbed harder as he tried to bring the location to mind. He screwed up his face, fighting to recall what he'd seen. It slipped from his grasp like a fresh caught trout. *How hard did I hit my head?*

Fey search parties and finding spells ate away the night. Despite his familiarity with Joe Franklin, something fouled his efforts. He swung by the sheriff's office the next morning for appearance's sake—tired, grumpy and with few facts.

Whoever abducted Joe Franklin had prepared an impressive array of defensive and cloaking magic to keep Jedediah away.

So, it's personal, but to what end? Perhaps worse, how to keep Stormfall from learning a wizard's ultimately responsible for Drake's injuries—assuming they're linked.

"Any word from Joe Franklin?"

Eddie sipped coffee and scowled. "Still hasn't checked in."

It grated Jedediah's nerves to waste time with Eddie, but he had to maintain visibility. Otherwise, they'd pin the abduction on him too.

Not about to ask Lanea to walk around as me again.

"Guess he and Nancy up and eloped. If he comes in, I still want a word."

Eddie nodded.

Muler had Joe Franklin. The deputies wouldn't find him. Jedediah had to find Muler and cohorts, rescue the sheriff and dump serious hurt into their lives.

I'll need another alibi, maybe lunch with Meadow—once I figure out where they've taken him.

Jedediah remembered Mason at the last moment. Keeping his promise to fetch the boy from school was important, but Joe Franklin was in trouble.

It's my fault he's wrapped up in this. I have to find him.

Jedediah pulled up in front of the middle school in his blue pickup.

Stop, breathe, smile—look like everything's normal just a while longer.

Mason leapt from a seat atop a brick flower box. "Thanks, Mr. Shine. I'd be here *forever* if I waited for Mom."

Jedediah smiled. "Yup, you're coming over for dinner anyway."

"Good, I'm starving," Mason said. "Can I ride in the bed with Drake?"

"Suit yourself."

Mason beamed. "Cool, Mom'd never let me."

Icy water struck Joe Franklin's face like a hammer. Points of pain, like stars burning on his skin, sighed then shrieked. Swollen eyes struggled to let in brilliant light. One eye remained foggy, but he knew Jedediah's fishing cabin.

Jedediah wouldn't have done this, besides we haven't been up here in forever.

Blood slathered his taste buds, jagged teeth cutting his tongue. A deep ache pined for food. Despite the broken path, he lapped what water he could from that running his face. Sharp pungence and discomfort reminded him he'd lost bladder control during the beatings.

How long?

He didn't know how long he'd been tied, beaten up. He didn't know why. Questions received orders of silence and more beating.

Nancy, where's Nancy?

Last time they'd woken him she'd been screaming somewhere close—calling out for him to help her. Imagination filled in details. A whimper reached him, or perhaps a choked sob.

Heat rose in his chest. He pulled at his restraints, reigniting the fire in his wrists.

"Careful. You're reopening the wounds."

He peaked through half-closed lashes.

A tall, fit man stood before him. Deep red hair fell to his shoulders in waves. The well-dressed man seemed familiar, but Joe Franklin didn't think they'd met before.

They studied each other.

"Bring him." He exited the room.

Black-clad men looked as one to Marc O'Steele. A deep discussion dominated Marc and a beautiful blond. She leaned against stacked plastic crates stenciled: U.S. Army.

Marc glanced up when no one moved. "You heard Zero."

They hesitated.

The woman whipped a pistol into the nearest face, addressing them with British malice. "Move."

Men grabbed Joe Franklin. Pains warred for prominence as they dragged him into the cabin's kitchen. He caught a flash of the bedroom. Ugly yellow bruises covered most of Nancy's nakedness. Fury flashed up and then back like a leaping salmon. He ordered his muscles to action. They responded only with agony.

Tears completed his blindness. *I have to help her. I have to do something.*

The dining area had been redone in bizarre fashion. Someone had pushed the old dining table to one side. A white cloth and golden place settings covered it.

How many times have Jedediah and I sat here after a day's fishing?

Medical equipment and a dentist chair had been squeezed into the tiny kitchenette. A man hidden behind a surgical mask stood beside it. More crates with U.S. Army stencils stacked against the wall.

Guards shoved Joe Franklin into a dining chair. A familiar glower flickered across the well-dressed man's expressions. Resigned determination replaced it.

"You've my apologies, Sheriff. The treatment you've received in response to my invitation defied my instructions. I'm afraid, these operatives have made poor choices."

Joe Franklin's attempted speech sounded muffled and incomprehensible.

The other man—Marc called him Zero—held a hand up. "Please leave until summoned, Doctor."

Joe Franklin eyed the steak knife in his place setting.

"I certainly wouldn't blame you. I know I'd try."

Zero stood and strolled into easy reach. He checked the exit, placed hands on Joe Franklin's face and closed his eyes.

Never get a better chance.

Joe Franklin snatched the knife. As he swept it forward to plunge into Zero, the man's hands glowed. Soothing cool spread from his face, long suffering's departure almost like pleasure itself.

Joe Franklin stabbed anyway.

Zero grunted.

For Nancy. He twisted the knife, looking into Zero's face for agony. Instead, he found himself facing an echo of Jedediah's sad smile.

Guards rushed into the room.

Zero glared. "Get out."

He stepped backward, blade slipping from his abdomen. He lowered glowing hands to his stomach. Flesh visible through the rip closed.

"Truly, I do understand," Zero said.

Wizard...could it be Jedediah masked? Glamour maybe?

"Who're you? What do you want with me?" Broken teeth slurred his questions, but they remained comprehensible.

"I'm afraid I'm less proficient with teeth." He seated himself, gesturing toward the door. "Hence the good doctor."

Joe Franklin narrowed his eyes. "You're either Jedediah behind glamour or related to him."

"Are those really my only two options?" Zero quirked an eyebrow. "You may call me Zero. I'd use Nobody, but Odysseus already took it."

"What have you done to Nancy?"

Zero examined his fingers. "Another sad bit of poor judgment. These men are more disposed to vulgarities than most of our employees. Troubling, but useful on occasion. None of them will leave here alive."

"Will we?"

Zero smiled—something hungry, dangerous, deadly. "One, Two, come in please."

Marc and the blond entered. Marc sat to Joe Franklin's right. The blond held out a hand for the knife. Joe Franklin handed it over. She rinsed it free of blood and handed it back.

These people are psychopaths.

She remained standing.

Zero cleared his throat.

Marc frowned at him.

Zero sighed, pulled out the blond's chair and seated himself once more. "There you are, Two."

"Thank you," she said.

Zero snapped his fingers.

An ancient looking woman with nearly transparent skin hobbled into the room pushing a cart.

How is she even still on her feet?

She uncovered the food and began serving.

Heavenly aroma filled the kitchen. Joe Franklin wasn't one for fancy meals— not that the steak and stuffed mushrooms, asparagus, creamed spinach, baked potatoes and steamed mussels set before him represented nouveau cuisine.

Probably couldn't have afforded the restaurant that made these, though.

"Hope medium rare suits you, Sheriff." Zero sipped wine the old woman set before him, inclining his head. "Suppose pureeing it might've been easier. It just seemed wrong."

"What do you want from me?"

Zero leaned back in his chair, cleared his throat and addressed the ceiling. *"For God's sake, let us sit upon the ground and tell sad stories of the death of kings; how some have been deposed; some slain in war, some haunted by the ghosts they have deposed; some poison'd by their wives: some sleeping kill'd; all murder'd."*

Joe Franklin stared.

"Shakespeare. Richard II." Zero chuckled. "Appropriate somehow."

Two leaned onto one of Joe Franklin's remaining wounds. "Tell us a story, love."

Pain twisted the sheriff's features.

Zero cleared his throat.

Marc leaned on the table. "Tell us everything you know about Jedediah Shine."

Joe Franklin blanched. "I don't know anything. Nothing important."

"Tell us anyway," Two said.

"He's a farmer. I knew his father. We've gone fishing here."

"How did Shine end up cleared of the murders?" Marc asked.

Joe Franklin's turned to Zero. "You arranged all this. Why?"

Zero chuckled. "I might've lent a guiding hand here and there, but my presence is a matter of happenstance and hospitality."

"I don't understand any of this," Joe Franklin said. "Why frame him and not just kill him?"

Zero sipped his wine. "That's proven...unwise."

"You've murdered innocent people to frame him. Why? What's he done that you'd escalate that far?"

"Sir," Marc cautioned.

Zero rolled his eyes. "It's a matter of family honor. Shine stole something very valuable from One's family. We want it back."

"This is a blood feud? Some generations old argument?"

"Sixteen," Marc said.

"Give or take," Zero smirked. "And yet far bigger than any mere blood feud."

Two leaned forward.

Joe Franklin almost fell out of his chair leaning away.

She smiled. "You had his shotgun, his shells, bodies. How did Shine escape prosecution?"

"You wouldn't believe me," Joe Franklin said.

"Try us," Marc said.

"Evidence proved circumstantial. The centaur's murders and your own never lined up right. Pretty half-assed frame job really. A decent lawyer would've rip our case to shreds."

Marc's brows furrowed. "Bianca, did you drug him?"

"No," she said.

"Continue," Zero interrupted.

"They'd killed Ronnie Gerald, then others after Jedediah confronted them," Joe Franklin said.

"What are you talking about? Who's Ronnie Gerald?" Marc asked.

Joe Franklin frowned. "The first murder."

Muler barged into the room. "I shot Shine twice in the chest. How'd he survive that? Hospital records showed arrow wounds, not bullets, how?"

Zero scowled.

"You shot his daughter," Joe Franklin said.

"Oh no, I had the old man in my sights," Muler said.

There's no way they're going to believe me. He studied Zero's pensive expression. *Well maybe.*

"He's a wizard. His daughter used something called glamour to look like him so we wouldn't know he left town. You shot her. A centaur attack hospitalized Jedediah."

"See," Muler pointed, nearly jumping up and down. "Wizard, demon, I told you there was something unnatural going on. No one can control the supernatural. I'm not to blame for worsening this mess, Shine is."

Bianca seized Muler and dragged him raving from the room.

"Magic, that's how he killed them, how he found me—"

Marc leaned in once again. "Look, this'll go a lot easier for Nancy if you just tell us the truth."

Bianca reentered.

"I *am* telling the truth," Joe Franklin said.

"Perhaps the beatings broke him," Bianca said.

"You know," Joe Franklin pointed at Zero. "You know I'm telling the truth. You used—"

A gun appeared in Zero's hand. The heavy shell blasted Joe Franklin's head backward, painting the far wall with red and greenish grey.

Awe filled Bianca's expression. "I've *never* seen so fast a draw."

Zero tucked the gun under his jacket. It didn't leave the slightest bulge—almost as if no gun rested there at all.

"Why did you do that?" Marc asked.

Fury crossed Zero's eyes for an infinitesimal moment. "He'd gone mad—useless."

Marc cradled his head. "I'd hoped for decent intel."

"Summon the good doctor. Let him fix the sheriff's teeth."

"You just blew his head off," Marc said.

"But not his mouth. Jedediah wouldn't torture his friend. We want the Feds to discover an easily read story, don't we?" Zero cut some steak and took a bite. He frowned. "Fetch the doctor and put the sheriff in the chair."

They turned to move the corpse.

Zero's hand passed over his plate. He took another bite, eyes closed, savoring its warm, rich flavor.

Memories nagged at Jedediah. He had seen where Joe Franklin was being held, but he couldn't bring it to mind. It had seemed familiar in the portrait, but even before he hit his head it wouldn't resolve into somewhere he could place. With Joe Franklin hidden behind magical walls, he chewed at his only clue.

Drake and Mason sat contentedly in the truck bed. Jedediah veered left onto a narrow bridge, surrendering space to its couple fisherman. He stared at them, something tugging at his attention so fiercely he had to jerk to one side to avoid running one down.

Mason knocked on the window.

Jedediah slid it open, answering distractedly. "Yup?"

"Would you take me fishing some time, Mr. Shine?"

Jedediah slammed on the brakes. Mason and Drake thumped against the back of the truck. For a moment, he'd had it. "Sorry. You two okay?"

Mason rubbed his head. "Yeah. I didn't mean to make you mad."

"What? No, son, you didn't make me angry."

Drake poked his head through the window. *<Master?>*

I had it, Drake. For a moment I knew where they took him.

<Did it have something to do with fishing?>

It came back in a flash but vanished once more.

Drake's brows knit together. *<Why are you forgetting?>*

What?

<You recognized your fishing cabin for a moment, but then forgot all about it.>

Jedediah swore enough to turn an awed Mason red.

"Mr. Shine?"

"Just a moment," Jedediah narrowed his eyes at Drake. *Do you see a cloud in my thoughts?*

<Yes, Master. It's spreading each time you remember your fishing cabin. Wait, the Namhaid's using your fishing cabin to hold the Sheriff? They wouldn't dare.>

Jedediah's jaw tightened. *Did Stormfall ever teach you how to do a psychic shock?*

<She never taught me anything.>

Jedediah thrust the knowledge into Drake's mind, making the dragonling reel. He erected a barrier around the cloud, leaving it the only exposed portion of his mind. *Hit me.*

<Master?>

Hit me, Drake, right where the cloud is.

Drake mind slashed Jedediah's consciousness. Jedediah's head snapped back. His nose bled. *Again, then tell me what I've forgotten.*

"Sir, are you all right?"

Drake told him about the cabin. The memory held.

"It's fine. We'll go fishing sometime soon, I've got just the place. Just hang on back there, Mason." Jedediah floored the accelerator. He whipped up the farm drive, kicking up rocks and dust. He bolted for the farmhouse without a word to his passengers.

"Lanea?"

She appeared in the bathroom mirror. "Da?"

"Get back here immediately."

"Da, I'm busy."

"Now!"

"What's happened?" Lanea said.

"I'll explain later." Jedediah stormed through the house, preparing the list of things for his assault. Mason sat on the porch. "Raid the fridge if you're hungry. Lanea's on her way. I've got to help a friend."

"Who's going to watch me until she gets here?" Mason asked.

"Drake."

CHAPTER FORTY-SIX

Wrong Place, Too Late

Zero sent Marc and Bianca back to their places. Muler left with a truckload of rocket launchers bound for a group of Syrian nationals hiding in Topeka. Others watched the perimeter, unaware they'd soon lie dead at their posts.

He finished his meal, watching the dentist work. He saw the Namhaid dentist and his equipment on its way.

"Come inside, please," Zero said.

The door guard complied.

"Stand right there," Zero said. "A little to the right. Perfect."

Zero's gun reappeared and fired, blasting the mercenary back over several weapon crates. His head splattered the cabin wall.

"Thank you."

Several guards entered at a run.

"Dispose of that turncoat."

They did.

Zero entered the kitchen and seated himself. Joe Franklin's body lay sprawled after its repair.

"Get up, please, Sheriff."

Joe Franklin—top of his head phantasmal—rose. "Why am I still here?"

"I haven't released you yet. Have a seat."

Joe Franklin sat opposite Zero. "I told you the truth."

"Yes, I know."

"Jedediah *is* a wizard."

"Yes."

"You killed me to prevent them learning you're one too."

"Death brings such clarity of mind, doesn't it?" Zero said. "Even enhances the senses to some degree."

"How would you know?"

Zero shrugged.

"What now?"

Zero gestured toward the bedroom. "Your women needs to be strangled."

"You wouldn't. She's innocent."

"You're right, very distasteful—that's why you'll do it for me."

260 | MICHAEL J. ALLEN

"Go to hell."

"Not if your death does what I intend."

Joe Franklin's remaining face frowned. "I don't understand."

"Police are eminently predictable. Always have been. I'm giving them what they want to see." Zero rose, pacing back and forth. His hands moved like a CEO speaking to a boardroom. "You got an anonymous tip, followed it up here and found an arms cache. Jedediah showed up and killed you to keep his secret. Simple."

"What about Nancy?"

Zero pursed his lips. "Her unexpected presence complicates things. Maybe infidelity turned you against her. Maybe you followed her, not a tip. Maybe you found her waiting on her lover, flew into a jealous rage, beat then strangled her."

"No one would buy that," Joe Franklin said.

Zero displayed his palm. The gun reappeared in it. "Why not? His gun shot you. His DNA on the girl. The easiest solution gets you cops back to your donuts. Nothing else matters."

Joe Franklin lurched out of the chair.

"*Sit.*"

Joe Franklin's body sat. "Not Jedediah's DNA. Yours."

Zero laughed. "Think you've figured it all out, do you? The DNA is an imperfect copy, but he's no family on record to offer confusion. It'll be enough considering the judges and jury selections I've purchased."

"What's to keep him from up and disappearing?"

"Jedediah believes in the system. He's too honorable and too out of touch to realize it's bought and paid for." Zero smiled. "Besides, I know how he thinks."

"What did he ever do to you?"

"It's what he didn't do, speaking of which. Go beat and strangle dear Nancy."

Joe Franklin's body rose and shambled into the bedroom. Nancy's expression softened. Shrieks replaced calm when she noticed his missing forehead. She fought her ropes. Joe Franklin wrapped fingers around her throat and squeezed.

Zero entered and snapped his fingers.

Her ropes untied. She clawed at Joe Franklin, trying to stop him. His body obeyed no matter how hard he fought. The sheriff wanted to stop. He had no eyes to cry.

Her face purpled. Her struggles lessened. Finally, she lay still. He pummeled her already bruised body.

"Excellent."

"Drop dead," Joe Franklin lunged for Zero's throat. His body ignored him.

"Now, be a good corpse and go lay across those weapon crates in the other room, just beneath the blood splatter," Zero slipped off his jacket and rolled up his sleeves. "The authorities will arrive soon, and I've got cleaning to do."

Jedediah appeared on the dirt road leading up to the cabin. A moment later, machine gun fire harried in his location. Masked men darted in and out of cover, firing controlled bursts.

He concentrated a disk of wind, bolstering it with an undercurrent of tidal force. He summoned flame.

Ianyss is going to throw a hissy fit.

Before he released the fire, two SUV's skidded to a stop behind him. Twice as many patrol cars flanked them. An eager highway patrolman leapt behind his car door. "Lower your weapons."

Jedediah glanced at his fire shrouded hands. Namhaid opened fire on the pompous officer.

FBI and police jumped into cover positions behind doors, returning fire.

Jedediah extinguished his flames. He opened his connection wider, swirling wind around himself as tightly as he could until it warped light and redirected bullets.

Against the Namhaid—those who'd hurt Lanea, Drake and Joe Franklin— he'd have laid waste and left no witnesses. He couldn't harm the authorities, nor slaughter the Namhaid in front of them.

Can't leave Joe Franklin in there either.

Jedediah bolted forward, raising as much dust and forest debris to hide his identity as possible. His new staff struck out as he went, a short blade of kinetic force atop the fresh black walnut.

He hit a protection boundary just beyond the Namhaid's gunmen.

Whoever had laid the circle had been weak but meticulous. Wooden posts, equally spaced, circled the cabin, stained with dark brown glyphs.

Jedediah altered his vision, examining the construct over several magical frequencies.

An imprisoned spirit screamed silently, bound to the nearest post. Its blood formed the glyph protecting his cabin and its woes distracted memory down forlorn paths. Woven chords rooted the circle into the trees for strength and power. The other posts imprisoned spirits too. Their raw magical energy combined into an inelegant but effective magical barrier. Demolishing the trees outside it would weaken the barrier, but those inside would keep it intact.

Could do with Sarah and her pups or that Kimberlite. He sighed. *Nothing an aeromancer loves better than solid earth suffocating him.*

He planted his staff and seized earth's power.

Jedediah slid down his staff like a fireman's pole. Rocks and pebbles grated against his skin as he swam through solid ground. The sandpaper sensation inside his skin evoked a sneeze.

Force of will pushed him along, leaving undisturbed earth in his wake. He cleared the circle and surfaced in a leap. A gunfight raged beyond barrier and his planted staff.

Hopefully enough to keep them from noticing.

A terramancy-enhanced kick splintered the nearest post. The circle collapsed, barrier vanishing. He smashed through the cabin door. Joe Franklin's corpse sprawled over military crates.

Pain slashed through him. *I'm so sorry, Joe Franklin. I should've realized sooner.*

Electricity surged through his veins. Heat hazed his vision. *Where's the son of a bitch that did this to you?*

Jedediah inhaled through his nose. He peeled lingering scents apart one layer at a time. A feminine scent brought him running to the bedroom door. What he saw crushed his chest.

Nancy, Maker, I didn't know.

He inhaled the lingering scent of spellcraft—sweet, rotted and cloying. *Necromancy. He's going to regret his birth.*

He swept his hand upward. His staff leapt through the wooden floor to fill it. Residue of a hastily erected portal evaporated on the wall beyond Nancy.

He slammed his staff into the wall, wedging a blade of force into the gateway's edges like a crowbar. He cursed and fought to pry it open.

Skilled construct, sealed on the opposite end.

Jedediah refused to be denied. He slammed his staff into it like a ram. The third blow blasted it open.

Gunfire died outside.

Now or deal with the survivors.

He leapt through the gate. It sealed after him.

A maze of mirrors reflected his scowl. He extended his senses, only to have enchanted glass thrown them back.

I hate mirror magic. He swung his staff at the nearest mirror.

The blow sounded a cacophonous gong, but didn't crack the surface. He struck another and another. Gongs filled the labyrinth, never falling silent between blows.

Jedediah's head pounded. He held his next blow. *Something's queer here.*

The ground shifted. Centripetal force threw him into a mirror, adding another gong to the tumult.

We're turning at high speed.

He invoked a short teleport meant to place him outside the room. Sound waves battered away the magic like beating a fire out.

Jedediah cursed himself. *Stupid, old moron! How many times have I lectured apprentices to think first, no matter their urgency?*

He'd stumbled into a custom tailored trap and made things worse by reacting. He gritted his teeth and examined it.

Portal's sealed. Mirrors reflect spell energy, attacking them created spell interference. Couldn't have planned a better wizard's bane. At least I hit the mirrors with a stick instead of filling this chamber with fire or lightning. A thought struck him. *No, VelSera's not this smart.*

He bent, placing hands on wall and floor. A forest's afterlife lurked beyond floor and impervious mirrors.

The room tilted through a harder, faster turn.

"*Llivoru.*"

Both ends of his staff emitted thin light beams. They hit mirrors and bounced over and over—drawing a floating, three-dimensional scale replica beside him.

Anyone who's ever bootlegged whiskey knows a tractor trailer's dimensions.

Weapon creation dominated feromancy's usefulness. Manipulating magnetic fields had limited use in an increasingly plastic world. Most aeromancers never bothered with the specialized facet of terramancy.

Practice can save your life, and here's the pudding.

A long breath filled his lungs, hot and stale. He chose his spot, summoning aeromancy in his right and feromancy with his left. Wielding antagonistic forces with haste, extreme care and razor-sharp control he attacked his cage.

Air expanded outward. Metal beyond wood and mirror strained.

All I need is a tiny gap.

A mist message lanced into his consciousness. His control wavered. He shoved away the summons, struggling to rebalance the forces in his stranglehold.

The world tilted forward. Gravity vanished.

Jedediah's heart skipped a beat. He shoved air outward and wrenched at the metal. Rising pressure blew a hole in the roof. He seized the outrush of air, letting it drag him free like a team of wild horses. He shot out through splintered wood like a bloody BB, whipping open wings of solidified air once free.

A mobile home slammed into the ocean far below, wide load sign floating atop the deep blue water.

Wings dispersed, leaving him breathing heavy atop a Pacific sea cliff.

Not sure whether the spell went wrong of my captor fooled me—again. Damned evil geometry nearly killed me.

CHAPTER FORTY-SEVEN

Run for Her Life

Jordan parked the old Charger in the state park's dappled green shade. Other than mud and the stairs, she'd been almost universally unsuccessful when it came to controlling elements beyond her skin. The car spell thwarted her again.

She chuckled. *Not a problem as long as my Cherry Coke stash holds out.*

She inhaled the fresh air, sweeter near the elven city than any other.

Guess it could be all the wild Fey instead. She loosened her laces, kicked off her sneakers and stretched out.

A soft whimper escaped the Charger's back seat.

"Damn it." She spun toward the car's back door, coming face to face with a really cute guy.

"Hello, beautiful." His voice slid into her ears like silk, masculine and vaguely familiar.

Jordan pushed a strand of hair from her face. "Um, hi."

"Seen *you* before."

Where? I'd sure as hell have remembered him. A forestry service t-shirt and green shorts covered muscled torso and runner's legs. A breeze tousled his short brown hair, lending him an actor's entrance.

"You work here?" Jordan asked.

"Sure. Associate junior park warden. Just finished a Cub Scout hiking trip. You a big sister or one of the single moms?"

"No. I run here sometimes. I'm on the cross country team, maybe you saw me compete?"

"Not sure, which college?"

She blushed. "High school."

His smile grew. "Are you good?"

"Better than most."

"I'm Trevor Ahn."

She extended a hand. "Jordan."

He took it. Nothing at all happened. *Normal, cute and interested, what a nice change.*

School contained normal boys, but she'd burned bridges. Worse, Jedediah dated her teacher. She ate lunches alone.

Cub Scouts started throwing rocks at signs. Trevor glanced over. He flashed her a smile. "Got to go entertain the little monsters until their moms show up. You doing anything tonight?"

She almost indulged the sudden urge to victory dance. She forced nonchalance. "Not that I know of. Why?"

"Great! You like wings? Foster's has the best around. How about nine?"

"I'll be there."

She watched him jog off to rein in the scouts, playing the cool adult for their benefit. *Or maybe he's showing off that beautiful ass for me.*

Trevor's shorts fell around his ankles.

Scouts burst out laughing.

Don't laugh. Don't laugh. His red face turned in her direction. She laughed.

Another whimper sidetracked her. She opened the back door. Two mudpuppies tumbled out: Nip and Nibble.

She sighed.

The male pups untangled themselves and jumped at her, tails going wild. They'd grown to the size of clumsy beagles. They'd also adopted her.

She placed a hand on their heads. "How on earth did you get into the car?"

One word yipped fast over and over again: *<Secret.>*

Jordan frowned.

The word changed: *<Run.>*

Jordan glared, hands on her hips. "I should take you back to Sarah."

They jumped and yipped, licked and wagged.

She glanced up. Scouts distracted Trevor enough for them to go unnoticed.

"Oh, all right, but keep up. And if someone comes close, hide. I can't even cover up a pimple with glamour."

Jordan restarted her stretching routine, gave the wrestling pups a sly grin and bolted for the trees. Despite short legs, they ran fast. She poured on the speed. They fell behind, then dove in and out of the earth—easily keeping up.

Wind whipped through leaf, branch and Jordan's hair. Trees sang. She usually blasted her iPod, but not in the forest. Certainly not the elven forest.

She eased into a rhythm, extending stride but slowing pace. Her thoughts drifted. *Magic sucks.*

Lanea encouraged her regularly, and even Jedediah offered occasional praise, but for nothing. She couldn't manage the tasks they expected. Aeromancy left her grasping at clouds. Water and fire soaked or burned her but never did what she desired. Terramancy—her element—slipped from her grasp with seldom exception.

Barefooted, she somehow drew in earth's strength. She had to struggle with it, but eventually, her athletic frame could Schwarzenegger most anything. She'd managed a change that equipped her tongue to pick out individual ingredients in a pizza. Her nose could pick fragrances out in a crowded room or dampen scents in a locker room. Strengthened limbs added speed and oftentimes balance she generally lacked. It all made her feel like a superhero.

Even if Jedediah says what I'm doing is marginal compared to using the elements best suited to power those characteristics. She reached for the rumble and split it between her senses.

Her hearing sharpened. Her eyesight stretched out, reaching not only farther away but further into light spectrums until the forest's living magical pulse grew visible. She extended it to her legs, faster longer strides.

Almost feels like flying. What more awaits me in a year? Five?

She laughed, a joyous giggle otherwise unuttered since childhood.

Nip and Nibble paced her. Their beagle shapes seemed slimmer, more whippet than scent hound.

Can they take whatever shape suits them? Drake does something similar. She laughed. *Though he never stops complaining about his shifting lessons.*

She pushed up her pace.

They fell behind.

Jordan danced through the forest, jumping logs, darting around trees, avoiding bush, bramble and gully.

Puppy barks pursued her.

Sorry, pups, keep up or give up.

Shapes paced her, appearing in and out of sight. Their barks seemed muffled.

Earthswimming's never muffled them before. She pushed power into her ears until they tingled. The barks didn't strengthen.

A sidelong glance informed her shadowcats had replaced Nip and Nibble. Three paced her right side and four her left.

Lanea said they wouldn't trouble me, especially here.

Her palms tingled.

Cats pressed closer on one side, the other side giving ground.

They're herding me, but why?"

She risked a feint to one side. A pair of fangs about to snap at her face vanished in a shaft of sunlight. She glanced over her shoulder for the mudpuppies, finding more shadowcats on her heels.

She let them herd her, scanning for the chance to break free.

Not like they're always there. They slid in and out of shadow. *Do they do it so instinctively that they don't realize they're going to open an opportunity sooner or later?*

Not too far left of their track a fallen tree leaned up against a much bigger tree. The gap in the canopy filled the spot with light. She darted left at the last moment and leapt into the light. Her bare feet raced up the mossy bark to the collision point. She turned around and assessed the situation.

She panted, a few dozen feet off the ground. Her position offered only one direction of approach or would have if they'd been something else.

Three cats sauntered up the tilted trees, a low growl in the last one's throat. Their bodies faded like a Cheshire cat, leaving smiling fangs to menace her.

The lead cat crouched.

"You best be on your way. I'm a wizard and from Jersey," Jordan sneered. "You don't want any of that."

Nip and Nibble burst out of the soil, slamming into the rearmost cat's side simultaneously. They left the spitting cat half buried. She caught a flash of husky or wolf before they vanished back underground. The cats waylaid them on their next strike. The smaller pups fought—snarls, growls and whirling limbs in a war of mud against smoke.

Smoke won.

Cat claws pinned their throats. The lead cat's tail twitched, daring her to dispute its claim to their necks.

"Dive. Get Jedediah," Jordan said.

They dissolved into the dirt. Cats advanced. Jordan placed her back to the bigger tree. She put a hand on its bark and reached for her strength.

Ianyss says you can hear me, Mister Tree. Please, shift your branches. Give me more light.

"Unsafe practice," a voice slurred. "Closing your eyes to concentrate."

Jordan's stomach plummeted to the forest floor.

The half burned centaur raised his bow.

"Of course, death's probably easier with them shut," SinDon said. "Goodbye, wizard."

Several things happened at once.

Jordan reached elbow deep into the rumble and yanked.

Paulie the fairy darted between Jordan and SinDon.

Nip vaulted out of the earth over the cats and raced up the tilted trunk carrying a long branch in his mouth.

SinDon unleashed four arrows with speed Jordan had only witnessed in movies.

Paulie cut down the first arrow. The second struck Nip's back. He yelped, tumbling from the tree. He hit the ground like a diver, sinking from sight.

Two arrows bounced off Jordan's stomach, splintering as if he'd shot them at a concrete wall. She snatched the teetering branch and presented it, trained in quarterstaff combat by Robin Hood movies and a few Daffy Duck cartoons.

"Kill her," SinDon snarled.

Shadowcats leapt up the trunk to meet wood in the sunlight. Others dove into shadows, raking claws and snapping jaws descending from darkness above her.

Paulie whirled through the air. He sliced and stabbed at leaping cats, snarling curses in a thick Jersey accent.

Centuries of human instinct turned stick into club. Solid blows coincided with raking claws, trading blood for bruise. She concentrated on her footing, otherwise swatting at shadows. She settled for intermittent glancing blows.

Arrows bounced off her mysteriously armored skin. Vicious claws left minor scratches.

Paulie gave about as well as Jordan got. Bright glowing light and pointy edges, the cats disliked him with feline intensity.

No way I can keep this up. Think or die. Wish I'd brought that dagger. Inspiration struck. "Paulie, right? Fetch Lirelaeli from the elven city. She'll help me."

"What about dem? I ain't gonna let anybody just rough you up."

"I'll probably be okay," Jordan said. *Wish I believed that.*

"You got it," he sped away, slicing cats along his path.

SinDon strode forward. "Stupid, arrogant *human*. No elves will help you."

"Which end holds your brain, wax face? I'm an elf."

SinDon braced himself and shoved the fallen tree with his hind legs. His purpled face reddened. The tree groaned.

If he brings me to ground level it's goodbye Jordan. Gods of rock-n-roll, make with the good reception. She opened up the channel between her and magic as best and as wide as she could. The rumble nearly shook her from her perch. She shoved the rumble down through her feet while defending with the club. *Grow, heal. You can do it. You're stronger than that old mule. Prove it.*

The tree responded, slow and sluggish, its pride rose. The old arbor heard her, took the offered strength and defied SinDon. It reached for its roots, new growth mending the break.

Trees start life ambitious, but soon learn not to hurry. Hurrying overextends roots. It causes starvation. The tree knew it needed to grow, so it did. It didn't recognize any need to rush. They struggled what seemed like forever.

It fell.

SinDon leveled a sword-lance for a charge.

"Do we have a problem, centaur?" Lirelaeli asked.

Paulie grinned insufferably, perched on her shoulders and surrounded by a squad of armed elves.

"Nay, forest cousin," SinDon said. "Merely ridding our world of another arrogant wizard."

"Understandable desire, but, this girl is my daughter's sister. She's under my protection."

SinDon pierced Jordan with a venomous glare. He bowed to Lirelaeli. "My apologies. I didn't know. If you would take no offense, I would leave in peace."

"Leave in peace," Lirelaeli said.

"You're letting him go?" Jordan asked. "He tried to kill me!"

"An understandable mistake." Lirelaeli smiled. "He apologized."

Jordan threw up her hands. "I can't believe this."

Lirelaeli extended a hand. "Come, child, we'll escort you home."

She glared at both, not daring to refuse.

CHAPTER FORTY-EIGHT

If Life were Simple

Lanea roared into the park on a motorcycle. Sarah and Nibble rode in the sidecar, enjoying the wind despite their urgency.

Nip lay beneath the Charger.

Lanea parked alongside.

Sarah leapt clear before the bike stopped. She licked him, and he whined.

"Where's Jordan?" Lanea set a hand on its head.

<Gone.>

"Where?"

Nip's head drooped. He didn't answer further.

Lanea leapt to her feet. Trevor smiled inches from her. "Hello, beautiful."

Conflicting emotions seized Lanea. Her fingers reached out to touch him of their own accord. Her tongue wetted her lips in preparation to kiss.

Jordan's...he's so handsome...what am I...I shouldn't be mad at him...Jordan needs me...just one little kiss.

She leaned in to kiss him. Sarah's low growl caught her, lips touching his. She inhaled, the subtle scent of magic unmistakable so close.

Shock, rage and hurt hit her all at once. She decked him. "How dare you! You seduced me with glamour!"

In a flash, Lanea understood the tension between Lirelaeli and her father. She felt weak and fierce, vulnerable and self-righteous all at once. She longed for him, his touch, his love while repulsed to her core by his betrayal.

"Calm down. Take a deep breath before—"

"I will not. I'm not falling under your influence again. Not now. Not ever."

"Lover."

Lanea stomped his crotch. "If you ever come near me or mine again I'll do that with ten-penny nails."

Lanea raced into the woods.

Jedediah stepped out of an old ramshackle shed, haloed in fumes. Somewhere a smart and powerful wizard wanted them dead.

And I've been lax.

He doffed his hat, wiped his forearm across his forehead, and seated himself on a stump next to the shed. Eyes closed, he picked up an old clay jug and hoisted it to his lips. He drank several large gulps and smacked his lips happily.

The cabin assault, escape and return from the Pacific Coast had taken a lot out of him. Rather than go home and rest, he'd come to the shed. He'd grown accustomed to Lanea's ability to fend for herself. He'd let Drake's tutelage then Jordan and Billie Jo fill his hours while their stock of potions dwindled.

He took another draft.

Ready potions can tip the advantage, particularly for Drake or Jordan.

"Too busy drinking to protect your charges?" Lirelaeli asked.

Jedediah jerked upright and teetered off the stump. He scrambled to his feet, stuffing down the eager flutter summoned by her voice. "What're you on about?"

"*Your* enemies attacked dear Jordan. Your dismal protection and instruction left her for dead—if it not for my graciousness."

"Hogwash. Nothing short of a magical being could penetrate those wards. Even they'd barely scratch her." He examined Jordan's shredded, blood stained clothes. A lead colonized his gut. "You all right, girl?"

Jordan nodded. "Thanks to Paulie and Lirelaeli."

"Mother," Lirelaeli corrected.

Jedediah's expression reddened. "You again, trickster?"

Paulie swept off his hat. "Yo. Dat'd be me, pops."

Jedediah sighed. "You both have my thanks. If you'll excuse us, we need to have a private father-daughter chat."

Jordan bristled.

He led her from them into the nearest wood. They'd follow or they wouldn't. He formed a soundproof bubble around them.

"You're not my father."

"Sadly so. Just wanted rid of them."

"Why?"

Jedediah arranged his thoughts. *Thought Lanea's gambit funnier than centaur face-plants, but that woman intends it as a license to scheme. I can't have her undermining Jordan.*

"Tell me what happened."

He listened, praising certain actions even if they're proved insufficient.

"Sometimes, surviving is all you can hope for. You did well. Thought on your feet. Used your resources, though Lirelaeli's help will doubtless come with strings."

"Like what?"

"Maker knows."

They walked in silence. Jedediah smiled at her bare feet. He led them back to the shack.

"Got to check something." He stepped inside.

"What're you doing in there?"

"Bit of brewing," he called back. "Come in and look."

Jordan peeked inside. "This is safe?"

"Yes and no."

Jordan entered a shack larger inside than it appeared. Shed walls boxed ledges over a small cavern. A stair wound along two sides to a stone floor. Mad science filled the cavern. Tables supported odd assortments of copper and glass tubes, flames, tubs, containers, jugs, vials, and beakers.

"Moonshine?"

Jedediah smirked. "Occasionally."

"You bootlegged during Prohibition, right?"

"Yup. I enjoy brewing moonshine, but I use the still's odor to disguise the alchemy fumes. Healing draughts, potions stink to high heaven." Jedediah shrugged. "It's their ingredients."

"Moonshine's illegal, how's that a good disguise?"

"Easier to explain away—assuming they find the place."

She laughed. "It's in an open field."

"Today," Jedediah said. "Shack moves about on occasion."

"How do you move a whole cavern?"

"Doesn't matter where the shack wanders, it connects back here once it settles."

Jordan rubbed her face. "Where'd you get a moving shack? What happens if you're inside when it moves?"

"Old Slavic witch sold it to me."

"Old Mauve?" Jordan asked.

Jedediah sucked his teeth. "Not advisable to use Mauve and witch in the same sentence. She can get a mite testy."

Jedediah led Jordan to a shelf-free wall. He touched a protruding rock and chanted. Stone slid into extra-dimensional space, present only as a transparent ghost. A high-tech vault lined with shelves, drawers and cubbyholes lay beyond.

"Vault and emergency exit."

"Moonshine still make good money?"

"Nah, can't compete with modern breweries."

A mischievous smirk lit her features. "Don't need money if you can simply make gold."

"Lanea talks too gorram much."

"You *can* make gold?"

"Yup."

Jordan glanced at her hands. "I thought maybe she pulled my leg."

"Mischievous, big-mouthed scamp likes you well enough to tell you straight—mostly."

"Why don't you live someplace nicer?"

"I like my home. Hell, I built that farmhouse from the ground up—three times. I don't ever want to move." He studied her. "There are other reasons you're not ready to know. Anyway, only figured out making gold a few years back."

"Don't those kinds of things get passed down father to son?"

"My Da was a hunter and war chief," Jedediah said. "Best not to pass such things down. Breeds the wrong attitude."

"How did you figure it out?"

Jedediah chuckled. "Like so many other significant discoveries in life, total accident."

"Tell me about it?" Jordan asked.

Jedediah considered her. *She's shown genuine interest fewer times than I can count on one hand. It's not like I'm giving her the recipe.*

"Wrestled with the gold transmutation for years—no success, but I liked the challenge. Had a dozen test formula's going, turning my lab—not this place—into a furnace. Pulled a Pepsi Gold from my cooler, tripped, and knocked over a beaker. Potion and Pepsi spilled everywhere: lead bars, floor and me."

"Lead to gold, just like that?"

"Hell, no. Turned lead into a goopy sludge." Jedediah laughed. "Where they both covered white dirt, the stuff transformed into real honest to goodness gold."

"No way, dirt?"

"You came from up north, probably never heard of white dirt. It ain't regular dirt, it's weird stuff—pregnant women eat it sometimes, no idea why. Best you just googley eyes it."

"Never heard of Pepsi Gold either," Jordan said.

He shrugged. "Discontinued. Worried me a bit, but turns out regular Pepsi does the job too. Anyway, want to lend a hand?"

"Yes." Jordan looked at her hands. "But I have a date."

"Now's not a good time to be out alone."

"Please, Master. You've no idea how long it's been since something good happened to me."

Jedediah cleared his throat.

"You know what I mean."

Jedediah considered. "Take the new Charger, leave your date's information just in case."

Jordan hugged him, rushed up the stairs and out of the shed. She poked her head back inside.

Jedediah pointed. "Farm's that way."

Muler ordered a pizza.

Hunger gnawed at him, driving him out of his hotel room to wait by his car. The delivery driver pulled up. Muler stepped forward to pay. The kid dropped the bill and Muler picked it up.

A blinking red light beneath the car caught his peripheral vision, reflected off a puddle of oil

He shoved the bill into the boy's hand, took his food, and rushed to his room.

Sweat ran down Muler's face. His heart pounded, and his mind raced through scenarios, counter-scenarios, and counter-counter possibilities.

One wants me dead. He usually gets what he wants. There's got to be a way out of this? Zero?

Zero scared One. He spoke for the Board. He could call One off—unless he ordered the hit.

Someone crossed his grave.

Muler grabbed food and a weapons case, racing from the extended-stay hotel. He crossed the highway to a Perkins restaurant. He stole a car. He tried to drive casually, but it kept accelerating.

Don't know how to contact Zero anyhow.

He considered going to ground. The Namhaid specialized in ferreting out well-defended targets gone into hiding. Two's renown built off that exact skill. They'd be watching his bank accounts. He had a few cash drops, but only because One insisted everyone keep them. Muler'd never taken them seriously. Cash went obsolete ages ago—why bother in a world full of anonymous online banks?

How long would that cash last me?

He pulled into a mall, stole an old car without GPS and drove on. A stomach grumble restarted his interest in the forgotten pizza.

Muler cursed.

Talk to One? Dead. Trap Two? Dead. Run? Dead. Dead. Dead.

He cursed again.

I need an ally, but loyal mercenaries cost.

His mother'd warned him to treat people well on the way up and never burn bridges—the mantra of those that never get ahead. He'd had her committed at fifteen.

I hurt people. I'm good at it, enjoy it. Killing Shine should've put me in a better position to hurt more people. How did it all go wrong?

He turned on the radio and cursed, Christian music. Other presets didn't improve things. It represented a message from on high: he'd stolen the wrong car.

He turned it off and focused on the road. It curved and wound through mountain and trees, not that he gave two pennies about the scenery. They offered places to hide, but rough living without the comforts he needed.

He passed a truck stop, almost stopping to change cars again.

Moving fast but no plan.

Go west toward where he grew up? They'd definitely expect it. Go east, opposite of home? They'd probably be on the lookout for that too. South? Skirt the Gulf and head into Mexico? Pretty much the same as going west. North?

I really hate Canadians.

His cell phone startled him. Caller ID displayed a blocked number. He removed the battery.

What if I could kill Shine? Would that buy my life?

In a word: No.

I'm out. There's no going back.

He turned east, thinking through harbors and small airports.

Maybe, I'll hijack a plane.

CHAPTER FORTY-NINE

Cover the Fan

Lanea rushed out of the farmhouse. "Da, thank the Creator, where've you been? I checked a half dozen of our properties, sent mist mirrors and tried a tracking spell to find you with no luck. We've got big problems."

"Mason all right?" Jedediah asked.

"He's fine," Lanea said. "There's trouble brewing."

"Yup. Namhaid's got a wizard," Jedediah lifted a milkman's cradle full of potion bottles. "Figured you girls needed some potions. Standard protectives: gazelle, spider, cheetah, ghost, and portable ley line. Ran out of bug juice bottles, so I brought them here. Billie Jo's due here for dinner soon anyway."

Lanea's jaw dropped. "Another wizard? This keeps getting worse."

"Care to be specific, girl?"

She dragged him into the boneyard and through an old Kelvinator, ignoring orange juice and toothpaste taste the gateway caused. They stepped out of the linen closet at Weems Road. She hurried him into the living room.

The television wall featured an attractive woman in a tailored blazer standing along an unremarkable country road.

"...we do know that this is one of several locations where bodies have been discovered. Details remain sketchy, but according to the anonymous tip faxed to news networks earlier today, burial sites may occupy as many as seven states. Rather than mass graves like recent funeral home scandals, dozens of small, unmarked graves seem spread throughout the properties.

"Police and forensics units continue investigating the provided locations as the victim count climbs toward fifty. Once again, we may be looking at the most prolific serial killer in Southeast history. Federal authorities continue to refuse comment, but public records link all the indicated properties to Jedediah Shine of Columbus, Georgia. Police haven't yet released victim identities—"

Lanea shut it off.

Jedediah rubbed his eyes, voice weary. "Gave serious thought to proposing, but now...."

"I, uh, haven't been able to reach Jordan."

"She's safe. Lirelaeli returned her mostly unscathed. I let her go on a date."

"With all this?" Lanea asked.

275

"Didn't know about it. Supposed to be a note with her date's info, fetch it from the farm while I call Billie Jo, would you?"

"What're you going to say to her?"

"I don't know, but it's probably safest if they join us there."

"We'd be safest in Sanctuary Hole," Lanea said.

He frowned. "Maybe, but I don't think there's any way to get her there."

"You could tell her the truth," Lanea said. "If you're going to propose, you have to anyway."

"I'll think about it."

Lanea followed him back and headed to Jordan's room. A small note in her neat scrawl held a name and a phone number.

Lanea mouthed silently, then shrieked with rage.

The Charger sat in Britt David Park's lot a few blocks away from Foster's Drive-In. Two other cars occupied the lot, all as far from one another as possible. Old street lamp bulbs offered little light.

Trevor's hands caressed Jordan's tingling skin. It'd been a phenomenal date. She'd never felt a stronger connection with anyone. He'd said all the right things, done all the right things. Even his invitation to neck had been phrased exactly as she'd always dreamed it.

His gaze beheld her as if finest gold. He leaned in for another kiss, her heart swelling at his touch. She'd received clumsy kisses from boys a few times. He planted strong and hungry man kisses on her lips that ignited her every desire.

A crack of thunder broke from the cloudless sky. She glanced up. Her palms tingled.

Trevor's hand tipped her face to meet his. Hunger swelled in her. *I want him so badly, more than I've ever wanted anyone. He's everything. Perfect, like out of a dream.*

"Don't worry, beautiful. No one's watching."

His kiss stole any objection. Jordan reached inside, enhancing her senses to explore their surroundings. His face blurred, probably from her joyful tears. His fingers caressed her magically sensitive skin.

Time slowed in equal measure with the acceleration of her heart. Her heartbeat pounded in her ears, but not loud enough to drown out Trevor's. Their beats varied only a mere hesitation from each other, his as rapid as hers.

He knew exactly how to touch her without going too far, teasing her in a way that drove her passion more and more ravenous. He kissed her again, and too far got farther away.

She seized his hands, pulling them to places he'd refused to touch. Desire redoubled. She wrapped her arms tighter around him, scratching her palms behind his back.

"Delicious," he whispered.

Wind rose in the background, a crowd cheering his kisses, cheering his touch. She couldn't agree more. She heard a whimper, probably from her own lips as his hungry touch drove her toward ecstasy. Each caress encouraged her to sing or cry.

Every noise he makes sounds as if he's nibbling a decadent sundae of hot fudge over caramel truffle ice cream—because he loves me, cherishes me. He's perfect and most important all mine. I'm the luckiest girl alive.

Jordan's heart beat with wild abandon. She hoped he hadn't noticed her clammy palms. She scratched them absently. She heard a scratching—his watch against the upholstery. His restraint drove her mad. She'd never felt so aroused, so sure of something that had previously intimidated her. She pulled him atop of her. He drowned her in his embrace. Their competing hungers tangled them in stubborn clothes. Fingers burned deliciously against her skin.

A sudden sense of perfection drowned a moment's indecision.

Everything is perfect. You want him. Take him. Hold nothing back.

The door behind her vanished in a screech of tearing metal. They tumbled to the ground, but her hunger continued unabated. She ripped at his clothes, blind to Jedediah towering above them haloed with electricity.

A spark leapt across her. Every nerve burned, clearing her thoughts. She gasped, pinned beneath his furious expression.

Oh, God, what am I doing? What have I done?

Jedediah's hand shot forward and snatched back. He didn't actually touch Trevor, but Trevor flew forward to land several paces away, dragging Jordan's shirt the rest of the way off in the process.

Time slowed.

Jedediah—almost always restrained, almost always preferring a quiet pointed word of rebuke—bellowed. "Treevoran spawn of Vysilar, what the hell do you think you're doing with another of my daughters?"

Trevor tried to get to his feet. "She consented, Wizard. The council won't allow you to touch me."

Another wave of Jedediah's hand slammed him into the Charger's side. "Think you'll live that long, elf?"

Elf?

Jordan scrambled to her discarded shirt. Lanea stood above it, white with shock, fear and fury. Nip cowered next to her.

"Elven council's ignored and excused you for preying on single mothers and girls a tenth your age. They've cried silently with no voice to defend them."

"Normals deserve no voice among the Lords of the Fey."

"Well, *Lord*, your perversions have crossed the line this time. I warned you to stay away from Lanea." Lightning melted the nearest streetlamp. Thunder roared. Treevoran slammed into a tree. "She shows up bleeding? You throw her out. That should've been the last of you."

Lightning split a tree into three smoking pieces. Thunder slammed across Jordan's skin.

That's pretty boy? Memory of his face blurring flashed across her thoughts. *Glamour. Oh, God, he tricked me into almost....*

Treevoran slammed into the Charger once more. "Now, you've seduced my underage daughter?"

Words slipped from Treevoran's dazed lips in a language she didn't recognize.

"I don't care what custom you invoke. I don't care what silk slides from your serpent tongue. This is the last girl you'll prey upon." Jedediah's staff leapt from nowhere. He raised it. "Cockroach might be too high an aspiration for your next life. Look me up when you make it that high."

The sky shattered with lightning enough to turn night to daylight.

Jordan threw herself against Jedediah's chest. "Jedediah, please stop!"

The sky held its breath. Blue lights flashed in the distance, growing closer.

"Get out of my way, girl. This bastard's got it coming."

"Dear God, Lanea, help me stop him."

Lanea spoke a single, icy word. "Why?"

The patrol car screeched to a halt. The driver aimed a spotlight at the scene. John leapt out. He approached cautiously a conciliatory hand extended and his other on his gun.

"Mr. Shine," John said. "Step away from him."

Blood bubbled from Treevoran's laughter. "You'll rot for this, *human.*"

Jedediah tightened his empty fist as if crushing a beer can.

Treevoran screamed.

John tackled Jedediah, driving him to the ground. Eddie pulled up, opened his car door and rushed to assist. A force pulse threw John into nearby bushes. Eddie and John hit Jedediah from opposite sides. Jedediah staggered to his feet despite the two weights wrestling him down.

Eddie lost his grip and fell. John wrapped his arms around Jedediah's head in a precinct-taught wrestler hold. Jedediah sucked in air and raised clenched fists.

"Da!"

Jedediah whipped around, sending John's legs swinging. Tears filled Lanea's eyes. She shook her head.

"Calm down, Mr. Shine," Eddie held his gun ready, aimed low.

John abandoned his apparently ill-executed hold and placed himself between Jedediah and Treevoran. "Just take a deep breath."

Jordan's enhanced sight saw Jedediah's limbs fill with power. She rushed to help Treevoran up, unsure why concern overwhelmed her.

John held his ground. "Get him behind the cruiser."

Jordan helped Treevoran half crawl to the cruiser. Eddie maintained a steady stream of calming patter long enough for them to reach the relative safety of the police car.

Jedediah glared at John, shot one last furious look at Trevor and stomped off. Once Eddie knew his direction, he let Jedediah go. He expected Jedediah to only take a few steps.

When he didn't stop, Eddie called after him. "Mr. Shine, you can't leave until you explain your actions."

"I stopped a crime."

Eddie and John looked at the Charger and then Jordan.

"What crime?" Eddie said.

"Statutory rape," Jedediah said.

"She initiated it," Treevoran said

Jedediah balled his fists and marched back toward the cruiser. John and Eddie got in the way. "You...drugged her."

"All right, Mr. Shine," John said. "I can see it, but you have to calm down. Things aren't the same as when we grew up. Teenagers—."

"He's older than you think. He uses those looks to prey on young girls," Jedediah smiled. "Check his ID."

"Fine, we'll take him too, but I'm arresting you for assault," John said.

Jedediah looked deep into John's eyes. He clenched his jaw. "Never laid a finger on him."

"What about damage to his car?" Eddie asked.

"My car," Jedediah said.

"Okay, we still have to bring you to the sheriff's office," John said.

Jedediah's gaze pinned Treevoran like a frog in biology class. "You pressing charges under human law?"

Eddie and John exchanged glances.

Treevoran looked from Jordan to Lanea back to Jedediah. "No."

"Then you ain't taking me nowhere," Jedediah said.

John pulled his handcuffs from his belt. "Mr. Shine, I'm citing you for causing a public disturbance—all that yelling. Put your hands on your head please."

Jedediah did as instructed. John took the first hand but jerked back—shocked by a massive charge of static electricity. John and Eddie put Jedediah in the back of a car. An ambulance arrived for Treevoran, but the EMTs found him uninjured. He declined a trip to the hospital. He stepped into the bushes, never meeting Lanea's venomous glower.

"Miss Jordan," Eddie said. "You need to answer some questions before you go."

She nodded, her heart in her mouth. She looked to Lanea for support. She found none. Lanea and Treevoran had vanished.

"Where did he go?" Eddie asked.

John cursed, reddening. "Sorry, Miss Jordan."

Lightning flashed overhead. Treevoran yelped, haloed and singed but otherwise unharmed.

Eddie rushed to him. "You've got to come with us too."

"I don't answer to you," Treevoran's brow wrinkled. "That didn't fill your ears as you should've heard it. What happened to my—"

Jedediah smirked.

Treevoran jerked from Eddie's grip. "Take your hand off me, primate."

Eddie whipped him around, pressing him against a tree. He pulled his cuffs.

Terror filled Treevoran's face. "No, please no, I'll come, how you say, quietly."

Eddie glanced at John.

"I'd cuff him anyway," John said.

Oh, God, if he's really an elf... An uncontrollable urge to protect Treevoran shoved her forward. "Someone abused him as a child, um, tied him up. Cuffing him would be cruel and unusual, it'd cause irreparable harm."

John shrugged.

Eddie studied her. "Okay. No cuffs, but the moment he tries *anything*, he earns a set of bracelets."

Why did I do that?

Nip lay his chin on Jordan's foot and whined.

"Yeah, you tried to warn me."

Bianca smiled at her phone. Had it been alive, it would've cowered. *Muler still won't answer, even a day since the spotter reported him haring off. He's better than I thought, discovering that explosive.*

One'd instructed her to feed him a new task, play dumb and ease his suspicions. They had the job location secure, ready to finish the little turd.

Her phone rang. She forced cheer into her voice. "Kaci."

"Zero."

"Yes, sir?"

"Ahn's no longer a priority."

"One wanted him for the plan," Bianca said.

"Shine's in jail. He couldn't be blamed for Ahn's death even if Ahn doesn't wind up in the next cell," Zero said. "Feds will take over before Shine's released."

Bianca frowned. She'd liked Ahn as a mark. Little men who thought women placed on Earth for them to paw, those topped her list of very favorite kills.

"Aw, I really wanted to play with him."

"A service to womankind, no doubt."

Bianca snorted. "Deserve what they get, letting themselves be victimized. I just *love* emasculating womanizers before they die."

"Indeed. Circumstances do not allow it. I have another task that should prove somewhat satisfying."

"I'm listening."

Zero outlined the new attack of opportunity. She forced down her mounting excitement. Zero hung up.

Bianca licked her lips. One would be disappointed they'd miss out on Ahn. She'd never said no to him before.

I'll make it up to him, after Zero's little job.

Lanea walked.

She paid no attention to where her feet led her. It didn't matter. Nothing mattered and everything mattered too much. The world fell in on her ears, and she couldn't force away the image of half-naked Jordan with Treevoran.

How can she have betrayed me like that? She should've known better. She witnessed me tell him it was over. Lanea chewed her lip. *If it's over, why do I care?*

Glamour.

He'd slipped the magic so deeply into her, she'd done things totally unlike herself.

Like Da.

Red haze tunneled her vision. Jordan had gone out on a date with him, chosen to kiss, no, more than kiss Treevoran after he'd ensorcelled her.

Forced me to do things I wouldn't otherwise have done.

They were supposed to be sisters. Lanea'd never had a sister, but sisters didn't whatever to each other's boyfriends.

He isn't my boyfriend. She asked about him, but I refused to talk about it. Is this my fault or did the glamour keep me from speaking out against him to possible prey?

She remembered the way Jordan had gazed at him before she'd started shouting at him. Treevoran's taken an immediate interest in Jordan as Lanea cast him off.

Jealousy surged to new heights.

We belonged together. She shouldn't have gone after him. Hell, she should've kept driving and never come back.

Flight

Muler stopped at a small town hotel near the coast. He'd been over it and over it. He swapped the license plate from the stolen car with the one next to it and went to the office by way of the vending machine.

There's no way out. Even killing Shine won't save me from One.

He stepped into the office and extended a wad of cash to the old Asian man behind the desk. "Welcome to the Sun Tzu Inn and restaurant. How long will we enjoy your friendship?"

Muler blinked at him. "Pardon?"

The desk clerk wheezed a chuckle. "We're all friends here, even our enemy's enemies."

"Whatever, I'm just here for the night," Muler said.

"Why can't you trust a man who lay on hillside with another man's wife?" the clerk slid the money into a drop safe and pushed a registration clipboard at Muler. "Because he's not on the level."

"Right." Muler filled out the form with false information and slid it back. "Keep that in mind."

"The restaurant opens for lunch at ten-thirty, our General Tso—"

"Can I just have the key?" Muler asked.

Muler hurried to his room, shaking his head. *That's what I need right now, some old gook mixing bad humor with worse philosophy.*

His room hadn't been redecorated in this century, probably not in several decades beyond that. Thumb-sized roaches raced for the bathroom when he approached the bed.

Muler crawled atop the bedspread. Sleep avoided him, but he faded into black dreams.

The Samoan twins chased him down deserted streets, clawed metallic gloves already stained with gore. He dodged down an alleyway, tipping debris into their path on his way by. He turned again, racing up the street to make one more turn and lose the great behemoths.

He turned. He raced. He turned again.

Tension eased. He bolted left and stopped short. A Godzilla-sized dragon with a dog collar snarled at him. He spun the other way. Shine marched up the street, dressed like Ian McClellan.

Muler bolted back the way he'd come.

The Samoans stepped into view at the block's opposite end. He raced on, desperate to reach the alley and elude all pursuit.

"Muler!" Shine thundered. "You hurt my dragon!"

Muler whipped a glance over his shoulder.

Shine pointed his long white stick.

Muler threw himself to the ground.

Lightning shot over him, raising every hair on his body. It hit Flash, or maybe Gordon. The Samoan lit up like a roman candle.

Another shot turned the twins into a firework's factory lit up for an insurance burn. Shine'd cleared his way. Muler bolted toward them and escape.

The dragon stomped into his path.

He spun, hopeful of an alley escape.

Lightning struck.

Muler bolted upright, drenched in cold sweat. He knew exactly what to do.

Muler stared through binoculars at Shine's farmhouse. A mob of press and police jockeyed for position at a newly erected gate. Through the tree lined drive, a barely visible minivan hid an old Charger in its shadow. News of One's latest trap filled every radio station.

I might be too late, unless I'm willing to break Shine out of jail.

Movement caught his eye. Shine's hound—the dragon—paced into view.

A chill ran Muler's spine.

It turned, looking directly at him.

Muler's mouth went dry. His pulse accelerated.

The beast glanced back toward the house, then loped toward him.

Muler dropped the binoculars, threw the car into gear and gunned it.

Drake understood every word escaping Billie Jo's mouth. Her tirade at finding Mason alone had been one thing, calmed by Mason's assurance of an emergency. But since the reporters had swarmed the house, the things escaping her lips made Drake want to tear out her throat.

Mason's attentions, instinctive or sincere, had kept Drake calm, but he'd finally had to flee her.

She should have more faith in Master, not fear the worst of him.

Deputies had driven the news people back to the highway just in time, shoving them behind a fence that had appeared only hours ago. One more accusation and he'd have dined on reporter tartare.

He paced the porch.

A wind blew toward him from the road. The deputies' failing patience tasted like burning marshmallow. The citrusy tang of frustrated reporter overpowered it.

Another scent lurked beneath.

Drake scanned for witnesses, enhanced his glamour a fraction, and extended his wings. He strengthened his senses and intoned a seeking spell in his mind.

The magic dragged his nose beyond the road and a bit left. A heat smudge inside the car faced his way.

Drake inhaled a scent indelibly etched into his memory. His blood bubbled and churned like magma. The scent had been his last before pain swallowed him.

There's pain to repay.

He loped toward the car parked opposite the fence. The scent intensified, spiced by fear's sharp bite.

Good.

The car and its driver fled.

A growling chuckle escaped Drake's throat. *You'll soon know real fear, my prey, and real pain.*

Drake raced into shadow, shifting talons into cat's paws. Agony met his call upon the source, pain added to Muler's account. His limbs lengthened, approximating a cheetah form Jedediah insisted upon before he'd abandoned Drake for Jordan.

Uneven strides followed in irregular rhythm until the last muscle slid into place. He extended his stride, weaving through trees at a breakneck pace. He attached a seeking spell to Muler's scent trail before releasing the agonizing magic.

His prey fled left, but Drake raced straight.

He burst from the treeline ahead of Muler's car. He leapt, restoring talons, intent to sink four claws into the car's bodywork.

Muler spun the car in an incomprehensible maneuver and raced back the way he'd come.

Drake opened himself back up to pain and roared.

Fire burned down his limbs, forcing his talons into quick feet. Muler's pungent, heady fear filled Drake's mouth with saliva.

His mind ripped Muler apart over and over, each time rending limbs in a different order.

The car turned hard down another side road.

Drake ran cross country, coming out of the woods close behind Muler. He gargled phlegm and spat a ball of concentrated fire. It clung where it struck the car's trunk. Paint bubbled and sheet metal underneath glowed.

The car shot forward.

Pain throbbed with Drake's every stride, taking breath became a labor.

Too much. If I'd thought, rationed my strength. Black smoke drew a trail across the horizon. *He won't escape.*

Drake envisioned the roads. Muler's flight took him down a road without turn offs or curves. It teed, offering two escapes and preventing certainty in cutting it off.

A thought sent phantom anguish through him. *Unless I fly.*

Drake extended strides into bounds. He shook out his wings. Stiff wing muscles complained at the small movement.

Will they even hold me aloft?

He extended them, bound into the air and flapped. He roared with agony.

His prey swerved. Its fear intensified.

Drake dropped his glamour. He shoved terramancy into his wings each time talons struck ground. He leapt.

Each wing beat felt like torture. Three beats, he hit the ground—still running.

Drake snarled. Flame spouted from each nostril. He leapt.

One wing beat, pain wracked him. He managed a second beat.

I'll rip him and his car into tiny unidentifiable pieces.

His wings beat a third time. His body arched downward. He pushed his wings down with all his might and roared.

No use. I've never managed before. I—elder fey—just don't have the strength.

He stiffened his wings, gliding into the inevitable landing.

After the things I said to Master, I've failed him, failed Lanea. She'll be madder I hurt myself than that I let Muler escape. His chest swelled at the thought of her, sudden ache adding to his pains as remembered bullet wounds bloodied her chest. *How many times has she helped me? Lessons? Fixing my mistakes? How many punishments has she suffered for me with that sisterly smile? How can I fail her?*

Strength surged to echo Drake's fury.

Drake's feet hit ground and immediately pushed him back into the air. One wing beat, two, pain, and a third. Four beats, five, agony and a roar. Six beats, seven and glide.

I'm flying! Rage and torment blinded him in equal amounts, but he rose into the air. *More important, I'm gaining.*

Muler couldn't believe his rear view mirror. *The little monster's flying.*

The fireball, its terrifying roar, his nightmares had told true. *It's a dragon...and it's going to eat me.*

Flame charred a black line along the cement highway and melted his bumper. Muler slammed on the brakes. It sped past, turning a graceful arc back to eat him.

Muler leapt out of the car to a kneeling position, hands up. "I surrender. I surrender. I'm here to help."

It landed. Flame flickered from his nostrils. Talons kneaded concrete like so much mud.

Muler's life flashed across his eyes. The cinematography seemed pretty poor, and the dialogue amateurish. It told a tough guy story, a bully inflicting pain for fun and profit—he'd never granted an ounce of mercy in his life.

"Mercy! Please! You're the good guys, you have to show me mercy."

The dragon stepped forward.

Muler flopped prostrate.

A huge claw pinned his neck.

Terror and a deep tenor radiated from it. "I don't have to show you anything but my teeth."

Urine ran down his thighs. Magic? Wizards? Weird, but okay. A talking dragon pegged the needle on his Bizarre-o-meter.

"Want me to crap your sorry remains anywhere special, Muler?"

"Please, I know everything. I came to help the wizard. I have a plan."

Pressure on his neck eased a moment. Smoke choked his breath. "You're as treacherous as a scorpion hitching a ride. Choose your next words with care."

Muler survived to tell him everything.

Eddie—Trevor still locked in his back seat—asked her questions and let her take a taxi home. She told the deputy what happened had been consensual even though she doubted her own words. She couldn't say a negative word against Trevor—even when she tried.

The taxi pulled up to a mob. Reporters rocked the cab, shouting questions about murder, torture and a thousand horrifying images. Deputies parted the crowd for it to enter the property. A tear-streaked Billie Jo descended. "Thank God you're safe. I'm so sorry. I did this to you. It's all my fault."

How does she figure she's at fault for Trever's—Treevoran's actions? Jordan's face scrunched together. "What are you talking about?"

"They say Jedediah's a serial killer."

"They're out of their frelling minds," Jordan snapped.

Billie Jo sobbed. "I just don't know. There's no television here, and phone reception is minimal, but what I saw, oh my god. Pack your things. I've got to get you out of here."

"I'm not going anywhere. Jedediah's a bastard sometimes, but he's not..." Words froze in her throat. She relived his rage, relived him torture Treevoran. Ice water bathed her.

"You'll have to return to group care." When Jordan didn't move, Billie Jo added, "Just while they figure this out."

Tears blurred her hazed vision. The rollercoaster of shocks and surprised she'd experienced at the farm played through her memory. Short time or not, it felt as if she'd always been there, as if she belonged. Screwed up as it might be, Jedediah wasn't a foster jailer, but a parent she didn't want to lose.

The park's horrors replayed. Warmth usurped ice.

He would've killed Treevoran to protect me. No one's ever cared about me like that. Jordan focused on Billie Jo through the tears. *You stupid woman. How can you turn away from that kind of love?* Jordan found her voice. "I'm not leaving."

"You may not have any choice," Billie Jo said.

"Has Lanea come back?"

"What? No, oh god, you're right. She might be a monster too. I'll call Angesa—"

"How stupid are you? He loves you. How can you believe the worst in him just like that? Where's your so-called faith?"

"Jordan, honey, when you're older—"

Jordan cut her off. "Where's Drake?"

"Who cares where the dog is?" Billie Jo snapped.

Jordan charged up to her room. Billie Jo followed, hanging up her phone while Jordan stuffed a duffel.

"I'm glad you've seen sense. Angesa's on her way."

"I'm going to Weems Road," Jordan lied. "There's a TV there."

"Let me wake Mason, and we'll go together. I can call Angesa on the way."

Jordan drove the old Charger through the gate. Flash bulbs and blue lights illuminated the interior. Jordan blinked her vision clear only to have it filled with fairy.

"Where're we going, my dame?" Paulie asked.

"I don't know," Jordan said. "Away."

CHAPTER FIFTY-ONE

Enemies & Allies

Two holding cells abutted those for the arrested and awaiting arraignment. They'd put Jedediah in the empty one. A drunk sleeping it off and a pair of adolescent shoplifters shared the other with Treevoran. A sparse population filled the other cells. Everyone else slept—except Jedediah and Treevoran.

"I won't forget this, wizard."

"Sorry, sonny, kind of deaf in one ear. Step closer to the bars and say that," Jedediah said.

Treevoran glared.

"What's the matter, honest life too hard for you?"

"Give me back my glamour."

Jedediah patted himself. "Where did I put that?"

"When the council hears—"

A wind whipped through the cells, shoving Treevoran toward the bars. He braced himself hard. Jedediah dismissed the wind. Treevoran stumbled.

A dark chuckled escaped Jedediah's throat. "I'd take care with threats, boy. There's little enough reason to let even your ashes leave this place."

"If I had my magic—"

Jedediah's brows rose.

A deputy entered the hall. "Ahn, you're being released on bond."

Jedediah frowned.

Treevoran smiled. "This isn't over, wizard."

"Oh, you're right about that, son."

Jedediah pressed his forehead against cool brick. He'd paced the cell all night, avoiding the game of stab-a-wizard the uncomfortable bunk's springs enjoyed.

I've been in here too long. I only did what any father—foster or otherwise—would do in the same situation. Who knows what the Namhaid's doing while I'm stuck here?

Trevor hadn't pressed charges, hell, he'd barely escaped deputies beating him without his glamour to transform his natural condescension.

John's just trying to knock a few ounces of humility into my thick skull. He'd been charged with disorderly conduct—not precisely murder. Probably enough to keep him overnight, but not enough to summon Meadow from Atlanta. *Kid's still got moxie.*

A deputy brought in a cart full of breakfast trays. Jedediah didn't remember the young man's name. He passed trays to everyone but Jedediah.

"Excuse me, boy," Jedediah asked. "What about me?"

"Sorry. Don't have you on my list."

A deputy named Wallace appeared before Jedediah could object. "Mr. Shine, your attorney's here. Step back from the door, and I'll take you to him."

Him?

Wallace led Jedediah to a small, empty room complete with tables, chairs and a television.

"They're walking him up now. Don't try anything. I'll be right outside."

Jedediah sat at one of the tables. An armored television advertised feminine products. The broadcast cut to a serious, telegenic anchor in a dark suit over the local news affiliate's logo.

"We have an update in the upsetting Shine serial killings. Police discovered two missing teenagers this morning in a hotel residence maintained by Shine. Authorities suspect the children—whose names are still being withheld— would've eventually joined other bodies unearthed on the Georgia farmer's properties."

Shock froze Jedediah thoughts, saving Muler's life.

"Your attorney, Mr. Shine," Wallace stepped aside to let Muler pass.

The face finally permeated Jedediah's glacial thoughts. He lunged across the table, grabbing Muler by his suit lapels. Sparking limbs seized Muler's throat.

Wallace tackled Jedediah, calling for help. Officers wrenched at Jedediah, but he refused to relax his grip.

Muler turned purple.

Nightsticks battered Jedediah. Tasers bit him, ineffectual through his electrified aura. Finally, an enterprising officer levered him backward with a nightstick across Jedediah's throat.

Muler wheezed for breath, eyes barely recovering from their last fall toward closed.

Deputies chained Jedediah down.

Muler coughed, managed to stand and took a seat opposite Jedediah. He took a deep breath. "That isn't necessary, gentleman. I'm sure it's just a matter of mistaken identity. Please release him."

"Keep him in hand a minute more," John countered.

Muler straightened his suit. "It's a pleasure to meet you, Mr. Shine. My name is Helmut Muler. I know you usually deal with Mr. Drake, but as he is otherwise indisposed, he sent me instead."

If he's killed Drake and come taunting, I'll fry him here and erase the deputies later. "Go on."

"I assure you, Mr. Shine, we at Stormfall, Drake and Muler will use every resource at our disposal to secure your release."

Stormfall? Joe Franklin didn't know that name. Only Drake could've told it to Muler.

"Right. Mistook you for a murdering, dog-killing, son of a bitch," he said. "My mistake."

John glanced at Wallace. "We'll leave a deputy in here anyway, to avoid further mistakes."

"In point of fact, this is a privileged conversation, and I require you to wait elsewhere while I confer with my client." Muler cleared his throat. "Should he kill me, charge him accordingly."

John gritted his teeth. "Fine, but we'll relocate him."

The new room featured frosted, steel reinforced windows, an all metal table bolted to the floor and a thick ring anchored to concrete. They fettered Jedediah to the ring before allowing Muler into the room.

John glowered, but stepped into the hall.

"None of this stops me from killing you," Jedediah growled. "It'll only save you the slow agony I've got planned."

"Or Drake eating me," Muler said.

"He doesn't need any more junk food. So for perversity's sake, why don't you tell me what's going on?"

Muler leaned forward, glanced at the door and spoke in whispers. "Look, there's a whole mountain of crap about to fall on you. Much bigger than a few murders. I have information you need."

"Out of the kindness of your sainted heart."

Muler snorted. "Not hardly. Can't go into it here, but One and Two have ensured you never leave custody again."

"One? Two?"

"One is Marc O'Steele, head of the Namhaid's U.S. operations."

A cold, black stone settled into the pit of Jedediah's stomach. "The scouting agent?"

Muler smiled. "Sucks being clueless, doesn't it?"

Jedediah grunted in the affirmative.

"You met Two at the hotel. Her real name is Bianca Norway, not Kaci."

"She checked me out."

Muler nodded. "Except she didn't check you out. Cops found runaways in your room there. They fed a grave map to the press so it couldn't be hushed. A contact said the Feds marked you at the cabin. You're as good as on death row."

"I'm innocent."

Muler snorted. "Think that matters? Judges? Juries? They're bought and paid for, *narr.* Being charged by the Feds means a move to higher security. That's when we'll break you out."

"We?"

"Me and Drake."

"You think I can't merely vanish from these cuffs, these walls, this country in the blink of an eye?"

Muler frowned. "I suppose you could, wizard, but I'm betting their plan took that into account."

"I can 'die' again. No one'd be the wiser."

"One isn't a good sport and Two's a psychopath. Disappear and everyone around you becomes a target," Muler said.

"I'd take them with me," Jedediah said.

"Either going to be crowded where you're going, or you'll miss someone who dies in your place."

Restraints prevented Jedediah folding his arms. "Why're you here?"

"They're trying to kill me," Muler said.

"I sympathize."

"You can protect me."

Jedediah laughed out loud.

Muler glanced at the door. "Yeah, I get it, over your dead body, but I've got information that can help you. We've got a common enemy."

Jedediah hoisted his most frightening grin. "Why don't I just kill you and enslave your soul? You'd obey my every command with no chance of double cross."

All color drained from Muler's face. His mouth opened and closed.

"Or better," Jedediah said. "Stop your heart and make your corpse confess."

Muler finally found his voice. "Look, I've seen the light. I'll mend my ways, join the good guys. Aren't you supposed to be grateful for my rehabilitation? Grant me clemency?"

"Who mislabeled me a good guy?" Jedediah asked. "This ain't a comic book. You want absolution, find a priest. I'm a wizard—we don't save souls. We use them."

"But, but," Muler stammered. "Merlin, the Wizard of Oz, Gandalf, Harry Potter..."

"Morgana le Fay, Elphaba the Wicked Witch of the West, Buckwart, Saruman, Voldemort, Meeks, Sedgrick," Jedediah looked up as if trying to recall the next evil sorcerer's name. "Jedediah Shine."

Panic permeated Muler's voice. "Drake promised you'd guarantee me protection if I helped the two of you."

"Drake doesn't speak for me."

"He's Elder Fey, he said that means you work for him."

Jedediah darkened. "It means I'm going to kick his ass between those nubs he calls horns and remind the arrogant, adolescent son of a bitch who's master."

A commotion in the hall moved their direction. Muler glanced nervously at the door. "Promise you won't kill me—or have me killed—and I'm yours with no effort."

Jedediah scrutinized Muler. "No holding back?"

"None," Muler said.

"Anything?"

"Well, I won't surrender my life."

The door flew open and careened off the wall. A woman dressed to the nines but scoring a ten barged into the room.

"What's going on in here, Jedediah?" Meadow March demanded. "Who is this charlatan?"

"Public defender's office must have made a mistake," Muler leapt to his feet. "I'll get out of the way."

"You said you worked for Stormfall, Drake and Muler," John said.

Muler shuffled toward the door, talking fast. "Yes, doing pro bono work for the Atlanta defender's office—sent down here because of a possible conflict of interest with local resources. Obviously, I'm not needed here. I'll just go."

"Mr. Shine," John said. "Would you be so kind as to tell me which lawyer is yours?"

"Who says they both aren't?" Jedediah said. "Mr. Muler and I are done. Ms. March will be staying."

Meadow's eyebrow arched.

"You intend to strangle this lawyer hello too?" John asked.

Meadow's brows scrunched together. "Jedediah?"

"I'll explain in a minute," Jedediah said.

John shook his head and left, shutting the door behind him.

"Why're you here, Meadow? What's going on?"

"Fill me in first."

"That man is a professional hit man. He shot my daughter and ran me off the road. Turns out his little unsanctioned adventures marked him for death. He came to confess his sins and beg my protection." Jedediah shrugged. "They've been trying to frame me for murder. I tried to strangle him. It seemed only fair."

"Hitman wants *his* protection?" Meadow mouthed. She licked her lips and stared him dead in the eye. "Are you a murderer?"

Jedediah met her gaze. "I've killed, but never in cold blood. What's more, the bodies on my land aren't my handiwork. Why're you here?"

"I saw the news and came running," Meadow said.

"Muler said something about runaways. I saw a report about missing kids, probably them," Jedediah said.

She nodded. "I don't know if they have anything firm yet, but the press is crucifying you. People are screaming for blood. It's bad."

Jedediah sighed and wished for some mint.

"Have they charged you with anything yet?" Meadow asked.

"Disorderly conduct," Jedediah said. "Found me with a roughed up boy, but I never touched him."

"That's not going to help matters," she said. "Anything else I should know about this Muler?"

"Besides a half-dozen attempts on my life? He's probably the man who kidnapped and killed Joe Franklin and Nancy."

Meadow shot a look of horror from Jedediah to the door and back. "Please tell me you're pulling my leg."

"Afraid not."

"Can you prove it?"

He chuckled. "We'll need a priest. I don't do miracles."

The itch of a mist mirror awoke Jedediah. Dim cell block lights indicated it still night.

"Da?"

"Here," Jedediah whispered. "How are you girls?"

"I'm fine," Lanea said.

"What about Jordan?"

"Don't know, don't care."

Jedediah glowered.

"What?"

"We're family—"

"She's not family. You and I are family. How can I help *you*?" Lanea asked.

"Start by taking you head out of your ass," Jedediah said. "Jordan's one of us. We're the only family she's got. I'm stuck here, so you got to watch out for her. Billie Jo and Mason too."

"If you care so much, why not gather them up and leave?" Lanea asked. "Take them to Sanctuary Hole."

"This is personal. Running and hiding don't sit right. Besides, what gives me the right to choose a life in exile for her?"

"Fine, I'll find Jordan. Should I talk to Billie Jo?"

"Appreciate it if you found out how she's coping," Jedediah said.

"Anything else?"

"You in cahoots with Drake and Muler?"

"What do you mean Drake *and* Muler?" Lanea asked. "Isn't Muler trying to kill us?"

"Muler changed sides. No idea what Drake's thinking, but I'm concerned he's in a bit deep for his years. He and Jordan will need your experience."

"Damn," Lanea cursed, "I left it in my other pants."

"Irreverent little scamp."

Her laughter eased his mind.

"What now, Da?"

"Meadow's working on things. Got to sit tight while she sorts it out."

Jedediah fell back asleep. A noisy rumble of power woke him, setting his teeth on edge. *Damn girl's throwing sheer power around noisiest way possible.*

Jordan slid up through the cell floor, one hand on Nip and one hand on Nibble.

"Y'all are damned noisy, girl."

Jordan blushed. "Come on, we're here to rescue you."

Jedediah looked her up and down. "Aren't you a little short for a sorceress?"

"Come on," Jordan pled.

"I take a short vacation on the county's tab and everyone turns into Bonnie and Clyde. Shouldn't you have waited until right before they hang me, Jordan James?"

Jordan glanced at the other sleeping inmates. "Jedediah, please, this is all my fault. I have to get you out of here."

He cupped her cheek and brushed some earth from her shoulder. "None of this is your doing. Now you get out of here before you get caught. Meet up with Lanea. She'll keep you safe."

"Right now I'm more afraid of Lanea than I am the cops," Jordan said.

"I talked to her."

"What about you?" Jordan asked

Jedediah fixed her with a disgusted look. "Might be I'm old to you, but what exactly makes you think I can't teleport from this cell for gelato in Italy, glimpse the Mona Lisa in the Louvre, swing by Shanghai for some moo shu pork and be back for soggy waffles without anyone noticing?"

He saw the implications of his rebuke fall into place behind her eyes.

"I appreciate the thought, and I'm proud of your execution—even if you need more practice. Please, do what I ask. I'll be fine."

"But what if they decide to execute you or something?" Jordan asked.

"Justice System doesn't work that fast any more. Why? You'd miss me?"

Jordan took a turn glaring.

He cleared his throat. "Glad you didn't run, but why didn't you?"

"Why do you think I'd run?"

"Things are pretty complicated just now. State will probably want you back until we resolve this mess. You've got money, clothes, a car and nobody to tell you no."

"I thought about it," she admitted.

"So?"

"Do we really have time for this now?" Jordan asked.

Jedediah gestured around them.

"Fine, as screwed up as life with you is, you'd kill a man...elf...whatever to protect me." Tears edged her eyes. "You're the first person since my parents that wants me for me instead of some angle."

Jedediah studied her, unsure how to phrase what came next. "We could see to it they would never take you back."

Her eyes swept his face.

"Just think about it. Now get."

Jordan seized him in a hug. She put a hand on Nip and Nibble and let them do their thing. They left, loud and clumsy.

CHAPTER FIFTY-TWO

Dominoes

Jedediah rubbed his shackled wrist. They'd chained him to an interrogation room floor—for everyone's safety. They'd moved him just before lunch but not before he could smell it.

Probably think it's torture.

The door opened. Scents of ozone, Old Spice, and overly sweet perfume wafted inside.

Jedediah glanced up.

A dark-haired, mid-thirties man in a government-standard suit strolled in burdened by innumerable folders. He laid them down, sat and adjusted spectacles over warm brown eyes.

The bookworm who would be Fed.

A similarly dressed woman reeking of perfume followed him. She glowered at Jedediah, paced behind the bookworm and too obviously disdained the other seat.

Jedediah smiled.

Irritation permeated her voice. "Something about this situation amuse you, Mr. Shine?"

"Ellouise, please." Bookworm leaned forward and extended a hand—a crucifix peeking from behind his tie. "I'm Agent Benjamin Ridley. My partner is Agent Ellouise Turner. Please forgive her, these kinds of things make her a bit testy."

Jedediah took his hand. A tiny current of electricity trickled up his arm.

Untrained, and weaker than Mason. Jedediah adjusted his vision. Power congregated around Ridley's senses, sharpening him into a natural bloodhound.

"Uh huh," Jedediah said. "Forgive poor bad-cop, soldiering on despite burdens that sour her disposition, says the innocuous, trustworthy bookworm. You revenuers should invest in new stereotypes for the twenty-first century."

Ridley smirked. "Perhaps."

"Why'd they send Feds to investigate a disorderly conduct and where's my lawyer?"

"This isn't about your altercation with Mr. Ahn," Ridley said. "Just wanted to ask you a few questions while in town—if you're not terribly busy."

"Should we've waited for your new boyfriend to finish?" Turner asked.

Jedediah's eyes fixed on her. "You're real good at playing the bitch. Take lessons or does it come naturally?"

Ridley adjusted his glasses and opened a folder. "The questions, Mr. Shine?"

Jedediah considered him. *Their questions might provide insight. I can always call Meadow before answering, and since we're playing the stereotype game....*

Jedediah beamed. "Call me Jedediah, son."

"All right, Jedediah, What can you tell me about Ronnie Gerald's murder?"

"Joe Franklin cleared me as a suspect."

Turner leaned close. "Sheriff's dead, Jedediah—as you know. He can't testify as to why he cleared a murderer."

"He can call me Jedediah. You'll say, Mr. Shine or Sir."

"Got a problem with women in power?" Turner asked.

"Nope, just don't like you," Jedediah turned to Ridley. "Bad-cop just voided the friendly chat. We'll continue my abuse with my lawyer present."

"Why, hiding something?" Turner demanded.

"Abuse complaints process easier when witnessed." Jedediah addressed Ridley. "I've invoked my right to counsel."

"This is just a general query, unrelated with your arrest," Ridley said. "We'd appreciate your cooperation."

Jedediah folded his arms.

Ridley smiled. "Bring her in."

Turner summoned Meadow from the hall. Meadow seated herself with a proud smile.

"If you were here," Jedediah said. "Why weren't you in here?"

Meadow glared at Turner. "Confusion over interview location."

Jedediah scrutinized Agent Ridley. "A simple mix-up, I'm sure."

"Ronnie Gerald?" Ridley asked.

"Found dead on my property. Drake," Jedediah narrowed eyes at Turner. "He'd love you."

"Jedediah," Meadow said.

"Drake's your bloodhound?" Ridley asked.

"When he wants to be," Jedediah said. "Called the Sheriff's office. Showed the deputies they sent out where Ronnie had been mauled. Granted permission for them to investigate and otherwise cooperated at every turn."

Ridley ran a finger down the report.

As if you haven't memorized it.

"Coroner's report identifies arrowheads as the cause of death."

Jedediah shrugged. "So Joe Franklin mentioned."

"You own a bow, Shine?" Turner asked.

"Yup, it'll be in the search warrant report."

"Right before being cleared, the hospital admitted you for similar wounds," Ridley said.

"Yup."

"How did you sustain those wounds?" Ridley asked.

"Someone shot me with an arrow," Jedediah said.

"Where'd the cash come from to pay your hospital bill?" Ridley asked.

"U.S. Mint."

"Did you call a Florida money firm?" Ridley said.

"Yup."

"You make a call, and hundreds of thousands ride to your disposal in an armored transport? You a drug lord? Mobster?" A wolfish grin spread over Turner's face. "Gunrunner killing trespassers who find your stash?"

"She done raving?" Jedediah asked.

Ridley smirked. "Perhaps, but they're good questions. Please answer them."

"Yup, no, no, no, and go take a Midol," Jedediah said.

"Jedediah," Meadow said.

Jedediah shrugged. "She's a bitch."

Turner's face reddened. She lunged, restrained just in time by Ridley.

"Practice that combo?" Jedediah asked.

Meadow scowled. "Thank you, agents. My client's too tired—"

"And hungry," Jedediah added.

Meadow's brow rose.

"They keep forgetting to feed me," Jedediah said.

Meadow stood, looking down at the agents. "That'll be all until my client's health needs are addressed."

Jedediah frowned. "But, Meadow, they've worked so hard to weaken and fool the simple farmer. Shouldn't I confess to the innocuous catholic bookworm now?"

"Frankly, I've had enough of the frothing hellhound act," Meadow said.

Jedediah chuckled. "Nice turn of phrase."

Meadow smirked.

"Ellouise, if you please," Ridley gestured.

They sat.

Jedediah leaned close. "Meadow, shouldn't we let them play a few more cards?"

"I don't like how they're playing this," Meadow whispered.

"Your call," Jedediah said.

"We'll entertain a few more questions while you arrange my client's meal," Meadow said.

Turner stepped outside, returning a moment later.

"Cash delivery?" Ridley asked.

"I fail to see the relevance," Meadow said.

"Recordings captured your client present at his Alabama fishing cabin during a firefight between federal agents responding to an anonymous tip and unknown gunmen," Ridley said. "Upon entering the premises, agents discovered stockpiled military grade weapons and the dead bodies of Joe Franklin Tomlinson and Nancy Radcliff."

"Sheriff discovered Mr. Shine's gun running operation," Turner said. "And your client shot him for it."

"We're investigating possible connections between illegal arms sales and moneys employed for hospital expenses, house purchases and other recent extravagant expenditures," Ridley said.

Well, shit. Does look suspicious piled together. Jedediah smiled. "Interesting theory."

"Where'd the money originate if not arms sales?" Ridley asked.

Jedediah shrugged. "Pappy buried a couple strongboxes of gold, been selling it off a bit at a time—wouldn't want to drive the price down."

"Where did he get it?" Turner asked.

"Can't say, agents. Discovered a safety deposit box with maps and the name of a money firm after he passed," Jedediah said.

"Convenient," Turner said. "Your simple, lucky farmer routine won't erase the corpses hanging over your head. You're not getting off this time."

"That is enough, agent," Meadow said.

"Ellouise." Ridley handed Meadow a folder. "We're charging your client with illegal arms sales, murder and the other charges listed here. This's a federal warrant for the search of his properties."

"Agent Ridley," Jedediah met the man's gaze. "Bad television plot or not, someone's trying to frame me. I've murdered no one."

"Do you know who and why?" Ridley asked.

"I think I know who, but I can't say why," Jedediah said.

Turner folded her arms across her chest. Ridley stepped closer. "Who?"

"Helmut Muler came posing as my lawyer, threatening my loved ones and bragging about the frame," Jedediah said.

"The lawyer you tried to strangle," Ridley said.

"Yup. He said Marc O'Steele and some organization set up the whole thing. I met O'Steele once and thought him a stand-up fellow. I've only Muler's word, but your people found mercenaries guarding those weapons.

"Maybe those gunmen are part of it. Talk to them. One'll roll to avoid prison," Jedediah said.

"None survived the firefight," Ridley said.

"You have any proof?" Meadow asked.

"No, but that's their job? Ferreting the truth and defending the innocent," Jedediah said.

Turner snorted.

"Agent Ridley," Jedediah's voice soften, becoming earnest. "Joe Franklin and I spent most of his life as friends. I want you to find his killers."

Ridley's searching gaze scoured Jedediah. "That's my job, Mr. Shine and I'm *very* good at it."

"Do your job then, Agent. Don't let lazy thinking blind you from the truth."

The agents left them alone. Meadow lowered her voice, glancing at the observation mirror. "Jedediah, these people aren't your friends. Let me do my job, or they're going to send you to prison—or worse."

"I'm sorry, Meadow, but that Ridley *cares* about the law. He's no witch hunter. I've put the possibility in his head. When the truth peeks out, might be his subconscious catches a glimpse now that it knows to look."

"What if you're wrong?" Meadow asked. "Let me bring Justin in on this."

Jedediah scratched his beard. "Good idea. If I got you the money, could you arrange protection for Jordan, Mason and Billie Jo?"

"They'll have frozen your accounts by now. Even so, none of them are your concern legally."

"Guess I'll handle it myself."

Ridley watched through the glass. Turner texted him again, eager to execute the warrant. Meadow left.

Jedediah stared back.

That farmer's sharp as razor blades. He's hiding something behind that likable façade. Ridley chuckled. *Takes one to know one. Maybe you're innocent. Maybe you're an incredibly clever villain.*

"Capelli, we're not waiting for Ridley. Head out there now and toss the property," Turner said. "Don't use any of the locals."

"We'll take care of it," Capelli said, "Why the rush? Don't we have enough for a conviction?"

Her eyes lit. "I want this bastard buried so deep hell's a move up."

Capelli studied her. *Any idea how fanatical that sounds?*

"Capelli?"

"If it's there, we'll find your evidence." He turned to the others. "Let's execute."

Capelli leapt into an SUV and glanced over as Deborah Flute pulled out of the lot. "Manufactured evidence would probably suit the she-bitch. What's she got against this guy?"

"He's a monster, Raul," Flute said.

"But that's the job. What makes him special?" Capelli asked.

Flute described the interview, drawing it out over the dull drive. "Then he told her to take a Midol."

"No kidding?"

"Honest."

Capelli laughed. "I'd have paid to see that."

"Priceless," Flute pulled onto the Shine property. "We're here. Let's catch a killer."

Fed SUVs filled the circular drive. Field officers spread out. Something black caught Capelli's peripheral vision. It vanished around a corner.

Capelli rushed after it. "See that?"

"I saw something," Flute said.

They pursued, others joining the sudden motion. Capelli rounded the corner. The greenhouse door shut.

He gestured. Agents took position on either side of the door, waiting for others to encircle the greenhouses.

"FBI," Capelli said. "Come out with your hands up."

They waited a few moments, then charged inside. A wide-eyed Jordan stood in the greenhouse rear. Muddy puppies milled around her feet.

"Ms. Jordan?" Flute gestured. "It's the foster girl."

"Leave me alone. I'm not going back to a group home."

"You take this," Capelli whispered.

"That's fine." Flute made her voice soft and reassuring. "But let's get you cleaned up, a meal, some shoes, doesn't that sound good?"

"No. You're trying to take me to a shelter," Jordan said.

"It's not safe here," Flute said. "We just want to protect you."

A hysterical note crept into Jordan's reply. "Nowhere is safer than here."

Capelli shook his head. *Stockholm.*

"I'm sure you feel safe here. We just want to make extra sure," Flute said.

Jordan raised both hands, but not in surrender. "Just stay back, I don't want to hurt you."

"There's nowhere to go," Capelli said. "The greenhouses are surrounded."

"Stop where you are," Jordan said. "I'm serious."

Flute glanced at him.

He shrugged slightly. *She's not armed. Those pups aren't a threat. What could she do?*

His earpiece informed him others approached via the other greenhouse to get behind her.

Jordan stepped backward, cracking the door to another section of greenhouse. A buzzing rose in volume. "Help me? For Jedediah?"

Capelli and Flute tensed. He spoke into his radio. "Possible accomplice in the far—"

Screams deafened him. People shouted gibberish about monsters and man-eating plants.

Bees swarmed past Jordan.

Capelli and Flute dove from the greenhouse, slammed the door shut and leaned against it. Bloodied agents staggered from the other greenhouse. Two struggling to keep the door shut while firing at leafy vines flailing around its edges.

"It ate Lin, just ate her," a bleeding men on the ground repeated in a hollow voice.

Bees swarmed over top of the greenhouse. They ran. Pain stabbed Capelli what seemed a thousand places. His tongue filled his mouth, copper tang polluting his labored breath. He staggered, grabbing at a holster behind his back with swelling limbs that refused his command.

"Raul!" Bees harried Flute. She seized Capelli's wrist, dragging him away while shouting into her radio. "Get us an ambulance. Capelli's gone into anaphylactic shock."

"This is Ridley," the radio squelched. "Give me a sitrep."

"We're under attack, sir," Flute said.

"Acknowledged, can you identify your attackers?" Ridley asked.

"Bees, plants, hell if I know," Flute's voice neared hysterical. "We've got men down, possible fatalities. Capelli's been stung a few hundred times. I think he's allergic."

"He'll have a syringe on him," Ridley said. "Inject him then get clear, help's on the way,"

Jordan peeked out the greenhouse door and slipped around its corner.

Flute caught sight of her and leapt after Jordan. "Help me. She's getting away."

Jordan fled toward the boneyard, cutting between Jedediah's workshop and the pond. "Stay away from me, please."

Jordan rounded the workshop and collided with Muler. The two tumbled. Jordan's color fled. She scrambled backward to the pond's edge, shrieking at the top of her lungs.

Flute came into view. "I've got eyes on that lawyer, Muler, I'm—"

Drake snarled. "Leave her alone, *human*."

Fear drowned Jordan. No glamour protected her or Flute from the absolute terror deluging off the dragon. His tail spikes gouged the ground in angry sweeps. Her throat closed off a squeak of warning. Muler scrambled into the oncoming Feds, ivory with horror.

Feds fell on Muler until the real threat slammed into them. Someone opened fire, setting off a chain-reaction of panic fire.

"No!" Jordan shrieked.

Rock thrust too slowly from the ground. Bullets ripped Drake's wings. They clipped frills from his head. They ricocheted off magic enhanced scales.

The sludge hydra—drawn from pond's bottom by Jordan cries—emerged from the far side of the pond. Horrified Feds fired at it. Enraged catfish heads opened wide, razor-toothed mouths

The fear exploded another octave.

Jordan curled into a tight, sobbing ball. Control fled her. Her earthen wall crumbled.

Drake slammed through its crumbling remains. He did as he'd been told. He defended Jordan without rules or limits.

The sludge hydra joined the Elder Fey.

They destroyed the Feds.

Ridley examined the remains of his field team.

Only those injured in the first assault survived the second.

Capelli floated in and out of consciousness on an ambulance gurney under the watchful eyes of EMTs forbidden to take him to the hospital until Turner released him.

"What in Christ's name happened here?" Ridley asked.

"You heard it, monsters, man-eating plants, nothing made any sense," Turner said. "Some sort of hallucinogenic gas?"

"Flute reported eyes on Muler." Ridley shook his head. "Gas or not, how does one man leave shredded flesh and melted Kevlar in place of all these agents."

"How'd he avoid getting gunned down?" Turner said. "Assuming they didn't hallucinate Muler too."

Ridley spotted a crucifix lying in bloody mud on a broken chain. He dusted it off, kissed it and tucked it into his shirt pocket.

"I've got more security coming down from Atlanta," Turner said. "It'll push Shine's relocation toward evening."

"We're only transporting him outside of town," Ridley said.

Turner gestured.

"You're right. No shortcuts." He circled the slaughter. He bent over footprints. "Small, barefoot."

"The girl?" Turner asked.

"Probably."

"Her and Muler together?"

"Hardly." Ridley's lips pushed to a fine line. "Handle the relocation. I'm going to follow these."

"You shouldn't follow her alone."

Ridley nodded. "Send me some locals, and see if they've got hounds."

"Drug lab?" Ridley asked.

304 | MICHAEL J. ALLEN

Eddie frowned through the doorway into the hollowed out cavern. "Moonshine still most likely."

"Strangest still I've ever seen," Wallace said. "Looks more like a chemistry set gone wacko."

Ridley climbed down and studied the cavern.

This is no still. It's not a meth lab or a bomber's setup. What the hell's he doing here?

"She came here," Eddie gestured to broken bottles beneath the small open refrigerator.

"How long ago?"

"Can't have much of a lead," Eddie said.

"Cordon this off. Keep a deputy here until our people arrive."

Eddie glanced at Wallace.

Wallace's shoulders fell. "New man, got it."

"What now?" Eddie asked.

"Spread out, deputy, there's got to be another trail here somewhere."

Jordan struggled to breathe. Stone pressed around and through her body formed a suffocating yet calming womb. Her fingers wrapped around Nip's and Nibble's scruffs. They took turns rising high enough to phase air into their earthswim pocket. The ground rumbled with their efforts to keep her melded with the rock.

Jordan shifted her sight, distracting herself by studying the way they managed the swim. *Wouldn't it be easier to just carve a little cave and some air holes—at least while we're stationary?*

Surprise flashed through Nip and Nibble. Nip held her in the swim. Nibble raced around her, building their new cave by moving earth elsewhere in mouthfuls. Nip released her into a cave far closer than swimming in solid earth had felt. The pups curled around her legs and promptly slept.

She watched through stone with magical sight. Feds exited Jedediah's shed, but one deputy stayed behind. He waited inside the entrance. Feds came, boxed up everything and left.

She breached the floor, gulped fresh air and flopped onto it like a landed fish. Nip and Nibble looked equally exhausted.

She dusted herself off and went to the fridge: empty.

What now?

Jordan shivered—exhausted, starved and as afraid as she'd ever been. *I need food, bed, definitely a shower. Where's safe? Where can I go? Maybe I should've left when I had the chance.*

"We'll stay here tonight," Jordan laid down upon a mostly smooth section of rock wishing for enough strength to soften it. Mudpuppies curled up next to her, dirty and warm.

The long, horrible night stretched on and on.

CHAPTER FIFTY-THREE

Appearances

Only occasional silent visits from Agent Ridley marked the passage of Jedediah's remaining day. They studied each other, a tension in the agent's face. They didn't speak.

He asked no more questions. He delayed no more meals.

Time flowed around the wizard in a cage.

They arraigned Jedediah the next morning, flanked by Meadow and Jedediah's ancient friend Justin.

"Not Guilty, Sir," Jedidiah announced with absolute confidence.

The judge remanded him without bond despite fervent argument by both his attorneys.

When Meadow used the little girl's room, Jedediah brought his old mentor up to speed.

"Muler said they've bought judge, jury and verdict," Jedediah said.

Justin placed a wrinkled hand on Jedediah's. "What do you say, young man?"

"That right and justice will prevail."

A dry chuckle escaped Justin. "Which one of us taught you that? You're too old for Superman comics."

"My Da. Dutchman too. When he passed the mantle to me, he promised the gates protected their rightful protectors."

"Old spells." Justin nodded. "Wily like a fairy lawyer."

"Maker save us from that fate." Jedediah chuckled.

"It'll be fine, boy. Charge that girl of yours to protect the Gate while we ride out this storm."

"She's not ready."

"Best way to see if a chick flies is throw it off a cliff."

Jedediah sobered. "Will you take the mantle, just until this is done?"

Justin shook his head. "I'm almost out of days. Besides, all those papers we prepared to ensure the property entrusted to only those intended would all have to be voided then redone."

"Have been wondering if I'd engineered a tough enough contingency geas."

Justin shook his head. "Jedediah, if you make that failsafe quest any tougher no one will be able to take Guardianship. You'll lock that corridor forever."

"Maybe that'd be better."

"No, boy. There are too few connections to the source already."

Angry protestors gathered around the courthouse and the jail. Security tightened around both. His escort reflected the change.

Farmhouse incident has got these boys hair-trigger tense.

They eased Jedediah up into the back of an armored van. He shuffled forward, manacles and fetters clinking. Two officers in full riot gear kept weapons point blank. A third bolted his chains through a retaining ring. The third slammed the doors shut behind him with ominous finality.

He shook off his unease. *Justice can't be bought.*

The rumor mill whispered about as quietly as Niagara Falls. The death of the federal agents ate at him. That resultant scrutiny kept him from checking up on Jordan's well-being chaffed that much worse.

How the hell does Muler figure he'll spring me from all this? He chuckled. *Not really my problem, is it? I can leave any time I want.*

The van pulled out through shouting, angry voices. Jedediah Shine, murderer and child who-knew-whater had to be protected so justice could send him to his death. There'd been an awful moment when one Fed had almost taken it upon himself to punish Jedediah.

Ridley saved him from another body on his conscience.

Lanea'd contacted him, asking a question that floated into his thoughts over and again. "Why don't we just leave?"

It tempted him, but whatever their intentions, the Namhaid needed not only trounced, but taught that integrity meant something—not just represented some weakness they could exploit.

Jedediah sighed.

Both guards jerked weapons toward him.

"Sorry, boys. Been a long day."

"Going to be longer once you get to prison," guard one said. "They love hurting guys who rape little girls."

"I empathize," Jedediah said.

Ridley rode two SUVs behind the armored transport. He scowled at the armored vehicle, something nagging at him.

Despise knowing something I don't know. Things should behave, act in an orderly manner. This damned case is like new math—no sense to it at all.

The convoy pulled onto an old, outbound highway. Civilization dwindled and his instincts ratcheted up.

Ridley spoke into the radio. "Everyone keep sharp."

"What's wrong?" Turner asked.

He shook his head. He didn't understand how or why, but he knew bad things filled their near future.

"I don't know, but something."

They managed another mile. Half way through a gentle bend, a missile hit the car directly in front of Ridley's. Chatter filled his ear. Drivers accelerated.

A fireball unlike any weapon Ridley's ever experienced slammed into the armored transport. Impact topped it and a second sent it spinning into a gully.

An armored dune buggy launched out of the wood, two men and a woman masked against identification. The buggy rushed up, circling the transport. The woman spun a heavy, mounted machine gun. She opened fire. Bullets and tracer round stitched the convoy.

The advanced escort skidded to a stop, blocking the road. Police poured from their vehicles. They took cover and returned fire. Rear escort split around Ridley's SUV. They blocked the rear escape.

The woman flipped forward and back. Tracer rounds a hand too high, drove police and agents for deeper cover.

Another missile flew in from the woods. It destroyed a police cruiser.

Ridley reached for his door. Terror gripped his throat. A small drone of some sort buzzed the convoy. It released the equivalent of small hellfire bombs, laying a wall of fire between Ridley and Shine.

The buggy screeched to a halt alongside the van. The passenger slapped something on its doors. He retreated around its side.

Explosives ripped off the back doors.

The bomber rushed into the smoking van. He stumbled back a moment later, firing inside.

Damn, have to put those men in for a commendation.

The bomber stumbled into burning doors. His mask caught fire. He ripped it off. A clean-cut man with soot-smudged blond hair glowered into the van, shooting with a vengeance. He glanced Ridley's direction before diving back into the van.

Gunfire and yelling echoed inside the truck.

The drone strafed the advance escort, pinning them down and dropping another flaming wall. Another missile launched a cruiser skyward.

Dear God, please let them have gotten to cover.

A voice rang out from inside the armored van oddly clear in the tumult. "Muler. Get in here."

The buggy driver said something to the woman enjoying her machine gun a bit too much. She swept the rear escort as the driver raced into the van.

They dragged Shine into view. The farmer fought them for every step. He dislodged the driver's mask before the blond knocked him unconscious with a pistol butt.

They shoved Shine beneath the laughing, masked gunner and sped back into the trees.

Ridley cursed. *Why'd Shine fight them? They offered escape from custody. He wanted to get away...didn't he?*

Muler cursed too, lowering a single expended missile launcher.

Marc O'Steele, a women who doubtless represented Bianca Norway, and his own doppelganger dragged Shine from the armored van. They clubbed Shine, shoved him into a buggy and escaped into the far wood.

What the hell? Why didn't they shoot him? Why the hell, shit, screw why, how the hell am I helping them while I'm right here?

He turned to the small, panting dragon. Regrown patches of wing almost camouflaging its lining.

"Explain what the hell just happened," Muler demanded.

Drake shrugged.

The motion gave Muler's spine an icy tickle.

"Let's go. Master will be waiting," Drake said.

"Waiting? I don't know why he doesn't already have a bullet in his skull." Muler swore more colorfully. "You're right. We've got to get out of here."

A swooping sensation nearly knocked Ridley from his feet. "No one? Not one fatality?"

"Mostly burns and scrapes from ricocheted debris," Agent Bridger said.

"What about the forward escort?" Ridley asked.

"Everyone in that first missile hit is alive. They're hurt, but the armor apparently protected them."

Ridley scowled. "It's not rated for that kind of ordinance. What about whatever hit the van?"

"Napalm weapon of some kind, again, just basic fire damage but minimal injury."

Ridley's fists tightened. *It's new math all over again.*

"I could've sworn two bullets from that big gun hit me. They sure as hell knocked me flat," Agent Bridger flushed. "Pardon my language, sir."

"Your new body armor stopped it," Turner said.

"No ma'am, not a scratch," he showed them.

"The guards inside with Shine?" Ridley asked.

"Shaken, bit disoriented, but otherwise fine."

"I heard gunfire inside the van. I saw the flashes," Ridley said.

Bridger shrugged. "Guess they missed."

Ridley rubbed his eyes.

"Take it easy, Ridley," Turner said. "We lost him, but no one died. Dash cams even got two of his accomplices."

"Muler and O'Steele?" Ridley said.

"Tech will verify, but they looked like the preliminary file images," Turner said. "We're going to nail the whole bunch."

"I hate this case," Ridley snarled. He paced back and forth in a fury, hand slicing the air. "Did Shine escape? Was he abducted, if so why? What killed our men at the farm? Property damage, but no casualties? How's that possible under that kind of assault? Nothing makes sense. Nothing fits. Nothing's right."

Jedediah waited in a fallow field.

This Keith's stretch or the Ireland farmstead?

Drake bounded across the field. Muler trailed behind in an obvious temper. Jedediah smirked.

Drake slammed into him, wrapping forelegs and wings around Jedediah. "Master! You're all right."

Jedediah chuckled and patted his shoulder. "When we're clear, you and I are jawing about your choice of companions, apprentice."

"How the hell are you alive?" Muler demanded.

O'Steele stepped out from behind Jedediah, aiming down a pistol at Muler. He opened fire.

Muler stumbled backward, whipping his own pistol out and fired his gun empty.

Jedediah flourished a hand. O'Steele dissipated in a sixties transporter effect.

Muler glowered. "You double-crossing bastard. You did some kind of magic that not only outed O'Steele, but me. The Feds saw me slaughter them. Do you have any idea what that means?"

"Yup," Jedediah smiled. "Though, no one died."

"How's that possible?" Muler asked.

"A little illusion, some kinetomancy, and defensive shields around the Feds in case you and Drake were sloppy, again."

Muler balled his fists. "Why would you protect the Feds?"

"They're good boys doing a hard job. Just because you and the Namhaid are murderous psychopaths, doesn't mean good men should end up hurt."

"They recorded me violate federal law. We had a deal."

"I promised not to kill you," Jedediah said. "You look pretty lively to me."

Muler fumed.

Jedediah folded his arms. "Drake, what happened at the farm?"

Drake's chest swelled. "I protected Jordan, like you said."

Jedediah scowled. *Damn, I did tell him to take the gloves off.*

Drake's head fell. He touched Jedediah. <*Did I do something wrong?*>

"I'm not happy you teamed up with this murderer and forced my hand. I'm really upset you killed all those officers."

Drake deflated.

"Still, that's partly my fault. You meant well, even if you did make things worse. You made the right choice defending Jordan, though more control would've enabled you to do it without a body count."

<I lost my temper, Master. I'm sorry.>

"Been guilty of that a time or two, got the guilty nightmares to prove it." Jedediah gestured to Muler. "I don't know what got into your head, but for all it's worth, I have to thank you for trying to protect me and mine."

Drake perked up. *<Ours, Master.>*

Jedediah snorted. "This whole household's gone rogue. I'm obviously too lenient on y'all."

"You two done getting cozy and insulting me in the process?" Muler asked. "Feds are searching for us by now. The Namhaid plant will have informed One. We need to move."

"Field's glamoured," Jedediah said.

"Why so large?" Drake asked.

A deep thrum like slow moving chopper blades filled the area. Muler goggled. A dragon bigger than a massive passenger jet settled behind Jedediah.

Jedediah turned, bowing to one knee. "Revered One."

Drake bowed his head. "Mother."

Stormfall's voice thundered. "This the mortal responsible for my son's injuries?"

Confusion played over Drake's face. "He is, Mother."

Jedediah turned to Muler. "Keep up your end. Tell me where to find the Namhaid."

"You and your illusions can go to hell. I'm not helping someone who double-crossed me," Muler said.

"Enough, I will taste justice," Stormfall said.

"A moment, Great One, please. We must have this information."

"Rip it from his soul," Stormfall said. "His flesh is mine."

"Go screw yourself," Muler said.

Stormfall's head shot down with striking speed. Muler's screams filled the air. She rolled him over her teeth, savoring his blood. A single decisive crunch shattered legs between her back teeth. His screams vanished down her throat.

"One and only one debt is paid, wizard. There'll yet be an accounting." Stormfall leapt into the air.

"Great, more to look forward to," Jedediah sighed. "At least she didn't try to shred my mind this time."

Drake studied him.

Jedediah transformed the corrections jumpsuit into a set of overalls and swished his newly created hat through the air. A faint blue form rose from where Muler's blood had sprayed.

"Rise, Helmut Muler, I compel thy spirit," Jedediah said. "Tell me where to find the Namhaid."

"You promised not to have anyone kill me," Muler's ghost said.

"I don't control dragons. Definitely not that one."

Jordan awoke.

What time is it? Her phone displayed four in the afternoon. Panic hit her. *I shouldn't have slept so long. What if the cops came back?*

She jumped to her feet. Pups leapt with her, immediately commencing play.

"No time—"

She stared upward, blood draining away. Solid rock roofed the cavern. The cops hadn't returned and found her sleeping because the hut had wandered off.

We're trapped.

She raced to the blank wall, scouring her mind for the incantation that opened the emergency exit vault.

Why didn't I pay better attention? If I get out of this, I swear I'll listen any time he says anything.

She tried a half dozen doomed combinations. The exit remained closed.

How far down is this cavern? Where is it? She looked at Nip and Nibble. *I don't have any choice.*

She knelt. They crouched, butt's high and tails going wild. They pounced on her, mock growls and excited tongues.

"I'm sorry, but we really can't play right now. I need you to swim me to the surface."

Nip and Nibble swam her through the ground. It took forever. They brought her up in a sparse wood she'd never seen before.

Her stomach grumbled.

Nip cocked his head, then dove back into the ground.

She reached into her power, trying to fill her stomach with magic. Energy crept into her, not sating her empty gut.

How much of my power comes from me rather than around me like Jedediah and Lanea?

Nip surfaced, laying a mouthful of earthworms at her feet. His tail wagged.

Jordan frowned.

His tail drooped. He nudged her. <Eat.>

"I appreciate it, Nip, but I can't eat that."

Nibble trotted over and slurped one up. He wagged up at her, half a worm flopping from his mouth.

"I don't eat worms." She pet Nip. "Thank you, but could you put them back, please?"

Nibble snapped up the partial before Nip could collect it too. Nip slipped into the ground once more.

"Come on, Nibble, let's run. Nip will catch up."

Running felt good. It didn't fill her gut, but it centered her.

"Can you find Lanea?" Jordan asked. "Jedediah said to find her."

Nibble veered left, bounding ahead of her.

"A fast food restaurant would be nice too."

Nibble froze, lip curling. He raced back toward her, sucking up mass as he ran. He hit her with all of his weight.

Pain sliced across Jordan's leg. She hit the ground. A line of blood burned along one thigh.

Nibble growled atop her. A long broadleaf arrow spitted him like a kabob. A second arrow joined the first. Nibble's growls died.

Heat erupted in her chest. She rolled over and leapt to her feet.

A massive, chestnut roan centaur glowered at her. He raised a horn to his lips and blew.

"Why'd you do that?" Jordan asked.

"The second arrow flew for mercy, sorceress. I meant the first for you, not the elemental—not that your like care about any Fey."

"Nibble was my friend," Tears burned down her face. "Who the hell do you think you are?"

He performed a mocking bow. "Velith'Seravin, chief of Wizard's Bane."

"Centaurs are led by council."

"Not Wizard's Bane."

She looked from his raised bow to her leg. "How'd you get through the barrier?"

He chuckled. "If you mean the property line, you're outside it—quite close to our encampment actually. Or did you mean how did I bloody you when SinDon failed?"

She glowered, rumble growing in her chest with magma heat.

"Dragonsteel," VelSera said. "A rare gift from our new benefactor. Perhaps you know him, Treevoran?"

Cold banked her rising temper.

VelSera smiled at her reaction. "The dragons ordered most of it hunted and destroyed after the last dragon war. You should be honored, dying thus."

"I'm not a dragon."

VelSera's tone rose. "No, you're a worthless, two-legger, barely better than the normals that plague our lands. You're a blight, an infestation too lowly to kill with such revered metal."

"Great, drop the bow and die." Jordan charged him, lights popping around her eyes.

VelSera stepped out of the way of her charge and loosed another arrow. It sliced into Jordan's right forearm and out the other side. "There's a little pain just for you. Meant these for Shine, as they're able like no other metal to penetrate magical protections. Perhaps bloodying them on his charge will increase the pain when they kill him."

Jordan's vision tunneled. She clutched her arm and charged him. Another arrow slid through her leg—perfectly placed to injure without rushing death.

She fell.

VelSera laughed. "How does it feel, witch, to reap what you deserve?"

He's playing with me. Jordan's blood boiled. "How'd Jedediah's staff feel shoved up your ass?"

VelSera darkened. He raised the bow.

A snarling Nip vaulted out of the ground and tore at the centaur's arm.

The shot went wide. VelSera kicked the mudpuppy from him.

Nip yelped.

"Insignificant bugs defended by inconsequential sycophants, call out to your imaginary deities. Tell them to prepare for your arrival."

Jordan saw hot, glowing, molten red. She couldn't get to him fast enough to avoid his arrows. She didn't know enough magic to strike like Jedediah might.

But I got an A in physics.

She opened herself to her accumulated rumble. She sent it into earth, into its core.

And a B in Earth Sciences.

She shoved magic into the earth, summoning its irresistible force: gravity.

VelSera's bow rose at a sluggish pace. Time seemingly slowing in her final moments.

She poured all her reserves into the spell.

VelSera's arms shook. His eyes widened. His arm fell, and his bow tumbled. His knees folded, slamming his weight to the ground.

Jordan crawled toward the struggling centaur. Sobs wracked her voice. "How's it feel being insignificant, huh? How do you like something bigger kicking you around?"

"Strike swiftly, if you dare, my tribesman near," VelSera said.

"Kiss Newton's human butt, frakhead," She slid free Lirelaeli's dagger and lifted it toward his throat. "And get ready to breathe through your neck."

Hoofbeats drummed the ground, thundering into a circle around her.

VelSera smiled.

Something tugged her pant leg.

Fury and delight filled SinDon's melted face. His bow flicked up and fired.

Something yanked her pants.

The arrow struck earth.

CHAPTER FIFTY-FOUR

Sanctuary

Jordan flopped from the ground like a beached whale and gasped. Every inch hurt, arrow wounds a sharp fire in the overall pain.

Nip limped toward her, ears pressed against his head. He'd dragged her from danger through the earth. He couldn't manage the whole job himself, leaving her feeling raked along the rocks despite her attempt to match his magic.

He curled against her. <*Pack mate.*>

Tears cleaned her face. *Nibble.*

Nip howled.

Inside, she howled too.

Pressure from the imperfect earthswim had slowed her bleeding. Her wounds leaked once more, but less than before. Her head spun. Lights not likely pixies danced before her.

Nip whimpered and licked his crooked leg.

Jordan dug out her smartphone. A shattered display dominated the dead phone.

She raised her head. "Where are we?"

She recognized the park between Billie Jo's and Weems Road. She stroked Nip's head. "Amazing. I figured you'd take us to safety, but we're nearly home."

The word struck her.

Rapid regular clicking sped toward her from behind. She turned. Darkness blurred her vision. A boy among others leapt from his bicycle and raced forward. His blur felt familiar.

Before her synapses connected, darkness swallowed her.

Someone kicked the door repeatedly. "Mom, let me in."

Billie Jo opened the front door. Mason struggled beneath Jordan's weight. He cradled Jordan—filthy, bloody and barefoot no less.

"Dear Lord," Billie Jo exclaimed. "What's happen to her?"

"I don't know, Mom. Some of us went riding in the park. We raced down that path only a few minutes before, but something made me glance back—like a weird tingle. Jordan lay there like this, where I'd have run her over otherwise."

314

They eased Jordan onto the living room floor. Billie Jo pushed Jordan's hair aside. One of the always filthy farm pups limped through the open door. It collapsed into a protective position at Jordan's head.

How many times have I told her to wash these mongrels?

She reached forward to move it from Jordan's hair.

A low earthy growl too deep for its size rumbled out of curled lips.

"It's all right, boy. I'll take care of her, I just need to move you."

Nip sank into the floor, leaving a pup-sized spot of bare concrete surrounded by raggedly torn carpet.

"Mom, did that—"

Hairs on her neck rose. Her stomach knotted. She wiped her eyes and crossed herself.

"Mom?"

Her voice rose higher than normal. "Yes?"

"Are you okay?"

Her head nodded up and down. "I don't think so."

"What happened to her?" Mason asked. "Why would someone stab her?"

Billie Jo shook her head. "Fetch my phone. Jordan, honey, wake up."

Jordan moaned.

"Tell me what happened, Honey. Did Jedediah hurt you?"

Mason handed her a phone. "Is she okay?"

"I'm calling an ambulance. She'll be fine."

Jordan pressed a shattered phone into Billie Jo's hands. "Please. Lanea."

Billie Jo frowned between Jordan's crumpled body and her useless phone. Her thoughts froze.

Angesa and a deputy had come around looking for Jordan. No one knew what had happened to her.

Everything had been so good. Her grades came up. She smiled, even talked to people other than Mary Ann. Jedediah had fixed everything. He'd made her happy.

Their near perfect life had disintegrated when the press identified Jedediah as a serial murderer.

I forced her into his clutches. Look what he did to her.

Even before Jordan's accusations, she'd wanted anything that might disprove Jedediah guilty. Wishful thinking had deluded her into a love blind fool. She wanted him to be real, not a monster. But men that nice never existed, no matter how old-fashioned they claimed. The evidence proved his villainy. Jedediah employed the same medieval values as feudal lords—taking privileges with innocent girls and killing anyone their whims deemed as lesser.

He didn't want to make love to me because...

She looked at Jordan and teared up. She couldn't even bring herself to think the possible horrors she'd inflicted upon Jordan.

She shook her head. Jedediah couldn't have done this. He's in jail, but who else could be to blame? Billie Jo flushed. *What's wrong with you? Stop sulking like a broken-hearted girl and help Jordan.*

She lifted her cell phone but hesitated.

Why would she want Lanea? Damn you, Jedediah, why'd you bring this mess into my life?

Jordan wanted Jedediah's daughter, or maybe Lanea lay hurt somewhere too.

"Mom, call Lanea. Hurry," Mason prompted.

"Jordan needs an ambulance," Billie Jo said.

"No, you need to call Lanea."

"Why?"

"I don't know, I just know it's the right thing to do."

Billie Jo frowned.

Mason's strange declarations grew more frequent as he aged. She'd passed them off as weird coincidences—like the time he insisted they stay off an elevator right before it crashed to the basement. Their frequency and uncanny accuracy left her hopeful the Holy Spirit touched him in some way.

From the mouths of babes, right? Not this time.

She dialed 911. "Ambulance is on the way, ma'am."

"Lanea," Jordan moaned.

"Mom, call Lanea."

What could it hurt? Billie Jo dialed Lanea.

An out of breath Lanea answered immediately. "Maker, Billie Jo, are you okay? Are you hurt? Where's Mason?"

Lanea's urgent concern wrong-footed Billie Jo. "I'm fine, Lanea, honey. So is Mason, but Jordan's hurt."

"How bad? What happened?"

"I think she's been stabbed. I've already called an ambulance, but she keeps asking for you."

"Frumious Bandersnatch! Da is gonna kill me," Lanea said. "Where are you?"

"At home."

"Be there in a few seconds."

"You nearby?" Billie Jo asked.

"No, got to go."

Lanea locked the phone and checked her pursuers. She leapt through a bramble, slipping through unscathed as dryads taught her.

Dogs closed on her. She'd stumbled upon them and the Feds following Jordan's tracks. They'd hunted her since. Their dogs refused elven persuasion to lose her trail. Glamour and cajoling the woodland's help failed to slip their pursuit.

Hell of a breed.

She needed water—more than she needed air. Lanea sprinted toward a nearby mire, stagnant and stinking.

No time to purify it. I'll just work around rot and mud. Ugh, I'm going to hate myself for this later.

She waded in and summoned her staff. As an afterthought, she checked for an alligator.

Be just my luck today.

Lanea verified dogs and their handlers out of sight, wishing for time to use a proper circle. She slammed magic into the mire, raising a mist.

The mirror rose—thin and translucent—showing Billie Jo, Mason and Jordan.

She ran lessons through her mind, struggling to find some way to complete a teleport without a circle. Water preferred to find its own way, not leap from place to place like lightning.

She opened herself to the Dragon Spring and leeched all the energy she could from her surroundings. Power raged through her, ripping along her limbs like a massive flash flood. She forced it into constructs with gestures, pure will and a primal scream.

A wave of putrid water exploded out of nowhere, covering Billie Jo. She gasped, swallowing some. She choked.

Lanea teetered in the wave's center, soaked and stinking of bog. She collapsed, holding her head and moaning a litany of curses strong enough to turn a church congregation to stone.

"Lanea?" Billie Jo clapped her hands over Mason's ears.

"Yeah, right," Lanea said. "That's who I used to be."

"Used to be?" Mason asked.

"Might be dead. No, that probably hurts less."

"Jordan's injured," Mason said.

Lanea forced herself to Jordan's side. "Oh, Jordan, what happened to you?"

Billie Jo's mind did backward summersaults.

She said she'd be here in a second, but I thought she'd meet us at the hospital. How'd she appear like that? Where'd the water come from? How— An all-encompassing terror chilled Billie Jo to her bones. Everything clarified in a moment. *Witchcraft.*

She tried to scream, but only succeeded in making a squeaky hiccup. "Get out!"

"What?" Lanea said.

"Mom?"

Billie Jo snapped up their family bible. "Get behind me, Satan. Be gone, foul witch."

Mason blanched. "Mom?"

"Mason," Lanea snapped. "Fetch clean water."

"What's wrong with Mom?" Mason asked.

Billie Jo seized Mason and pushed him behind her. "Stay away from her, Mason. She's a devil worshipper."

"Not hardly," Lanea said. "And people say *elves* are insufferable."

Billie Jo brandished the Bible

Lanea rolled her eyes, snatched it from her hands and shouted in her face. "Jordan needs clean water. Now!"

Mason dashed to the kitchen, returning with two bottled waters.

"Thanks." Lanea poured them onto Jordan.

But she's already wet.

Lanea placed hands over Jordan. Strange words escaped Lanea's mouth, solidifying Billie Jo's worst fears. She raced to the mantle and snapped up a crucifix.

Lanea's hands glowed blue. Clean water pooled together, rising from Jordan's soaked clothes like a translucent serpent.

Billie Jo gaped. *I knew it. Jedediah's a Satanist. All those lovely words came from Lucifer, the Flatterer.*

The snake bobbed its head at Lanea and split into smaller snakes. They slithered over Jordan's body in opposite directions.

"No, no!" Billie Jo waved her crucifix. "Get them off her."

The cross splashed through one. The coiled water took one moment to put itself back together, another to glare, and headed down toward Jordan's leg.

"Mason, stop your mother before she hurts someone," Lanea said weakly.

Waterworms slithered into arrow holes. Jordan's wounds glowed, the blue light intensifying.

Billie Jo collapsed to the carpet, squelching as she landed. "Hellspawn...in my house...raising the dead."

"Mom, Jordan looks better. Lanea's healing her with magic."

"Witchcraft! Fruits of the Devil!"

Lanea mumbled, pale to the point of near transparency. Her body swayed— not in some trance rhythm but as if losing a fight to maintain consciousness.

An ambulance siren reached Billie Jo.

Jordan's wounds closed.

It's a reality show, an elaborate gag. It can't be real. Lanea can't be a witch. God protects me. The Devil can't be in my house. He'd never let the Devil into my house.

Fog rose around them.

Billie Jo seized Mason. *Merciful God, protect us. Send your angels to fight off these evils.*

Lanea whimpered. "No, Da, I need to finish the spell."

"Mom?" Mason asked.

A tsunami of vertigo pummeled Billie Jo's senses. One of her hands held a branding iron's wrong end. The other held dry ice. Pressure squeezed her ears.

Wiggling her jaw made it worse. Toothpaste and orange juice slathered her tongue.

Hope the ambulance has room for me too.

Everything went dark.

Billie Jo's head pounded. Her eyes hurt. Her tongue felt burnt. She opened her eyes.

Jedediah stood over her.

She screamed. "Devil worshiper! Oh, God, deliver me. Get away from me, Murderer! Satanist!"

"Easy there, Billie Jo."

Billie Jo rolled to her knees and folded her hands. "Please, God. I don't ask for much. I've been abducted by your enemy, *please* deliver me..." Her head snapped up. "Oh, God, Mason. Where's Mason? What've you done to him, monster?"

Jedediah's lips pressed a thin line on his face.

She scanned her surroundings. No ambulance raced toward them. No house sheltered them. Not even Georgia surrounded them. A cavern with steep walls surrounded her as if she sat in a huge well.

I'm in The Pit.

A waterfall issued down three sides of the cavern. Mason stood at the edge of an oblong pool, staring up at the waterfall. She rushed to him, wrapping him in protective arms.

"Look at it, Mom. It's all so amazing."

"It's Hell, Mason, we—"

"It's Africa," Jedediah snapped.

She turned toward him.

The pool stretched across the cavern to a small stream carving a path into a hole in the stone well. Lush, verdant grass—watered by copious mist—cushioned his steps.

Light cast a divine radiance from the blue sky high above.

Lies of the Devil.

"Calm down," Jedediah said.

Terror, panic, affection, repulsion and several dozen emotions she didn't even know how to name rushed through her all at once. She seized Mason, who gazed around in wonderment, and dragged him away from Jedediah.

"You just stay away from us," Billie Jo stepped back, foot slipping on the pool's edge.

Jedediah moved faster than humanly possible. He snatched her out of her tumble. Released her and held up empty hands. "You need to calm down."

"Da."

Jordan lay blood-soaked in Lanea's lap. Jedediah knelt beside them. He withdrew a bug juice bottle of mint-silver liquid and handed it to Lanea.

He rubbed hands together, lowering them toward Jordan's wounds.

Billie Jo's shrill voice cut through the cavern. "Don't touch her!"

"Girl."

Lanea wiped glowing liquid from her lips and nodded wearily. She inhaled mist rich air and struggled to her feet.

"It's all going to be just fine, Billie Jo. Let Da heal her, and I'll try to explain," Lanea said.

"Mom, why's your picture in the waterfall? Twice?"

Billie Jo's gaze crept up the waterfall. Silver frames hovered in the cascade, each portraying one of many people. A topmost portrait displayed her.

No, not me.

Her doppelganger laughed and smiled, living a life disconnected from circumstance. She aged through flashing scenes, growing ancient before becoming a teen once more. In the next frame, a centaur lived the same cycle in larger jumps.

"That's not your Ma, Mason," Lanea said. "Billie Jo? Billie Jo?"

Billie Jo's eyes followed the portraits down to one of herself laughing and blushing. It changed to she and Mason picnicking with Jedediah. Mason hung in his own portrait, happy and smiling.

Warmth stretched her face in a smile. It shattered.

"Dear God, he's trying to steal our souls!" She cast around. "Where's my crucifix?"

Drake trotted over to her with it in his beak.

Her eyes widened. "It's a dragon! Get away from me, Beast. I rebuke you in Jesus' Name."

Drake shrugged, set the crucifix near her and lay near Lanea.

I'm drugged. This isn't real. Or it is, and my mortal soul is in danger. Her eyes flashed up to the portraits, searching them for faces she might recognize that had gone missing. *I'll show the police. It'll prove he murdered those people and devoured their souls.*

Lanea watched her, arms folded. "Whenever you're done."

"Get out of my mind, witch!" Billie Jo said.

"Da, she's not coping."

"Give her a minute," Jedediah said.

Billie Jo scooped up the crucifix, shielding her and Mason with it.

"Looks like a lost cause," Lanea said.

"Talk to her, Jordan's in bad shape," Jedediah said.

Billie Jo's gaze flickered to Jordan. Her heart jumped into her throat. *I can't let them have her.*

She rushed Jedediah, dragging Mason by a wrist.

"Mom!"

"Da."

"Girl."

Billie Jo slammed the crucifix down onto Jedediah's head, or tried. A blue mist coalesced into a sparkling sphere around him. Billie Jo whirled around.

Lanea wavered on her feet, glowing hands extended. "You're just fine, Billie Jo. Jordan's not in any danger—"

"Drake! Fetch Mama Yamai," Jedediah interrupted.

Drake hurried down a cave.

"—from us," Lanea said.

"Explain that." Billie Jo shrieked. "I won't let you steal our happiness. God will protect us. You won't feed on our souls."

"You want an explanation or would you rather keep ranting?" Lanea asked.

Billie Jo held the crucifix toward Lanea.

"You're here because he wanted you out of danger." Lanea gestured. "You're there because Da loves you."

"Like her better when she's calm," Jedediah mumbled.

"Da," Lanea softened her voice. "The woman who looks like you is Da's first wife, Elsabeth."

"So that's it?" Billie Jo asked. "He marries them then murders them and buries them on his land?"

"Starting to feel a mite insulted," Jedediah climbed to his feet.

Billie Jo swung the crucifix back and forth.

Jedediah's expression sobered. "I've married three times. Elsabeth died of old age. A dragon slew Samantha in the last Dragon War. Jocelynn and Esme perished in an accident."

"That's four, not three. Liar! You said Lanea's mother was still alive."

"My *daughter* Esme. Lirelaeli is Lanea's mother and she's definitely alive," Jedediah said. "I ain't murdered no one, leastwise not in a very long time."

"Explain all the bodies they found then," She shrieked.

"You sent for me, *Jedaiha*? Shall I calm this one's spirit?"

Billie Jo whirled her crucifix.

An ancient, dark-skinned woman watched her from fathomless brown eyes surrounded by considerable bulk. The much shorter woman moved fluidly despite being nearly spherical. Neon markings painted copious naked flesh. A rope pinched her waist, gourds and bags hung from it. More rope supported oddments around her biceps and calves.

A crowd of men and women surrounded her, dressed like primitive tribes in National Geographic—right down to the handmade spears. Hulking dark skinned centaur wearing similar garb mingled in their ranks.

The whole world crashed down around Billie Jo as if the cascading water falling nearby slammed into just her.

Everything faded to black.

CHAPTER FIFTY-FIVE

Subtle Forces

Jedediah sighed. "Mason, look after your ma a moment, all right?"

"Mr. Shine?"

"Yup?" Jedediah said.

"It's real, isn't it?" Mason said. "All this, magic and Drake being a dragon?"

"Do you not trust your eyes, boy?" Mama Yamai asked.

"Yes, Mason, it's real," Jedediah said.

"I knew it," Mason goggled at the huge woman, blush creeping to his cheeks.

"Don't you stare at Mama Yamai, boy, unless you intend woo or challenge," Mama Yamai said.

"Sorry," he mumbled at his feet.

"I need your help with this girl," Jedediah waved her toward Jordan.

"Looks to me, *Jedaiha*, like your own girl be skirting the Scytheman."

Lanea resembled a walking corpse. She'd exhausted what the potion restored protecting him. "Look at Jordan. I can't figure out why she's not recovering. I'll take Lanea inside."

"Can you not feel it, *Jedaiha*?"

"Mama, I'm too tired for lessons."

Drake leaned close to Jordan.

Mama Yamai's petrified wood staff appeared from nowhere, striking his beak. He darted backward, lip curled. "Too close, Rydari Phriel."

"Drake wouldn't have hurt her," Jedediah said.

"No, but she would've hurt him," Mama Yamai said.

Jedediah stopped. A tribesman spoke to him in their native tongue. The tribesman took Lanea from him. He inclined his head in thanks and returned to Jordan. He scowled at Mama Yamai, but her expression never flickered. He looked at Jordan, examining her in every method he knew.

His heart seized. "It can't be."

"Oh, but can and is. A sliver foretelling coming doom," Mama Yamai said.

Jedediah leaned in close, reversing Lanea's and his own healing. He pushed a finger into her wound, mouthing incantations.

"Hopeless, *Jedaiha*," She shoved him from her way and cupped a hand over the open wound. A sliver of metal flew into her palm. She presented it. "Your foes wield Dragonsteel."

Drake's eyes flew wide. He whimpered.

"See to Mason," Jedediah said.

Drake's beak swung back and forth, his frill raised.

"See to the boy," Jedediah's voice allowed no debate. "Teach him everything he needs to know."

Drake went to Mason with several backward glances. Mason hugged him, wearing an overjoyed expression that bespoke too rare innocence.

Billie Jo woke in a fairytale bedroom which returned her sense of nightmare. Jedediah sat in a chair at the far wall. Panic washed over her. She snapped up the covers to find herself fully clothed.

"If I'm not going to bed you willingly, I'm certainly not doing so when you're unconscious," Jedediah said.

"Who knows what a monster like you is capable of," Billie Jo whipped her head back and forth.

"On your left."

She scooped up her crucifix, laid atop a gigantic Bible. She grabbed it too, hugging it to her chest while brandishing the cross.

He sighed. "I'm a Guardian, a wizard. My lands protect the Fey from humanity and humanity from them. Sometimes I find a body on my land—someone trespassing who ran afoul of some animal or a Fey creature."

"You mean demons and ghosts and witches."

"No, more fairies, elves, centaurs—you know those things you like in movies?"

"Those aren't real."

"No, but the ideas came from real encounters. Just the same, not all Fey are Tinkerbell and Mr. Tumnus. Normals have treated them foul, and many hold grudges a very long time."

"So you protect monsters for Lucifer."

Jedediah took a deep breath. "First off, more often than not, normals—human beings—are the monsters."

"How do you figure?"

A dark chuckle escaped him. "Personal experience. Humanity drove the tribes from their homes, force marched them to reservations of land no one wanted. Tell me that isn't monstrous."

"That's ancient history."

"Not for me. I lived it."

"See, Lucifer's power sustained your unholy lifespan."

"I don't work for Lucifer."

"Don't split hairs. It doesn't matter which demon or devil you serve. Let me go. You won't have my soul..." Her eyes widened. "Where's Mason? What've you done with Mason?"

"He's having lunch with Drake."

She bound out of bed.

"Sit. Down." Jedediah's voice filled the room.

She froze.

"I love you, but I've had about enough of your small-minded accusations," Jedediah said. "If you can be civil, I will explain everything."

She covered her ears. "I don't want to hear your lies. Let us go."

"You're in danger."

"From you."

"Because of me. I brought you here to protect you."

Fury, terror, worst of all, helplessness filled her. Even through her marriage and the horrors that entailed she'd managed to keep her calm, keep a handle on her emotions. She had no handles. She wanted to scream, to throw things, to beat her fists against Jedediah.

Why won't he just admit it's all lies? Why does he have to sound so damned sincere, so damned caring?

"I hate you. I don't care what you say. Magic's witchcraft and witchcraft is evil."

"Because God didn't bother to keep any magic for his own. He gave Lucifer all the power and left you helpless."

"Just let us go home. Please. I don't ever want to see you again."

Jedediah opened the door. "I'm no monster. I wanted to protect you, but I won't keep you here."

She started toward the door and stopped. "How do I get home?"

"That's going to be a bit more difficult. I could send you home, but that'd be 'evil magic.' I wouldn't want to taint you," Jedediah folded his arms. "Exit's down the stairs two flights, big stone foyer, can't miss it."

She descended, calling for Mason. He emerged from a modern kitchen a floor below.

"Here, Mom, I made you a sandwich."

She slapped it from his hand then knocked the half eaten one from his other. "Don't eat that. You'll invite their evil into yourself."

"It's tuna."

She grabbed his wrist and dragged him out the front door. "It's *evil* tuna."

Mason rolled his eyes.

Her eyes traveled up the building they'd just exited. A fairy tale structure somewhere between a castle and a wizard's tower rose up the cavern wall. She searched the cavern for an exit.

"How do we get out of here?"

"Teleport," Mason said.

She gaped at him. "Don't say such things. Magic's evil."

"Why?" Mason said.

"The Bible says so."

He scowled. "So everyone with magic is evil? They're born that way?"

"Yes. No. I don't know how they get it, but they're witches. They serve Satan."

"I thought you told me that once we confessed our sins, Jesus protected our souls," Mason said.

"You're right. I'm so scared I forgot they couldn't steal our souls after all."

"And I'm saved, right?"

She patted his arm, trying to figure out how to leave. "Of course you are."

Mason extended a hand, a Cheetos bobbed weakly in his palm. "Then how am I evil?"

Blackness returned.

Jordan stared at the waterfall. Magical portraits hung in its mist. Staring at each left her feeling as if she'd somehow connected to their subject.

Lanea approached, walking noisily enough to be heard.

"What's this thing?" Jordan asked.

"Waterfall of Memories. It's an old spell."

Jordan gestured at her own portrait. "When do you think he did that?"

"Consciously, he didn't. It's bound to him, preserving cherished memories."

"Why am I up there?" Jordan asked.

Lanea smirked. "Very funny."

"Tell me about Elsabeth?"

Lanea took a deep breath. "He doesn't talk much about her, I'm sure you noticed her portrait."

Jordan nodded. "He touches it each time he passes, as well as a few others."

"Wives and daughters," Lanea said.

Jordan faced Lanea. "We have sisters but no brothers?"

A sad smile touched Lanea's face. "We had brothers too. Way Ma tells it, when his Jocelynn and Esme died, Da closed himself off. Pushed everyone away for half a century. She wanted his attention, but he refused her. She ensorcelled him. I'm the result."

"That's kind of like—eew!"

Lanea made a face. "I know."

"Why does Elsabeth resemble Billie Jo? I mean not totally, but damn."

"Coincidence?"

"Doesn't sound like you believe that?"

"Old Mauve thinks Billie Jo's Elsabeth reborn—reincarnated."

"What do you think?"

Lanea strolled to the fall's edge and trailed fingers in the water. "Most Fey believe they're reincarnated back into nature. Humans don't believe that. I've talked with a few dead. Something happens after we die."

Jordan glanced at her hands. "What?"

Lanea sucked the water from her fingertips. "I don't know. They penetrate the veil until their spirits are just gone. Maybe there's a final rest. Maybe they expire. Maybe they're reborn."

"What about half-elves?" Jordan asked.

Lanea paled, turning away. "Elves are Fey. Human's believe their immortal soul reaches heaven or hell."

"Where does that leave you?"

Lanea shrugged. "Da wants us inside."

Jordan preceded Lanea into the immense tower library. Books, scrolls and tomes filled four stories. Floating disks created stairs at need to reach upper shelves. Latin and other languages labeled books of all sizes. The eclectic collection matched that in Jedediah's study. Entire bibliographies of a given author leaned against books on potion ingredients, Reader's Digests and Mad Libs.

"We're here," Lanea said.

Jordan turned away from the shelves.

Jedediah bent over a desk. A massive window behind him changed scenes every few minutes.

He looks tiny—deflated somehow. Jordan bit her lip. "Where're Billie Jo and Mason?"

"Gone," Jedediah said.

Drake curled near Jedediah, doleful eyes watching him.

"They're in danger, Da."

"Yup," he whispered.

"They'll be a target."

He nodded.

"You're just going to let that happen?" Jordan asked.

Jedediah raised a somehow hollow gaze to her face. "She forbade me to help her."

"She's upset. She doesn't know what she's saying. You can't abandon them."

"In this, I have to respect her wishes," Jedediah said.

"You can't. It'll be your fault if they get hurt."

Jedediah jerked upright. "Don't you think I know that? She's protected by a ward—y'all are—but I've lost her. Her beliefs won't change just because I rescue her."

"What's the plan, Da?"

"I'm going to hand myself over to the Namhaid," he said.

Both girls stared.

Jedediah took a deep breath. "Drake, get Jordan settled. Lanea take care of Jordan's foster records. Come straight back."

"She's exhausted. You can't send her alone," Jordan said.

"VelSera nearly ended you. There's a wizard hunting us. You're staying here. Drake can go if Lanea insists." Jedediah turned to Lanea. "Modify Angesa Cooper's memory too."

Lanea nodded.

"Mama Yamai will watch over you until I get back, which probably won't be soon. She'll teach you too, so obey her."

He studied them in silence.

"I'll take care of this," he said. "Please, just stay here where it's safe."

He touched his staff to the changing window. The farmhouse den froze in its frame. Jedediah stepped through.

Jordan paced.

"He should've incinerated those bodies," Drake said.

"Maybe," Lanea said. "He returned them to Mother because it's his way."

Jordan snarled under her breath. "He can't do this. It isn't right!"

"Let's get some food," Lanea said.

"Food? We have to protect Billie Jo and Mason."

Lanea held up her palms. "Da's made up his mind. I've got to remove you from the system."

"You and I can do it," Jordan said.

"What?" Lanea asked.

"Protect them," Jordan said.

"We're both being hunted. I'm exhausted. You can barely control your powers. We're no match for an army of professional killers."

"I'm not hiding while Ms. Bartlett dies," Tears brimmed her eyes. "She brought me to you guys."

Lanea chewed her lip.

Jordan sniffed. "Please, Lanea. We have to help them."

"No, look I'm sorry, but it isn't a good idea."

"Because of Treevoran?" Jordan asked.

"I'm sorry I got mad at you. What happened wasn't your fault, but you need to stay. You can barely use magic," Lanea said.

"I almost killed that centaur," Jordan said.

"You got lucky," Lanea said. "Nibble did not."

Jordan's chest compacted.

Lanea stepped across the room, took a dark grey staff from an umbrella holder and brought it to Jordan.

"This is your wizard's staff. It'll occupy you until I return. Drake doesn't use staves, but he can show you how to focus through it," Lanea held out her hand and plucked her own staff from the air.

"It's heavy," Jordan said.

"Petrified oak."

"Petrified?"

Lanea raised an eyebrow.

Jordan considered the staves. Wood composed both. Water had changed one. Earth hers. She raised her staff. "Wood to earth."

Lanea smiled. "Wood tempered by water."

"Why doesn't mine have any markings?"

"Because you haven't marked it yet?" Lanea asked. "Don't worry, it's got all the basic protections. Runes will appear in your first year of attuning it. After that, augments will be up to you."

The portrait, the staff, he really does care.

"Once you're attuned, it'll come when called," Lanea said.

"You know petrified wood isn't actually wood anymore, right?"

Lanea rolled her eyes.

"How do you attune it?" Jordan said.

"Practice, a lot. I'll teach you the basics over lunch."

CHAPTER FIFTY-SIX

In Plain Sight

Jedediah followed Muler's directions to a large, private hunting reserve not far from where he'd first met Elsabeth. His thoughts turned to Billie Jo as he hid a small duffel.

Despite everything, I hope she comes around. She's precious enough to risk snatching her to safety, well, she's worth protecting this way too—though I'd have preferred her safely in Sanctuary Hole while I dealt with this.

High stone walls and metal gates surrounded the private hunting club's entrance. Twin guardhouses flanked the gate, built into the wall's stonework and capped with old fashioned battlements.

More functional than a casual observer might expect.

Guards in hunting fatigues watched him. A man emerged from the guardhouse. His mixed attire suggested both security and concierge. "Can I help you, sir?"

"I'd like you to open the gate," Jedediah said.

"Are you a new member? Perhaps someone's guest?"

"I've an invitation of sorts, as to guest, well, depends on your observance of the Rules of Hospitality."

"I don't understand."

Jedediah let temper sound in his voice. "If you're a guest by Fey law, it'd be unthinkable to kill your host."

Guards above mumbled into radios and shifted positions. The greeter paused a moment, listening to his ear bud. "Could I have your name and the name of your inviting member?"

"One, Marc O'Steele, invited me when he killed my friend. Stand aside."

"I don't know where you think you are, sir, but I suggest you turn around and walk back the way you came."

Jedediah leaned in, trusting in his shielding spell to block bullets from over anxious guards. "Escort me to your cell leader, or make peace with your God."

A squad of men armed, uniformed and masked like at his cabin emerged from the guardhouse. "Hands up. Search him."

Jedediah raised his hands and smiled at the greeter. "My ride's here."

They searched Jedediah, shoved him into a jeep at gunpoint and drove him into the complex.

Nice cabins and bungalows dotted the landscape between tall trees and mostly cleared underbrush. Asphalt paved the initial roads but faded to dirt and gravel the farther in they went. Another squad waited before a huge lodge.

They assumed guardianship and escorted him not into the lodge, but around back to a building marked infirmary. Guns prodded him into a well-equipped mini-hospital, into a medical dispensary and through a high tech security door hidden behind the medicine cooler.

A stair led underground, switching back on themselves in engineered kill zones. Cameras watched him from behind armored mounts. Four stories down, the stairs dumped into an unremarkable corridor with nothing to offer cover.

"Guess you guys get a lot cardio around here."

A gun shoved him forward past unmanned gun emplacements without comment.

Jedediah marked a gymnasium, a weight room, several conference rooms and even a spacious auditorium.

Their numbers exceeded his expectations, most masked even indoors. More stairwells descended deeper into the compound. They arrived at a thick glass wall, steering him into a huge executive office. An attractive secretary stood from behind her huge high-tech station. Leather twin shoulder holsters hung over a white blouse matched to a professionally tailored black skirt.

"One's expecting Mr. Shine. Take him inside," she said.

They led him to a mantrap. A gun shoved him into the small armored room. Walls closed around him and his two guards. Jedediah sucked in breath before the door sealed them inside. The opposite door opened, letting him into a plush office.

A masked figure in a business suit gestured from behind a mahogany desk. "Handcuff him there, then leave us."

They seated Jedediah and handcuffed him to the chair's thick arms. A guard laid a small bag of copper birdshot on the desk. "This is all he had on him."

"Fine. You may go."

They exited through the mantrap.

Marc O'Steele pulled the mask off, pausing to straighten his hair. "You're supposed to be in jail."

Jedediah smirked. "Then Muler, Bianca and you shouldn't have abducted me from federal custody."

"Preposterous," Marc said.

Jedediah shrugged. "Check with your contacts."

"Is Muler working for you now?" Marc asked.

"He's a bit busy being digested by a dragon," Jedediah said.

"Your pet dragon?" Marc asked.

"No, his mother."

"Are you here to feed me to a dragon?"

"I'm here to protect those I care about," Jedediah said. "What will make you go away?"

"Making us go away won't solve your legal issues."

I'm taking care of that. Jedediah smiled. "What do you want?"

"Your land."

"All of it?"

Marc fetched a map from a wall cabinet and unrolled it on the desk. "This piece."

Cold washed over Jedediah. *The Gate to Mythela'Raemyn? That can't be coincidence.* Jedediah narrowed his eyes. "Why that piece?"

Marc folded his hands. "I work for people who don't trust me with all the details."

"Is your wizard in charge?"

"What're you talking about?"

Jedediah's brow creased. "You really don't know—interesting. I tried to teleport into the cabin before you killed Joe Franklin. Magic stopped me."

Marc stared.

"Who planted the posts around my cabin and enchanted them with blood magic?" Jedediah asked.

"Compartmentalization, Mr. Shine. Shall I have Patricia put together a property transfer agreement or would you prefer we imprison you until the Board provides instructions."

Someone controlling things behind the scenes, how very wizardly. Jedediah met Marc's eyes. "I cannot sign that property over to you."

"Even if we hold your loved ones?" Marc asked.

Jedediah flipped his wrists out of the cuffs and stood.

Marc jerked a pistol from behind his back.

"You could threaten the entire eastern seaboard, and I wouldn't sign that property over to you," Jedediah said. "I'd like to be taken to my cell now."

"You don't want anything else?" Marc asked.

Jedediah shrugged. "You should probably know, I'm going to kill you."

"After lunch, I hope."

Jedediah smiled. "Once my plans reach fruition."

"Oh, good. I'll update my will." Marc donned the mask and pressed the intercom. "Have Gordon escort Mr. Shine to a holding cell."

Muler's confessions predicted Marc's responses pretty close to the mark. Mythela'Raemyn, why does a mercenary organization want access to the sacred valley?

A huge Samoan entered.

Gordon escorted Jedediah deeper underground to a small, high-security holding facility. He locked Jedediah into one of a handful of transparent cells.

Guess they don't entertain much.

Jedediah finished lunch before he started killing people. He stuck fingers through the holes in the cell door. Lightning arced through the surveillance cameras. Guards leapt to alert drawing weapons. A blast of air slammed into his cell door. The clear material shot across the room, end over end, plowing through several of them.

Bullets slammed into his protective shield, a thousand angry hornets beating on his flesh.

Jedediah sank into the wind, letting it carry him with its haste. He flashed around the room, clotheslining necks hard enough to snap them against his shield-reinforced arm.

Fury, held at bay too long, rose. He grappled men firing point-blank into his chest without effect. Jedediah rampaged through the prison's security team, leaving them broken toys for someone else to clean up.

He regained his temper. *I have to stop. Slaughtering these men won't end things.*

Jedediah drew in strength, fixing his mind for a teleport.

Gordon stepped into the room. He bared his teeth, jumping on Jedediah faster than should've been possible. Reflexes still accelerated by wind's power, Jedediah dodged. Gordon's massive arms caught him anyway. A shock knocked Gordon free. They circled one another, martial arts stance against raised fists.

"I'm in a bit of a rush," Jedediah said. "Mind just falling down so I can be about my business?"

Gordon drove a fist toward him. Jedediah sidestepped, but Gordon corrected. The fist hammered Jedediah. He stumbled backward, his shield cracked where the fist struck.

Lightning haloed Jedediah's hand. He brought the charged haymaker in against Gordon's jaw. Lightning coursed over the struck Samoan.

Gordon shook it off and countered with a left then an uppercut right.

Jedediah careened into the security desk. His hand fell upon the bag of copper birdshot. He flung it forward. Wind gathered the tiny balls, shooting them deep into Gordon. He fell, bleeding from a dozen wounds.

Jedediah gathered power for his teleport.

Gordon struggled to his feet, wounds closing.

"You're getting a mite annoying," Jedediah sighed. "Guessing you work for the wizard."

Gordon barred his teeth.

Jedediah threw out both arms, reaching into the walls. Electricity arched out of outlets on every wall. It lanced into Gordon, burning between the copper BBs. Spasms wracked him. His limbs flailed left and right. Burnt flesh choked the air. Power flickered.

Jedediah's follow up jolt knocked out the power. "You done?"

The fluorescent lights relit, while security electronics rebooted.

Gordon shifted.

Jedediah hit him again with power from the lights. Bulbs exploded. Arcs playing over Gordon lit the darkened room in flickers. He double-checked the twitching body.

About damned time.

A teleport took him outside the complex. He ripped his clothes, mussed his hair, and layered an illusions to worsen his bruises.

A highway patrol car sat where he'd seen it earlier.

Jedediah stumbled into the highway, waving his hands and shouting to alert the napping patrolman.

"Please, I surrender. I'm Jedediah Shine, they abducted me from federal custody. You've got to take me in, please, call FBI Agent Benjamin Ridley. I surrender. Contact the FBI—they're monsters."

The third FBI mention alerted the groggy patrolman. He handcuffed Jedediah and sped him to their nearest office.

Agent Ridley appeared outside the cell bars. "Let me get this straight. These mercenaries abducted you, took you to their secret base and though they managed to free you from our custody you still managed to escape."

"Charmed life?" Jedediah asked.

"You're lying to me, Shine."

"They're there, Agent. They stuck me in a cell, and I fought my way out."

Ridley scrutinized him. "We'll check it out."

"Go in force, Agent. These men are dangerous," Jedediah said.

"Yet, you escaped." Ridley walked away. The wind brought his discussion to Jedediah's ears. "I know, but I want a full contingent on scene just in case. If his claims prove out, any delay may let them slip away."

Jedediah exhaled. *Good. I hate throwing these men into the teeth of military-trained mercenaries.*

Ridley exited the highway patrol station. A young, blond agent glanced after him then stepped up to the bars. "I don't care what lies you tell, you're going down."

Jedediah's brows rose. "For what?"

"Murder. A lot of good men and women died on your farm."

"While I remained in custody, remember?" Jedediah asked.

"You're responsible. You'd better hope they never leave you with only one guard."

"Why's that?"

"Someone might decide to take justice into their own hands."

Jedediah rose. "Like you? Murder is illegal."

The agent stepped closer, still out of arm's reach. "Putting down a rabid dog is an ugly necessity. Maybe less so in some cases."

Jedediah smiled for the cameras and turned back to his bunk. A dark cloud coalesced, blocking video lenses. The agent slumped to the ground, caught at the last moment by a cushion of air. The cell door clicked open and slid out of the way.

Jedediah rushed through the open door, grabbed the agent and dropped him on the bunk. He stepped out, cloaked them both in glamour and closed the cell door.

Ridley rushed into the holding area. Two agents and a patrolman flanked him, weapons ready. The young agent glared at Shine through the cell doors.

"Everything all right, Agent Pine?"

"Yup."

CHAPTER FIFTY-SEVEN

Storming the Castle

Despite Agent Ridley's call for reinforcements, the Namhaid outnumbered the officers four to one.

If I hadn't come, they'd have been slaughtered.

Ridley and Turner pulled up to the staging area. They lingered in the SUV, arguing about something.

Turner jumped out of the vehicle and slammed the door. She marched over to the waiting agents.

"What's the call, Agent?" a man on Jedediah's left asked.

Turner gritted her teeth.

"We're going in," Ridley said as he approached.

Turner rounded on him. "Demanding a warrant before granting access to a private hunting club isn't a crime."

"You saw their armaments, their defenses. Something isn't right," Ridley said.

"Not right doesn't make them some mercenary enclave. Shine's manipulating you, trying to create reasonable doubt."

"Perimeter reconnaissance reported armed men on all the fence lines. Something illegal is going on," Ridley said.

"You've got nothing but a murderer's word," Turner said.

"Highway patrol picked him up less than a mile from here. If he's lying, why turn himself in? Why surrender instead of fleeing?"

"That's it? That's all you've got?"

"I've got a feeling," Ridley said.

She threw up her hands.

Ridley turned to the others. "We're a go. Team leaders coordinate with your people. We're going back to serve the warrant. If they cooperate, only a few of us go in. If they don't, we go in hot."

Jedediah met up with his team leader. Pine and an assault team fell under Agent Harris's command. Jedediah spread a kinetic shield over all of them. The thin shield reinforced their body armor—even extended it over areas without protection—but over an entire assault force, he could only add so much protection without the shields flaring to visibility when struck. He drifted behind the group, adding the contents of his cached duffel to his pockets.

335

Ridley served the warrant.

They didn't cooperate.

Mercenaries poured onto the walls in battle regalia. Assault weapons hiccupped trios of bullets. Their own assault teams opened fire.

Jedediah's team stayed close to Ridley and his men. Despite Turner's protests, Ridley let her spread through the compound with the vast majority of forces while Ridley's and Jedediah's teams—chosen under magical influence—stormed into the infirmary. They found the entrance in short order.

"Turner, Ridley. The entrance is where Shine said."

"What says he's not part of all this, maybe turned traitor over some slight?" Turner asked.

"Arrest now, argue later," Jedediah snapped.

Ridley frowned at him. "Send us another team as soon as you can spare them."

"There's a lot of ground to cover," Turner said.

"Do your best." Ridley turned to those around him. "Intelligence reports kill zones at each stairwell and gun emplacements at ground floor."

"I volunteer to go first," Jedediah said.

"Green," Agent Harris chuckled. "Pine, we don't charge kill zones."

"Yes, sir," Jedediah said.

One of Ridley's men opened a long flat case Jedediah had taken as a sniper rifle. Its interior's base held multiple small drones and a keyboard. Screens stretched across its top.

He withdrew two of the drones and knelt next to the keyboard. Tiny propellers whirled to life. Lasers flickered this way and that, drawing a three-dimensional map on the computer screen. The agent tapped an icon then a spot on the map. He did it again as the drone flew down the stairwell in its upper left corner.

Have to remember those.

Jedediah watched the twin video feeds as the map expanded. Thermal imagery detected ghostly gunmen behind thick walls and tiny gun ports. Ridley gestured.

The drones pulled back, and two tactical agents dropped flash bang grenades down the stair. They followed the flash, but before they could reach whatever their objective, the gun ports opened fire.

They pulled back, one grunting as a round hit his armor.

Ridley looked at the drone pilot. "Blind them, Dietrich. Three men follow, two Moratex right and left. Third prep the breach."

Jedediah glanced at Dietrich. He pulled an odd sort of connector from his case and connected it to the two drones. He added an inverted canister into the cradle suspended by the connector. "Moratex?"

One of the men who'd gone down the stairs held a lump of shiny putty out to him. "Moratex Shear-thickening fluid—STF—same as in our armor, Agent. Hardens only on kinetic impact. More impact, harder it gets."

Jedediah took the blob and squeezed it. It made a rude noise. "Fart putty?" Others snickered.

"Just let him do his job, Pine," Harris shared a look with Ridley, but the senior agent studied Jedediah.

The drones flew back into the stairwell along the ceiling. Paint whirled every direction in a fine mist, surprisingly opaque for such a thin coat. Two men rushed in its wake, slapping fart putty over the gun ports while the third man drew a line of explosive gel along the far wall in a doorway shape.

In and out in moments, they retreated to cover and blew a hole in the wall. The Namhaid awaited them, taking cover several steps down a far stairwell.

Jedediah threw a wedge of air between the waiting gunmen and the Feds. Bullets shied left or right, losing velocity in the nearly solid wind. He tossed a concussion grenade from the gear he'd been provided, adding enough kinetic force to catapult Namhaid like an A-Team episode.

Tactical units pushed forward, peeling right and left to cover the extended kill zone alcoves. Jedediah seized a moment's distraction and bolted through the bodies down the stairs, picking up the air wedge as he ran through it.

Another ambush awaited him on the next flight. He slapped hands together. The walls forming the air wedge unfolded, mimicking Jedediah's movements to slap against the waiting gunmen like a giant's hands. Footsteps rushed his wake. He held his pistol with his right hand, left bracing it with a handful of copper birdshot. He fired the unfamiliar weapon, dropping a single BB which shattered tactical optics with unerring headshots.

He hurled himself forward before Agent Ridley could reprimand him. He turned hard to descend the next stair only to have a combat knife plunge into his chest. The armor caught the blow. The knifeman caught a reflexive bolt of lightning.

Crap. I can't leave evidence like that.

He opened himself to Magic's source and disintegrated the man, armor and all. His delay let the tactical team catch him.

"Jesus, Pine, we're supposed to take prisoners."

He glanced back to the shot Namhaid. "I-I just reacted. I d-don't know what happened."

"Maybe you should sit down," Fart Putty said. "You've got no business charging ahead like that anyway, Agent."

A fallen Namhaid gunman fired.

Fart Putty placed himself between Jedediah and the gunman, taking the round on his Moratex armor.

Man saves my life. I ought to learn his name. Jedediah scowled. *Later. Right now I need the distraction.*

Jedediah descended another layer, expecting gunmen lined up at the bottom of the stairs. He had a few moments of peace before Namhaid opened fired from angled positions right and left.

Jedediah jerked out of their angled crossfire. He hurled two handfuls of copper birdshot into the room. Tiny BBs rolled over the whole lower floor. Fart Putty's boots thundered down the stairs.

Jedediah lobbed a stun grenade from his arsenal and raced up around the stair's bend. "Fire in the hole."

Namhaid took cover from the grenade, paying the ineffectual BBs no mind. Power arched through the room, the BBs and the Namhaid in an interconnected web that knocked out lighting.

Fart Putty peered around the corner. Namhaid gunmen moaned on the ground.

"Jesus, Pine, I don't know who equipped you, but I want what you got," Fart Putty said. "Ridley ordered me to detain you."

"Sorry," Jedediah panted. "I got excited."

"Guess so."

"Not sure I caught your name."

"Aaron Snyder."

"Thanks for the help back there," Jedediah said.

"Got to keep you pretty boys safe," Snyder said.

Jedediah endured Ridley's dressing down, half convinced he'd still ended up earning a commendation for the arrogant ass back at the jail. Tactical teams pressed on into the complex, surviving Namhaid defenses on skill, training and magic reinforced Moratex.

Turner's reinforcements arrived to find Jedediah still in the bottom kill zone blind.

"What the hell happened here?" Turner asked. "What's with the Scooby Doo defense?"

Jedediah shrugged.

"And why are you here, Pine?"

Jedediah smiled. "Ridley asked me to wait for you."

"We're here. Stop goldbricking and get back in the fight."

"Yes, ma'am."

The radio in Jedediah's ear informed him of hot spots. Instead, he turned down a stairway toward the prison. A mercenary jumped out from behind him and discharged his pistol into Jedediah's skull.

Jedediah's ears rang and the impact through his shield hurt—though it probably wouldn't even bruise. He turned an angry glare on the stunned gunman.

"You should be—"

"Dead. Yup. Brain's splattered. Kind of like this." Air shot a handful of birdshot through the man's head. Jedediah squeezed the bridge of his nose. "Jackass gave me a splitting headache."

He continued down the corridor, trying to listen for mercenaries lurking in his near future. He misremembered how to find his destination, but he finally came to the records room door he'd passed on the way to Namhaid jail.

Maybe now I'll get some answers.

He pushed the door open. Cold air hit him. Jedediah cursed.

An enormous curved desk separated him from a great labyrinth of futuristic boxes stacked in some sort of rack. They stretched out in the distance, blinking lights speaking gibberish to his untrained eye. He hurried behind the desk to find it less comprehensible than the stations on the old Enterprise—television starship, not the aircraft carrier.

He stared at keyboards and screens somewhere between the mess Mason had selected for Lanea and the device Alden took three weeks teaching him how to operate.

"Who the hell would've believed an overgrown arcade game would stand between life and death." He reached a finger down, then pulled it back. "If I break the damned thing I'll never learn what I need to know."

He snorted. "Won't learn shit if I just sit here losing a staring contest with the—"

Movement and fabric brushing fabric brought him about. He dove sideways as Kaci the Assistant Manager sprayed bullets at him.

"You'd be Bianca."

"And you're just another dead Fed."

Forgot the glamour. Let's see if she's the woman Muler claims.

He raised his hands. "I surrender."

Another spray of bullets forced him back into cover.

"Yup. Muler called it. You're a psychotic bitch."

"That where the little worm disappeared to? Turned state's evidence?"

"Surrender and you won't find out first hand," Jedediah said.

Her voice came from his right. "Kiss my ass, Fed."

She opened fire. Bullets slammed into Jedediah, sending him reeling. He fell behind the desk.

Hells, she's quieter than a shifty elf. She actually snuck up on me.

Bianca rounded into view and leveled the submachine gun at him. "Goodbye, handsome."

Jedediah flash froze her in mirror mist. Eyes widened and shifted to wild panic as every other part of her refused to move.

Jedediah rose, thickening the mist holding her tight. "Well, now. I think it's time you and I had a little chat."

Noises escaped her. He didn't need to release her mouth to get the gist.

Jedediah parted his glamour, keeping it up in case others arrived but letting her see through it. He gestured. "I'm thinking you can help me with this overgrown calculator. Think we can work that out?"

He released her mouth.

"Eat me, Shine."

"Huh, insults not wild questions about how I've got you froze so neat," Jedediah studied her. "You're either real adaptable, or you've worked with magic before."

"Muler's a fucking nuisance, but he's no druggie, and he's not delusional. There had to be something to his claims. Add that to your file, and let's say flexibility keeps me alive." She licked her lips. "I can be *very* flexible."

Jedediah snorted. "Rather screw a three-tailed scorpion. Safer too."

She scowled.

"You going to help me with this computer?"

"Sure," she smiled.

"You kill those kids in the hotel?"

"Flash did."

"You have a hand in it?" Jedediah asked.

"I helped set you up. You already know that."

"What I want to know is why. Killing innocents is bad enough, but kids?"

"Who the hell cares? Means to an end. That's all."

"Yup." Jedediah's eyes narrowed. "Like agreeing to help me with the computer so I'll release your limbs."

Jedediah pried the gun from her hands. He drew a knife across her palm and let the blood drip into his hand. An idle finger drew patterns in the blood as he met her eye. "Tell me one thing, Bianca Norway. Are you going to help me?"

She smiled. "Of course."

Blood writhed in his palm.

"Seems you're about as trustworthy as that scorpion too." Jedediah drew symbols across her face with her blood.

"What're you doing?"

"Stay still, a mistake might burn your face off."

She fell silent.

Jedediah stepped back, admiring his work. He added a dab here and there to the symbols with her remaining blood. "That ought to do it."

"Do what?"

Jedediah recited the old witchdoctor's working. Light glowed from his lips, wafting out in a mist which clung to Bianca's head and throat. The light died.

"What did you do?"

"Why?"

"I'm frightened." Words died on her lips.

"I cursed you."

"Warts? STDs? A craving for junk food?"

"Truth. You're compelled to tell only the truth."

"I believe you. I mean, I don't...see any way to deny you're telling me the truth." She glared. "Remove it. Take it off me."

"Why?"

"Telling only the truth will get me killed."

Jedediah smiled. "Means to an end. Tell me your Name."

"Bianca Ellaine Yves."

"Not Norway?"

"No."

"I'll remember that." Jedediah sat at the desk. "If I'd let you help me without this compulsion to tell the truth, what would've happened?"

She fought it, but the words escaped her. "I'd have tricked you into wiping the core and deleting everything."

"Tell me what to do to unlock the information in this thing and access it without causing any of it to be lost."

She cursed, but the instructions tumbled out of her lips.

A giant Samoan sprinted into the room, dove over the desk and tackled Jedediah.

"Thought I killed you," Jedediah said.

"Flash, help me," Bianca called.

Jedediah threw the hulking man off of him. He dug into his pocket for birdshot.

"Freeze," Ridley said.

Flash slowed, holding his hands up. Turner entered the room. The moment she crossed into Ridley's field of fire, Flash leapt to a sprint. He veered to one side, scooping up Bianca and racing into the rack labyrinth.

Jedediah bolted after him. "Oh, no you don't, jumbo."

Even wind-enhanced, this twin to the Samoan he'd killed kept just ahead. Jedediah held onto his rising temper, all too aware that sparking wouldn't just reveal him to Ridley, it might destroy the information necessary to prove his innocence. He didn't know much about technology, but it'd only taken two heated lectures for Lanea to impress upon him what happened to her iPod song library when he sparked too close to it.

Flash yanked down a fire extinguisher.

Jedediah readied himself to jump it, but it hung upside down from its pillar. The far wall split apart.

No.

Jedediah whipped an invisible lasso after the two. It hooked Bianca, jerking her off of Flash's shoulder. He turned back as Jedediah and the two slower FBI agents rushed to catch him.

"Flash, help me. I'm ordering you."

"Not Zero," Flash leapt through the doors and slammed something that snapped the walls shut in a flash.

Jedediah dug fingers into the wall, pouring earth strength into his limbs.

"Pine," Turner said.

He turned toward her. She pushed the extinguisher back up then pulled it down. The wall parted to show a deep shaft leading who knew where. Jedediah psyched himself for the leap, gathering wind to catch him. Ridley's hand stopped him. Static electricity discharged between them.

"You did your best," Ridley said. "Made me feel like an old man trying to keep up."

"Who do we have here?" Turner asked.

Jedediah cut across her. "Admitted to being Kaci the Assistant Manager from that hotel where they found those murdered kids. Goes by Bianca Norway. Isn't that correct, Bianca?"

"Yes," Bianca said through gritted teeth.

"She's a European cell leader for the Namhaid, going by the name Two. She helped kill Joe Franklin and frame Jedediah Shine," Jedediah said.

"Is that true?" Ridley asked.

"Yes," Bianca slapped a hand over her mouth, shocked to be able to move it. "I want a lawyer."

Jedediah smiled. "I headed her off from accessing that terminal back there. Guessing she wanted to delete everything, but she didn't get the chance."

"Good work, Pine," Ridley said.

CHAPTER FIFTY-EIGHT

Fixed Verdict

Jedediah remained incarcerated while awaiting trial. Justin and Meadow championed him in court. The evidence in the Namhaid fortress should've been enough to clear him, but the judge insisted the trial go ahead, citing the numerous bodies found that hadn't correlated with murders found in the Namhaid records.

The trial itself stretched for months. Accusations of child murder forced Ridley to arrange protective custody. He refused to allow Jedediah visitors by ordinary means. Drake and Lanea attended the trial—a blind woman and her service animal.

<Master?>

Jedediah rubbed his eyes and regarded the mist mirror.

This is new.

<Lanea's been helping me.>

What is it, Drake?

<I'm worried. The scent of the jury is wrong.>

Justice will be done, Drake. Don't fret, I'll be back making your life miserable soon.

<I'd like that.>

There anything else?

<No, I just wanted you to know.>

I've smelled it, Drake, but everything will be fine. Watch the girls for me.

<Yes, Master. Good night.>

Drake paced Sanctuary Hole, wearing a path along the lake. Jedediah echoed Lanea. They both believed that justice, judge and jury would acquit Jedediah. He'd be free, and the nightmare would end.

I just don't trust the normals.

He used the library portal to return to the farm. It felt dead without Jedediah. The crowds no longer picketed the fence line. Deputies no longer watched the gate. Bees went about their happy routine, asking about Jedediah. He shared what news he had. Sarah and her pups whined after Jordan. He promised to ask her to visit.

Drake ran across overgrown fields gone to seed toward the wood's edge. Shadowcats and darker Fey moved about the wood, unrestrained by Jedediah's

343

watchful eye. He snarled reminders of their place and warned of Jedediah's wrath if they misbehaved.

I'll have to talk to Lanea. She's supposed to keep them in line while Master's away.

Familiar woods felt strange, but he found his way to Fleet Hoof. Centaurs parted for him, bowing and saluting where they'd threatened Jedediah so long ago. He came to the pavilion and Fleet Hoof's elders. Four stood at its entrance, the fifth forbidden them under censure. All decisions came from the High Tribe until the *Mythela'Raemyn* centaur declared Fleet Hoof rehabilitated.

"Welcome, Lordling," WaphRae said. "Why do you honor us?"

Drake imitated Midall E'Cru's bow. "I ask a boon."

TharHa stepped closer. "How can we serve you?"

"I wish to speak to my mother, but can neither fly nor leave the area."

"We're not allowed to leave," WaphRae said. "You know that."

"I do, but can't you use your fire to send a message, tribe to tribe?" Drake asked.

TharHa saluted. "It shall be done for you, Lordling. What message do you send?"

"I need her help."

The trial dragged on several more weeks before Stormfall deigned to fly over Jedediah's farm. Drake met her on the lawn before the farmhouse.

<You dare summon me, whelp?>

I'm honored that you came, mother.

<Speak while my patience endures.>

I fear for my Master—

<No kine is your master, child.>

They circled each other on the lawn.

I misspoke, Great Mother. My teacher's fate rests in normal hands. My abilities are not enough to force their minds.

<What have you been doing here these years? If your teacher has done such a poor job, let them burn him at the stake and be done with it.>

Mother. It's my own folly, my own arrogance that slowed my studies. Please, help me protect my teacher.

Stormfall snorted. *<I'd rather he burned.>*

Very well, then I'll return with you to your lair.

<You'll do no such thing. I live alone and will not suffer you under talon.>

Round and round they argued, circling for advantage physical and verbal.

If you won't help me continue my lessons here, then what else can I do but come home?

<We'll find you another mentor.>

I doubt you'll be able to manufacture another life debt to exploit.

She narrowed her gaze. *<Careful with your threats, child, lest I choose to simply end you.>*

No threat, Mother, merely stating that another teacher might not be so easily obtained.

<I don't care. I won't help that kine—talented or not. He threatened your being, invoked your Name.>

Drake shuddered. Jedediah knew his Name, had ultimate control of him—at least until his Name changed as Drake's definition of himself evolved.

Fly me home or not, if you do not help my teacher, I'll find my way home to our lair.

<My lair.>

What would the others say if they heard Stormfall turned out her own child after her poor choice of fosterage left him abandoned in the normals' world?

She launched herself airborne. *<I'll not help him. Enjoy your walk.>*

Drake watched her shrink into the distance. *Guess I'm on my own.*

The trial came to a close. Meadow held Jedediah's hand under the table. Justin, his health fading, kept up a confident air despite the energy it cost him. Word of a verdict brought them back to the courtroom, but a courtroom unique in all the long trial.

A palatable wall of power hit Jedediah as he stepped into the room. He scanned the occupants.

Press filled the edges, ever-ravenous. Drake and Lanea sat in the back corner as they often did. Mauve filed her nails just behind the defender's table, a wiry youth anxiously glancing around. Agent Ridley sat next to her, casting unsure glances as his instincts probably found something about her that put them on edge. Guardians from around the world filled seats, apprentices at hand. Lirelaeli Ermyn'Phir sat behind the prosecution. Treevoran sat with her, casting occasional glances at Lanea despite her glamour. Velith'Seravin maintained a glamour wheelchair, sneering at Jedediah with anxious glee.

Jedediah instinctively brought a shield to bear, adding to the overwhelming, almost blinding cacophony of power in the room.

Drake strained to see the paper in the foreman's hands through the pixie's eyes high overhead: Guilty.

He cringed inwardly. *I'd hoped Master would prove right.*

He looked at Jedediah. The old man seemed in a daze, distracted by those assembled. Meadow's hand prompted him to stand or sit.

Five words snapped his attention back into focus

"Have you reached a verdict?"

Drake didn't bother to glamour the paper. He reached for the jury foreman's mind, using the mist mirror trick Lanea'd helped him practice as a means of telepathy without touch. He pushed his mind into the normal's, cautious not to break the feeble thing but trying to gain control of its slippery strings.

The courtroom inhaled a breath. The bailiff took a folded paper from the jury foreman.

A thick gloom fell over the room. Tiny ripples topped pitcher and glass upon Jedediah's table. Hairs stood up along Drake's skin. Jedediah scratched his beard madly. Justin's gaze shot back and forth.

Silence fell over the crowd, but the thrum of magic intensified.

Jedediah's head shifted side to side. The judge smirked as he read the paper.

He returned the paper to the jury.

Drake wrapped mental talons around the foreman's will.

Gloom intensified to oppression. Whatever ill omen the magical gravity portended, it neared to strike its blow. Practitioners around the room shrouded self or apprentice in protective magic.

The strings slipped from Drake's grasp.

The jury foreman took the note and opened it. He read the words. "We the jury find the defendant, Jedediah Shine..."

Drake scrambled to regain control, but something blocked his reach—a thick, viscous shield of some sort. Panic filled the dragon. *They're going to find him guilty. I'm going to lose him, lose everything important.*

Oppression grew indomitable. The foreman stiffened.

"Yes?" the judge asked. "How do you find?"

"We, the normals designated judgment rights, find the wi-defendant, not guilty on all counts."

The press murmured.

What the hell?

"What?" a juror echoed him.

Ridley's eyes narrowed.

"You found the defendant not guilty by unanimous vote?" the judge asked.

The jury stiffened as one. They stood as one. They nodded as one.

Drake looked at Lanea. She seemed as confused as he felt.

The judge gestured. "Give me that back."

The bailiff retrieved the paper.

The judge scowled at the paper then the jury. He opened his mouth.

He's going to overturn it. Drake reached for the judge's mind, too fearful to take care with the fragile thing. He sunk his talons. The judge slipped free.

His body stiffened. "The accused is acquitted of all charges and released with the apologies of we who are unworthy to judge him. Court is adjourned."

Drake goggled. *What just happened?*

Lanea beamed, hugging Drake. Her closeness drove uncertainty from his thoughts.

Jedediah redoubled his shields, searching for the culprit who'd robbed him of a fair verdict. Lirelaeli stepped across the aisle to him. She offered him a gloating smile. "Dear Jedediah, you'll never repay this debt."

"You?"

She laughed, leading Treevoran away on one arm. The younger elf shook his head.

Jedediah turned to Justin. "What just happened?"

"They acquitted you," Meadow beamed. "Touch and go there a while, but we did it. You're free."

"He'll have to be processed first," Ridley gestured to the confused bailiff trying to get the judge's attention. Another bailiff took the first's job, taking Jedediah from the courtroom.

Mauve winked at him as he exited.

A tiny pink sprite flew up to Drake. "You owe her."

It flew off.

CHAPTER FIFTY-NINE

Vengeful Talon

Jedediah drove up the farm drive, glad to be back home once more. The farmhouse appeared through the trees. Jedediah's breath caught in his throat. Jordan, Lanea and Drake stood before it. He'd expected a welcome home party, but he had also expected to have a home.

The farmhouse lay in ruins, surrounded by gigantic talon marks. Crushed cars grown back to full size lay at odd angles. Clothing exploded when she'd destroyed his extra-dimensional closet space spread to the horizon in every direction.

His heart seized in his chest. He leapt from the truck, not even bothering to set the brake. Countless treasures lay beneath the rubble. Portraits of wives and daughters, irreplaceable and in unknown states. Tears streamed down his cheeks.

I've lost it all. She destroyed everything.

Lanea rushed to him, tears flowing double of his.

Jedediah reined in his feelings. *No sense in panic. It'll be all right. Maybe she broke some things, but things could be worse.*

Marc O'Steele watched from the tree line far across unkempt fields. He watched the strange reunion through a rifle scope. He looked up, scanning the area. The Feds hadn't left Jedediah alone just because he'd been acquitted. SUV's drove too often up and down the rural highway.

They're waiting to catch him again. Too bad for them.

Marc escaped their raid using the executive office emergency sled, but it'd been a near thing. Shine and the Feds had stolen everything: his cover life, his girlfriend, even his job as a talent scout.

He'd waited months for the trial to end. He'd arranged death for Shine in prison, but they'd kept him secluded. He'd paid to have it done when protection ended, but Shine'd been acquitted. Zero wouldn't have approved, but Marc had to regain his number. Shine's death paved that way.

Must've been how Muler felt, knowing his only way back meant killing this one impossible farmer.

Shine and the girlfriend seemed estranged, and the foster girl wouldn't inherit, but the farmhand? No bribe had turned up a solid will.

I'm not taking a chance. Zero's getting his land, and I'm getting my number back.

Marc's heartbeat rose. The shot he'd awaited gift wrapped itself. Farmer and farmhand lined up in the scope.

Marc squeezed the trigger.

Something smashed into Jedediah, driving him backward.

A crack of thunder rent the air.

Red mist filled his eyes. He wiped it away, searching for a gunman.

He rushed forward, shielding Jordan and Lanea with his body. "Lanea, get Jordan to Sanctuary Hole."

Jordan's cry ripped his attention from the horizon. "Lanea."

Lanea sprawled on the ground, crawling toward the pond in blood-soaked clothes. She paled toward translucent. Ugly green veins reached from beneath her sundress.

"Drake, potions."

Jedediah ran to her where she collapsed at pond's edge.

Jedediah threw open his connection, sucking power from around him in addition to Magic's source.

"They're gone, Master. Mother destroyed everything."

"Find that cockamamie shed then!" He placed glowing hands on her. A single wound flooded his fingers with blood. *Hells, that bullet can't have missed her heart by the breadth of a fairy's wing.*

Drake didn't run. He stared at Lanea. Tears ran his beak.

Jedediah seized her. He waded into the water. She floated, cradled in his arms. He poured healing magic into her.

Tears streaked down Jedediah's cheeks. His own skin lightened progressively as he pushed more and more power into Lanea's body. Her life drained away faster than he could refill it. The centaur on his chest galloped down his arm. It leapt from his skin onto hers.

Jedediah glimpsed it raise a horn through the tear in her dress. Sound and smoke billowed from beneath her hems. They coalesced into a ghostly centaur. Sorrow etched its face. It took Lanea. It placed her on its back. A Gothic arch bubbled out of the water one carved skull at a time, growing high enough to permit the centaur. The phantom centaur blew a somber note and marched through the arch.

Jedediah charged after it. He slammed into the surface of the black tunnel like a bad cartoon. Blows powerful enough to shatter thick fortress walls pounded against it. It resisted his fury. The water around him boiled. Fish floated to the top. Steam hazed the pond's surface.

The sludge hydra bolted from the pond, running from Jedediah with many backward glances.

Jedediah raised his head to the heavens and screamed.

The arch crumbled. The pond exploded, water to superheated steam in an instant. Jedediah knelt in its dry depression surrounded by cooked fish.

Drake howled a low, mournful sound that vibrated Jedediah's leadened bones. He sniffed back tears and howl turned to snarl. His wings snapped open.

Jedediah's head shot up. Tears blinded wild eyes. "Where?"

"This way, pops. Follow me." Paulie led the charge, Jedediah paces behind.

Shock froze Marc's heart. His mind ground to a halt, unable to process the scene before him. Jedediah whirled his direction and charged, haloed in a ball of lightning.

He sighted on Jedediah's chest, the target blurred by a brown smudge on his scope.

He fired again.

Jedediah staggered. The lightning fizzled. He regained his feet and with it the lightning. *I shot him...twice...armor piercing rounds. I've got nothing short of a rocket launcher to top that.*

The hound glided over Jedediah on wings. Terror slammed into him, but rather than freeze him, it woke his battle instincts.

The sudden impact had been a truck slamming into Jedediah. He rubbed his chest, worried about broken ribs. Splattered Paulie come away on his fingers.

It's not real. It can't be real.

Marc sprang toward his motorcycle, stopping at the last minute to aim down his sight once more. He squeezed the trigger, and ran to his waiting transport, breaking the rifle down into its two largest pieces. He shoved it into custom saddlebag and urged the motorcycle to carry him from the waking nightmare.

FBI might end up being my only hope.

A flash of blond disappeared deeper into the tree line. Jedediah summoned a mist walk and poured on speed. Sprites darted to him from all sides. High pitched squeaks pointed the way.

Jordan screamed

A third shot broke the silent tension.

Ha, missed me, corpse. I'll...Jordan?

He whirled. Jordan lay flat on her back. Magic kept him upright as he changed direction without slowing. He raced to her, cursing the gunman getting away.

Sirens filled the distant air.

"Drake!"

The dragon didn't respond.

Jedediah paused his breakneck pace only long enough to scoop Jordan into his arms. He sprinted into the boneyard. Curious faces popped from hiding. He ripped the door from the Weems Road fridge.

Manic laughter bubbled from his lips. *Jordan'll be happy I took at least one door off.*

The bike wove and vaulted through woods. Strange shadows shifted around him. Hair stood tall amongst raging gooseflesh. Fireflies buzzed him, jabbing at buttons until he swatted or smashed them.

The road came into view. He vaulted out of a gully, hit it hard and spun. He gunned the throttle and gave the bike literally all it could accept.

Jedediah laid her onto the theater seating. A dark red welt colored her forehead. He pushed her eyelids back, checking for concussion.

Ward protected her. She's going to be fine.

Jedediah stood, frowning down at Jordan surrounded by the theater he'd built Lanea.

She's gone. She'll never again lounge on the couch next to Jordan throwing popcorn.

A tear-blind gaze swept the room, not seeing it. His knees crumpled beneath him. He scooped an empty box of Lanea's favorite candy from a garbage pail, clutching it to his chest.

Lanea's light had been extinguished

They'd killed the daughter he'd never intended.

Lost, gone, they'd taken the precious child who'd filled his life.

He'd lost her, failed her somehow.

He'd let her killer escape.

Despair overwhelmed his anger, robbing him of strength. Grief and guilt rained down upon him, crushing him to the ground. He sobbed and wailed and beat his hands against carpet.

A deathly still replaced rage. He stared at Jordan. Turmoil and panic distilled to disbelief.

Impossible. I protected Lanea and Jordan the same. I can't have lost her. I can't. Sobs wracked him once more. *I triple checked my wards perfect upon completion. Nothing should've been able to steal another daughter. I protected her, protected all of them.*

One Resurrection

Bianca sulked in her cell's corner. Her arms held knees tight to her chest. Many of One's people filled the surrounding cells.

It's my fault. I told them where. I gave them the codes.

Heat rose. "No, it's Shine's fault. He did this to me. I'll make him remove it."

"That's the woman I know," Zero said. "Started to wonder, though, all that sulking."

Her eyes rose to meet Zero's. He stood inside her cell, a swirling doorway freestanding just behind him. He extended a hand.

"I'm cursed. I've ruined the Namhaid," Bianca said.

Zero smirked. "We've survived three centuries. We won't be undone by an errant arch magus and a few FBI storming a single fortress."

"How can we recover from what I did?"

"Survival rule number one: never put all your eggs in one basket."

"Shine forced me to unlock the servers," Bianca said.

"In olden days, townspeople feared disease. They'd never have congregated in millions like today."

Bianca nodded. "European villages kept separate to prevent plagues emptying the countryside."

"Precisely. I need a new One to rebuild us and destroy Shine."

"Did Marc get captured?" she asked.

"No, incarceration would've been better for poor Marc."

"What could be worse? Death?"

Zero frowned. "No, Marc's fate will be worse than death."

"Why? How?"

"I know Shine better than you can imagine. Marc killed Shine's daughter. Nothing, not heaven, hell or a thousand of their agents could save Marc now."

Acknowledgements:

Well, we've made it to the end of another book, and I genuinely hope you've enjoyed the journey—those of you who didn't just flip to the back, dirty rotten cheaters.

We—story, characters and scribbler—have delighted in shared laughter and maybe even shared tears. We started the journey alone, but with you in mind. Your enjoyment—and occasional frustration or tears—motivate every moment which went into providing you the best story possible. After all, without you this journey wouldn't have been half as much fun.

Once more the list of people involved in bringing Jedediah and his world to life is a long one. Life and adulthood have stolen many over the long years, but they're still near my heart. I wouldn't have met Jedediah if not for some of them. Proofreaders, sounding boards, editors and people who contributed by simply oohing and aahing in the right places have helped give you this story.

My thanks and love first go to B, B & J, who've suffered through the most story babble. Next Mike and Shannon, still around from the early days and the unnamed who told me to quit because I'd never see publish or an audience. Their naysaying contributed almost as much, if only to drive me toward proving them wrong with your help. Troy and Trint, Justin and Jason, Simeon and Lynette, Bryan and Big Frank—each contributors in their own way. I can't imagine many writers get very far without a group of fellow writers. I appreciate mine: Kimberly, Katherine, Kelsey, Rus, Sean, Benjamin & Kristen, another Mike, and my extended writer group Trish, Sunder and Anthony.

So many pros's lent their wisdom and guidance, it's impossible to name them all. I can only hope to repay them through hard work and eventually passing on what I've learned. I'm proud to be at the table, still starry-eyed, but a little less green.

To Jedediah, Lanea, Jordan, Drake and the rest of the cast. Thanks for a grand adventure. I look forward to seeing them and you in the next book. Thank you for reading.

Coming Soon...

THE WIZARD'S BANE

BITTERGATE: BOOK TWO

Michael J. Allen

Delirious
Scribbles Ink

Delirious Scribbles Ink

CHAPTER ONE

Dia de lo Muerto Mago

A cream-colored lounge chair hovered atop an open grave under a clear blue late autumn sky. The scent of fresh cut marigolds floated in a soft breeze. A voluptuous woman lay beneath the warm rays, bronze skin shining and honey-brown hair fanned out like a halo. Her tiny white bikini hid as little flesh as possible. She'd have forgone the top, but going topless had produced disastrous distraction to her new apprentice.

Mauve raised her head, glancing around for the boy.

Around her the cemetery buzzed with activity, families cleaning graves, preparing altars and arranging offerings for the evening's festivities. Happy chatter and sung prayers overlaid the graveyard's usual hush. Despite the bustle, none of it encroached on her sunbathing island. Around them, frowning spirits stared forlorn at their activities.

A scowling bandito reached spectral hands toward a young woman.

"No." Mauve's sultry voice cracked like a whip. Every dead head shot up her direction, but no living soul seemed to hear. "Hands off the living."

The bandito narrowed his eyes and snatched a long knife from its belt.

"Don't sass me, Juan," she raised a warning finger his direction and scanned the crowd. "Lane?! Where is that boy?"

An adolescent boy slunk out of the crowd. Tiny for twelve and rail thin, black swathed his pale skin from his boots to a padre's hat he'd lifted from a preacher's tomb. He didn't look at her directly, though she could tell by the pinking of his cheeks when he snuck a glance her direction.

Stuffed cheeks garbled his words. "Yes, Mistress?"

"You're supposed to be minding the dead, not stealing candied pumpkin from the altars," Mauve said.

"I'm hungry," he said to her feet. "It's not like the dead can eat it."

"They eat its spirit...forget it. Stop stealing candy and deal with Juan."

Lane glanced toward the bandito. "Again?"

Juan sneered at him. An exaggerated sigh shifted Lane's slumped shoulders. He stomped toward the bandito, flexing his fingers. Juan stepped back from him.

"Stand right there," Lane whined. "I'm not chasing you again."

1

Juan darted for cover.

"Stop," a whisper of command invaded Lane's whine. "Damn it, Juan, I said *stop*."

The specter froze.

Lane pointed to his shirt. Grimacing skulls and tormented spectral faces covered his black t-shirt. "In."

"No," Juan said.

Lane stomped across the intervening distance. Juan slashed his knife across Lane's face. The blow dislodged his black ring glasses and left a white line on already white skin.

Lane thrust both hands into the specter, hooking his fingers into claws. "*In!*"

Juan screamed as Lane balled up his spectral body and shoved into the shirt. His cries joined other spirits crying out for release in the moment when Juan's spirit rippled the imprisonment spell's barrier plane.

Lane cradled his cheek and mumbled his way through a dozen curses. He looked up to see a little girl gaping at him. "Mind your own—"

"Lane," Mauve snapped.

Lane shot her a dirty look, forced a smile onto his face and dug a piece candied pumpkin out of his pocket. He offered it to the little girl. Her expression grew more shocked. He dusted it off and offered it again. "Here?"

"Mama!"

Lane watched her flee to a position behind her mother's skirts.

Mauve rose, drawing his quickly retreating gaze. She swept hands down her body, replacing the white bikini with a curve-hugging silk dress. "It's safe to look now, darling."

Lane glanced up at her, wide eyes shot back to the ground. "M-mistress, your...um, I can see...um..."

"Pay attention to your spell," she said. "You've got a pair about to escape your shoulder."

She shook her head, using his distraction to conjure underwear beneath her attire. *How long must I coddle his awkwardness?*

A girl screamed, then another. More screams rent the air, and people fled toward them. Mauve craned to see what sent them into flight, expecting a ghoul or some other dead malcontent causing trouble to spite those celebrating life around it. Several dozen mounted figures galloped toward them.

"This isn't the old west, boys," Mauve said. "If you're going to come around scaring people and stealing candy you could at least act like you live in this century."

"Mistress?"

The concern in his voice felt sharper than normal. She looked again, noticing the double image of glamour hiding a band of heavily armed centaur. Movement flashed in her peripheral vision. A faun landed a gigantic leap just behind her.

Another landed on the other side followed by two other before her. The four—half bare-chested teenage girl and half doe—circled her in a flouncing skip. Each had hair of shoulder length long curls matching the soft coat that clothed their lower half. Softest flax colored hair on two fauns. The third shone honey-brown to match Mauve's own. Brindled hair covered the fourth's head and legs—the color of sand with clumps of honey brown. Reed pipes bounced between breasts too-ample for their short, lithe frames.

The first curtseyed to Mauve, introducing herself in a high alto. "Jiji, Sorceress."

A girlish bosom-jiggling laugh accompanied the second's curtsey. "Kiki."

Lane's red face shot to the ground.

Mauve slapped him upside his head, sending his hat flying. "Eyes up."

"But they're *naked*," Lane said.

Centaurs fanned out around them.

"I don't care if they're writhing around in an orgy, never look away from danger," Mauve said.

"But—"

The third cupped her bosom toward Lane, addressing him in a husky contralto. "Do you think Lili's breasts are dangerous little man?"

Lane responded with incoherent stammers.

The last faun curtseyed and introduced herself in a sweet soprano. "Mimi, Lady Mauve."

"Quiet," the sleek black mare Glent Se'Lailos said. "Mauve Cortez, you are under arrest for crimes against the Fey. You and the boy will surrender or face summary execution."

Mauve laughed. "You're not High Tribe, and even then I don't answer to any Fey."

"Kill them," Glent Se'Lailos said.

The fauns' skip turned into a complicated dance, each raising their reed pipes. Grasses and flowers sprung up in a ring they wore into the grave dirt, the path laced with a braid of auras.

Mauve shoved Lane behind her, though she couldn't truly protect him from all angles. "Stay down and out of the way, Lane."

Despite superior numbers, the centaur held fire while the four faun wove around her. Jedediah might've tried to reason with them, but Mauve lived by the simple creed of do unto others before they get a chance to do unto you. She reached out to the dead filled cemetery and felt her reach blocked at the dancing circle. She altered her reach, but the thoughts commanding her power waded through a rising fog.

Mauve cursed. "Cover your ears, boy."

"I've heard that kind of language before," Lane said.

"Block out the music, child."

The four faun stopped, extending hands as if commanding them to stay. In each of the upraised palms, a different colored light pulsed. Mauve had a split second for her thoughts to catch up before four energy bolts streaked toward them.

Mauve threw Lane and herself to the ground just ahead of the coursing magic. The scent of ozone filled the air, accompanied by freshly turned soil, new rain and singed hair. Mauve pushed herself up, brushing dirt from her gown.

"You girls are talented," Mauve said, "but you know what all of those elements share in common? Death."

She threw her hands forward, a fan of light-sucking violet power knocking two of the faun from their feet. She reached downward before they could recover and sent her will into the grave soil.

"There's a reason I have to watch this place on the Day of the Dead." Mauve lifted her hands as if dragging a great weight from the earth. "They've buried a lot of really bad boys here."

Skeletal hands thrust from the ground around them, sending up a shower of dirt. Ghouls clawed their way from the broken earth, wild-eyed monsters wearing the tattered remains of their former clothes and shredded flesh from their last victims caught in jagged piranha teeth. One ghoul lashed out at the honey brown faun, Jiji, slicing through her hamstrings. It brought back a bloodied claw to its mouth, licking it clean with a two-foot tongue.

The centaur opened fire.

The first volley tore through the rising skeletons, shattering skulls and splintering bone by sheer volume. Mauve threw a scythe of flame around the circle's interior, cutting off most of the second volley and forcing the fauns back from the heat.

Lane rushed past a ghoul, snatching up two jagged femurs and slashed at the downed Jiji. A blast of electricity slammed into him, driving him back but not before he added another pair of jagged cuts.

"Stay down so I can protect you, boy," Mauve gestured at the ghouls.

As a man, the ghouls each snatched up a spine from a fallen skeleton. The attached ribs vibrated a moment, shifting together and unfolding into skeletal shields which thickened without respect to the amount of bone to be consumed. Bones jiggled across the ground, assembling into jagged spears and presenting themselves to the ghouls.

Mauve pirouetted on the spot, hands waving like a conductor pulling a hundred puppet strings.

A shard of stone lanced up from beneath her feet. She sidestepped, feinting forward and jogging right as two others followed the first. Lili rushed to Jiji's side, setting a rippling blue aura over the wounds already stinking of rot.

"The fauns have failed, first flank charge," Glent Se'Lailos said.

"We have not," A deep melody floated from Mimi's pipe ahead of rumbling earth.

Lightning slashed out from Kiki's hands, blackening rib-bone shields and filling the air with static.

Arrows lead the charge, followed close by a dozen centaurs with light lances tipped with serrated blades. The ghouls dropped their spear butts to the ground, receiving the charge in pikeman fashion. Against normal horseman, it would have proved deadly, but the centaur differed from men atop simple steeds. They jogged to the side of the spears, cutting them in angles, leaping their tips and making a path for their brothers. Three still fell to the spears, writhing and screaming as the ghouls discarded defense to fall upon them with eternal hunger.

Lane stood at Mauve's back, hands outstretched. His voice cracked halfway through his shout. "Kill them for your freedom."

The collective, imprisoned dead flooded out of his shirt in a mad horde. In moments a small arc of centaurs disappeared under the wave of ravening spirits.

"Jiji!" Kiki shrieked.

Mauve ripped the souls from dying centaur and forced them back into their former bodies regardless of their condition. Her centaur soldiers waded into their former comrades with twice their earlier ferocity.

Jiji wobbled to her feet beside Lane. "Here, sister."

Lane stared, an odd expression on his face.

Kiki fought her way forward, throwing a wave of ice shards at Lane. "Get away from her, monster boy."

Mauve appeared over the boy in a moment, two shield bearing ghouls rushing to protect their flank.

Jiji extended her arms toward Kiki. "I thought you hurt."

"No, you got...how are you're standing," Kiki said.

Jiji's smile grew piranha teeth. Jiji's entire body seemed to slither in a thousand directions at once. Her hands thrust out, gouging a chunk of flesh from Kiki's gut and shoving it into her mouth. Mimi and Lili appeared at her side, blasting the ghoul backward with stone and wind.

Mauve lent Lane heat stolen from an animated centaur, tapping the last lingering life as she made it her slave.

Despite her seizure of the centaur dead, her defense crumbled under their onslaught. She taxed her energies to their limits. The number of dead within the fauns' warded circle dwindled. Without the boy to protect she might have a chance, but as long as he remained she suffered a disadvantage.

Lane stirred as the heat finally won out over the ice spell from the faun struggling to heal herself mere yards away. Mauve grabbed the boy and shoved him into the arms of her newest convert. "Take him to Jedediah. Warn Jed, boy, tell him what's happened."

"But Mistress—"

"Do as you're told," she pushed as much energy as she could contain in the centaur corpse. "You'll have to sustain him when he starts to crumble. You can do it."

"M-mistress you're—"

"Sexy as hell and just as mad, now get going."

Mauve slapped the centaur's rump, feeling stupid for the unnecessary encouragement for it to bolt. Lane disappeared through the press, his mount's face, buying enough confusion for him to win clear. Mauve turned back to the centaur. She scooped up a pair of bones, pushing energy into them to reshape them into short, sharp blades.

She twirled her bone swords. "Okay, mules, Mama's ready for the next dance..."

Ghouls and dead centaur flourished their weapons.

The centaur swarmed her.

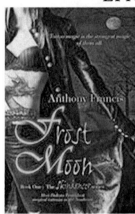 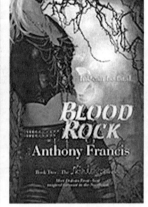 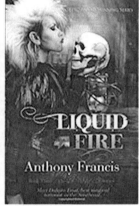
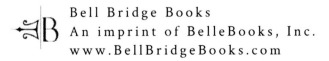

If you enjoyed this book, try out my other titles:

THE SCION SERIES
Michael J. Allen
www.deliriousscribbles.com

Scion of Conquered Earth ISBN: 978-9443557009

Stolen Lives ISBN: 978-9443557108

Delirious
Scribbles Ink

Delirious Scribbles Ink

ABOUT THE SCRIBBLER

(Photo credit: Jim Cawthorne)

Originally from Oregon, Michael J. Allen is a pluviophile masquerading as a vampire IT professional in rural Georgia. Warped from youth by the likes of Jerry Lewis, Robin Williams, Gene Wilder and Danny Kay, his sense of humor leads to occasional surrender, communicable insanity, a sweet tooth and periodic launch into nonsensical song. He loves books, movies, the occasional video game, playing with his Labradors—Myth and Magesty. He knows almost nothing about music.

A recovering Game Master, he gave up running RPG's for writing because the players didn't play out the story in his head like book characters would—we know how that worked out.

Suddenly fresh out of teenagers, his days are spent writing in restaurants, people watching and warring over keyboard control with the voices in his head.

For more information about Michael or expanded book lore, visit:
www.deliriousscribbles.com
Or like him at:
http://www.facebook.com/DeliriousScribbler

CPSIA information can be obtained
at www.ICGtesting.com
Printed in the USA
FFOW03n1807250218
45272553-45914FF